"What?" was all I had time to say.

A klaxon sounded, loud and pulsing.

Lord Ashington's face changed in an instant. "Clark, are you on the damned boilers?"

There was noise below as men shouted and ran.

The scaffolding lurched beneath my feet. I staggered. Lord Ashington wrapped his arm around my waist to steady me and grabbed for one of the braces with his free hand. He clasped me tight in a most inappropriate manner.

The machine he had been working on moved, lurching to rise to its feet. It was an automaton, fully twenty feet tall, and it turned a copper face toward the klaxon.

There'd be no help from below, as men raced to what appeared to be a boiler on the verge of boiling dry. Once again the automaton lurched. Ashington released me, thrusting me behind him as he turned to confront his creation, wrench in hand. The platform shuddered beneath our feet. "We have to stop it," he yelled to me. "Or else it will—"

The automaton raised its hand, and whirling blades emerged inches from Ashington's face.

I gripped my parasol and leaped to the attack.

—From "For Queen and Country"
by Elizabeth A. Vaughan

Also Available from DAW Books:

Boondocks Fantasy, edited by Jean Rabe and Martin H. Greenberg
Urban fantasy is popular, but what if you took that modern fantasy and moved it to the "sticks," with no big city in sight? Trailer parks, fishing shacks, sleepy little towns, or specks on the map so small that if you blink while driving through you'll miss them. Vampires, wizards, aliens, and elves might be tired of all that urban sprawl and prefer a spot in the country—someplace where they can truly be themselves without worrying about what the neighbors think! With stories by tale-spinners such as Gene Wolfe, Timothy Zahn, Mickey Zucker Reichert, Anton Strout, Linda P. Baker and others.

Zombiesque, edited by Stephen L. Antczak, James C. Bassett, and Martin H. Greenberg
Zombies have long stalked and staggered through the darkest depths of human imagination, pandering to our fears about death and what lies beyond. But must zombies always be just shambling, brain-obsessed ghouls? If zombies actually maintained some level of personality and intelligence, what would they want more than anything? Could zombies integrate themselves into society? Could society accept zombies? What if a zombie fell in love? These are just some of the questions explored in original stories by Seanan McGuire, Nancy A. Collins, Tim Waggoner, Richard Lee Byers, Jim C. Hines, Jean Rabe, and Del Stone Jr. with others. Here's your chance to take a walk on the undead side in these unforgettable tales told from a zombie's point of view.

Steampunk'd, edited by Jean Rabe and Martin H. Greenberg
Science fiction is the literature of what if, and steampunk takes the what if along a particular time stream. What if steam power was the prime force in the Victorian era? How would that era change, and how would it change the future? From a Franco-British race for Kentucky coal to one woman's determination to let no man come between her and her inventions . . . from "machine whisperers" to a Thomas Edison experiment gone awry, here are fourteen original tales of what might have been had steam powered the world in an earlier age, from Michael A. Stackpole, Donald J., Bingle, Robert Vardeman, Paul Genesse, Jody Lynn Nye, and others.

After Hours: Tales from the Ur-Bar, edited by Joshua Palmatier and Patricia Bray
The first bar, created by the Sumerians after they were given the gift of beer by the gods, was known as the Ur-Bar. Although it has since been destroyed, its spirit lives on. In each age there is one bar that captures the essence of the original Ur-Bar, where drinks are mixed with magic and served with a side of destiny and intrigue. Now some of today's most inventive scriveners, such as Benjamin Tate, Kari Sperring, Anton Strout, and Avery Shade, among others, have decided to belly up to the Ur-Bar and tell their own tall tales—from an alewife's attempt to transfer the gods' curse to Gilgamesh, to Odin's decision to introduce Vikings to the Ur-Bar . . . from the Holy Roman Emperor's barroom bargain, to a demon hunter who may just have met his match in the ultimate magic bar, to a bouncer who discovers you should never let anyone in after hours in a world terrorized by zombies. . . .

HOT AND STEAMY

Tales of Steampunk Romance

Edited by Jean Rabe and
Martin H. Greenberg

DAW BOOKS, INC.
DONALD A. WOLLHEIM, FOUNDER
375 Hudson Street, New York, NY 10014

ELIZABETH R. WOLLHEIM
SHEILA E. GILBERT
PUBLISHERS
www.dawbooks.com

First Printing, June 2011

1   2   3   4   5   6   7   8   9

DAW TRADEMARK REGISTERED
U.S. PAT. AND TM. OFF. AND FOREIGN COUNTRIES
—MARCA REGISTRADA
HECHO EN U.S.A.

PRINTED IN THE U.S.A.

ACKNOWLEDGMENTS

CONTENTS

INTRODUCTION
Jean Rabe   1

CHANCE CORRIGAN AND THE QUEEN OF HEARTS
Michael A. Stackpole   3

ABSINTHE-MINDED ARCHAEOLOGIST
Vicki Johnson-Steger   28

THE PROBLEM OF TRYSTAN
Maurice Broaddus   46

CLOCKWORKS
Jody Lynn Nye   64

IN THE BELLY OF THE BEHEMOTH
Matt Forbeck   82

AUTOMATA FUTURA
Stephen D. Sullivan   99

LOVE COMES TO ABYSSAL CITY
Tobias S. Buckell   117

FOR THE LOVE OF BYRON
Mickey Zucker Reichert   139

FOR QUEEN AND COUNTRY
Elizabeth A. Vaughan   169

GRASPING AT SHADOWS
  C.J. Henderson   188

GO FORWARD WITH COURAGE
  Dean Leggett   212

HER FAITH IS FIXT
  Robert E. Vardeman   228

KINETIC DREAMS
  C.A. Verstraete   246

FOR THE LOVE OF COPPER
  Marc Tassin   257

CASSANDRA'S KISS
  Mary Louise Eklund   275

DASHED HOPES
  Donald J. Bingle   290

INTRODUCTION

To me, the Victorian era is romantic all on its own. The dresses and music, lace doilies on decorative little tables, fluted glasses for wine, the soft glow of oil lamps ... ah, to be transported there. But to be transported there with the use of a time machine, such as is available in "Kinetic Dreams," is even better. The Victorian era is a little more interesting with a good dose of science fiction, steampunk style, thrown in.

Some of the authors in this collection were in DAW's previous offering—*Steampunk'd*. They even revisit their favorite characters in a romantic light.

As the title implies, these are all love stories—with varying degrees of steam to suit most tastes. But the tales are more than smoochy scenes filled with tender embraces and a few sweaty sheets. They are also filled with intrigue, danger, pyrotechnics, and plenty of gadgets. It wouldn't be proper steampunk without some gadgets and airships and automatons and the like. There are even a few pairs of goggles in the mix.

The stories weave their way from England to the New World to Egypt and back again, from high above the earth to deep beneath it.

And all are centered on the heart—from Michael A. Stackpole's Queen of Hearts to the one beating in Jody Lynn Nye's tale.

This one's for you, Marty.

Enjoy! I certainly did.

—Jean

CHANCE CORRIGAN AND THE QUEEN OF HEARTS

Michael A. Stackpole

Michael A. Stackpole is an award-winning writer, screenwriter, podcaster, game and computer game designer, and graphic novelist. One of his recent novels, At the Queen's Command, *is the first in his Crown Colonies series. He lives in Arizona and, in his spare time, enjoys indoor soccer and dancing. His website is www.stormwolf.com.*

I

Chance Corrigan emerged from the shadowed doorway and fell in step with the woman. None too gently, he took her right elbow in his left hand. "Keep walking, my lady."

Her blue eyes sparked hotly. "How dare . . ."

"I'm not with them." Chance cast a glance back over

3

his left shoulder, the mechanical eye clicking once. "I'm here to save you."

She failed to wrench her arm free, so she raised a heel to kick him. Chance, expecting that, leaned into her, throwing her off balance. Her gown's long skirts would have rendered the kick less than effective, but now they tangled her legs. Save for his hand on her arm, and his right hand quickly slipping around her waist, she would have fallen onto a wet Monaco street.

Her two pursuers sprinted forward. Both wore evening clothes, the trailing man having donned a thick overcoat and bowler hat. The younger man, wasp-waisted, his blond hair slicked back in the manner of the day, raised a hand. "I say, you there, unhand her." His accent, the product of generational inbreeding and the finest of British public schools, rendered his English all but incomprehensible.

Chance turned, interposing himself between them and their petite, flame-haired prey. "'Unhand her?' I ain't gonna hurt her. Or are you afraid I'll do a better job than you?"

"Beastly American idiot." The gentleman snapped fingers. "Stockton, the *convincers*, please."

The larger man mutely raised the valise and managed to open it, all the while keeping his master's coat folded across his left forearm and his hat balanced on top. The gentleman reached into the leather handbag and pulled out two stainless steel rectangles about the size of a cigarette case, with the thickness of two stacked card decks. He set one on the back of his left hand and punched a button, then did the same with the other on his right hand.

With a whirring of gears, flaps opened and levers flipped. Metal rods covered the man's fingers to the first knuckle. More steel looped his palm, and then the boxes began to flip backward, somersaulting over his forearm and past his elbow. Slender rails clicked into place, paralleling his bones. Other metal hoops shot out, encircling his limbs. The skeletal supports covered him to just above his biceps, the stainless steel flashing in the streetlight.

Chance released the woman and clapped politely. "Those'll wrinkle your jacket."

The slender man snorted. "Stockton is good with wrinkles."

Chance's good eye narrowed as he shoved his hands into his coat pockets. "You couldn't have known I'd be here. You brought them to use on her."

The aristocrat gave him a thin smile. "I am always prepared in case of chicanery. Virginia Greene defrauded me of £5,000."

Chance smiled and looked back at her. "Ginnie, you've been very bad. Worse than Bremen. Who's the sport?"

He answered before she could. "I am Reginald Trent, Viscount Moulton."

Chance canted his head. "Your reputation says you're a gentleman. You're just a common thug."

Trent banged his fists together and smiled at the din. "I prefer to think of myself as pragmatic."

Chance stepped back, exposing Virginia to her pursuer's view. "I ain't here to be her champion. I'll just hold her cloak as she cleans your clock."

That got a chuckle from her and a hiss from Trent.

"Of course, for a sporting guy, there is an alternative. How'd she swindle you?"

"Chemin de fer."

"Only £5,000?" Chance slowly shook his head. "Surprised you're bothered. That ain't much at all."

The viscount hesitated. "It is the principle of the thing."

"Yeah, I had you pegged as a man of principle. Here's the game, sport. Double or nothing on your losses." Chance pointed up toward the well-lit body of the orbiting *HMAS Fortune.* "I'll stake you, then whip you for my money back. That's if you really is a gaming man."

Trent sniffed. "As if they would even allow you aboard."

"Wanna bet they won't?" Chance's right hand came out of his pocket and flipped something toward Trent. "You'll lose."

The nobleman caught the disk awkwardly, then slowly turned it over in his palm. His lips parted and eyes widened. "A £10,000 chip from the *Fortune?*"

"That do as proof?"

"Marginally." Trent lifted his head and sniffed. "I would have your name."

"Tomorrow night, if I figure you earned it."

"It shall be a pleasure to take your money."

"A pleasure you ain't likely to know." Chance turned and this time, instead of grabbing the woman's arm, he presented his to her. She smiled and slipped her right hand inside his elbow. She rested her head on his shoulder as they paraded off into the darkness.

Beyond the next corner, Virginia Greene, her eyes tight, looked up at him. "I would have known you even without the mention of Bremen. Shall I just use your old name?"

"The old one is fine." She continued to watch his face, unseen, she thought, by him since his mechanical eye remained focused straight ahead. He shifted his voice, draining the growl from it. "'Virginia Greene' suits you. I like it better than the other one. Good to see you're doing well."

She laughed easily. "And you have come up in the world. No longer a mere stevedore."

"Luck favors the bold."

"I doubt you were ever a *mere* stevedore."

"Charming as always." Chance patted her hand, relishing its softness. "So how is it that Trent figured out your swindle? Taking money off him should have been simple. You were working the build-the-banco swindle, yes?"

"I don't know how he twigged to it. He fully believed I was blackmailing the man who maintains the Grand Casino's automaton dealers." She frowned. The severe expression accentuated her vulpine beauty, inspiring a flutter in Chance's belly. "I took my exit at the right time, but he followed me instead of waiting for the kill. I appreciate your intervention. No hard feelings over Bremen?"

"Which part? Your seducing the Chief of the Constabulary to get out of jail or your abandoning me to the agents of the Lithverian prince?"

She stopped, turning to face him, her hand pressed against his chest. "I tried, but the Chief was jealous and thought you were my lover. Then the prince's men arrived." She glanced down. "It broke my heart . . ."

The growl returned. "They worked on other bits of me."

She lifted her face again, tears welling. "I am so very sorry."

"I healed." He nodded. "I gave as good as I got."

"That was *you?* Oh, God," she shivered. Her hand shifted, grabbing a handful of his wool coat's lapel. "Now you've come for me?"

"I need someone with your skills." Chance smiled broadly. "I have some big fish to fry."

Her face lit up. "I do so want to make amends." She pointed toward the center of the principality. "I'll just return to my hotel—these events have fatigued me. We can meet for breakfast."

"Ginnie, I was born at night, but not *last* night." He led her across the square to *La Maison Rouge*. "I have the Imperial Suite. Wonderful view of the sea. I already sent for your things. The concierge was beside himself with joy that my *fiancée* was able to join me."

"You presume greatly."

"The Josephine Suite is yours. The hotel's top floor is ours and ours alone."

"Oh." Her lower lip pushed out into a pout and he resisted the urge to caress it. He led her up the hotel's broad granite steps and into a cavernous lobby. Marble pillars upheld a vaulted ceiling. Murals with cherubs and scenes from Greek mythology adorned the walls. Chance's heels clicked on the checkerboard marble of the foyer.

The lift operator, very sharp in his dark green uniform, touched his cap's visor. "*Bonsoir, mademoiselle. Bonsoir, Monsieur* Corrigan."

"*Bonsoir*, Philippe. The suite, please. No one to go up or down until I call in the morning? No visitors."

"*Oui, Monsieur. Je comprend.*"

She said nothing as the operator closed the brass gate, then cranked the lever. The lift started upward with a squeal. Chance pulled her back with him against the warm walnut panels. Philippe stared straight ahead, but she remained quiet. Still, she watched him, searching his face with renewed interest.

They exited on the penthouse floor. When the lift began its descent, she tugged him around to face her. "You'll keep me a prisoner, will you?"

"Nope. Figured on Trent having half-an-idea that he could get his money back from you *and* steal my chip." Chance raised his hands. "If you want to go, I'll get the lift. But I don't think you will."

"How can you be so certain?"

"You may have run from Bremen but . . ." Chance unlocked her suite and threw the door open. "Run now and you miss the opportunity to take Reginald Trent for every cent he can beg, borrow or steal."

II

A hint of fear slithered through Chance's guts as he entered Virginia's suite. While he counted on avarice and curiosity to keep her in the hotel, it was entirely possible that she might have seen the virtue of escaping while he slept. In bringing her things over from her hotel, he had supplied her with the tools she needed to descend to the ground and vanish into thin air.

His original plan hadn't involved her. He'd not expected to find her in Monaco, but when he spotted her, he followed her and quickly learned of her association with his target. Having seen her at work before, and finding her a delicious distraction for Trent, he opted to bring her into things. To set it up, Chance had sent Trent the anonymous note exposing the swindle, precipitating the events of the previous night.

And yet, it was not just her utility that had made him seek her out. He knew better than to fool himself. The Lithverian adventure had indeed left him with painful memories, and yet they vanished when first he saw her again. His breath had caught, his scrotum tightened, when she'd come into view.

Unfinished business.

Chance, wearing a dark suit, white shirt with a blue ascot, held his head high. A folded paper was on the front room table beside a discarded napkin and her breakfast dishes. Beyond it, the door to her boudoir remained half open. A softly hummed tune drifted through it.

Without asking permission, or any expectation of receiving it, he crossed the front room and pushed the door open. "I hope the accommodations were to your satisfaction."

She sat there before a vanity. The triptych mirror reflected her surprise—feigned at his arrival, genuine at his appearance and proper diction. She studied him for a moment, then quickly glanced down.

She had lowered her diaphanous white gown to the padded bench and had been brushing her long red tresses when he entered. Her hair, having been pulled forward of her shoulder, provided him a clear view of rounded hips, narrow waist, and strong shoulders. Supple muscles moved beneath creamy skin as she resumed brushing her long locks.

"A gentleman should have knocked."

"Blame the stevedore."

She laughed lightly, lifting her chin, exposing her throat. "I've missed that stevedore."

"You've found other people to amuse you." Chance smiled. "I understand swindling Trent. I just don't see how you can stand to do it."

"Better that than surrendering to ennui." She guided the brush through a copper cascade. "How is it that you'll take him for so much? I've left him with nothing."

"It's simple. You'll go to him, apologize, and tell him that you knew me when I was a *luckless* stevedore. You'll say I got lucky and, on my travels, discovered a diamond mine that makes the Kimberley mines look like mud-puddles."

"I'll convince him that I'll let him swindle you, and we split it all later, using the build-a-banco trick."

Chance nodded. "I know you're more comfortable with cat-burglary, unless you've retired since Lithveria, but this will be an easy job. Your piece is £50,000. For an evening, that's not bad."

She brushed with renewed vigor. "Acceptable. Why him?"

"Link in a chain."

Virginia's lips pursed. "Assuming my split is half, you'd have to convince him that you've got at least £100,000. The chip was a nice start."

"He has his convincers, I have mine." Chance withdrew a small velvet sack from his pocket. The contents sparkled and rustled as he poured them into his left palm. With a magician's flourish, he let the ruby and diamond necklace dangle from his hand.

Her eyes widened. Her voice dropped to a reverent whisper. "The Queen of Hearts."

"You've seen it before?"

"Not seen, but every woman in the world knows it. A one-hundred-fifty-carat, pigeon-blood Ceylonese ruby, heart-shaped, surrounded by a dozen thirty-carat diamonds, all set in white gold. Napoleon designed it for his Empress, basing it on tomb paintings of a necklace Pharaoh Seti I looted from Kadesh." She stared at the necklace in the mirror. "That one was lost to antiquity. The Napoleonic necklace belongs to an American industrialist, Theodore Caine."

Chance crossed to her, staring down at her reflection. He looped the necklace about her throat as she pulled her hair up. The ruby, darker than her rose-petal nipples, nestled between her soft breasts. Her hair spread into a veil against her back as a hand came up, trembling, to touch the stone. Her fingers drew back quickly, as if it were molten, and then pressed to it again.

"How did you . . . ?"

"Steal it?" Chance rested his hands on her shoulders. "I've not your skill for that sort of thing. I had this one manufactured. Its appearance should be enough for Trent to bring the real one out of hiding."

"What?"

"Your blush betrays you, Virginia." Chance kissed the top of her head. "Caine became overextended. He is using Trent as an agent to secure financing from the Rothschilds. The Queen of Hearts is meant as collateral of sorts. I don't know how you learned Trent had it, but I know you wished to steal it."

"Trent is a fool, but not utterly stupid, curse my fortune." Her blue eyes met his in the looking glass. "He has it locked away in the vault of the Royal Bank of Monaco."

"And this will draw it out."

Her hands came up, covering his. "And how shall we free him of it?"

"You work your swindle just as you planned. Leave everything else to me."

Her smile grew, as did the pressure of her hands on his. How simple a thing it would have been to run his hands slowly down over her alabaster flesh. His thumbs would brush the ruby as his fingers caressed her nipples. She would draw him down into a kiss. He would fill his hands, squeezing firmly, his tongue seeking hers. She would turn on the bench to face him. Her robe would slip to the floor, seconds before she knelt on it. Those blue eyes looking up at him, at one moment widely innocent, in the next devilishly lusty..

He wanted that. He wanted it very badly. Memories stirred him, warming his flesh. His body reacted and she could feel it against her back. Her hands became more insistent, her reflected expression pleased. She wanted it, too. She remembered; she had to remember. They had lost themselves in each other for too brief a time. It almost seemed as if it hadn't happened, and this would be their chance to prove it had.

And yet, because she wants it, I cannot.

Chance reluctantly slipped his hands from beneath hers.

Her hands fell to modestly censor her reflection. Her eyes filled with confusion. "I hurt you terribly, didn't I? I'm horrible, I know it." She raised her brush to smash the mirrors.

Chance caught her wrist. "Pleasure would erase those memories."

"Then why?"

He smiled confidently, taking the brush and beginning to stroke her hair. "Tonight, when we are victorious. It will be that much sweeter. And we will have more time. There's still a lot to do."

She took the brush from him. "Then go do it. I shall take care of Trent." Her smile returned. "And try not to let thoughts of our victory celebration distract you too much."

III

Virginia Greene, in an empire-waisted gown of scarlet silk with a sweetheart neckline, was breathtaking. It was not that the Queen of Hearts made her more beautiful; it was that in combination with it, she became stunning. The dirigible's powerful engines sent a thrumming through the whole of the airborne casino and brilliant light flashed from the necklace in synch with it. She did not fail to catch a single eye. Heads, once turned in her direction, did not surrender sight of her willingly.

The Viscount Moulton's reaction did not mirror any other. Whereas lust and appreciation had animated most faces, his expression tightened with rage. He thrust a finger at her. "You can't . . . that . . . you are a thief!"

Chance clapped his hands politely. "She would not be the thief, sir. I made her a gift of the necklace this morning."

"Then you are the thief!" Perspiration dappled Trent's forehead. "That is the Queen of Hearts. It's in the vault at the Royal Bank. I don't know what your game is, but it shall not succeed. We need the manager here and the police."

Chance cocked the eyebrow above his mechanical eye. "I think, sir, you should be certain of your facts. Perhaps you will send your man Stockton to see if the necklace has indeed been stolen. You may, in fact, wish to go yourself, and return here with it. I will accept your apology then."

Trent's eyes narrowed. "I shall do just that."

"Excellent." Chance caught him by the upper arm. "But, before you go, the chip."

The nobleman blinked, as if he'd been splashed with ice water. "I am a *gentleman*, sir!"

"You've just called me a thief."

He dug in a pocket and handed Chance the chip. "I shall have that back off you."

Chance watched him and his manservant go, and then flipped the chip to the manager. "The Grand Salon, the main table, reserved for us alone. We shall play when he returns."

"Very good, sir."

Chance escorted Virginia to the saloon at the airship's bow. One entered on either side of the ornate mahogany bar—a veritable mountain of shelves crowded with every odd shape and color of bottle, and ladders to ascend to the upper reaches. Opposite, the forward bulkhead glass and bronze construction provided a breathtaking view of the city. Lights winked and moonlight frosted the sea's light chop. A tiny dirigible—likely the aero-brougham carrying Trent—slowly spiraled toward the ground.

They sat at a candlelit table nearest the bow. Her gloved hand sought his. "You did that masterfully."

"He's low-hanging fruit." Chance smiled up at the waiter. "Champagne for the lady. Macallan for me with a glass of water on the side."

"Not what I remember you drinking."

"An old habit." Chance squeezed her fingers. "And after tonight, you shall never want for champagne again."

She smiled. "You will keep me in the style to which I wish to be accustomed?"

Chance sat back. "I hadn't . . . yes, I will."

Virginia's smile broadened. "You might cling to the idea that you're more the stevedore than anything else, but you are *more*. That's what sets you apart from men like Trent. Why did I decide to swindle him? Not to fight off boredom, but because he bored me. You, on the other hand, challenge me. I like that. It intrigues me. You will not, I am afraid, be easily rid of me."

Chance stared into her eyes, holding her hand in both of his. "I'd like that very much."

"Good." She fell silent as the waiter served their drinks. As he departed, she lifted the flute. "To a long future of successes together."

Chance had to resist punching that smug smile off Trent's face. "You have the necklace?"

Trent nodded and Stockton placed a box on the chemin-de-fer table. He opened it. A twin Queen of Hearts glittered from its white-satin bed.

"As long as I was about rousing bank managers, I also summoned *Monsieur* LaPointe." Trent waved a small, nervous man forward. His bushy moustaches boasted more hair than the top of his head, but he had diligently combed and slicked the few strands down. "LaPointe is the finest jeweler in Monaco—perhaps on the Continent. Your necklace is paste, and he shall prove it."

The jeweler glanced up at Chance, his shoulders hunched and eyes moist. "If you will permit me, sir."

"Of course." Chance crossed to where Virginia sat at the table and removed her necklace. He handed it to LaPointe. "Give us an honest opinion now."

The small man produced a loupe and raised the necklace into the light. He studied the ruby first, then each of the diamonds in turn. He began slowly, and then more quickly spun the necklace. Finally he turned it over and studied the setting. He laid it down on the table again as gently as if it were a newborn baby, then ran a finger around his collar.

"Well, man? Paste, isn't it?"

LaPointe's lower lip trembled. "You will forgive me, my lord, but every stone is genuine. Flawless. Save for one tiny mark, a jeweler's mark on the setting, I could not tell this from your necklace."

Trent shook his head. "This isn't possible."

Chance nodded. "It *is* possible. Very possible."

"Where did you find the stones? A discovery that big ..."

"I didn't discover the stones." Chance smiled broadly. "I *manufactured* them."

Virginia blinked with surprise. "You said you manufactured the necklace."

"A slight omission, darling." Chance picked up his Queen of Hearts and cavalierly tossed it into the air, catching it deftly. "I told you I'd give you my name. It's Chance Corrigan. Check on it later. I was a good little inventor ten years ago before an accident cost me ... everything. Over the past decade I've spent my time well, perfecting a process to create artificial diamonds. Use enough heat, and use magnets for the high-speed linear-acceleration of pressure plates and you have diamonds. Right mix of corundum and chromium will give you rubies. Hannay and Moissan were on the right track, but they never thought of the power of linear acceleration."

LaPointe half-fainted, catching himself on the table's edge. "*Mon Dieu.* If this is true, we are ruined."

Chance helped the jeweler to a chair. "Yes, the De Beers monopoly would be broken. Were I not a reasonable man."

Blood had drained from Trent's face. Even he could understand the threat. If Chance could produce gemstones so easily, the value of any of them dropped to insignificance. "You're lying."

Chance cocked his head. "You've called me a liar and a thief. Have you no honor, sir?"

Trent's nostrils flared. "I am most honorable."

"Ah, just a coward, then."

The noble turned toward Stockton and his valise.

"You're an idiot, too. I'm not challenging you to a duel." Chance nodded toward the table. "One game. Virginia is the bank. Your necklace against hers."

"But this is not my . . ."

"Coward and idiot, as I said." Chance snorted. "If I am a liar, then both necklaces are of equal and inestimable value. You have an even chance of winning and losing. If I am telling the truth, then your necklace might as well be paste. Caine and his allies will forgive your losing it when you bring them news of my process. The only way you lose is if Miss Greene wins."

Trent almost covered his reaction. Chance gave no indication he'd noticed anything amiss. Since Trent and Virginia had agreed to swindle Chance, there was no way he could lose. The very worst outcome would be his walking away with the real Queen of Hearts. *And were he to win . . .*

Trent sat and pushed the jeweler's box to the center of the table. "I want a new deck in the dealer. And you . . ." Trent pointed at Chance's left eye. "A blindfold. Who knows what he can see with that eye."

Virginia sat up straight. "Chance would not cheat."

Chance rested a hand on her shoulder, savoring her warmth. "Fine. And not just a new deck. I want a deck from a new case of cards."

The salon manager dispatched staff. The man bearing the blindfold arrived first. The opaque black wool scratched as it went over the mechanical eye and across Chance's forehead. One lace looped beneath his left ear-lobe and the other met it toward the back of his head. The man tied it firmly, but not so tightly that it tore at his ear.

The manager himself took custody of the box of cards. He slit the paper-tape and pulled two decks from the box—one red and one blue. He displayed them front and back and let Trent choose. He selected a red deck. The manager matched it with five more red decks from the case, broke the seal on each and fanned the cards. Virginia nodded.

The manager turned his attention to the dealer. The automaton only existed from the waist up and had been perched on the table. Only by looking at the bronze face and the hands could one see the intricacy of its construction. It had been clad in a bright blue silk blouse and had an ivory turban wrapped around its head—giving it the look of an Ottoman Turk. The eyes—painted wooden balls with brown irises—moved back and forth slowly enough to provide the illusion that the dealer studied the cards.

The manager lowered the collar and pressed the first of four buttons on the neck. Gears whirred from within, and then a drawer slid forward from the base. The manager pulled the remnants of the previous deck from it, the closed it with a click. Hitting the second button, he opened the automaton's mouth and fed it each red deck in turn. The mouth closed and more gears ground away inside. As the cards cascaded through what passed for its stomach, the automaton's gearing thoroughly shuffled them.

"*Mesdames et monsieurs*, the lady is the bank. The wager is . . ." He hesitated.

The jeweler mopped his head with a handkerchief. "Oh, dear, at current market value that would be £1.5 million. But if *Monsieur* Corrigan is telling the truth... *mon Dieu.*"

The manager hit the third button. The automaton's right hand came forward, grasped a card protruding through a slit in its blouse, and slid it toward Virginia. It followed with a second, then dealt two cards to Trent.

Virginia peeled her cards off the green felt. The quick twitch of the corners of her mouth heralded good news. She flipped over her hand, revealing a king and an eight. Because face cards counted as zero, the game valued her hand at eight—the second-best hand possible.

Trent stiffened as he looked from her cards to his. His initial reaction had been genuine. Chance figured his hand totaled four or five. Then Trent remembered that he couldn't lose. After a moment's hesitation, he forced more nervousness. "Card, please."

Pressing the last button produced another card. The automaton plucked it from his torso and rotated his wrist.

A three.

Trent's cards fell. Queen and four.

"*Monsieur* has seven. The bank wins."

Trent sat there, blinking, staring at the cards. "Oh, God, I am undone."

Chance laughed easily. "You before your masters."

Again overplaying things, Trent half-stumbled as he rose. His man steadied him.

Chance shook his head. "No need to pretend for my benefit, Trent."

"What?"

"You and Virginia. Your deal to split everything. I know all about it." Chance smiled. "But she can't split what she doesn't have. I call 'Banco.'"

Virginia, who had leaned forward to gather both necklaces to her, froze. "What? You can't possibly. . . ."

"I have a letter of credit good for £5,000,000 on record with the *Fortune.*" His good eye tightened. "Care to try your luck?"

"But of course." She looked up at Trent. "Our deal still stands. Half of everything."

Chance nodded. "Just remember, half of nothing is nothing."

"Nothing ventured, nothing gained." Virginia shrugged. "After all, you've made these baubles worthless, so I venture nothing against your cash."

Chance's mouth opened for a second, and then his shoulders slumped. "I'd better win, then."

The manager opened his hands. "*Monsieur* Corrigan is the bank. The wager is £3,000,000." He hit the button. The automaton whirred and dealt.

Chance lifted his cards. *Too much color.*

Virginia flipped her cards over. A deuce and a six. "Eight seems to be my lucky number."

Chance exhaled slowly, laying his cards face up on the felt. "Jack and queen. Zero." He glanced at the manager. "A card, please. A nine would be convenient."

The manager patted the automaton's shoulder. "The choice of card is not up to me, *Monsieur.* I do wish you good luck."

"Most kind."

The manager touched the fourth button. Gears ground. The automaton's hand slowly drew back. A card thrust forward. The brass hand delicately plucked the card, and then rotated at the wrist.

A nine.

Chance clapped his hands. Virginia gasped and Trent groaned.

"I believe, my dear, the *nothing* you ventured is now *mine.*"

Virginia nodded slowly. She turned in her chair. Stockton quickly moved to draw it back for her. She smiled at him then, standing, started down at Chance. "So you really *did* want revenge for Bremen."

He removed the blindfold. "We all pay for our sins, Ginnie."

She brushed a single tear away. "Such a bitter price."

"Oh, yes, your price." Chance plucked five of the £10,000 chips from the caddy before the manager and tossed them toward her. "I keep my promises. Your things have been packed. The airship *Vesuvius* leaves for Naples at dawn. You'll enjoy your berth."

Virginia's hand hovered for a heartbeat before she scooped up the chips. "I would say, *Monsieur*, that it has been a pleasure, but I shan't add prevarication to my list of sins. Gentlemen, good night." She turned and departed in a rustle of scarlet silk.

Chance closed the jewel box and slipped it into his pocket. He returned the other necklace to a velvet bag and pocketed it as well. Standing, he smiled. "I should be happy, *Monsieur* LaPointe, to offer you champagne in the saloon. Too bad, Trent, you won't be able to join us. You've been entertaining but, I do believe, your value in that department is at an end."

IV

Clicks and snaps gave Chance the warning he'd have denied Trent had their roles been reversed. The nobleman, his bow tie askew, his cheeks flushed with drink, and his arms sheathed with the *convincers*, blocked the companionway deep in the *Fortune's* bowels. Stockton stood further down the passage, his expression almost apologetic.

Trent, white froth at the corners of his mouth, pointed with a quivering finger. "You aren't getting away with this, Corrigan. You can cheat that witch. I don't care. But you can't cheat me."

Chance sank his hands into his pants pockets. "Seems I already have."

"Give me the Queen of Hearts." The man hesitated. "And £50,000, same as you gave her."

The one-eyed man laughed. "Take a lot of convincing before I do that."

Trent balled metal-clad fists. "I shall enjoy this."

"Doubt it." Chance shrugged and drew a flat, silver metal disk from his pocket. The diameter of a silver dollar, but three times as thick, the disk traveled effortlessly back and forth over Chance's knuckles. "Go away. I don't want to hurt you."

Trent set himself. "I'll beat you to within an inch of your life."

Chance flipped the disk at Trent.

The nobleman contemptuously backhanded it out of air. "That was supposed to hurt me?"

"Stockton, he says you're good with wrinkles." Chance smiled. "How good are you with scorch-marks?"

Trent's mouth fell open, incomprehension softening his expression. He looked at his right hand. The disk, instead of flying off, had attached itself to the back of his hand. Trent shook it, trying to flick it away. He then brought his left hand over to pry it loose, but the steel wristband clicked tight to the disk.

Chance nodded. "Magnets. My specialty. Oh, and electricity, too."

Jagged blue-white electric tendrils raced along the *convincers*. Trent bounced up and down, and then capered around. His jacket smoked. He slammed into one bulkhead, then rebounded into another and slumped to the deck. A couple more sparks engendered twitches. His head lolled to the side.

Chance looked through the thin vapor. "Your master will be fine in a few minutes. A stiff brandy or two, and he'll be calculating how to explain all this."

The manservant nodded mutely.

Chance hesitated, then fished into his jacket pocket. He tossed the jeweler's box onto Trent's chest. "It's worthless now. Just like him. Call it a souvenir. Something for his pains." Chance laughed at his own joke, eclipsing Trent's groans, and made his way unmolested to the ground and his bed.

She came to him through the balcony's French doors. "You need to be more careful with valuable treasure in your room."

Chance shook his head. "Why lock doors you'd have been through in an eyeblink?"

Virginia smiled and crossed to the sideboard, where a magnum of champagne cooled in an ice bucket. "Shall we celebrate our success?"

"I'm going to disappoint you." Chance sat in the wingback chair in the room's opposite corner. "I gave the Queen of Hearts back to Trent."

"You what?" She glanced back at him over her left shoulder. "You had £750,000 and gave it back?"

Chance pointed at the velvet sack in the middle of the bed. "I was playing a bigger game, Ginnie. Trent is a link. I want his bosses terrified. The Queen of Hearts you wore, the one LaPointe authenticated, it was paste. I paid LaPointe to create it and claim it was real. Caine and the Rothschilds had chosen LaPointe to value the real Queen of Hearts, so his word wouldn't be challenged."

She turned slowly, still somehow incredibly feminine despite wearing a black woolen sweater, dark knickers, socks, and slippers. "If Trent hadn't thought to bring LaPointe, you would have demanded, as a point of honor, his coming to verify things?"

"Trent would have thought it was his idea."

"And LaPointe worked with you because?"

"Money. And an incident in the Sudan, when I was with Somerset."

Virginia brought him a glass of champagne. "You give back the necklace, proving it's worthless. Trent's bosses believe in your manufacturing process. Wanting to beat a market collapse, they will divest themselves of jewelry and gem businesses. Prices will crash. Lot of money to be made buying what they sell off."

"Clever girl. Might want to invest there, too."

She slowly lowered herself into his lap, straddling his thighs. "These men, they must have hurt you terribly. More than I did in Bremen?"

"You hurt me. They *murdered* me."

She touched her flute to his. "To evil men reaping what they have sown; and a penitent woman making amends."

Chance nodded and drank.

Virginia set her flute aside and lowered her face to his. "I will earn your forgiveness, Chance."

Her breath warm on his face, her scent filling his head, made Chance smile. He circled his arms around her waist and drew her to him. She slid forward along his thighs, her hands firmly on the chair's back. She kissed him, lips parted. The tip of her tongue danced quickly against his lips.

His arms tightened, crushing her against his chest. He sucked her tongue into his mouth. One hand rose to her head, loosening thick copper curls. His other hand slipped beneath her sweater's hem, sliding up along soft, warm flesh, exposing her belly.

She raised her arms, letting him free her from the garment. She sank her fingers into his hair, jerking his head back. She dipped forward, licking up along his jugular until her lips brushed his ear. "Yes," she whispered, "I will earn forgiveness, no matter how long it takes. And you will enjoy every second of it."

V

LaPointe smiled at Chance over demitasse at an outdoor cafe the next morning. "It was as you suggested, *Monsieur*. *Mademoiselle* Greene had a woman pose as herself and board the *Vesuvius*. She then made her way to the railway station and is bound on a coach for Paris. You are certain the rest of your plan will work?"

"Nothing's certain, but all looks good." Chance added another sugar cube to his coffee and stirred. "You create the paste Queen and substitute it for the real one when you appraise it. I use the real one to convince Virginia and Trent that I can manufacture gems. I give Trent back the fake, then Virginia drugs me, steals Trent's Queen, and leaves the real one in its place. She'll contact you as a go-between with the owners, since you can authenticate it and already have the contacts to broker a deal."

"And the narcotic she gave you? It has left you with no ill effects?"

"Mild headache. I didn't drink much." Chance tapped his left eye. "Sees in the ultraviolet wavelength. The champagne in my glass glowed eerily. After a while I slowly fell asleep."

"But not too soon, as your smile suggests."

"A gentleman does not kiss and tell." Chance's smile broadened. "Neither do I."

LaPointe set his cup down. "I do not understand, however, how you were able to draw a nine when you needed it."

"Magnets. The card decks were specially printed. The nines were done in a separate run, printed with an ink containing a high concentration of iron. As the automaton shuffled, it retained the nines in a stack. When I needed a nine, the manager touched the automaton's shoulder. That turned off an electromagnet. The nines dropped on top of the deck." Chance shrugged. "That was insurance only. Had Virginia won, Trent would have demanded the necklace. She would have managed to swap the two of them, and the result would have been the same."

The jeweler smiled. "And your enemies will fear for their fortunes."

"Most of them, yes." Chance nodded. The others—his most powerful enemies—upon hearing how Chance claimed to have made diamonds would understand he'd actually developed a new weapon: a magnetically driven linear accelerator. Krups, Springfield, Colt, and every other man who profited from war would see the value of their weapons evaporate. They'd pour money into research and development of their own linear accelerators. They'd ruin themselves trying to duplicate a device for which Chance had only scribbled some rudimentary diagrams.

The jeweler shivered. "That smile, my friend, is a terrible thing. No mirth and no mercy."

"Don't worry, it's not for you." Chance raised his cup in a salute. "It's for the evil men who destroyed my life ten years ago. They'll rue the day they failed to finish the job."

"And for the woman, for her you have another smile?" LaPointe sat poised with cup and saucer in hand. "Would it not be better to abandon revenge and instead go to Paris?"

"It would, except for one thing." Chance nodded slowly, focusing his good eye distantly. "All this revenge is *because* of a woman."

The Frenchman smiled. "Unfinished business . . ."

"Exactly. And a debt to be collected in blood."

ABSINTHE-MINDED ARCHAEOLOGIST

Vicki Johnson-Steger

Vicki Johnson-Steger lives in Mount Pleasant, Wisconsin, with Dale, her husband of many years. They have three grown offspring and four adorable grandkids. Some of her other stories have been published in the DAW anthologies Spells of the City, Timeshares, *and* Boondocks Fantasy. *Vicki just finished a fairytale book and is working on several YA projects. She volunteers as an interpreter at the Kenosha Public Museum and Dinosaur Museum . . . when not finding other ways to get out of the house. The idea for this story came from taking several fascinating classes in Egyptian hieroglyphs taught by Peter Chiappori, architect, sculptor, artist, archaeologist and expert on all things Egyptian. This one's for you, Pete.*

Jameson Watts, deep in thought as he usually was, failed to notice the bullet that whizzed past. He mistook it for a large insect, and shook his unkempt gray hair as he waved a hand by his ear. The middle-aged archaeologist stood at the rail of the *SS Evangeline,* flagship of his family's steamboat fleet, an unseen figure in a lavender bustle melted into the shadows behind him.

Jameson fished into the pocket of his stained lab coat and slid out a large watch, its fob a shiny golden ankh; it always reminded him of his first expedition to Egypt when he was still a teenager. There he'd discovered a small straw-colored scarab beetle carved from desert glass. He'd kept it with him ever since, superstitious that the talisman protected him. During the many decades since that first adventure to the Valley of the Kings, he'd unearthed, liberated, studied, and cataloged countless treasures from dusty dark tombs. But the beetle was his favorite piece; it was the symbol of the rising sun, the source of all life.

It dangled from a chain around his neck and he ab-sent-mindedly stroked it as he mulled over his life's project. Ever since he had opened the tomb where his first discoveries were made, Jameson had felt that a strange aura surround him—some sort of electromag-netic force that not only seemed to keep him out of harm's way but coaxed him back to the desert time after time.

He flicked open the back of the large watch, and there on the indigo surface ciphers whirled, forming stick figures and ancient symbols. Against the dark blue glow small silver markings produced blinking hiero-glyphs. With a slight shake of his head he snapped the gadget shut, mumbling, "Cap'n Keel worries too much."

The state of the river was what Jameson worried about this morning as he strolled back to his cabin's laboratory. Muffled sounds of a train whistle could be heard through the dissipating morning fog. The river had become wider and shallower from years of clear cutting trees along the banks. Steamships consumed wood—and lots of it—and this resulted in increased flooding, making the waterway more treacherous and requiring the use of added river pilots for navigation. What was happening to the river due to all the traffic and commerce festered in his bones.

The mournful sound of a rival steamboat reached him as he opened his door. He inhaled the faint aroma of wood smoke curling from fires along the banks. This, mixed with the stench of a bloating cow carcass wedged against a log jam, lent an interesting pong to the heavy morning air. He closed the door tight behind him.

Jameson cleared his workbench of jeweler's tools and an accumulation of miniature gears, tiny springs, and various parts. He was assembling a new navigation device that would chart the movement of the stars as well as river currents. The archaeologist smoothed out a rather worn parchment rubbing he'd made of the stone tablet on his first Egyptian expedition. Through the lighted magnifying loupe of his monocle, he examined the marks scribed onto a tablet eons ago. He'd discovered the ancient tablet along with the scarab beetle, a canopic jar, and other trinkets in his first tomb.

He'd managed to conceal the scarab and a few other artifacts in the many pockets of his safari jacket, but the tablet was too heavy and large. There had been barely enough time to make a rubbing and escape with his life from a league of murderous desert thugs that preyed on foreigners.

It had taken decades, but he knew he was so very close to finally deciphering every last bit of it, completing his life's puzzle. The canopic jar he'd smuggled from the tomb contained a strange coal-like rock and a chunk of brittle silvery white metal hidden beneath the mummy's liver. Perhaps they were connected, he'd thought then.

Now he was certain of it.

Jameson had devoted months to testing these materials, secretly so no one would discover his theft. In the end, he learned that the rock with the brownish-black crust was a meteorite, and contained the smooth cool metal he named Isidium, after Isis, his favorite Egyptian deity. Deciphering enough of the glyphs from the tablet revealed a formula to extract this metal from celestial rubble.

Jameson stumbled on the power of this silvery element quite by accident. When his pocket watch was close to this mysterious metal the hands sped up until they became nothing but a blur. He repeatedly tested this compact power source and found it would animate other objects . . . such as his automaton deck scrubbers and dishwashers. Best of all, this strange metal was powering the *Evangeline's* large steam engine without burning wood as fuel. When the metal was under extreme pressure it produced heat, which in turn produced steam in the boilers.

The ancient Egyptians—at least the ones buried with his finds—must have used this amazing energy source. Soon Jameson would share their knowledge with the world.

Markings carved into the canopic jar, such as a scepter, represented dominion. This didn't seem to be the same kind of power reserved for pharaohs and rulers but power that could be held in one's palm. So Jameson believed that the tomb had not been the final resting place of a king—but a scientist. The archaeologist felt a kinship with the man whose jar he held.

What had the ancient scientist powered with the Isidium? And why had the tablet with the formula for extracting it been buried? Had someone—the scientist perhaps—in those long-ago days not wanted the discovery revealed? The answers were lost beneath a mummy's liver and lay undisturbed in the desert's shifting sands in the Valley of the Kings.

Jameson used shavings of this incredibly hard metal to animate his inventions, and with a slightly larger piece the *Evangeline's* steam engine served as a prototype for all engines and machinery. Only Captain Keel knew of this magnificent energy source that made Jameson's shipping line the most successful one on the river. Rumors circulated in the waterfront taverns that angry competitors were meeting to stop the Jameson Packet Company from taking over the entire river with its boats.

The scuttlebutt did not bother Jameson. He was preoccupied with getting the Isidium discovery out to the world.

It wouldn't be much longer now before he could do just that. Since meteorites laced with Isidium were not readily available, he sought an alternative source for the rare element. He found that Isidium was a byproduct of copper and nickel mining. Jameson and his investors had secured several copper and nickel mines in Canada that he was confident could provide a steady supply.

Soon he'd be in Washington D.C. to present his findings to the President of the United States. Then he intended to celebrate; first stop would be Denmark to visit his late mother's relatives, next a chartered airship to the Valley of Kings where he would pay a visit to his first tomb. After that, he'd start a new dig.

He tidied his workspace and locked his cabin door. Jameson usually took his meals in his room, but today he ventured to his private table in the corner of the main dining salon. In the salon, paneled in cherry, passengers ate at beautifully decorated tables with fine linens, fresh bouquets of flowers, and brass hurricane lamps. Men in coats and ties summoned waiters, while dainty women under elaborate hats sipped fine wine from small crystal glasses. Seemingly out of nowhere a large man wearing a white cap and navy blue jacket appeared.

"Cap'n Keel, what brings you out of the wheelhouse?" Jameson asked the man he'd known since childhood.

"Mind if I join you?"

Before he had a chance to refuse, Keel hailed the waiter and ordered pot roast and red potatoes. "And bring me a bourbon right away. And not one of those thimble-sized ones neither," he growled. Soon his burly hand gripped a tumbler and he scanned the dining room, then lowered his head.

"Listen, Watts, you gotta to be more careful. Someone's tryin' to kill you," he whispered. "Although why they'd bother is a mystery, you'll do the job for 'em soon enough—drinkin' that vile green stuff."

Jameson could see that the captain was staring at the lime green stains that dotted his white shirt like tiny tracks.

"I'll be careful," Jameson said, humoring him.

He spent a few more hours in his cabin scouring his notes and papers before he ventured out for fresh air again. On the deck round-bellied men in top hats talked business while waiters delivered drinks to ladies discussing whatever women discussed. Jameson paid little attention as he mentally polished his presentation. Then something caught his eye.

A red-haired woman in her mid-twenties held a thin green book, while a lace parasol deflected the afternoon sun from her long neck.

With a look of amazement, Jameson dropped to his knees beside her.

"Excuse me, Miss, I don't mean to interrupt . . . but I

couldn't help noticing you're reading *Egyptian Antiquities* by Auguste Mariette." Jameson's voice was thick with excitement.

She looked up, and without any expression answered, "Why, yes."

Jameson's heart caught. This woman . . . this stunning woman with a flawless complexion and ice blue eyes that sparkled like stars . . . was reading his favorite book. It was this book that led him to Egypt many years ago and fueled his strange addiction for the place. After devouring it a half-dozen times, he taught himself hieroglyphs and had become a self-made authority on ancient Egypt.

And it all started with that small book.

Her fingers were perfectly manicured, the nails painted a shade of pink that reminded him of the first blush of a rose. She reached an index finger up and rubbed at a cameo attached to a ribbon around her neck. She must've felt the penetration of his gaze because she gave him a furtive glance, smiled ever-so-slightly, and returned to the page.

Jameson was not willing to give up the opportunity to speak with someone interested in his passion for Egyptian antiquities. "That's the best book on ancient artifacts ever written," he blurted.

"I agree, Professor Watts."

"H–h–how is it that you know my name?" He didn't bother to hide the surprise in his voice.

"Don't be silly, Professor Watts, everyone on this steamer knows who you are." She tossed her head and offered her dainty hand. "Miss Sinclair Upchurch. Pleased to make your acquaintance."

Her fingers were pleasantly warm to the touch, and he held them longer than proper. His chest grew tight and his mouth went instantly dry. Still, he managed to work up enough saliva so he could speak. "Join me for supper, Miss Upchurch? Seven o'clock, my private table?" After a moment, he added, "Please."

"That would be lovely." She promptly lowered her eyes to the book.

He released a breath he'd been holding and took in another filled with the essence of her, the sweet mellow fragrance of sandalwood and vanilla.

When he returned to his cabin something felt out of place, but nothing seemed to be missing. His satchel, research papers, and other valuables were as he'd left them. *I should never clean my desk,* he thought, and vowed not to make that mistake again. He might have investigated further were he not so preoccupied with the notion of dining with the marvelous Miss Sinclair Upchurch.

That evening when Sinclair arrived, Jameson jumped to his feet to welcome her and pulled out a chair. While she arranged her voluminous satin skirt the waiter stood at attention.

"I'll have a sherry," she said sweetly.

"The usual for you, Mr. Watts?"

"Yes, thank you, Finley." Jameson's eyes never left his guest.

Moments later the black-vested waiter offered the woman a small glass of sherry, which she delicately sipped as she watched Jameson concoct his. He poured a pale green liquid from a cruet onto a sugar cube held by a fine slotted silver spoon, and followed this with a splash of water. He raised his small crystal glass, "to Egypt."

"So I can see you've been bitten by the green fairy, Professor Watts."

"I must admit I love this stuff more than I should. But I feel it focuses the mind in a way that nothing else can."

He took another sip, savoring both the licorice essence and the presence of this beautiful woman.

"To Egypt," she echoed. "I love Egypt."

He fought for breath. Jameson had never met another whose love of Egypt equaled his.

"I would live there, I think," she continued. "So I could be near the pyramids and the Nile."

Jameson felt his skin flush and he stared at her hands, making sure there was no wedding band or promise ring. Dare he hope . . .

The waiter presented a tureen of fish chowder, followed by roast venison and creamed peas, but the couple was so lost in conversation about Egypt and each other that they barely touched their meals. The other diners had gone; the room was now dim; the candles inside the hurricane lamps had nearly all burned out. The couple didn't seem to notice the blackberry cordial and lemon chess tarts on a silver tray in the middle of the table.

A massive brass chandelier suspended above added a warm glow to the rich cherry paneling and reflected bits of light around them like stars.

None brighter than her eyes, Jameson thought. Her lilac gown was the color of his mother's favorite flower.

It was nearly midnight when Jameson felt a familiar flutter. He pulled his watch-communicator from his vest pocket and read the coded dispatch while Sinclair craned her neck to look at the device.

"Important message?"

"Just my captain," he sighed.

"Professor Watts . . . how many books have you read on Egypt?"

"Oh . . . a few more than I've written." He hoped he hadn't sounded arrogant.

"I should like to read them all," she said.

He leaned in close, taking her hands, his lips inches from hers.

"Professor Watts, it's after midnight. I really must be going." She leveled her gaze. "I do have my reputation to consider. Thank you for a lovely evening, and I hope we see each other again."

Before the archaeologist could beg her to stay, she'd vanished.

The next morning Jameson tried to concentrate on deciphering a parchment rubbing. He swore he could still smell her perfume. He'd had trouble sleeping last night, so consumed with thoughts of her; he'd dampened the sheets with his dreams. Why hadn't he leaned in all the way and kissed her after dinner? Had she left because he'd hesitated? Because he didn't have the courage or presence to . . . .

He was startled by a knock at his cabin door. He'd trimmed his goatee, combed his thinning hair and changed his shirt, secretly hoping to run into Sinclair. Was it she at the door?

After a quick peek into his looking glass, he pulled the door open. His heart leapt.

"Good morning, Miss Upchurch."

"Sinclair, please." She poked her head into the dimly lit cabin overflowing with all things Egyptian. A small baboon carved from carnelian sat on the corner of his desk and a pomegranate-shaped vase, mud seals, vials of tiny springs, and brass gears littered shelves among alabaster jars, jeweler's tools, and funerary artifacts. A small gold-leafed statue of Horus perched on a bookcase piled with fragments of clay tablets, potsherds, papyrus, and well-read books.

"Why, Professor Watts—it looks like you live in a tomb."

She looked radiant, and the fragrance of sandalwood

floated into the cabin. Her long red hair was tucked under a cream-colored silk hat wrapped in chiffon. A few tendrils fell at the nape of her long neck. Jade and pearl earrings dangled against her pale skin, and she clutched a small beaded bag in her dainty gloved hand.

"I wondered if you'd accompany me onshore . . . if you are not otherwise busy. The captain told me the boat would dock soon at Ephraim for the day while the supplies are loaded, and I have business there. I'd feel much safer if you'd come with me to town."

Jameson stammered his acceptance, donned his tweed jacket, and strolled at her side off the boat.

The city bustled: barrels and supplies were loaded, and passengers waved to those waiting for them on the dock. The breeze drew spicy scents of late autumn as they walked along the streets of the old river town. For the first time in years Jameson noticed the rich colors blazing from the maple trees. Leaves that looked like gold coins shimmered from tall white-barked trees that lined the main street.

Sinclair and Jameson arrived at the green-shuttered law office of Rabe and Perlman.

"This is the place. Professor, I have a bit of business to attend to this morning, it shouldn't take long. Would you meet me at the end of Canal Road? At the edge of town there's a warehouse I'm interested in leasing for my new millinery business. Once my meeting is over I'll meet you there at say . . . one thirty? My lawyer has a key and will show us through the place, and I'd like to get your expert opinion."

"But . . . I'm no expert on ladies' hats."

"Ah, but you are an expert, Professor."

He felt the heat of a blush spread over his face. "I–I need a few provisions for my trip anyway, so of course I'll meet you at the warehouse . . . at one thirty . . . and maybe we can dine afterward at the Blue Oyster. It's the best restaurant in Ephraim." He watched Sinclair disappear through the front door of a red brick building. As he reluctantly turned to leave, he noticed a shabbily dressed man watching him from across the street.

"Sinclair," he said to himself, realizing the fellow must have been watching her. Jameson wondered if everyone noticed her great beauty and stared. "Now . . . for those provisions."

He hadn't needed anything, but went shopping anyway. With a new coat and shirt wrapped in brown paper under his arm, he wandered the streets looking into the shop windows. Shortly after one o'clock he sped toward Canal Road.

Out of the corner of his eye he thought he saw someone step over the curb behind him. He had a strange feeling that he was being followed as he rushed down the sidewalk, but then dismissed the notion as silly. "Ah, there it is." Nearly a half mile away towered a dilapidated warehouse. He arrived out of breath.

"Sinclair?" He didn't see her.

Jameson wiped a spot on the grimy window to see if Sinclair and her lawyer were inside. At the same time he noticed the acrid smell of something burning and heard a faint hiss. He spun, fully intending to leap out of the way of a snake, when out of nowhere a man tackled him and pushed him face down in the dirt. Before he could react, he felt the ground shake. An explosion rocked the earth and glass shards and splinters of wood pelted them from every direction. He felt his assailant roll off him and heard him coughing, but he couldn't see through the thick smoke.

The stranger groped his way toward Jameson, both men still choking on the smell of gunpowder in the thick air. "I got my orders from Cap'n Keel to get you back to the boat right away."

Jameson made a connection; it was the shabbily dressed man, who was now even filthier than before. He managed to hoist Jameson under his arm and hustle the archaeologist back onboard the *Evangeline.*

"Sinclair . . ." Jameson wheezed.

"She's all right. Wasn't near the explosion. I'll go find her," the man answered. "Just see to yourself."

Jameson had no intention of abandoning the comely woman, but he would change his jacket before returning to shore. He'd just reached his cabin, stripped off his shredded tweed, and decided to have a swallow of absinthe to steady his nerves before searching for Sinclair. As he prepared the drink, his door flew open with such force he was surprised it remained on the hinges.

Captain Keel's large frame filled the doorway.

"Dammit, Watts. What's it gonna take for you to get serious that someone's out to kill you?" His eyes blazed as he blew an exasperated puff of air that fluttered his wide walrus mustache. Gold buttons threatened to explode from the vest stretched tightly over his large belly, and his face blazed a disturbing shade of red.

Momentarily, thoughts of Sinclair fled and Jameson stared, dazed. He poked a finger in his ear, opened and shut his mouth, but he was still unable to hear much after Keel's outburst.

The captain stomped over the threshold in the dimly lit cabin just as the archaeologist raised a shaking glass of chartreuse liquid to his lips. Captain Keel reached his ham-sized hand across the desk and knocked the glass of absinthe across the room.

"Watts, are you listening to me?"

Jameson watched slack-jawed as the spilled green liquor smoked for a moment before it burst into flames, igniting a crumpled newspaper that lay on the floor.

Keel's large foot stomped out the fire, then he quickly

whisked the decanter of green liquid off the desk. Jameson followed the captain, hanging his head like a scolded dog. Absentmindedly, he pinched the bridge of his nose and rubbed it while a thousand random thoughts threaded through his head as his heart thundered in his chest.

"Why would someone try to kill me?" he whispered. "And Sinclair . . . Miss Upchurch . . . I need to know she's all right."

"She's fine," Keel blustered. "She's finishing some business in town and will be onboard the ship before we sail."

Jameson spent the rest of the afternoon under Captain Keel's watchful dark eyes, and he was "allowed" back to his cabin to change for supper, one of the captain's men keeping watch outside the door.

He changed his shirt and tie, buttoned his vest, and paged through a portfolio of pen and ink sketches and pencil drawings he'd made of ruins and artifacts that were cataloged on his last expedition to Egypt, hoping these would interest Sinclair. By messenger, he sent her an invitation to join him for the evening meal. "Please," he'd ended the message.

The dining salon was full of passengers, not an empty table anywhere. Under other circumstances this would have made Jameson happy that his steamboat was doing such a brisk trade, but he was more consumed with thoughts of her. Her absence tore at his heart. The chandelier cast its glow over the crisp white table linen, the exquisite hand-painted china, and shimmering crystal goblets. He sipped on some whiskey and checked his watch. The captain had tossed out all of the absinthe. Lost in thought, and trying to keep his mind off Sinclair, he scribbled into a notebook. He didn't hear the slight creaking from the enormous chandelier that hovered above his head.

Every few moments he nervously checked to see if Sinclair had arrived. He'd confirmed that she'd returned to the ship, but she hadn't returned his message.

The bodyguard who was ordered to stay nearby was lighting his pipe when Jameson dipped under the table to fetch his fallen pen. In that instant the brass chandelier crashed onto the table. Glass flew and the thick maple table split neatly in two.

Jameson moaned from under the wreckage.

Diners rushed to dig him out just as Sinclair stepped into the room, shrieked at the sight, and promptly fainted.

Battered and bruised and suitably bandaged, the archaeologist limped to answer his cabin door the following morning. His broken arm was trussed in a sling. A lovely shade of purple bloomed around his left eye below a lump large enough to cast a shadow.

Sinclair flinched when she saw his face in the dim light. "Oh, dear," was all she said.

Jameson felt his temperature rise. She was lovely, an angel come to ground.

She held out her hand and offered him a small package. "I'm so sorry to see you hurt," she said in a concerned voice. "I brought you a small token. It's nothing, really. Don't try to talk." She touched his swollen lip with her finger. "Oh, this is my fault. If I hadn't asked you to come to shore with me . . ."

He shook off her words and held her fingers in his good hand, trying to draw her close, but the motion was awkward with his bandages and he practically stumbled into her.

"Maybe we could meet later, Professor? Say this evening, after you've had the day to rest. I'll be leaving as soon as we dock in the morning, and I'd hate to go without a proper farewell . . . a long, proper farewell."

His blood pounded in his ears. "Leaving?" the word came out as a croak.

"Unfortunately, yes. Business, you understand. But that doesn't mean we can't . . . you know . . . if you feel up to it."

A smile crept to his swollen lips.

"It's settled then. I'll be on deck . . . say . . . around ten. We'll watch the stars on the water and then . . . retire . . . for the rest of the night."

Jameson watched her sway away and closed the cabin door behind her. He swallowed a powerful pain remedy with some bourbon sent by Captain Keel and woke not knowing if he'd slept an hour or an entire day. As he swung his stiff legs over the side of the bed and gathered the strength to stand, his blood tingled with the thought of seeing the willowy redhead for perhaps the final time.

He scratched his whiskers, remembering the scent of her exotic perfume, and thought, *Maybe she'd come with me to Egypt. Maybe this won't be the last time. Maybe it will be forever.*

The pain had somewhat subsided, he felt hungry, and the lump on his head no longer stung. Maybe she could see past his infirmaries and idiosyncrasies . . . and the ugliness of his mottled black eye.

It was nearly ten when he made his way along the deck awash in silvery moonlight. He slowly limped toward the stern where the water splashed off the paddlewheel with a whooshing rhythm. Between the posts of the railing something familiar glistened—Sinclair's cameo. As he tried to grab it, a gunshot ripped through the peaceful night, followed by a thud. He turned around to see Sinclair face down—dark blood slowly staining the back of her gown. The blade of a Bowie knife gleamed in the moonlight, the handle clutched in her leather-gloved fist.

He didn't need to look closer; he knew she was dead.

Behind her Captain Keel held a smoking pistol. The sharp scent of gunpowder hung like a cloud around the captain as he looked sadly at the archaeologist.

"Come on, Watts," Keel said. "Let's have a drink."

In the wheelhouse the archaeologist stared straight ahead in shock. Tears stained his bruised face.

The captain threw back a large bourbon. "She was about to run you through with that Bowie knife when I showed up."

Jameson lifted his bloodshot eyes.

"Her real name was Stella Rechow, a black widow for hire—so to speak, sent to kill you. A pack of Texas oil-men put her on their payroll. Word must've got out about your trip to Washington and your energy metal, and it seems they weren't going to let your discovery put them out of business. I contacted the authorities and had them do a check on every passenger onboard. The information about our 'Miss Upchurch' had just come over my communicator, so I went to her cabin to confront her—but she'd gone. Found this on her bed." The captain held out a green antiquities book. "It's yours—she must have taken the book from your cabin."

Taken it, as she had taken his heart. Jameson sniffed as he opened the green cover and saw *J. Watts* scribbled in the corner.

"The police'll be waitin' for us at Exeter in the morning. Seems they've been chasing her for a while. She's got a list of aliases, murders, and felonies long as your arm. My best guess is she was gonna stab you and throw you overboard. I reckon she left that cameo for you to find right where you'd reach over the rail. She'd have been long gone before your body washed ashore."

Jameson regarded him numbly and finished his bourbon.

"You better get some sleep now, Watts." The captain grabbed Jameson by the shoulder and steered the shaken man toward his cabin.

Dawn was seeping over the horizon when the archaeologist finally fell asleep.

Several months later, after his meeting with the president, Jameson traveled back to Egypt. He visited the final resting place of the ancient scientist he'd discovered decades ago, stood at the sarcophagus, and gazed steadily while his eyes adjusted to the flickering torchlight.

The hieroglyphs on the walls spelled out the necessary incantations for the mummy seeking the afterlife. The Ankh and Shen symbols meant life eternal, and beneath it the deity Ma'at wore the feather of truth next to Heh, the god of millions of years. The colorful spells that adorned the dusty walls had barely faded through eons of time.

Jameson pried open the sarcophagus. He carefully placed the canopic jar and all but one of the artifacts he'd found there decades ago back inside. He idly wondered if the mummy had been murdered for the energy discovery.

He rubbed the scarab beetle dangling around his neck for luck.

Before he crawled out of the tomb for the last time, the archaeologist reverently said a prayer that the ancient man had found eternal life.

THE PROBLEM OF TRYSTAN

Maurice Broaddus

Maurice Broaddus is the author of the novel series The Knights of Breton Court. His dark fiction has been published in numerous magazines, anthologies, and web sites, most recently including Dark Dreams II *and* III, Apex Magazine, Black Static, *and* Weird Tales Magazine. *He is the co-editor of the* Dark Faith *anthology. Visit him at www.mauricebroaddus.com.*

The Tejas Express was a monstrosity of gleaming metal, though in its own way beautiful to behold. Large and cumbersome, with steam curling around it like caressing tendrils, the carriage rumbled along on an intricate system of toothed tracks. It moved with a great thrumming sound, much like a racing heart attempting to be restrained. Winston Jefferson jostled about in the car, one eye on the group of soldiers milling as if they were not on duty. Part of him resented the scarlet bleed of their red soldier uniforms. The antithesis of camouflage by design, it let the enemy know who was coming for them in the name of Her Majesty Queen Diana.

His other eye rested on his charge, who the soldiers amiably chatted up. Winston's hand tightened its grip on his cane handle as she sauntered toward him.

With an olive complexion and long brown hair framing aristocratic features from her piercing brown eyes to her aquiline nose, Lady Trystan stood at a formidable six feet. He couldn't quite place her origin, but he didn't care enough to ask. He simply appreciated the view and thanked God for whatever country that could produce such a resplendent specimen. Lips glossed to an exaggerated redness were pursed tightly, not betraying a hint of her feelings. She had a regal presence in her green and blue gown in a kente cloth pattern; a crinoline supported her dress with its slight train. It had a high neck with a tatted collar and soutache trim. She walked toward the bench. For a moment his eyes met hers. She held the gaze.

"Mr. Jefferson," she said in her demure drawl, pretending she didn't know him. One of the little games she liked to play.

"Colonel." He tipped his top hat.

"My . . . colonel. We are proud of our titles."

"Only the ones 'we' have earned."

Winston still wore a gray sack coat, copper buttons running up each side, left open in order to display a four-in-hand necktie and collared shirt. The veneer of respectability. He began his career as a soldier when he was seventeen. For ten years he served queen and country, earning a battlefield promotion to colonel during the Five Civilized Nations uprising. Not that the title was anything more than honorific, as one of his station couldn't hope to command men. A moot point as, wounded as he was, he was soon discharged for his troubles. His cane, a lacquered black rod with copper fittings beginning midway up its shank to its hilt, an open-mouthed copper dragon's head, allowed him to hide the slightest of limps.

"Lady Trystan." He nodded toward the wrought iron table bedecked with a silver tray set with tea and cream in matching pots next to a plate of strawberries. "A magnificent name."

"LaDashia Rachel Brown Willoughby of the Virginia Willoughbys." She dipped a strawberry into the cream then rolled it in the sugar—a slow, deliberate action—before popping it into her mouth.

"A family of noble bearing. Your father, Sir Anthony Willoughby, must be proud."

"Adopted father. My mother was widowed soon after I was born."

"Still, he's a member of the Royal Academy of Sciences. A rare honor."

"We both took his name when they married. I took Rachel as my confirmation name."

"So where does the name Trystan come from?"

"Are we the sum of our names, or can we choose to own some of them but not others?"

"You tell me."

"I had no say in my birth name. No say in my mother's remarriage. And my religion was thrust upon me. Trystan is what I choose to call myself."

"To my ear, it almost sounds like Trickster."

"We all could use some of Br'er Nanci's spirit sometimes." She chatted to mask her unease, perhaps discomfited by the weight of his scrutiny. Her over-creamed coffee complexion allowed those who wanted to let her pass for a white woman. However, despite careful make-up and the distraction of her peculiar framed glasses, her features favored the Negro. A keen intelligence laid in wait behind the beguiling playfulness in her hazel eyes and mischievous humor was hinted about in her lips.

"My mother was Caucasian. My natural father was African. He passed away soon after my birth. But I was so fair, none were the wiser when we relocated to Virginia, where Mother met Sir Anthony. My heritage would be an embarrassment to him, my mother impressed upon me."

"So why entrust your secret to me?"

"You have one of those faces."

"What kind of face is that?"

"Handsome. Intelligent. And something just short of trustworthy." She smiled, a terribly enticing thing.

He never imagined his oval shaped face, with low-cropped hair matching the length of his closely shorn beard, little longer than a week's stubble, as a particularly pleasant countenance. At best, he tried to carry himself as a nobleman, a proud oak of a man with a complexion to match. She differed from most of the ladies of society he had encountered, with their insipidity and air of self-importance which accompanied most of the people of high society. They reeked of privilege and uselessness, and he listened to their chatter with perfect indifference. Inane white noise which heavied his eyelids. Lady Trystan was cautious in her praise of any man, he imagined, and with her insouciant demeanor—both flippant and wry—she would make a poor wife by most men's standards. Not used to so bold a woman—sarcastic humor with a keen mind and no care for others' thoughts on her manner—she intrigued him.

"Men are such foolish creatures. Unsure of what you feel or if you should feel it. It was good for you that God chose to create women to help you along."

"I can sort my own feelings just fine, miss."

"Oh, I hardly believe that. You don't even realize how much attraction you feel for me right now."

Winston found it difficult to disengage from her commanding gaze. Suddenly he straightened in his seat, conscious of where he was and what he was supposed to be doing. He was a man with a job to do, and it wasn't to be caught up in the spell of this woman.

"You look as if you've swallowed a turnip," Lady Trystan said.

"Merely reminded of my duty."

"Sorry if I distracted you."

"Your father entrusted me to guarantee your safe passage."

"Are your coterie of soldiers not enough?"

"They serve their function."

"Which is?"

"To distract."

Winston studied the faces of the people who shared their car, searching for anything or anyone that looked out of place. He read their eyes. A gaunt, swarthy gentleman buried his face in a newspaper. On the short side of average, in his brown suit and bowler he had the build of a rodent dressed as a dandy. The newspaper's headlines declared the beginnings of The Troubles—how everyone referred to the Jamaican uprising—as well as the Queen's preparation to appoint Viceroy Reagan to rule the American colony in the name of Albion and carry the banner for the Empire. A former actor as puppet sounded about right to him, but he didn't have the benefit of an A-level education. A young boy quavered as his father scolded him. The tone rose in volume and the tenor in harshness, a critical barrage fueled by anger and maybe a little drink. The rest of the passengers turned away in polite deference. The man's contempt erupted as he drew back to beat the boy, when Winston rose and, heedless of the pain which caused him to limp, sprang to the boy's side. His cane may have stayed his father's blow, but it was the steel of his gaze which stilled the man.

"There's no need to take so stern a hand to the boy," Winston said.

"The boy," the man started, swallowed hard, and then found his voice again. "The boy needed a lesson in quieting his manner."

"A lesson already delivered. Do not let me find this boy bruised."

"What business of it is yours to interfere with a father doing his duty?"

Winston came from a family of five children; the responsibility of the older siblings was to protect the younger ones. Funny, the number of his family was six actually, but his brother, Auldwyn, had died when he was two. Though Winston was barely old enough to know him when he died, the thought of Auldwyn, more than the actual memory of his loss, continued to pain him. "I can't abide bullies. They . . . vex me. You don't want to vex me."

Trystan looked at him as if seeing him for the first time. A frightfully insufferable woman who had a predilection for revealing all of her teeth when she smiled, she quickly turned away, her long hair curled up into a tight coif, and she fanned herself as she stared out the window.

"As I was saying, my duty was to deliver you to the hand of Sir Melbourne."

"Such was my father's wish."

"He is a powerful man, your father, with many enemies."

"And he sought to mollify some of them with this ill-conceived arrangement. My parents are quite cross with me at the moment."

"I couldn't hazard a guess why."

"I was to marry Sir Melbourne, the archduke of Georgia. A nobleman of noble family."

"And?"

"He bored me."

"And a husband's duty is to entertain his wife."

"Your sarcasm has been duly noted. He wanted a wife interested in keeping a home, organizing social events, to be a trophy attached to his arm when at a party and placed on the mantel when at home."

"And such is not the calling for your life." Winston had no use for a wife. Marriage was a kind of ownership, one person belonging to another. Freedom was too precious a commodity for him to forfeit any.

"No, it most certainly is not. However, I have more to do than just find a husband. The problem is that it is unseemly to have your daughters marry out of order."

"I trust that your younger sisters are vexed with you also?"

"All four of them."

"You broke off all marriage talk with Sir Melbourne?"

"Sir, my heart is my own. And it tarries ... elsewhere."

"You still have time to change your mind."

"I know. A lot can happen in a fortnight."

The dynamo of Albion, the American colony, was a proud beacon that stretched from the Atlantic to the Pacific, between the Five Civilized Nations of the Northwest Territories and the Tejas Free Republic of the Southwest Territories. The Tejas Express was a product of American revolutionary design. A luxurious vehicle, with an interior of lacquered mahogany, polished brass, and brushed velvet. To Winston's mind, it was like a brothel decorated with decadent designer's eye. His tastes ran to the simple. The engine snorted a continuous billow of steam as it bustled forward toward Indianapolis on its way to Chicago. For every burgeoning overcity like Indianapolis, there was a burgeoning undercity; in Indianapolis' case, the residents referred to it as Atlantis.

Winston imagined himself starting over in a place like Indianapolis. Nondescript, a blank slate where he could disappear and redefine himself. As of this moment, he was a forcibly retired—as forcibly as he was conscripted—soldier. His station was enough to spare him toiling away in the undercities shoveling coal or assembling small machines in the industrial shops, the clockwork gears biting into scabbed fingertips, for hours on end. He might be able to find a low-ranking position in the overcity, something he was overqualified for, but it'd be a place to start. Winston wondered why he couldn't just be content with his lot in life. No, the nagging fear that he ought to be doing something other than his father's profession dogged him. He had inherited an estate of $750,000 from his father, but his father had made his fortune in trafficking. Money made selling their own people into indentureship; the weight of the shame was not worth his soul. He used some of the credits to free others from indenture then gave the rest away. He was meant for greater things, to have it all, and he wanted to be beholden to no one. Perhaps his destiny awaited him as a businessman. If he could grow a business to the point where he wasn't needed to run it day-to-day, then he could expand into other ventures. To dabble in airships was his dream, but it all began with starting a business. Only then could he hope to be with someone like Lady Trystan.

"Mr. Jefferson." She leaned on her frilly parasol in tacit imitation of him and his cane.

"Colonel."

"Where are you from? Kentucky, perhaps?"

"Why do you ask?"

"Your manner and speech betray you. Too affected."
A furtive glance. A less attentive gentleman may have
missed it. But she tracked the movements of the soldiers.
"A hint of accent to your words. They don't slip out often,
but they're there. You've worked hard to hide your roots."

"Your impertinence begins to irritate me." By nature
he eluded any attempts by others to get to know him.
He hated the way she saw through him, knowing him
with a glance.

"There's no shame in it. Or you."

She locked onto his eyes as if her very being de-
pended on maintaining the intensity of their gaze. More
powerful than lust, it was magic. Their world was the
train. Here they could pretend they had no outside responsibilities. Distance meant nothing, time meant nothing; even though he was across the table from her, she
was probably unaware that he had slipped his fingers
between hers.

Winston turned away and sought to master the emotions threatening to distract him from his appointed
task. He noticed a gentleman in his early fifties with an
athletic build with silver hair and beard. A silver and
blue eye patch matched not only the pocket handkerchief tucked into the breast pocket of his black suit, but
also his elegant silk tie. He cut a striking figure though
wearing perhaps too much toilet water. The man took
the moment to saunter over to them. Winston stood and
composed his demeanor.

"Allow me to introduce myself. My name is Richard
St. Ives." He had a queer lilting resonance to his voice, as
if speaking through his nose at a high altitude.

"Pleased to meet your acquaintance, Mr. St. Ives."
Lady Trystan offered her hand.

"Oh, I very much doubt that. You see, I'm an agent of Sir Melbourne."

"Then whatever business you have is between you and him."

"Would that it were so, but often the claims of family tread all over our well-intentioned designs."

"The lady says she has no business with you." Winston rested both of his palms on his cane. Not even the joggling of the train's movement budged him.

St. Ives smoothed his gloves, the corresponding gesture in their voiceless dance of intimidation and veiled threat. "But I fear I've business with her, as I have been retained to sort out matters. That is what I do."

"You sort out things. You should know that I am under the employ of Sir Anthony. I, too, sort out things."

It was a bold maneuver to approach Lady Trystan so openly, especially with the occasional soldier wandering about. Winston scanned the car on the hunch that St. Ives didn't work alone. The swarthy gentleman feigned attention at his newspaper, making too much effort to appear inconspicuous.

"What is it you want, Mr. St. Ives?" Lady Trystan asked.

"Your father has all manner of secret contraptions, not all of them built through his own ingenuity. Sir Melbourne's demands are simple. Either go through with the proposed marriage, so that the two families be enjoined . . ."

"Or . . ." Winston asked.

"Or turn over all patents pertaining to his micro-clockwork project."

"My father would never agree to that."

"Your father finds himself in a precarious position. At odds with his government, at odds with his business, and at odds with his religion. He is in need of allies, not further enemies." St. Ives' eyes grew flat and cold. "Your father should not have meddled with the inventions of others. Only Sir Anthony's resources could keep the kabbalists from pursuing your family."

"None of this has anything to do with me," Lady Trystan protested.

"But it does, I fear. For the sins of the father shall pass on to the next generation. And the next and the next." St. Ives turned to Winston. "Tell your man he has one day."

"What was that about?" Winston asked as he watched St. Ives depart the car. He did not acknowledge knowing the man who pressed his nose back into the newspaper.

"I don't know."

"I know a few things about the business of fathers, the secrets they keep in the name of building a family's fortune, and how much children can know. No matter how well their parents guard against their learning ..."

"... secrets win out," Trystan finished.

"As you say."

She worried the kerchief in her lap. "I fear Albion rots from its own wealth and bloat. The sun never sets on the Albion empire, yet its very strength is its weakness."

"How so?"

"Intellectual laziness comes with a lifestyle of ease. We don't advance as fast as we should."

"You sound like an insurrectionist. A Jamaican sympathizer."

"Keep your voice down. You do me an injustice, sir."

"My apologies, milady. Then the rumors about your father ..."

"Do you now traffic in rumors, Mr. Jefferson? My father is loyal to the crown."

"I would hope should I ever become the object of

unwarranted speculation that I have so staunch a defender."

"Do you mock me?"

"I do not."

"I always speak what I think."

"That can be a dangerous trait in a lady."

"Good, because I have dangerous thoughts. All I am saying is that America is the heart that pumps the life-blood of resources and invention to Albion. It is they who should fear us breaking away."

Lady Trystan reminded him of a prized flower kept under glass. To be viewed and kept as a piece of living art, but cut off from the world. Never touched. He was careful not to let their hands brush one another.

"We are both playing the role expected of us."

"Trapped by them, you mean."

Winston slept for a few hours. His dreams, though unre-membered, left him unsettled, his clothes damp with per-spiration, and he, curiously, in a state of mild arousal. The pungent scent of bodily exudations filled the air. Yet the thought that something was amiss lingered. He dressed hurriedly to check on his charge. He slipped out of his car, hand steady on his cane as he ambled toward Lady Trystan's compartment. Once he caught sight of the crumpled bodies of the two unconscious soldiers outside it, he knew what he'd find inside. Her suite—filled with embroidered sofas, an armoire, and stacked trunks of memorabilia—greatly disheveled. Her bed asunder.

Winston ducked out of the car and passed through the other passenger cars as he made his way through the train. His heart raced, pained with anxiety. Winston sur-veyed each car as he strode, inspecting them for any sign of his charge. He cursed himself for not doubling her guard after their encounter with Mr. St. Ives. He closed his eyes and forced himself to remain calm. Not wanting to alarm the other passengers—nor create greater chaos—he didn't rouse his soldiers. He had to be the one to find her.

The passengers of the train slept soundly at this late hour. The train rumbled around a bend, throwing off Winston's gait, then straightened out as it crossed a bridge traversing the Ohio River. He pulled the door to enter the small portico that bookended each car. It allowed the passengers to be undisturbed by the noise of the outside as porters entered and left the car. Winston opened the next to last car. The wind scraped at him. The cacophony of the rush of air, the clangor of the engine, and the rattle along the tracks rose to a near physical assault. He clutched his cane as he leaped from car to car, latching onto the rail with his free hand. Once inside, it took a moment for his ears to adjust to the eerie silence once more. The engine room wasn't what he expected. He remembered the days of coal-shoveling engine jockeys crying black tears as soot mixed with perspiration around their goggles. This engine room gleamed with polished metal. Two figures struggled at the far end of the car. The swarthy man glanced at pressure gauges, flipping levers like a mad man as he turned a wayward crank. Lady Trystan, in a red silk dressing gown, was held fast under one arm. His stomach bottomed out. His heart lurched, so desperately afraid she might be hurt. Or taken away.

"Unhand her, cur," Winston shouted.

The man turned and revealed a weapon aimed at Lady Trystan: a pistol of some sort with a glass sphere where the cylinder should be. Energy crackled in it like a miniature plasma ball. Winston has seen such weapons before, cognizant of the charred remains to which they could reduce a body.

"I have no wish to harm the young lady. However, my employer does wish her to be delivered to him. So while this train may make a detour so that we may depart, her condition upon arrival was not . . . specified." The man yanked her, tightening his grip to drive home his point.

Leaning on his cane, Winston raised his left hand to show that he was unarmed and for the man to relax. He caught Lady Trystan's eye, counting on her intelligence and resourcefulness. "You'll get no trouble out of me. I actually feel sorry for your client. Lady Trystan is a handful. A vexing woman prone to outburst."

He nodded.

Lady Trystan bit the man's arm. In a savage hurl, he flung her into the control panel. He raised his weapon to take aim at her, but Winston drew a bead with his cane first. He squeezed the open mouth of his dragon head handle, and the cane discharged with a sharp report. A wisp of smoke drifted from the tip of Winston's cane. The bullet pierced the man's heart, and the man stared at him in mild disbelief. He staggered back one step, touching his vest as if checking the measure of his wound and determining it as fatal. For a moment, he seemed to waver, enough life in him to fire one shot of his weapon. But as Winston scampered to get between the man and Lady Trystan, the weapon fell from his fingertips as if he'd decided it would be unsporting of him.

Winston offered his hand to help Lady Trystan from the ground. She rose to her feet with an awkward dignity.

"I turn my back on you for a moment and you get into all manner of trouble."

"I find I must ever seek to draw attention to myself to keep the men in my life entertained."

"But it's not your job to keep your husband entertained." Caught up in their droll banter, the ill-considered intimation of spousehood tripped from his tongue before he could stop it. Were he a man prone to blushing, he might have beamed a torrid crimson. As it was, he fumbled at his pocket to find a new cartridge to reload into the breech of his cane.

"Kiss me." Lady Trystan leaned close to him, her voice husky in his ear. She touched his shoulder.

"God save you. You're a complete romantic. People like me aren't meant to be with people like you. It isn't . . . proper. Our roles . . ."

"*Their* roles be damned. *Our* role is to love. There's not enough of it in our world, so when we find it, no matter how proper society finds it, we must embrace it."

Winston kissed her tenderly.

Mr. St. Ives' private car featured a bench of crimson velvet on which he sat reading a book and smoking a briar pipe. Music poured out of a small contraption with a gleaming carapace. At Winston's entry, St. Ives leaned over to shut off the electro-transmitter device.

"Your agent failed."

"An agent of an agent? Surely I have no idea what you're talking about," St. Ives said. "I will say this: the pursuit won't cease. Lady Trystan, as she calls herself, is still her father's daughter. As such, ever the most visible pawn to move."

"And if she should disappear?"

"It is a complicated world we live in. However, a pawn out of play is of no concern to me. Or my employer."

Lady Trystan carried herself with the bearing of a woman prone to athletics. With a seductive modesty, her gown was snug enough to reveal every curve of her voluptuous breasts and fitted to show off the flatness of her belly, without exposing any skin. In stark contrast to Winston's mannered fastidiousness, her eyes sparkled with an arcane fire, a vivaciousness that threatened to consume him. The curious curl of her lips added a certain coquettishness to her manner, a coy edge compounded in her posture. Something about her scent captivated him, rushed straight to his head like a fog settling on his brain. No one should radiate so much sexual energy simply by sitting down.

"I have an acquaintance in Indianapolis I was due to call upon after delivering you to your father," Winston said.

"I do so wish the men in my world would quit discussing me as if I were a sack of potatoes being shipped somewhere."

"After some careful consideration, a clear mind would determine that a fortnight of acquaintance is no basis for any claim of intimacy."

"You're quite circumspect. I imagine it takes you hours to convey the cleverest of anecdotes." Lady Trystan leaned closer, running her fingertips along his hand. He jumped, snatching his hand back as if bitten. She smiled. "Do you wish me to go with you?"

"You delight in vexing me."

"I delight in being me. Perhaps you are too easily vexed. Led by your nose from passion to passion, spending it recklessly on any passing fancy."

Lord have mercy, the way that woman stared at him, Winston thought. His own eyes drank her in. Large, brown pupils danced in a pool that reflected only her. He attempted not to conspicuously gaze on the curve of her body, her dress barely contained. His mouth grew dry, his tongue a swollen useless thing that choked back any words his brain managed to string together. He couldn't imagine what to say, not to a woman like that.

All woman—confident, unapologetically sexual, and with a devouring seductiveness. Someone who knew the power of her sex and wielded it like an expert martial artist. Winston's hands labored to remain fixed on his cane handle. Instead, he consulted his pocket watch, and then blew on its pewter finish to polish it with a handkerchief, avoiding the power of her gaze. "I thought perhaps it might be prudent for you to accompany me. Away from the schemes of your father and his enemies. Somewhere you could determine your own course."

"With you?"

"It would honor me to accompany you." Most women concerned themselves with the attentions and fortunes of available men and their standing in society. She was a woman of deep reflection. A woman of no discretion, as proud of it as she was difficult. A woman who preoccupied his thoughts.

"Would there be horses? I love to ride."

"Surely we could find a horse for you." He donned his top hat, and then tugged at the vest that covered his white shirt left open at the neck.

"You carry on like a brooding old man."

"I have enough vitality left in me to keep up with you."

"Come on then."

The Tejas Express slowed as it pulled into the Indianapolis station. Its gears ground and clanged as the rattletrap box of their car shook. Winston directed his soldiers to carry Lady Trystan's belongings from the train and gave his number two a message to give to Sir Anthony upon their arrival in Chicago. Lady Trystan also gave him a note to pass along, informing her father of her decision to go her own way. That pursuit of her would only put her in further danger, though he shouldn't worry. She'd be in touch soon and in the mean-

time, she was in perfectly safe hands. Winston spied the
father who he stopped from beating his son. As they
both disembarked at the same stop, he gestured that he
would have his eye on him. Finally, he turned to Lady
Trystan.

"Do you believe in love at first sight?" she asked.

"Only inasmuch as I believe in the tooth fairy and
leprechauns. It is the domain of fanciful schoolgirls and
bored housewives."

"You are quite the romantic." She crossed her arms
and turned her head in a feigned pout.

"Indeed I am. I believe in love, deep and unbridled,
not the turn of a pretty phrase, polite gestures, and
barely engaged feelings which pass for courtship. I believe in putting in the work for love than contenting myself with the dream of romance."

"You still manage to turn the pretty phrase, nonethe-
less."

"I have my moments."

CLOCKWORKS

Jody Lynn Nye

Jody Lynn Nye lists her main career activity as "spoiling cats." She lives northwest of Chicago with two of the above and her husband, author and packager Bill Fawcett. She has published more than thirty-five books, including six contemporary fantasies, four SF novels, four novels in collaboration with Anne McCaffrey, including The Ship Who Won; *edited a humorous anthology about mothers,* Don't Forget Your Spacesuit, Dear!; *and written more than a hundred short stories. Her latest books are* A Forthcoming Wizard, *and* Myth-Fortunes, *co-written with Robert Asprin.*

Rosa sighed as the last man passed her by to dance with another young lady. She knew the chances were slim that any of these handsome gentlemen in black tailcoats and crisp white shirtfronts would reach for her hand and draw her out onto the dance floor—not when doing so meant being followed by a large, whirring, gasping device on wheels. You could have set a timer going as each man cast eyes upon her: how pretty was her shining black hair swept high on her head. How lovely her large brown eyes. Her pert, pointed chin had attracted many a whispered compliment that she was careful not to show she had overheard. Her graceful neck turned into a charming décolletage swathed modestly in her best lace wrapper. Then the large black disk attached just above the bodice of her pale blue dress caught their attention, drew it along the flexible brown umbilical to the bronze and steel machine, and the gentlemen, sometimes blushing at their own fears, would nod politely to her and pass along with somewhat indecent haste. Like the clockwork that kept her alive, the reactions were predictable and unfailing.

She withdrew into the curve of the gold velvet couch, and watched the dozens of couples sweep by her around the high-ceilinged white ballroom. How she wished she had not let her aunt talk her into coming to the dance! Jean Rabenski was aware how few opportunities for socializing that Rosa had. For that kindness, Rosa was grateful. But it was futile to hope that attendance might lead to courtship and matrimony.

Oh, God, she thought, *let me not die an old maid, or at least not a maiden!*

Her aunt would undoubtedly have been shocked. She came from a different generation, when a young lady's dreams of equality in matters of mind, body, and soul were just dreams. The advent of the machine age had brought forth the new notion that women were just as capable of invention and achievement as men, so holding women to be a secondary creation of God was foolish. It had opened the eyes of young ladies to exciting possibilities.

Still, Rosa was unlikely to put her hopes to the test. By all standards of public decency, or, more honestly, public fear, she should remain at home, quietly living out of sight of other people, so as not to remind them of the frailty of the human body. Rosa did not want to be decent any longer. She wanted to live. She wanted to dance with a different partner than the infernal gas-powered machine that kept her heart beating. Aunt Jean understood that part. She and Uncle Bruce, who had invented the cardiac regulator, were as devoted and loving a couple as anyone had ever known.

Here she came, her large blue eyes wide with delight. The rapid rasp of Jean Rabenski's dark blue taffeta gown almost drowned out the waltz music played by the orchestra as she towed a tall man behind her.

"Rosa, my darling, this lovely man would like to meet you!" she said. The blonde hair piled into a pumpkin shape on her head threatened to shake loose as she nodded vigorously at her escort. Rosa smiled politely at the newcomer. He didn't look 'lovely.' In fact, he was a bit plain, if Rosa could be so bold. He might have been tall, but he was somewhat stout, and though he looked not much more than Rosa's own age, he was already losing the hair on his domelike head. "Miss Lind, may I present Mr. Greenberg? Mr. Greenberg, this is my dear niece, Rosa Lind."

Rosa put out a gloved hand. To her surprise she felt it tremble. Mr. Greenberg wore thick pebble-lensed glasses, but when he bent down to take her fingers she saw the kindly blue eyes behind them. His grasp was warm and gentle.

"Mr. Greenberg, I am pleased to make your acquaintance," Rosa said.

"Thank you, Miss Lind," he said, his face shining with eagerness. "When I saw you from across the room, I knew I could not wait to speak to you. Your aunt was kind enough to introduce us." He nodded to Aunt Jean, who beamed. "I wonder, if it would not be an intrusion, if I might . . . it would mean a great deal to me . . ." He swallowed. Rosa held her breath, preparing herself to say yes, yes, yes! ". . .If you would permit me to examine the device at your side."

Rosa's heart, the flesh-and-blood one, sank to her dancing pumps. "Oh."

"Not here, of course," Mr. Greenberg continued, reading the disappointment and dismay in her face as potential embarrassment. "I am fascinated by modern machinery, and I am interested in its workings."

"You do understand that this is not a toy," Rosa said, unable to keep asperity out of her voice. She shot a speaking look at her aunt, who smiled blandly at her. She would have a lot to say to her later!

"Of course I do," Mr. Greenberg said earnestly. "It would be useless to deny that I have heard, er, some talk about the purpose of the machine. I know that it is continually saving your life. Not only would I want it to continue in its purpose, but it would be my aim to better it if I could. I am a clockmaker, you see, and I believe that miniaturization is the wave of the future. If you would be so very kind to allow me to visit you at home, perhaps tomorrow, or any other day that would suit your convenience?"

On the way home in the horseless carriage, Rosa felt her rage reaching a boiling point. If it were not for the quiet hiss-thump of the regulator beside her that kept it slow and steady, her heart would have been pounding like a tom-tom. She didn't trust herself to speak.

"You are very quiet," Aunt Jean said, steering the car with the electrostatic reins through the gaslit night toward the Rabenskis' town house, where Rosa was living during the season.

Rosa could not contain herself any longer. "How could you subject me to such a ridiculous person?"

Aunt Jean's face turned various colors as they passed electric advertisement signs lit by neon gas. "Well, my darling, he did ask to meet you. I had no good reason to say no. Everyone can see that you spend every single ball by yourself. Besides, if he can do anything to shrink your 'companion' there, I see no reason not to let him try. He is well known in his field. He trained in Switzerland, and his inventions have made him rather wealthy. Even you have heard of Tekno-Clocks."

"I . . . have," Rosa admitted. Another thought struck her and made her cheeks burn. "But now everyone will think me a fortune-hunter!"

"What do you care?" Aunt Jean said practically. "You have defied Death himself every day of your life. If nothing else, enjoy the novelty of having a gentleman caller."

It was no good saying Rosa didn't want one. The essence of normality was an elusive scent she had pursued all of her life. Her friends did their best not to treat her with pity, fearing her scorn, but she knew they felt it. She missed having private little notes dropped casually beside her on a couch or tucked into a bouquet. She longed for stolen kisses in the cinema or theater. But the heart regulator was the fiercest possible chaperone. No young man could pretend he didn't know it was there. And, perversely, she was insulted that it was the regulator that drew Mr. Greenberg's admiration.

Even so, the next afternoon, Rosa fussed over her garments and her toilette like any other young lady. She had just settled herself and the hissing regulator in a fetching tableau when the uniformed automaton strutted out of his sentry box in the timepiece on the mantel and announced, "Three o'clock post-meridian, madam and miss."

"Thank you, Joyeaux," Aunt Jean said. The mannequin bowed and retired. Almost as soon as she did, the doorbell rang. "There he is, like a clockwork himself!"

Mr. Greenberg's appearance did not keep with the theme of his precise arrival. His coat and trousers were slightly rumpled, and the brown leather valise in his left hand was battered by time and much usage. He bowed over Aunt Jean's hand and turned to Rosa.

"Miss Lind, how kind of you to let me come."

"My pleasure, Mr. Greenberg," Rosa said. In spite of herself, she did enjoy having a caller. Aunt Jean had gone to some trouble to whisper the news around the ballroom the night before. The speculative looks in Rosa's way gave her a frisson of excitement. "Will you sit down?"

"Thank you." The young man pulled a footstool up to Rosa's knee and sat on it. He was so tall that his knees stuck up like a grasshopper's. He opened the valise, and she saw neat rows of shining steel instruments, lenses, calipers and other small tools. "May I?" he asked.

No clever small talk, nor inquiries as to whether she had enjoyed the previous evening's entertainment. Ah, well, what in this world was perfect?

"Yes, of course," Rosa said. She watched as he put on a set of rubber-rimmed goggles with lenses several times thicker than his eyeglasses, and took out an oblong device the size of his hand. He turned a knob at the side. The device made a zooming noise and a glass-fronted gauge on the top lit up. Mr. Greenberg drew the regulator a little closer to himself and began to go over it carefully, taking readings from the gauge or peering even more closely with a large, handheld lens.

"Who made this device, Miss Lind?" Mr. Greenberg

asked, his face very close to the control panel. He ran a careful forefinger over the ceramic knobs and bakelite switches, and then moved on to the hissing pistons cycling up and down in the valves that drove the dynamo.

"My uncle, Professor Rabenski," Rosa replied, watching him with growing curiosity. "He is an electrical engineer and inventor."

He turned, his wide eyes magnified enormously by the lenses. "Ah, yes! I have heard of Bruce Rabenski."

"And he of you, sir," Aunt Jean put in, with a smile. "I asked him about you last evening when we returned home."

Mr. Greenberg looked pleased. "I would love to consult him about his design."

Aunt Jean shook her head. "I'm very sorry, but he is in Africa on a research trip. We consulted him by means of long-distance wireless. He will be back in a month. He'd be pleased to speak with you then."

"I hope that I can conclude my analysis long before then," he said, ruefully. "I must go to America in two weeks to defend one of my inventions before the Patent Board. Might I see a schematic of the device?"

"Of course," Aunt Jean said. "There is one in his desk. I will fetch it."

With the document in hand he resumed his studies. Aunt Jean rang for tea. The parlormaid who brought the tray fixed an interested eye on the gentleman caller seated so close to Miss Rosa. Impatiently, Rosa waved her out of the room. The visitor would be the subject of much talk during the servants' tea, and no doubt with the tradesmen. Aunt Jean should have sent for one of the mechanical valets, who, as they only had rudimentary prerecorded speech, never gossiped. It was a good thing they didn't know how little interest the man had in her or they would have pitied her.

"Fascinating," Mr. Greenberg said, referring between the regulator and its plans. "But so inefficient."

"I beg your pardon!" Aunt Jean boomed.

"No, please let me beg yours," Mr. Greenberg said, taking off the goggles. He wiped them with an absent expression on his good-natured face. "I forget myself. Professor Rabenski's invention is wonderful, but I feel that it could be a good deal more, er, compact."

"Do you know anything about heart stimulation machines?" Aunt Jean asked, annoyed. "This is the smallest portable unit available to date! Until we made this, my niece was tethered to her room, because the machine and its power source took up half of it!"

Mr. Greenberg nodded. "But all it is meant to do is deliver a minute electrical charge, is it not? Your electric bell does the same thing, in a device a mere fraction of the size. I think I could adapt the design to work with my newest technology." He held out the schematics to her. "I think vital economies could be made here, here, and here."

"Could you, sir?" Rosa asked. She had a momentary vision of her freed of her tether, to run down the streets like an urchin. "I would be in your debt."

He glanced at her, then down at the magnifying spectacles on his lap. "The debt is mine. Thank you for indulging my interest."

"Go ahead, if you wish," Rosa said.

Mr. Greenberg smiled. He flipped the small levers that held the faceplate on the control panel and began to examine the interior of the device with the aid of the plans. Though Rosa held her breath, he never touched anything that might cause the machine to halt or slow down. Aunt Jean, a skilled fabricator of devices from Uncle Bruce's designs including the regulator, kept a close eye on him. Mr. Greenberg unwound cables from their clips and ran his gauge over them, hmmming to himself over the readings.

"What does that do, sir?" she asked.

He didn't answer. Perhaps her voice had been drowned out by the droning of the machine. Instead, he delved further into its workings. His touch was gentle, insistent, but firm. Rosa felt almost as if he was examining her own body. She felt her cheeks grow warm. No one of her acquaintance had ever opened the machine. It was surprisingly . . . intimate. She could almost sense the long, flexible fingertips as they ran over the surface of the vacuum-sealed tubes and boards. They tickled their way along the dials that adjusted the speed of her heart rate. Rosa heard the pounding as her own feeble heart reacted to the caress and the machine responded with increased vigor. Her skin pricked as though stimulated with electricity. She felt as though she might faint from delight.

Mr. Greenberg was unaware of the sensation he was causing but Aunt Jean was not. Her fair eyebrows lowered on her forehead for a moment, and then she relented. The gentleman was behaving exactly like Uncle Bruce might when faced with a fascinating subject in his field. No doubt she was thinking too far ahead as to how nice it would be to have a second inventor in the family. Rosa poured tea for all of them. Mr. Greenberg took his cup and set it on the small table untasted.

With the gauge in one hand, he ran a hand down the face of the miniature dynamo. The reading must have pleased him, because he broke into a wide smile of wonder. Rosa smiled back. He didn't look up. His hand traced the negative and positive leads from opposite ends of the capacitor it fed, to the insulated connector at the base of the umbilical, and out along the thick cord to Rosa's breast. His long fingers spread out gently upon the disk attached to her skin. They probed the small connections that led to the wires that penetrated to her heart. Rosa could feel his hand's warmth and slight pressure through the thin bakelite, and lightning ran through her body. No man had ever touched her in that fashion in her entire life. She wished that he would continue his gentle explorations to the flesh on either side. Her body tingled, aching for more. Rosa realized how seldom someone touched her: only the chambermaid who helped her dress and an occasional hug from her aunt. She wanted a lover and husband. She turned her face up to Mr. Greenberg's, seeing that calm curiosity and fervent interest that was focused so intently upon the regulator's workings, and leaned toward him. *Look at me*, she willed him. *Look at me. See me.*

"A-hem!" Aunt Jean cleared her throat.

Mr. Greenberg came out of his reverie, and realized he had his hand planted on the chest of a respectable young lady. He jumped backward, his face suffused with scarlet.

"I am so sorry, Miss Lind. Please forgive me!"

I am sorry you stopped, Rosa thought. She swallowed her disappointment. He really didn't see that the machine was attached to a living woman. "I understand scientists, Mr. Greenberg. No offense was taken."

"Thank you," Mr. Greenberg said. He paused, clearing his throat uncomfortably. "It is as I suspected. This machine is brilliant in concept. No other device has managed to keep a damaged heart beating—for years, I believe?" Rosa nodded. "It is a technological wonder, but it is like a very large shoe over a very tiny foot. It is so much larger than required for its purpose that it almost causes harm to what it protects. It's old technology."

"Sir!" Aunt Jean protested. "That device took us five years to create!"

The gentleman dipped his head abashed. "My apologies, madam. I do keep speaking out of turn. To paraphrase a friend of mine, Dr. Louis Moore, scientific applications double in power as they halve in size every year or two. If you had kept on reinventing the regulator, by now it would be the size of a mantel clock, or even smaller. As it is, this is compact for its day and most well-made."

"What do you propose, Mr. Greenberg?" Aunt Jean asked. She was only partly mollified at the compliment.

"What is the charge that it dispenses?"

"Ninety millivolts."

He beamed. "Then I have the answer to the problem of size. My company, Tekno-Clocks, has a new pocket watch that has an alternating circuit to allow it to light up, for telling time in the dark. The lamp is driven by a small dynamo that winds up by means of a coiled spring."

"Just like any other watch," Aunt Jean marveled.

Mr. Greenberg nodded. "Just so. It would be my privilege to attempt to duplicate this machine in miniature, using the new technology."

"When could it be done?" Rosa asked, suddenly interested. His visit might not yet be wasted. Even if *he* was not interested in her, he could free her enough that perhaps another man might look her way.

He turned to her. "I have prototype machines on my workbench. I could begin tomorrow, if you would like."

Rosa was breathless at the thought of near-freedom. "Oh, yes!"

"Please call upon us at four," Aunt Jean said. "Will that give you enough time? Then you may stay to dinner afterwards."

Mr. Greenberg put away his tools and rose, the now-cold tea forgotten. "That would be perfect, Mrs. Rabenski. Miss Lind, until tomorrow?" He took her hand and bowed over it. Rosa felt his long fingers close over her small ones and smiled.

"Until then, sir," she said.

Rosa knew from correspondence with her aunt and uncle that scientific progress took a long time, but it seemed absolutely endless when one was the subject of investigation. Mr. Greenberg knelt at her feet, a dozen small gadgets each with a clock face and twin bolts sticking out of the top ticking and humming on the floor where he had discarded them. He had come to the Rabenskis' town house daily for a week. He said little to her during his visits, but applied himself diligently to his investigations. Rosa was beginning to wish she could leave the regulator and her heart there in the sitting room and go read a book instead. She was never so aware of the oppressive noise the machine made, and how it obviated conversation. With a key he wound up a gold-cased device the size of a melon.

"The speed seems right, and it would run for eight days," Mr. Greenberg muttered to himself, not for the first time. He listened, and then set the device down. "Too weak, and too great a variation in tempo."

"What is it you are doing now, Mr. Greenberg?" Rosa asked.

He glanced up at her briefly, but continued to wind up another mechanism from his case, this one shaped like a huge walnut. "I am testing each of these units to see which might carry the voltage for the longest possible time in the smallest possible volume, Miss Lind. To carry out the test successfully, it will be necessary to attach one beside your regulator, and then briefly switch input from that to the unit. There is some risk involved, but I believe no pain."

Rosa sat up bravely. "My life has little meaning as it is, Mr. Greenberg. And I am not afraid of pain."

Mr. Greenberg appeared to be about to say something, then paused. He smiled slightly, took off his glasses and polished them on a handkerchief. "I, er, am glad to hear that. I applaud your courage, Miss Lind." He put the glasses back on. "Let us try this unit, then." He wound it up.

The patronizing devil! Rosa fumed to herself, but she sat still as he clipped leads running from the golden device to her regulator and to the base of the umbilical on her breast. How dare he say that as if it *amused* him! She was ready to throw him out of the house. Only the prospect of going about the town virtually unburdened kept her from doing it. Every one of the devices he tested was smaller than a marketing basket, some only the size of a large orange. It was all she kept her hopes on. Her friends were already asking how serious Mr. Greenberg's suit was, since he was spending so many afternoons with her. She was humiliated to have nothing to tell them.

More gadgets and devices joined the first, until there was a veritable electrical laboratory arrayed on the tea table between Rosa and her regulator. Mr. Greenberg held his hand above a large black switch.

"Ready?"

Rosa sat up straight and nodded her head. He moved the lever.

The regulator went on hissing and pumping, but the current coming from it ceased. Rosa sensed an absence, not a presence, as the gadget took over stimulating her heart. It was not strong enough. Her heart began to flail at her ribs. She clutched them. Mr. Greenberg hastily threw the switch to its original position. She gasped with relief as the regulator's power resumed its task.

"Not that one, then," he said. He disconnected the walnut device and picked another out of his bag.

"If I were not tethered to this tinker's cart of machinery, I would remove myself from here, Mr. Greenberg!" Rosa snapped. "Don't you have the decency to inquire after my health?"

"But I can see that you are all right," he said, frowning so that lines formed across his broad brow. "Should I ring for your aunt?"

"No," Rosa said, in exasperation. "No, go on." She wanted the whole situation over with as soon as possible. Thankfully, Mr. Greenberg would be on his way to America in a week, and she wouldn't have to look at the top of his head any longer.

Aunt Jean had stopped sitting by them every minute. She dipped into the room occasionally to ask after the visitor's needs and take the temperature of Rosa's mood. Promptly at four, she whisked in just ahead of the parlormaid pushing the tea cart.

"And how is your progress?" she asked Mr. Greenberg. She settled herself in a chair covered with flowered chintz that went well with the green tea gown she had donned.

He pushed the goggles up on his forehead, giving him the air of a coal miner. "Slowly but steadily. I don't seem to be balancing the alternating current properly."

"Well, perhaps I can assist you," Aunt Jean said, pitching her voice over the regulator. "I am often my husband's second pair of hands."

"That would be very helpful," Mr. Greenberg replied.

"If you would care to wash up a bit, I'll fix you a plate. You must be starving!" Aunt Jean said.

Mr. Greenberg looked down at his front. Bits of wire, insulation and metal shavings decorated his waistcoat and trousers. He smiled at her. "If you will both excuse me for a moment, I will rejoin you as soon as I can."

The parlormaid escorted him out of the room toward the lavatory. Rosa watched the door close behind him with annoyance.

"Not going well?" Aunt Jean murmured under the noise of the pistoning regulator.

"Not in any way," Rosa said. "He acts as if I am not here, when he purports to be building a new regulator for me."

Aunt Jean smiled. "He knows you are here, my dear. I'll prove it."

After tea, Mr. Greenberg unwrapped one more gadget. Its copper-colored case was the size of a coconut shell and almost heart-shaped. He held it out to Rosa.

"This is a unit I am very proud of," he said. "It is adjustable, and runs on a spring made for an eight-day clock that is one of my finest timepieces. The dynamo is one of the most reliable I have ever made. Shall we give it a try?"

"Yes, of course."

He wound it with a small gold key. It let out a softly comforting tick-tock sound, exactly as all the others had. Rosa wondered why, if this mechanism was his finest, he hadn't tried it first, but watched as he turned the adjustment switch on the face to the right, from sixty beats per minute up to seventy-two, and set the dynamo's power lever to ninety millivolts. With Aunt Jean's help, he hooked it to the leads and all the gauges. When he rose to attach the black switch to the umbilical near the body of the regulator, Aunt Jean reached over to the ticking device and tweaked the lever ever so slightly up. She shot a significant look at Rosa, who frowned. Mr. Greenberg sat down on the stool at her knee and held up the switch.

"Ready, Miss Lind?" he asked.

"Yes."

Aunt Jean took her hand and squeezed it. Rosa held on as Mr. Greenberg threw the switch.

There was no shock, as there had been with several of the devices. The ease of transition surprised her. She breathed normally. Mr. Greenberg beamed at her.

"How are you doing?"

"Very well," she said, pleased. "Very well indeed." Her heart was getting the proper stimulus. Blood moved as it was meant to by nature. She smiled. Mr. Greenberg smiled back.

Then the stimulus became too much. Her heart was beating faster than usual. Not enough that anyone but she would be aware of it. Blackness rose in her eye and her blood pounded in her ears. Too fast. Her aunt had increased the pace of the clock regulator. She reached for the device to turn it down. Aunt Jean shook her head and held her hands firmly. Rosa tried to speak, but it felt as if her heart was in her throat.

Mr. Greenberg saw that she was in distress. "What is it? What is it, Miss Lind?" he asked.

Rosa opened her mouth to tell him, but the room went dark, and she heard nothing more.

When her vision cleared, she was reclining in a very warm chair scented with bay rum. A scratchy cloth was being applied to her cheeks and forehead, and something was puffing warm air on her face.

"Darling Miss Lind, are you all right? Can you speak? What did I do?"

The scratchy cloth was Mr. Greenberg's unshaven face, as he kissed her again and again. The warm air was his breath. She tilted her head back.

"What happened?" she asked.

He looked relieved and abashed. "Are you all right?"

Rosa tried to sit up. He took her arms and righted her against the sofa back. She leaned away from his grasp.

He seemed reluctant to let her go. "I am fine. What happened?"

"When I switched from your regulator to my device, I must have miscalculated the voltage," he said. "I am so sorry! Have I done you harm? I would never want anything ill to happen to you. I would rather wish all the woes of the world on myself instead." His brow was wrinkled with concern. He clutched her hand. "My dear, dear young lady."

Rosa frowned, looking down on their joined hands in confusion. Was this the distant man who for a week had only had eyes for her machinery? "Your declaration puzzles me, sir. We've only just met."

Mr. Greenberg smiled a little shyly. "The truth is that I have seen you across the room on many an occasion over these last months, Miss Lind. You are so very beautiful, but you seemed to me as remote as a mountaintop. I felt that I could not approach you until I could offer you something tangible, to prove I might be worth your interest. It was only last week I was ready to ask your aunt to introduce me to you."

Rosa laughed bitterly. "My dear sir, you have seen how few gentlemen I attract. Anyone who would brave my clockwork companion, not to mention my chaperone, is worth my interest. I thought that you were not interested in me."

Mr. Greenberg kissed her hand. "You should see more value in yourself, my dear Miss Lind. I hope that you will allow me to continue to call upon you, even though it seems that this last machine of mine does indeed do the job that your previous mechanical servant did."

"What?" Rosa asked. She looked down. The ruddy-colored, heart-shaped device was on a ribbon around her neck. It probably weighed a pound, but compared with the gigantic regulator, now silent at her side, it was lighter than air. She touched its gleaming surface, and ran a finger around the keyhole in its small clock face. "It works?"

"It works," Mr. Greenberg said simply. Aunt Jean beamed at her over his shoulder. "I thought that it would. It only has to be wound every eight days. I admit I have stretched the task out so I could spend time close to you." He placed the golden key in her palm and stood up. "But now you are free of both of us, if you choose to be." He crossed to the door. "I will take my leave now. Send for me if you wish me to come back."

Rosa stood up. The soft ticking was so different than the wheezing and groaning of the old regulator. She was filled with gratitude and relief, as well as amazement that this kind, brilliant man had worked in secret for her. That spoke of a passion that she never dreamed she could elicit in a man. Boldly, she went to him. With a smile, she folded the key into his hands and held them tightly.

"I think, dear Martin, that as you have won it, you should keep the key to my heart. You must come to see me at least once every eight days to wind it up."

The kind blue eyes twinkled behind the spectacles, and he enfolded her in his arms. The clock-regulator ticked triumphantly between them as she reached up to kiss him. She poured all the pent-up emotion of her lonely, tethered days into the kiss. Rosa was delighted when he returned the embrace with ardor. She nestled her head against his chest and listened to the soft ticking and his pounding heart. His hands ran softly up and down her back. She closed her eyes, feeling she could never have enough of that sensation.

"Well, it's about time!" Aunt Jean said.

IN THE BELLY OF THE BEHEMOTH

Matt Forbeck

*Matt Forbeck has been a full-time creator of award-winning games and fiction since 1989. His latest novels—*Amortals* and* Vegas Knights*—are on sale now. He has designed collectible card games, role-playing games, miniatures games, board games, and toys, and has written novels, short fiction, comic books, motion comics, nonfiction, magazine articles, and computer game scripts and stories. For more about him and his work, visit Forbeck.com.*

Dusky didn't hear the Union soldier until he tumbled out of the bushes near the main house on the plantation that she'd never left her entire life. She'd never seen one of the boys in blue up till that point, but from the way the style of his clothing matched that of the Confederate soldiers regularly trooping in and out of Dr. Tucker's barn she recognized right away that he had to be part of the Union invaders that were charging through Georgia on their way to the sea. Gunshots had been cracking in the distance for days, getting closer all the time, but the thought that they were here, on the plantation's doorstep, still stunned her.

Dusky dropped the bucket of mop water she'd been carrying and put a hand over her mouth to stifle a scream. The water slopped over her bare feet, but she ignored it as she stared at the bloody mess a bullet had made of the man's neck. Other than the crimson splashing his face, his complexion was paler than that of anyone she'd ever seen—even Dr. Tucker—especially when contrasted with her coffee-colored skin.

"Ma'am." The solder staggered toward her and collapsed to his knees. "I've been—could you help me, please?"

With that, he toppled over backward at an awkward angle and bled into the dirt.

Dusky knelt next to the man. She hadn't seen someone hurt so bad since her daddy had gotten his arm caught in the cotton gin last spring, and he hadn't survived the night. She hadn't been able to help her daddy then, and she had no idea what to do now.

Dusky jumped back up and started toward the house. After a few steps, she caught herself, spun around, and headed back in the other direction, back toward the shack that she and the other slaves called home. She didn't know who she expected to find there, but anyone in the shack would have to be more help than Dr. Tucker and his friends.

She burst into the shack, out of breath, and found it empty. Of course, she realized, the men—the ones who hadn't run off yet or been shot trying—would be out in the fields right now, picking cotton right up until dark—or until the Union soldiers arrived. She turned to leave again and ran straight into Obadiah's bare chest. As she bounced off of him, he reached out to steady her with his hands. Dressed only in tattered pants, his dark brown skin dripped with sweat in the steamy July heat.

She looked up into the young man's inquisitive brown eyes, and her tongue froze in her mouth. For months, she'd been watching him watch her, wondering about him with strange, wonderful new thoughts roaming through her head. While they'd grown up on the plantation together, Dusky and most of the other women lived in the house with Dr. Tucker, leaving the men alone down here in the shack. There were damned few of them left at all anymore.

Dr. Tucker frowned on any interaction between the sexes, and he limited contact of any sort to the absolute minimum. Because of that, Dusky and Obadiah had barely spoken a score of words to each other over the past year. Still, her interest in the strong, handsome man he'd transformed into during that time had grown, and as she looked up at him her breath caught in her chest.

"What is it?" Obadiah grabbed her by the shoulders, and Dusky realized she'd been about to swoon. He stared into her eyes for some hint of what might be wrong.

Dusky could only point out the door and back up toward the main house. "Soldier," she stammered out.

That one word sent Obadiah sprinting toward the two-story, white-pillared house, leaving Dusky behind. A moment later, she chased after him. By the time she reached him, he was already kneeling next to the wounded soldier.

"He's hurt bad," Obadiah said. "Real bad."

"We got to help him," Dusky said. "He'll die if we don't."

Obadiah looked up at her, his jaw set and determined. Without a word, he picked up the soldier in his bare arms and cradled him like a baby. "Go get Mamma Esther," he said. "Run!"

Dusky charged toward the house, but before she got a hundred feet from Obadiah, she heard a shot ring out. She froze in her tracks and turned toward the barn. What she saw there made her scream.

Dr. Tucker stood there on his one good leg and his prosthetic one, dressed in his grime-streaked work clothes, which he'd had shortened on one side to prevent the fabric from catching in his fake limb. He had pushed his tinted goggles—the ones he always wore when welding his contraptions together—back on his head, toward his mane of graying hair, and he blinked out at the world with ice-cold eyes unused to being so exposed to the evening sun. He held a smoking gun in his hand, and it pointed toward Obadiah. He ignored Dusky, not sparing her a first glance much less a second.

"Put that filthy Yankee down, boy." Dr. Tucker strode toward Obadiah, who had not moved a single one of his bulging muscles. As he walked, the servomotors in the brassy replacement Dr. Tucker had built for his left leg whirred and clicked in sequence.

Whirr-click. Whirr-click. Whirr-click.

"I said, put him down." Dr. Tucker never raised his voice. He let his gun do all his shouting for him.

Obadiah let the Union soldier's legs down and stood the man up on his wobbly feet, leaving the soldier's arm over his shoulders.

The tubby doctor ambled closer to Obadiah and the soldier. "Where'd you find this one, boy?"

Obadiah pointed over to where the soldier's pooling blood had darkened the dirt. He knew better than to answer Dr. Tucker directly. He bore livid scars on his back from the first and last time he'd made such a mistake.

"And just what did you plan to do with him?"

Obadiah shook his head and shrugged.

"Step aside, boy." Dr. Tucker waved Obadiah off with his gun, and Obadiah took three steps to the side.

Dr. Tucker stepped up to the Union soldier. Whirr-click. Whirr-click. Whirr-click.

Even from as far away as she stood, Dusky could see the soldier's legs trembling. He licked his bone-dry lips before he spoke.

"I surrender to you, sir."

"You're a Union scout," Dr. Tucker said. It wasn't a question, but the soldier nodded to affirm it.

"How far?" Dr. Tucker asked. The soldier shook his head and teetered back on his heels before righting himself.

Dr. Tucker took another step forward. Whirr-click. "Sherman," he said. "How far away is he?"

The soldier shrugged. Dusky couldn't tell if the man had refused to answer or couldn't. Dr. Tucker cocked his revolver and pointed it at the dying man's face.

"A day's march," the soldier said. "No more." He struggled to take a new breath. "I throw myself on your mercy."

Dr. Tucker shot the man between the eyes, knocking him to the ground.

Dusky let out a little scream, then stifled it by clapping her hands over her face.

Dr. Tucker looked at her then with a cold eye. "He's the first Yankee to die on my land," he said. "He won't be the last."

Dr. Tucker pivoted on his good heel, swung his machine leg around, and headed back into the barn.

Whirr-click. Whirr-click. Whirr-click.

Dr. Tucker closed the door behind him. Obadiah rushed over to Dusky, who still stood watching the dead soldier, her hands clamped over her mouth.

"It's all right," he said to her. "Come with me."

He put a strong arm around her and walked her down to the shack. As they neared the door, she began to shake. "But the doctor," she started.

Obadiah shushed her. "Don't worry none about that," he said as he guided her in through the door. "Come this time tomorrow, we all going to be past worrying about that." She shut the door to the shack. "What do you mean?"

Obadiah swallowed. "You know the machine the doctor been working on so long?"

Dusky nodded. She had never seen it, but she had heard the men talking about it: a massive machine of battle that the doctor claimed would bring about the end of the war and deliver the South from the Union's aggression. She hadn't believed Dr. Tucker's wild claims, figuring them to be the rantings of a madman still in grief over losing his leg at Sharpsburg.

"It can't be real," she said.

Obadiah frowned. "It's real, all right. I seen it."

Dusky shuddered. "But—but "

She sat on one of the beds and held herself, rubbing her hands over her shoulders. She'd been foolish enough to let hope take root in her heart. Hope that the Union might somehow win the war. Hope that she might someday put this plantation far behind.

Obadiah sat next to her and put his arms around her. She turned toward him and buried her face in his shoulder and wept. When she finished, he reached under her chin and tilted her face up so that he could look into it.

She saw that he had tears glittering his eyes too, although none of them had spilled down onto his face.

"It's gonna be all right," he said. And she believed him.

He brought his face closer to hers, and their lips brushed together in a tender kiss. She drew back.

"What's wrong?" he asked.

A smile broke through as she wiped away her tears. "I—I just never kissed a man before."

He smiled, showing all his teeth. "You think I'm a man?"

She felt a hunger leap up inside of her. She leaned upward and kissed him again. "Do you think I'm a woman?"

His eyes shone at her, the tears that had welled there gone, replaced with a warmth that Dusky now realized she'd longed to see. He brought his face down to hers again. "For sure."

Dusky felt her body arch toward Obadiah's, pressing his chest against her breasts. Their tongues came together, and she discovered that he tasted sweeter than any berry. She felt herself being carried away, body and soul.

Then a sound came outside the door.

"Obadiah!" a voice came. "You in there?"

The heat between Dusky and Obadiah evaporated. She recognized the voice. It belonged to Emmanuel, the man who'd taken over as the head of the men after her daddy died.

Obadiah looked at Dusky and froze, unable to open his mouth. Dusky stood and headed for the back door. If Emmanuel caught her in here, the best she could expect was a whipping. She stopped to give Obadiah one last kiss, though, and that's when the door burst open.

"Obadiah!"

Emmanuel stood silhouetted in the doorway, his bulk occupying the entire frame from edge to edge. Without a moment's thought, Dusky fled, her feet carrying her out the back door and up the low hill toward the main house. She was halfway home before she regained control.

She stopped and looked back at the shack and its empty front door. Emmanuel was shouting something at Obadiah, but Dusky couldn't quite make out his words. When his form appeared in the doorway again, she turned back toward the main house and sprinted away, not stopping until she was safe in the room she shared with the other girls.

When Missy and Sandy came in later, they found Dusky curled up on her bed. The tears she'd wept had long since dried, and she'd spent the time since then lying there, thinking about what had happened and what she could hope to do about it. The girls tittered about the excitement, the gunshots they'd heard, but to them it was just a story someone had told them. They hadn't seen the soldier die. Someone—Obadiah, Dusky guessed—had removed the body so the only evidence the other girls had seen of the incident had been the soldier's blood.

"This ain't nothing for you girls to laugh about," Mamma Esther said when she stormed into the room. "You got your things packed? Y'all ready to go?"

"I thought we wasn't going nowhere," Missy said. "After Martha got herself shot, we said we gave up on that."

"Gonna happen one way or the other," Mamma Esther said. "That soldier didn't come all the way down to Georgia by his lonesome. Soldiers are like mice. See one, there's bound to be more."

"But what we gonna do if they come here?" Sandy's voice squeaked as she spoke. She was only eleven.

"Get," said Mamma Esther. "That's why you need to be packed. When the bullets start flying, we best be on our way. We can come back when it's over and see who won."

"Or just keep heading north." Dusky sat up in her bed as she spoke. Everyone's eyes turned to her. "To be free."

Mamma Esther grimaced at her. "Now, don't be talking like that. Don't be getting your hopes up, none of you. There ain't no telling who's gonna win this war, and either way you can bet we're gonna be on the losing side."

Dusky opened her mouth to speak, but before the words could come out, a gunshot cracked in the distance. Then several more came, until it sounded like a barrage of lightning had struck the plantation, bringing with it a rolling thunder that seemed as if it might never end. Missy and Sandy clutched at each other and screeched in fear. Mamma Esther's frown deepened as she shuffled over to comfort them.

Dusky ran to the window and peered outside. The sun was setting over Stone Mountain in the west, leaving the land shrouded in darkness and the sky turning a brilliant pink and orange. She could see most of the plantation from here, all the way to the clearing in front of the barn, down past that to the shack, and from there to the half-picked cotton fields beyond.

The doors to the barn stood open. There, framed in the massive entrance, Dusky saw the great machine.

It stood taller than a man on a horse, and it was wide around as a Conestoga wagon, but it was made of polished metal that covered it from end to end and gleamed in the dying rays of the sun. It rolled forward out of the barn on great metal wheels shaped like massive versions of the cogs that Dusky had once seen sitting inside a broken wristwatch. A demonic glow surrounded it, reflected off the ground below it and shoving back the encroaching night. Gun barrels bristled from every side of the machine. A pair of Gatling guns sat atop its shoulders, smoke wafting out of each of their multiple barrels, and it bore a massive cowcatcher strapped across its front. The machine spewed steam through a giant whistle that stabbed from its rear. The horrible noise caused Dusky to cover her ears while Missy and Sandy screeched once again in fear.

Emmanuel lay dead in front of the machine. Isaiah, Jebediah, and Aaron were sprawled along the trampled grass nearby, the life bleeding out of each of them so fast that it left them without even a moan.

Obadiah sat twenty yards in front of the machine, clutching at his leg and hollering in pain. He struggled to his feet, tried his weight on his injured leg, and collapsed once more.

Dusky pushed herself away from the window and headed for the bedroom door.

"Where you think you're going?" Mamma Esther asked.

"I can't just let him die like that," Dusky said. She wiped the tears away from her face, unaware until then that they'd been blurring her vision.

"There ain't no good you can do that boy now," Mamma Esther said. "Ain't no use in getting yourself killed too."

Dusky pushed open the door. "I love him." As the words left her lips, she knew them to be true. "I got to try."

Leaving Mamma Esther to comfort the whimpering girls, Dusky made her way through the house until she reached the front door. Slipping out between the tall white columns, she crept around until she could see the field in front of the barn.

Obadiah stood there, still alive—for now.

Dr. Tucker stood next to him, fastening a pair of man-acles around Obadiah's hands and trussing them behind his back. Dusky had seen him use this sadistic invention on recaptured slaves before. The interior rims of the manacles had been sharpened, and anyone who strug-gled against them was likely to cut his wrists to the bone.

Obadiah grunted in agony as he tried to maintain his balance on his one good leg and failed. Dusky's heart ached for him. She knew she had to do something to save him, but what? Maybe, she thought, Dr. Tucker would see that he'd had enough by now and would leave him be. Maybe he'd satiated his anger and his madness by murdering the other men whose bodies lay sprawled about the field.

Or maybe not.

Staying to the edge of the field, Dusky crawled her way through the taller grass, making her way toward the barn. The weeds pricked her legs and pulled at her skirt, but she ignored them and concentrated on keeping her head low. As long as Dr. Tucker was busy with Obadiah, she stood a chance. If the man managed to spot her, though, they were all doomed.

The doctor reached down into the grass and pro-duced a rope that terminated in a noose. He tossed it up over a sturdy tree branch that hung high overhead, then placed the loop over Obadiah's head. He sneered as he tightened it around Obadiah's neck.

"You and the rest of those boys figured you'd just walk right in and take the Behemoth from me?" he said. "You think I'm stupid. That I didn't know that you'd been watching me? That I didn't know that you'd try to do something to stop me?"

Dr. Tucker gave the rope a fierce tug, and Obadiah gagged.

"You think I wasn't ready for you, boy?"

Dusky reached the barn and stared up at the machine—the Behemoth, as Dr. Tucker had called it. She had never seen anything so magnificent and terrifying in her life. Now that she was close enough, she realized that the glow from the thing's underbelly came from a fire that had been stoked in a boiler down there. As she noticed this, she wondered if the machine's invulnerable metal hide wasn't quite so impenetrable from below.

Dusky got on her hands and knees and crawled underneath the Behemoth. There she spotted a trap door that had been left open, a hole in the great beast's suit of armor.

"Take heart, boy," Dr. Tucker said. "You're going to go down in history as the first man to ever be hanged by use of a steam engine."

The doctor strode over to the front of the behemoth and began to fasten the open end of the rope there. As he worked, Dusky held her breath, hoping he couldn't hear her, no matter how hard her heart might be pounding.

"Don't worry, though," Dr. Tucker called back to Obadiah. "You won't be up there long. While you're hanging there, struggling for your last breath, I'll help you find it. I need a target to help me calibrate my guns. After all, when I take on Sherman's men tomorrow, I need to make sure the Behemoth is in top shape."

Dusky's blood ran cold. While the plantation's men were hardly well-trained soldiers, she'd seen what the machine had done to them. If Dr. Tucker managed to deploy his Behemoth against the Union invaders, she didn't see how they could stand against it. It would mow them down like dry summer grass.

She couldn't let that happen.

As Dusky eyed the hatch that led into the machine, Dr. Tucker leaned down to examine his knot and gasped. "Hello there," he said.

Startled, Dusky did the only thing she could think of. She scrambled up into the belly of the Behemoth.

"No, no, no, no, no!" Dr. Tucker said as Dusky disappeared into the machine.

She reached over and slammed the trapdoor shut before he could reach her. Then she sat down on top of the hatch, pushing all her weight down onto it.

Dr. Tucker smashed into the trapdoor from below, lifting Dusky into the air. A moment later, though, she came crashing right back down. It was dark inside the machine, lit only by the glow of the stoked fire. Dusky felt around with her hands, finding the edges of the trapdoor and following them with her fingers until she found a latch.

Dr. Tucker smacked into the trapdoor again, and Dusky screamed as the impact lifted her into the air again. The sound seemed to shock the man so much that he dropped back once more. When he did, Dusky found the thick bolt for the latch and slammed it home.

Dr. Tucker threw himself into the trapdoor once more, but this time it held tight. From below, Dusky heard a groan of pain that grew into a howl of frustration and fury.

"Come on out of there, you witch!" Dr. Tucker said. "You come out of there *right now!*"

Dusky scrambled away from the trapdoor. She didn't know much about Dr. Tucker's fearsome contraption, but she knew she wasn't leaving it to face his wrath. So far, she'd somehow managed to make it through her life without taking a good whipping, but if she came out of here now, she knew that thirty-nine lashes would be the best she could hope for.

She glanced around the interior of the machine. The flickering flames from the boiler's stove cast everything in a hellish orange light.

Levers and switches of all types bristled from the walls inside the Behemoth. Dusky didn't know what any of them might do. One might save Obadiah. Another might kill him. A third might blow the entire metal beast up and destroy them all.

A leather chair sat fixed higher up in the contraption, and Dusky crawled into it and looked around. From here, she could see out of the machine through thin slits that had been cut into the metal plating. Straight before her, she saw Obadiah hanging from a noose, and she fought back a full-throated scream that threatened to break free right up until she spotted the fact that his feet were still on the ground.

"I said, get out of there, or I swear to God in Heaven I'll kill every last damn one of you!" Dr. Tucker banged on the belly of the Behemoth with something hard, and the clanging rang throughout the entire machine. Dusky felt like she'd been made into the clapper of a gigantic bell.

She scanned the controls in front of her, and she recognized some of them. Dr. Tucker had been driving a steam-powered horseless carriage around the plantation for the past year, and Dusky had sometimes watched him manipulate the controls to get the machine in motion. This lever in front looked familiar, like it should kick this contraption forward.

Dusky reached out and clasped the handle, squeezing the hand lever that released the mechanism. Then she shoved it.

The Behemoth surged backward, and Dusky pitched forward into the control rods with a squeal. She looked up through the slit and saw the rope pulling tight and hauling Obadiah into the air. She'd been trying to save him, but she was killing him instead.

A stream of curses erupted from beneath the machine. Dusky shared their sentiment, although she would not have aimed them at the same target. She shoved herself back and fumbled for the same lever again. Finding it, she hauled backward on it, and it pivoted back into the neutral position, where it stopped with a solid clunk.

Obadiah still hung there in the air, his feet well off the ground and flailing about for purchase on the earth below. Dusky allowed herself a little curse too. If she didn't do something soon, Obadiah would die—at her hand! But she also didn't want to make everything worse.

Dusky put her hand back on the control lever. Should she use that one or another? There were so many to choose from. Or should she just get out of the machine and go cut Obadiah down?

Dr. Tucker strode in front of the machine now and leveled his pistol at her. He thumbed back the hammer on it and fired.

Dusky shrieked as the bullet ricocheted off the Behemoth's metal skin. Obadiah gave out a strangled cry of anguish worse than any he'd uttered for himself.

Dr. Tucker threw back his head and laughed.

"Come on out of there now, Dusky." He pointed the gun straight at her, as if he could see her through the slender slits and would put his next bullet right between her eyes, just like he'd done to that poor Union soldier. "You do, and maybe I'll just beat you half to death and wait to see if God wants to leave you with me or bring you home."

The sneer on the man's face set Dusky off. She could tell he was bluffing. He'd built this damned machine of his too well. He couldn't hurt her, no matter how much he might want to.

That realization raised her spirits a bit, but she knew

that if she didn't get out of there and cut Obadiah loose he'd be dead in a matter of seconds. She couldn't just sit here safe inside this metal can and wait. She had to take action, or the man she loved would die in a horrible, painful way.

Dr. Tucker seemed to sense she was about to take action. He opened fire at her again.

Dusky squeezed the hand lever on the handle before her as the bullets glanced and pinged off of the Behemoth's skin. This time, instead of pushing forward, she pulled back on the long-handled lever with all her might.

The lever gave, and the machine lurched forward like a gigantic, ravenous monster. Dr. Tucker kept firing until his gun was empty, refusing to give ground to his slave inside his own machine. Behind him, Obadiah's twitching form touched down on the ground and collapsed.

A horrible cry went up from the front of the machine as Dr. Tucker disappeared beneath it. His pride, Dusky guessed, kept his feet in place when he should rather have been running away. Quick as she could, Dusky pushed the lever forward again until it clunked back into its place. It rolled to a stop just before it might have run over Obadiah.

Dusky threw herself out of the seat and toward the trapdoor. Flinging it open, she dropped to the scorched ground beneath the Behemoth. Dr. Tucker—or what was left of him—lay there, mangled by the cowcatcher as it had shoved forward along the lawn. She turned her head away.

Scrambling from under the machine, Dusky dashed over to where Obadiah lay, still as death. She fell to her knees and pulled the noose from around his throat. It had made livid red marks upon his neck, but once she removed it, he started hacking and coughing, struggling to get the air back into his lungs.

Dusky thought she had never heard such a wonderful sound in her life. She leaned over and kissed Obadiah's face again and again as tears flowed down her face.

"You're alive," she said. "Oh, thank the Lord, you're alive."

"My arms," Obadiah said weakly.

"Oh!" Dusky said. She looked over at Dr. Tucker's stone-still form. She cringed at the thought of having to touch his body, but she had no other choice. She found the key to his cruel manacles in one of his blood-soaked pockets, and in a moment she had Obadiah freed.

He brought his arms around and held her in them tight, his shoulders shaking with the release of his emotions. "The worst part wasn't hanging there," he said. "It was the thought I wouldn't be able to stop him from killing you."

"We're safe now," Dusky said. "Right?"

Obadiah craned back his neck to peer into her eyes, and he nodded. He let his eyes roam the body-littered field, where many of his friends lay.

"Well," Dusky said. "Mamma Esther, Missy, and Sandy are still here. And we got this machine up and running and ready to go. Where we gonna take her?"

Obadiah smiled at her then, and she felt her heart melt from the sheer heat of it. "Out of here," he said. "Any place we can find that's somewhere new. Someplace you and I can call our own."

She brought her mouth up to his again and tasted the sweat tang of the sweat on his lips. "Let's go north," she said. "Let's find us a home."

AUTOMATA FUTURA

Stephen D. Sullivan

I've loved steampunk since the first run of The Wild Wild West TV show. Yet this is only my second steampunk story, after last year's "Of a Feather" in Steampunk'd. Why? Mostly because I've been so darn busy working on other publishing ventures and writing about women warriors, alchemists, dinosaurs, and demons (though not all at once). When my old friend Jean Rabe asked me to submit a tale for this book, I immediately decided to return to the cast from "Of a Feather." Oddly, the resulting story was not any of the numerous sequels I'd planned to follow that tale. Instead, what tumbled out of my keyboard was a mad scientist story with an unlikely romantic lead, plus a touch of classic cinema. I hope you enjoy it. You can discover more about me and my latest mad experiment at www.stephendsullivan.com.

Zoe stood outside the Great Man's door, her references clutched in her left hand, along with the cablegram that had summoned her to this ramshackle structure. The hall of the building was dingy, its once-ornate carpet musty, dust-filled, and stained. The sole light came from a grime-covered window at the far end. It seemed odd that Doctor Von Lang, the famed inventor, should live in a deserted tenement, though he was a renowned eccentric. Yet, Zoe had checked, and the city registry definitely said he owned the building, so . . .

Maybe I should have brought Armstrong or CC with me, Zoe thought. *No! You can do this! We need this job so Kit can continue her research, so all of us can—so we don't go broke. You can do it!*

She remembered Ray Armstrong's confident smile from earlier that day. . . . "If Victor Von Lang wants to see you, it must be important. And if he's got work, so much the better."

"But what could he possibly want with me?" Zoe had asked.

"Zoe, you're brilliant," Kit Chapman-Challenger, whom Zoe called "CC," put in. "Bring your references, in case he wants them."

"B–but . . ." Zoe stuttered.

Armstrong cut her off. "No 'buts,' kiddo. Just keep the rendezvous and knock him dead."

Dead, Zoe thought. *I wish I were dead.*

She stretched out her trembling right hand and pressed the doorbell. Somewhere in the unplumbed recesses beyond the battered mahogany door, a distant buzzer sounded.

Suddenly, the door flew open, and the face of a wild man poked out. His shocking blond hair protruded in all directions; grease-smeared goggles covered his frantic blue eyes. Zoe jumped back and nearly lost her glasses.

"Can't you see I'm busy?" the man said, fairly spitting the words. Then he looked Zoe up and down, and his gaunt face brightened. "Miz Tesla?"

Zoe nodded mutely.

The madman grinned from ear to ear. "Welcome! Welcome! Do come right in." He held the door open and motioned for Zoe to enter. "I'm Victor Von Lang."

"I–I'm Zoe. I got your cablegram."

"Of course, of course." Doctor Von Lang laid one greasy, glove-clad hand atop the shoulder of Zoe's freshly cleaned blouse. Despite his apparent mania, his touch felt surprisingly gentle. "I know who you are, Miz Tesla: aide-de-camp and chief mechanic for the world-renowned Kit Chapman-Challenger."

World-renowned but perpetually strapped for cash, Zoe thought.

"That's why I cabled you," Doctor Von Lang continued. "Do step inside. We have so much to talk about." He gently moved Zoe through the doorway and into the cluttered laboratory beyond.

She gawked. Beakers, tubes, electrical engines, lathes, drills, cutting equipment, and more filled the huge space to overflowing. The ceiling in the lab stood easily thirty feet tall.

It looked as though Von Lang's lab took up the entire floor . . . maybe the entire structure. *No wonder the building seemed deserted!*

Zoe held out the papers clutched in her hand. "I brought references . . ."

"References? Don't be silly! Why would a mechanic of your caliber need references? I wouldn't have cabled you if I thought you needed references."

"Why did you cable me, Doctor? You said something about a job. . ."

Von Lang pulled off his dirty goggles and gloves and smoothed back his hair. "Yes, of course. I almost forgot in the excitement of the moment." He removed his chemical-stained lab coat and hung it on a mahogany coat rack. "You've heard of me, I suppose?"

"Everybody's heard of you, Doctor Von Lang—"

"Call me 'Victor.'"

"You invented the ionic storage battery, the electro-steam converter, the micro-motor, the artificial skin used to treat burn victims during the war . . . all before you were twenty-five."

Von Lang waved his hand dismissively as he washed up at one of the lab's many soapstone sinks. "Child's play. Anyone could have done all that."

"Don't be absurd, Doctor. Your inventions have changed the world—"

"Poppycock!" He straightened and looked her directly in the eye. "People sing of my accomplishments every day, yet the world remains full of chaos and greed. If anything, I've merely accelerated human-kind's inhumanity toward its fellows. That is why I have withdrawn—retired, as it were—to these humble chambers."

I'd give my right eye for a lab this humble, Zoe thought.

He looked away from her, out the lab's tall windows, and his blue eyes grew distant. In that moment, Zoe realized how truly handsome he was—once he'd cleaned himself up.

"Yet," he said quietly, "it's this very isolation that vexes me now. One person, no matter how brilliant, no matter how talented, cannot do everything." Somehow, despite all his money and property and patents, Von Lang seemed terribly sad and vulnerable. Zoe remembered, then, how he'd lost his wife in an industrial accident, several years before.

He must be lonely living here all alone.

"That, Miz Tesla, is why I cabled you. I need your help."

"Zoe. You can call me Zoe. But why do you need my help?"

"Because you are the best mechanic in Manhattan, if not the entire country—or perhaps even the world."

Zoe blushed from the tip of her nose right down to her toes. Von Lang didn't seem to notice. "I–I'm not—"

"Of course you are. Do you think I can't afford to hire the best?"

"So you're hiring me?"

"Of course! Why did you think you were here? What is your usual rate?"

"I don't really have a usual rate. I usually just work for CC."

"Miz Chapman-Challenger, yes. How foolish of me."

"She usually handles all my negotiations," Zoe fibbed. *Even though no one's ever tried to hire me before.*

"I'll have my solicitor contact her, then. I'm sure we can come to a mutually beneficial agreement. How soon can you start? Immediately, I hope?"

Zoe glanced down at her white blouse, one shoulder now dirtied from Von Lang's hand, and her neatly pressed skirt. "I really didn't come dressed for—"

"Never mind. There are some spare jumpsuits in the locker room. I'm sure one of them will fit you."

"You have a locker room? I thought you worked alone?"

"I work alone now . . ." His eyes grew sad and distant once more. "Find something you like. I'll call my solicitor and we can begin work in, say . . ." He fished out an ornate golden pocket watch and checked it. "Twenty minutes?"

Zoe nodded. "I . . . I guess."

"Splendid!"

He's really not as strange as he seemed at first, Zoe thought as she buttoned the top button of the khaki-green jumper. The outfit didn't fit very well, but it was the best she'd been able to turn up in the dusty locker room adjoining the lab. She gazed at her reflection in a grimy mirror and adjusted the belt. *He doesn't care how you look,* she told herself. *It's your mind he admires, and your dexterity, and your . . . craftsmanship.*

Taking a deep breath, she returned to the lab, where Von Lang, in a new white coat, stood waiting.

"All set?" he asked. "Excellent. Everything is arranged. You're working for me full time until such time as either Miz Chapman-Challenger urgently needs your services or our project is complete."

"How soon do you think that might be?"

He shrugged. "It depends on how well-deserved your reputation for brilliance is, Zoe."

Again, she blushed, and this time he definitely noticed.

"I have few rules in this laboratory. The only absolute one is that you must *not* touch any of my ongoing experiments."

She looked around. The lab was a mess of boiling liquids and sparking coils. "How will I know what not to touch?"

"I have only one ongoing project right now, and it lies inside that armoire." He pointed to a tall wooden cabinet on the far side of the room, between two blue velvet curtains.

"W–what is it?"

"I . . . I'm testing the longevity on a new type of battery. I've been working on it for several years now, so it's imperative that the cabinet not be disturbed. Do you understand?"

"Yes."

He stared into the distance, lost in thought, until she cleared her throat.

"What are we working on, Dr. Von Lang?"

His blue eyes lit up. "Let me show you." He walked across the laboratory to a large table, draped in burgundy velvet. The tabletop was tilted nearly vertical, and the whole surface was taller than either Zoe or Von Lang. The doctor removed the velvet drapery with a flourish, like a magician completing a trick. "I've been working on this for a long time. . . ."

Zoe gasped and stared at the life-size drawing pinned to what she now realized was a huge drawing board. It was the schematic for a machine, but a machine like nothing she'd ever seen before—a machine in the shape of a human being.

"This," Von Lang announced, "has become my life's work—the fully functional human automaton. I call it the *Automata Futura*."

Zoe looked the schematic up and down; it was, without a doubt, the most complicated set of plans she had ever seen. It made her own automaton inventions—including the self-propelled *spider grapnel*—look like tinker toys. "Th–that's amazing, Doctor—"

"Victor."

"Victor. But . . . why?"

He clasped his hands behind his back and looked at the floor, his shoulders slumping. "You've heard about the . . . industrial accident that took my wife from me."

"Yes. I'm very sorry."

"Well, what if things like that never had to happen again? What if people never had to labor in the shadow of death—in mines and factories? What if all such dangerous jobs could, instead, be done by machines? Imagine the revolution that such an invention could bring. Imagine the working classes elevated to the leisure class. Imagine the power of all those brains set free from day-to-day drudgery. Imagine working on what you loved—your passion—liberated from worldly cares and danger and loss."

As he spoke, imagery of the world set free from toil and suffering blossomed in Zoe's mind. It was beautiful; Victor's grand scheme was even more glorious than the plans pinned to his drawing board. She gasped at the plan's brilliance. "I . . . I can see it!"

"If all that could be true—if we could make it happen—what a glorious, shining metropolis this city, indeed, the whole world, would become! Will you help me, Zoe?"

She took his hand, and his fingers felt soft and kind and oh-so-warm.

"I will. Of course I will."

Von Lang put his hands on Zoe's shoulders and massaged the tight muscles along the top of her back. "How's it going?" he asked.

Zoe pushed the magnifier away from her face and pulled her glasses down from her brow. "I've never worked on a micro-motor this small—"

"Nobody has. Nobody even dreamed of it before we did."

"Before *you* did. I'm just a mechanic."

"And the best machinist in the world."

"Anyway, I think we've just about got it. Whether the silicon-based oil you've formulated will hold up to the stress on so tiny a scale, that's the key."

"I assure you, it will. I didn't make my fortune by screwing up basic chemistry." He smiled at Zoe and her heart fluttered. In the twelve weeks they'd been working on Project Automata Futura, she'd come to admire Von Lang not only as an inventor but also as a man. Zoe hoped, with a complete lack of certainty, that Victor might feel the same way.

She flashed him a brief, nervous grin and then returned to her work. "And the alloy for the skeleton?"

"The foreman at my foundry says they'll be ready to deliver the first batch by the end of the week. Then things can really get going." He kept massaging her shoulders.

"That feels w–wonderful," she cooed.

"I'm glad."

"But my hands need to be completely steady to finish this delicate work."

He turned her toward him, swiveling the work stool she sat on, and looked at her upturned face. "Then maybe we should finish the work later."

Under the gaze of his sea-blue eyes, Zoe's heart melted. She tried to stop herself from quivering as he leaned down and kissed her.

She failed in her attempt, so, still trembling, she threw her arms around him and kissed him back with all her might.

"Victor?" Zoe said, sitting up in the bed they'd shared for the past seven weeks.

His side was empty save for the shadows of the window panes cast in a checkerboard grid across the satin sheets.

She rose, naked, and tiptoed to the adjoining master bathroom. Victor's quarters had been a mess when she'd first arrived at the laboratory, but the bedroom had transformed into a clean and sparkling retreat from the lab—as if by magic—the first night they slept together. It had remained neat and tidy ever since.

"Victor?" she called quietly outside the bathroom door.

She gently pushed the door open, but he wasn't there—only darkness.

She took a silk robe from the dresser near the bed and threw it around her shoulders. A dim light shone from beneath the door that led to the laboratory.

A tingle ran up Zoe's spine as she opened the door and padded across the lab floor. She knew where she'd find him: at the drawing board. She and Victor had run into a design problem with powering all the discrete elements in the mechanical skeleton, and he'd been tormenting himself about it for weeks. Often, she would get up in the night and find him working. It wasn't that he didn't love her, or want to be with her; it was just that his work—their work—kept driving him forward.

She tiptoed around the lab tables, the generators, and the machine tools, to the far side of the lab. Sure enough, Victor lay with his head on the drawing board, diagrams scattered around him, exhausted, sleeping. His eyelids twitched with troubled dreams. He hadn't even bothered to dress.

Zoe's heart went out to him. *Poor darling*. She gently stroked his forehead; he felt deathly cold.

She took off her robe and draped it around his shoulders. Then she put his right arm over her own shoulders and tried to ease him off the stool. "Come on, darling. Time for bed."

He opened bleary eyes and gazed at her. "I have to work."

"I know," she said sympathetically. "But not tonight. Tonight you need to rest. Come back to bed. No more work."

"But I have to," he said. "Time . . . our time is so short!"

Though the lab was warm, goosebumps prickled Zoe's skin. "Victor, is something wrong? Are you . . . ill? Is there something you're not telling me?"

"I . . . No. I'm fine. It's just. . . ."

She embraced him, pressing his head to her naked breast. "Don't worry, darling," she said. "I won't leave. We'll see this through right to the end."

He threw his arms around her, clinging, his body trembling as though he were crying, though his cheeks remained dry.

"Oh, Zoe . . . I . . . I don't deserve you."

She stroked his hair. "The world won't end if we don't solve this tonight—or even tomorrow or next week. The world's survived without automata this long. It can survive until we get this done."

He smiled at her, but she could see in his haggard eyes that he didn't believe her.

"And we *will* get it done, *together*," she said, leading him to the bedroom. "Don't worry. We can start again tomorrow."

Victor was up before Zoe the next morning, and working late again after she went to bed that night. In the days that followed, the pattern continued. She tried to keep up with him, tried to support him, but though they worked practically side-by-side, she felt more distant from her lover each day.

Even after they'd solved the power distribution problem, Victor's mania did not stop. "Now we need to finish constructing the skeleton."

"But it won't even move without the clockwork brain," Zoe said, "and we've barely begun designing that yet. Without the brain, the automaton won't walk, it won't move, it won't do *anything*."

"I have some thoughts about that," Victor replied feverishly. "Once the skeleton is finished, I will supply the motive force. It will work. It *has* to!"

Her heart ached to see him like this. Yet what else could she do but support him and work as hard as possible?

Over the course of a week, the final form of the automaton took shape. Victor revised the designs as they went, tweaking here and there to make the form more functional. The hips flared out for more leverage and strength. The arms bowed slightly to carry objects. The chest cavity grew larger to house the ion batteries, the large electro-steam generator, and the interlinked series of micro-motors to supply energy to the machine's powerful arms and the rest of its body. Tiny arrays of light-and-shape sensors, like miniature cameras, glistened in the automaton's metallic eyes.

Zoe looked up at the glittering, nearly complete skeleton standing on a curtain-draped pedestal in the machine shop portion of Victor's lab. "I–it's beautiful."

"Yes," Victor agreed. "She is." He looked exhausted but, for the first time in weeks, pleased.

"How long do you think the batteries will power it?"

"As long as the generator has fuel."

"And if the fuel runs out?"

Victor scratched his chin. "It depends on energy usage. These ion batteries are not like those powering the city's motor vehicles. I've made considerable advances in energy storage since . . . during my seclusion."

A shadow of bitter memories flashed across his face, so she hugged him.

"The experiment in the cabinet?" she asked.

For a moment, his eyes widened with surprise, but then he merely nodded.

"What's the upper energy storage limit?"

"Three years, perhaps," he said, glancing toward the

curtain-flanked cabinet. "Under optimal conditions, that's the longest I've managed to ..." He trailed off and looked away.

Zoe smiled and kissed him on the cheek. "You know," she said, cocking her head to get a different view of the automaton, "our machine *does* look like a girl." All of the design adjustments they'd made to it the over the weeks had given the automaton the classic hourglass shape of a woman. "I hadn't really noticed it until you said, 'she.'"

"Yes," he replied thoughtfully. "I will call her Hella."

A chill ran down Zoe's spine. "After your late wife."

Victor blushed. "It ... It wouldn't seem right to name it after you. I mean, we're not even married."

Now Zoe blushed. "Are ... are you asking me to...?"

Victor turned away suddenly. "No! I mean ... not yet. I *can't*. I can't, until ..."

She bit her lip, and tears beaded at the corners of her eyes. "Until what?"

He turned back and embraced her, crushing her body against his. "Not until we're finished. Not until we know whether I've succeeded ... or failed."

He felt hot, almost feverish, but she hugged him back, losing herself in the embrace. "Don't worry," she whispered. "I'm sure it will all work. We'll *make* it work."

"Victor?"

Again, the bed next to her lay empty. Tonight, though, the moon was dark, and only shadows kept Zoe company. A strange, throbbing hum came from the other room.

"Victor?" she said, getting up and pulling on her robe. "We *can't* do this every night." Anger and worry fighting within her, she threw open the laboratory door and strode inside. Then she stopped, frozen, her wide eyes glued to the far side of the room, where Victor worked.

Every piece of equipment in the laboratory whined

and hummed, harnessed in series, their power building to maximum capacity. The cabinet containing Victor's battery experiment stood open. Inside, a strange battery, like a transparent Leyden jar, pulsed with eerie greenish light. It looked like the glow from a radium experiment Zoe had once seen in electro-mechanics class.

Wires, like intricate networks of blood vessels, ran from the humming machines to both the body of the automaton and to the pulsing battery. A heavier wire, the thickness of Zoe's thumb, ran from the battery directly to the machine's head.

"Just a moment longer," Victor said to himself. "It won't be long now, my darling."

"Victor!"

He turned, madness blazing in his blue eyes. "Zoe!" he cried. "Get back."

She walked toward him.

"Don't come any closer!" He threw a big switch on a panel of circuitry next to the automaton.

ZAM! Artificial lightning filled the room, arcing between automaton and generators and pulsing battery. The automaton bucked and shook, twitching like an insect on a collector's pin.

Before Zoe could process any of it, a stray bolt of electricity flashed out and hit her in the chest, knocking her off her feet.

She skidded across the laboratory floor, crashed against the wall, and the world went dark and silent.

"Zoe! Are you all right?" Victor's voice. Not manic now, but sane, compassionate. "Get a wet towel, would you? Zoe, can you hear me?"

How can I get you a wet towel when the whole world's spinning? she wondered.

Something damp mopped across her forehead.

"Good. Now something to drink. There's brandy in the kitchen cabinet—in the usual place." A vague whirring sound, like distant machinery. Was the humming just in her head?

"Zoe?"

"I–I can hear you, Victor." Slowly she opened her eyes. She was lying in her bed, Victor's bed. Bright afternoon sunlight streamed through the big bedroom windows. Victor was swabbing her forehead with a cool, wet towel. He smiled at her.

"Pretty bad shock you had."

"Yes, I . . . Victor, what happened?"

"It worked!" he replied, somehow appearing both jubilant and sheepish.

"It did?" she said, sitting up so fast her head hurt. Then the whole crazy scene of the night before came back to her. "Victor, what were you doing? What worked? Is the automaton—"

Victor beamed. "She's alive, Zoe. We did it!"

"But we can't have! We didn't finish designing her brain. There's nothing to run her control systems!"

"We didn't need a brain, Zoe, because we already had one."

Zoe's guts twisted, and she suddenly felt terribly cold.

"A *soul*, to be more precise—trapped in my experimental battery."

"Trapped since . . . since t–the accident."

Victor's face remained radiant. "She has a body now, and she's back!"

Zoe turned away, tears springing to her eyes and running down her cheeks. "Oh . . . Victor!" She squeezed her eyes closed, trying to shut out the world, trying to shut down her brain.

The bedroom door creaked open and soft, mechanical footfalls crossed to the bed.

"The brandy, Victor," said a woman's voice. It was sweet, gentle, but it buzzed slightly, like the voice of a singer coming over the wireless.

"Thank you. Here, Zoe, drink this. It will make you feel better."

Zoe felt a tumbler pressed into her hands. She put the glass to her lips and downed the whole thing, though she knew that—at this moment—nothing would make her feel better. Finally, when she'd drained all the liquor, she opened her eyes.

Next to the bed, beside Victor, stood the automaton, all gleaming metal and softly whirring motors. She looked stunning. Perfect. Venus as a machine.

"Zoe," Victor said, "I'd like you to meet Hella. My wife."

The automaton regarded Zoe with shiny, metallic eyes. "Pleased to meet you," the machine said. "My husband has told me about all you've done for us."

All? Zoe wondered. *How . . . open-minded of you.*

Victor looked lovingly at Hella, and Zoe couldn't help herself—even now, in the midst of all her pain and sorrow, the mechanic's heart went out to him.

"After the accident," he said, "when Hella lay dying, I captured her soul in that special battery. I couldn't tell if my experiment had worked, not until . . . not until last night, when I transferred her into the automaton. I couldn't wait any longer, you see. Her energy was fading, but now . . . now Hella and I can finish our lives together."

The machine put her hand in his. "As we should have."

Victor gazed lovingly at her. "I know she's not much to look at now, but once I've applied my artificial skin. . . ."

"What about *our* dream?" Zoe asked. "A world without fear and death and drudgery?"

"I've conquered death," Victor said, a sheepish grin spreading across his face. "I think the rest can wait a little while longer."

The steamer-cab pulled up outside the Chapman-Challenger mansion, in one of the city's less-fashionable districts, and let Zoe out. She stared up at the crumbling stone and sagging Victorian roofline.

It's good to be home.

"So the prodigal mechanic returns," Armstrong said, appearing in the mansion's door. He grabbed a pair of Zoe's bags from the cab's trunk and hefted them toward the front door. "I was beginning to wonder whether you'd ever grace us with your presence again."

Zoe punched him in the shoulder. "Nice to see you, too, y–you big lug!"

Armstrong grinned at Zoe as Kit Chapman-Challenger strode out the entryway; she held the door open for her mechanic.

"I hope you had a nice rest," Kit said, "'cause I've booked us passage on a freighter to the Congo, day after tomorrow. An archaeobiologist's work is never done!"

"Give the kid a break, Kitty! She just got home."

"No," Zoe said. "I need to work. Working would be good right now." It would take a long time for the heartache to disappear completely, but, surrounded by her friends, the sorrow was already beginning to fade.

The three of them walked together into the mansion's foyer. Armstrong put the bags down next to the stairs that led to Zoe's room and workshop.

"You'll be happy to know you made out like a bandit while you were away, working for Von Lang," Kit said. "I drive a very hard bargain—if I do say so myself. Not only did you receive a great salary, but you also get a cut of any patents resulting from the work you did with him.

And the small stipend I get for representing you will get us all the way to Africa—and back, hopefully."

"That's great, CC. Really great."

Armstrong put one beefy arm around Zoe's shoulder. "What's the matter, kid? Did the project not work out the way Von Lang planned?"

"No, things worked out exactly the way he planned. Just not the way *I* planned."

Kit arched one eyebrow. "Why? What happened?"

Zoe took a deep breath and put one arm around Armstrong's shoulder and the other around Kit's. "Well, I helped Victor Von Lang piece together his heart's desire, and, at the same time, managed to break my own heart."

"That sounds like it calls for a drink," Armstrong suggested, heading for the liquor cabinet.

Zoe sighed. "You can say that again. And Ray. . . ?"

"Yeah?"

"Make mine a double."

LOVE COMES TO ABYSSAL CITY

Tobias S. Buckell

*Tobias S. Buckell is a Caribbean-born speculative fic-
tion writer who grew up in Grenada, the British Virgin
Islands, and the U.S. Virgin Islands. He has published
short stories in various magazines and anthologies. He
has four novels published, including a bestselling novel
set in the Halo videogame universe—Halo: The Cole
Protocol. Visit him at www.tobiasbuckell.com.*

To be an ambassador meant to face outsiders, and Tia
was well prepared for it. There was the overpowered,
heavy, high-caliber pistol ever strapped to her right
thigh. Sure, it was filigreed with brass and polished wood
inlay, a gunsmith's masterpiece, but it was still able to
stop many threats in their tracks. A similarly crafted-
but-functional blade swung from her hip. And then
there was the flamethrower strapped to her back.

This was not so much for threats, but for contraband
and outside material forbidden in the Abyssal City.

Today she'd taken the elevators up the edges of the

ravine that split the ground all the way down to the hot, steamy streets a mile below. Overhead, tall, wrought-iron arches and glass ceilings spanned the top of the ravine, keeping life-giving air capped in. Up here, near the great airlocks, the air bit at her skin: cold and low enough on oxygen that you sometimes had to stop and pant to catch your breath.

"Ambassador?" the Port Specialist asked, his long red robes swirling around the pair of emergency air tanks he wore on his back, his eyes hidden behind the silvered orbs of his rubber facemask. His voice was muffled and distant. "Are you ready?"

"Proceed," Tia ordered.

Today they examined the long, segmented iron parts of a train that hissed inside the outer bays. The skin of the mechanical transporter cracked and, shifted, readjusting itself to pressurized air. From the platform she stood on, she surveyed the entire length of the quarantined contraption.

It had thundered in, unannounced, on one of the many rails that crisscrossed the rocky, airless void of the planetary crust.

It was a possible threat.

"Time of arrival," the Port Specialist intoned, and turned his back to her to grab the long levered handles of an Interface set into the wall. He pulled the right handles, pushed in the right pins, and created a card containing that data.

"Length," Tia called out. She bent her eyes to a small device mounted on the rim of a greening railing. "One quarter of a mile. One main motor unit. Three cabs. No markings. Black outer paint."

Behind her the Port Specialist clicked and clacked the information into more cards.

A photograph was taken, and the plate shaved down to the same size as the cards and added.

A phonograph was etched into wax of the sound of the idling motor that filled the cavernous bay.

All this information was then put into a canister, which was put into a vacuum tube, which was then sucked into the city's pipes. "The profile of the visiting machine has been submitted," intoned the Port Specialist.

"We wait for Society's judgment," replied Tia, and pulled up a chair. She sat and looked at the train, wondering what was inside.

The reply came back up the tube fifteen minutes later. The Port Specialist retrieved the card.

"What does Society say?" Tia asked.

"There is a seventy percent threat level," the Port Specialist said.

"Time to send them on their way," Tia said. "I will help you vent the bay."

But the Port Specialist was shaking his head. "The threat level is high, but the command on the card is to allow the visitors into the sandbox. Full containment protocol."

Tia groaned. "This is the worst possible timing. I had a party I was supposed to attend."

The Port Specialist shrugged and checked the straps on his air mask. He tightened them, as if imagining the possible danger of the train to be in the air around him, right this moment. "And I have a family to attend," he said. "But we have a higher duty right now."

"I was going to be introduced to my cardmate," Tia said. The first step on a young woman's life outside her family home. The great machine had found the person best suited for her to spend the rest of her life with.

It would disappoint her family and her friends that she would be stuck in lockdown in the sandbox with some foreign people waiting to make sure they cleared quarantine.

The Port Specialist handed her the orders. "Verify the orders," he said.

Tia looked down at the markings, familiar with the patterns and colors after a lifetime of reading in Society Code.

A large chance of danger.

But they were to welcome in this threat.

"Hand me an air mask and a spare bottle," Tia sighed.

The Port Specialist did so, and Tia buckled them on. She checked the silvered glasses on the eyeholes and patted down her body armor. She put in earplugs, pulled on leather gloves, and then connected a long hose to the base of her special gas mask.

"Hello?" she said. "This is Tia."

The sounds and sights of what she saw would be communicated back through, and monitored by Port Control, with the aid of a significant part of Society's processing power. Crankshafts and machinery deep in the lower levels of the city, powered by the steam created from pipes below even that, would apply the city's hundreds of years of algorithms and calculations to her situation and determine what she would do next.

And Port Control, really someone sitting in a darkened room in front of a series of flashing lights, would relay that to her.

"This is Port Control, you are clear to engage," came the somewhat muffled reply from the speaking hose.

Tia walked up to the train, stopping occasionally to yank the bulk of the hose along with her, and rapped on the side of the steel door.

Pneumatics hissed and the door scraped open. Tia's hand was on the butt of her gun as a man, clad in full rubber outer gear and wearing a mask much like hers

stepped forward, a piece of parchment held out before
him.

He had a gun on his waist, and his hand on it as well.
They approached each other like crabs, cautiously scut-
tling forward.

Tia snatched the parchment, and they retreated away
from each other. She read the parchment by holding it
up where she could both read it, one handed, and keep
an eye on the other man.

Manifest: three passengers.

Passenger one and two, loyal and vetted citizens of a
chasm town two stops up along the track. Affiliation:
Chasm Confederation.

Passenger three was an unknown who had ridden down
the track from places unknown. Affiliation: unknown.

Tia reported this all back to Port Control.

"Go ahead and let them in," Port Control said.

Tia nervously waved her assent at the man in rubber,
and he turned around and waved the passengers out of
the car.

The first two, a husband and wife team with matching
gold-plated lifemate cards dangling from their necks,
were diplomats. They carried briefcases full of paper
network protocols, and rode up and down the rail to
pass on packets of information between the cities and
towns. They stepped down, the tips of the tails of their
bright red diplomat suits dragging on the ground slightly
as they walked past.

Tia bowed to them, somewhat clumsily in her gear.

"What is the threat level?" the male diplomat asked.

"Sandbox," Tia told him.

With a sigh they walked around her toward the air-
lock leading out.

The third passenger stepped down.

He had long hair cut to just above his ears and dark

eyes partially hidden by wire-rimmed glasses. He pulled a giant trunk with wheels mounted on the corners. A leather-bound notebook dangled from a gold chain looped around his neck, as did a mechanical pen.

With a cautious step forward, he bowed, and then straightened. "My name is Riun," he announced.

He went to walk around her and follow the diplomats, but then realized he'd let go of his wheeled trunk. He awkwardly turned back for it.

Tia smiled beneath the heavy mask.

The sandbox was a hall that could seat two hundred. The center was dominated by several long tables, while the periphery had cots that folded out from the wall.

By the far end, clear one-way mirrors allowed observers to view the sandbox.

Overhead, large metal balconies allowed Society's Reporters to look down on the sandbox and constantly file new cards with the machinery of Society, updating the computing machine that ruled them all with all the moves the quarantined made.

Every fifteen minutes the reporters would change shifts, to prevent contamination.

As the diplomats huddled together in the far side of the room, not interested in company, Tia removed her cumbersome protective gear and joined Riun at the table.

"Your city is strict about outside influence," Riun observed, looking around the sandbox.

"There are murals on the lower alleyways," Tia said. "Some of the cityfolk believe that during the Ascendance Wars the city's programs, during the great Downshifting, became somewhat paranoid of outside infection."

"The Ascendance Wars?" Riun asked, looking puzzled.

Tia stared at him. How much of an outsider was he?

Suddenly she thought about the warning, and wondered if maybe Rium was something far more dangerous than she realized.

Should she even be talking to him?

But the machine hadn't flagged Riun to be separately sandboxed. Nor had Tia been handed any warnings to shun him.

"Were you schooled in your city's history?" she asked.

He smiled. "Of course. But I am not schooled in yours."

"The great thinking cities of the world tried to reach for the stars, but fought among each other to reach them first and over control of the skies. The fighting grew so perilous and killed so many people that the machines that ran the cities decided to Downshift. They would only use mechanical technology, slow thought, to run the systems of their cities. The city used to use 'quantum chips' but now only uses steam and gears and cards."

Riun chuckled. "Always different stories."

"What?"

"I find, from city to city, there are different stories and variations on the stories," Riun said.

"And what is the story *your* city tells?" Tia asked loudly, while thinking to herself that surely this was auditory contamination, and why wasn't the city flagging this conversation yet? Hearing that the city's histories were false was dangerous.

Wasn't it?

Then again, Tia realized, she'd only seen the murals or heard tales. She'd never heard the city give an official history.

Riun cleared his throat. "According to the histories of my city, the Downshift came when the great Minds of this world created a shield to save us from a war with the other minds out in the Great Beyond. In order to save us, they banned all methods of information that could be transmitted through the air."

"And which one do you believe?" Tia asked.

Riun smiled again, large and welcoming. "I think they're all shards of some older truth we've forgotten," he said. "That's why I travel the world, listening, gathering, and meeting the citizens of the cities."

He opened a case of notes and showed her hand-drawn sketches of other cities, other night skies. Hand-written notes of tales, and descriptions of systems.

"Why?" Tia asked. "Why leave your city?"

"Why not?" he shrugged.

The hours dragged on. Food was delivered by chutes, and they ate on the large, empty tables in silence.

Afterward Tia sat and watched Riun read a leather-bound book he pulled out of his large trunk until she couldn't stand the boredom. "Do you play Gorithms?" she finally asked.

"Of course."

"There're several playing stands near the far walls," she said. "Care to join me?"

They set up on the small playing table, connected the pneumatic tubes, and a few seconds later the dual packs of cards appeared.

Tia unwrapped hers and laid them down with a thwack as Riun delicately laid his out behind the dark glass of his privacy shield.

They looked at each other over the rim of the shields.

"You play?" he asked. She couldn't see his smile, but the eyes twinkled.

"Always."

Today's game was five flowchart sequences with

equations, solvable by sub games with the cards. Tia quickly solved her sequences, passed on the marker cards, and looked up.

"You're quick."

"Five points," Riun said. "If my results agree."

Which they didn't. One of the sequences tied.

Tia crosschecked with his cards and he rechecked hers. No tie; they came to the same conclusion by playing out the math. Tia was right.

Riun placed the markers in the tube and watched them get sucked away. "You're quick," he said. "And accurate."

"Ninety percent accuracy rate on simple sub games like that."

Down in the belly of the beast their results would be tabulated, the result of a low-priority calculation request. Maybe they'd just helped calculate which lights should be left on above some city street. Or regulated the pressure of a valve somewhere. You never really knew. All you knew was that the thousands of games constantly being played helped comprise the total computational capacity of the entire city.

Streets released traffic along paths that helped simulate equations, games were tied into the city's calculations, and some suspected that even lives had some sort of calculating function, in the cities.

Some Gorithim games were checkerboards, or mazes, or just patterns. You never knew what the tubes would hand you. But playing them was usually fun, if not sometimes puzzling, and it gave you something to do.

Particularly when stuck in the sandbox.

"Another game?" Tia asked.

"I don't know if I should," Riun's eyes crinkled. Was he smiling? "I think your mind is far quicker than mine."

Tia looked around pointedly. "I'll be gentle. Besides, do you see anything else you could be doing with your time?"

Riun conceded the point and tapped the delivery button. "Since you promised," he muttered.

As they waited for the next game to arrive, Tia craned over the shield to get a better look at his whole face. He did have the remains of a smile still. "Tell me about the places you've visited," she suggested.

And Riun began to spin tales of cities perched near cliffs with pipes dug far into the crust of the world to deliver steam, or dug into giant pits, and even one at the top of a tame volcano.

Quarantine broke. Three days of playing Gorithims, eating, and putting up with the diplomats pointedly ignoring them. All the while, the fifteen-minute shift changes of observers continued in the gantries overhead, shuffling in and out to observe them all.

It wasn't all that unusual for Tia, who enjoyed the gentle rhythm. She'd done several quarantines already. And to be honest, there were worse people than Riun to get stuck with. He was easy on the eyes, and he could chatter on about the rails he'd traveled, the citypeople he'd met, and the places he'd been. But in a neutral manner, not a boasting one.

She liked that.

When the doors cracked open, Riun excitedly packed his things. "Thank you for the company," he said, and gave her a half bow.

"My pleasure."

And they parted ways, Tia headed for the south switchbacks, threading her way down through the houses clustered on the ravine's steep walls. Riun would be headed for the guest houses, from where he'd launch a campaign of interviews and his explorations of the new city.

It felt, Tia thought, vaguely treasonous to wonder whether she could submit herself as Riun's minder to the city while she was getting ready to meet her family and her new cardmate.

At the card ceremony, Tia arrived stripped out of her ambassador's garb. She now wore her red leathers, with a bustle designed to shove and prod and push her into what her mother called a more pleasing shape, though Tia preferred the comfortable fit of her work clothes. Her hair had been carefully brushed down, and adorned with brass clips.

Here she was, an ambassador, an elite trainee tasked with the city's defense, and her parents had spent money to have her mate-card bronzed; they were not powerful nor rich enough to afford gold. Tia carried it in her gloved hands up the street toward the sub-routines check palace and Gorithims parlor that dominated the nearest intersection.

There, in black leathers and a tie, was her cardmate.

According to the lifelong database kept by the city, her life in punched out rows and marks, this was the unmarried city man with the best statistical chance of making her happy.

Actually, that wasn't technically true, was it?

No, this *pairing* was the most statistically valid and most likely to work. There might be someone else better for her, but who wouldn't be interested in her.

Could she fall in love with this man? He cut a fine figure. Dashing dark hair and large eyes. A certain precision to his movements that spoke of self control and quickness. Those were qualities she loved in a person.

It was long a tradition to know nothing about your cardmate. Getting to know each other was half the excitement. Who was this person you were matched to by the great city?

That was something to discover.

But did it make her another switch or lever? Was this truly the person she would love, if left alone? Or was this another calculated move by a greater calculation, testing some subroutine?

The two families moved together, their center of focus the two cardmates.

Tia held out her bronzed card. "It says we are most compatible."

Her cardmate held out his silvered card. "Then let us verify it."

They put the two cards into a machine, and it whirred and clicked, and then a green light glowed.

Compatible.

"My name is Owyn," the man said.

"I'm Tia."

She hung his silvered card around her neck, and he her bronzed card.

It was done.

On the first night, she was expected only to eat a dinner with Owyn. A celebration of a new life that was to slowly bloom. She'd done that, sitting politely in place, and asking after his family. They were a family of silk merchants, and Owyn occasionally rode the rails to other towns and even some cities in order to trade for the city. And normally . . . that would have been fascinating and exotic to her.

Tomorrow there would be a banquet, with dancing and instruments. And on the third day . . .

Well, on the third day, her parents and friends and extended family would walk in a procession down the road, and Owyn's parents and friends and extended family would do so as well, all carrying possessions to the new couple's home, where there would be yet another celebration.

And after that, everyone would withdraw, leaving them alone.

It should have been all she was focused on. So why was she wondering how Riun was doing, his first night alone in the city?

Her stomach full of rich food and tea, Tia climbed up on her roof and looked up at the atrium lights far overhead. Somewhere else Riun might be looking back at the same lights, she thought.

And then she swore at herself and climbed down the wrought iron ladder along the side of her parent's house and sneaked off into the night.

Riun answered the door to the guest houses with a frown. "Tia?"

She slid right past him.

He was puzzled, but offered her tea from a side-table and lit some lights. His hair was disheveled, and he wore his nightrobe tied tight around his waist.

They sat in the large foyer near the coolant fans. At night, this close to the city's lower depths, it grew hot.

"What's wrong?" Riun asked.

"What makes you think anything's wrong?" she asked.

"You're an ambassador, here in the middle of the night." He looked guarded, and tired. "Should I begin repacking?"

"You've done nothing wrong." She curled up on a small couch and hugged her knees.

"Then why are you here?"

Tia sighed. Typical of men, to miss the obvious and wallow in their own confusion. It was no wonder the great City Minds took to giving out cards that told you who your best match was. "To see you," she said, a bit more angrily than she'd meant.

And why hadn't he picked up on that? Or did city women who'd just met him show up at his door at odd hours of the night all the time?

Riun downed the last of his tea and stood. He walked over and sat next to her, and Tia felt a thrill of excitement run through her as the couch shifted from the added weight.

But Riun didn't look happy. A weary look had replaced what she had hoped was intrigue. He reached over to her neck and held up the silvered card. "That isn't wise," he murmured. "I am here at the courtesy of your city, and I will be expelled if I violate that hospitality. Your city has computed the best possible match already for you. I will not endanger that."

He let go of the card suddenly and pulled his hand back.

For that, she found herself even more interested in him. "You're right," she said.

He relaxed, slightly.

But Tia grabbed his hand. "You're right: you're an outsider. The city never had a chance to run your profile. Maybe we would have been a good match. But we'll never know. We could never know. And maybe the city made a mistake. There are mistakes made, that's why there are error checks." That's why every game of Gorithims involved cross checks for secondary points.

Riun pulled his hand gently away and stood up. "Tia, I'm something new and exciting. An outsider. Maybe even a little scary. Many are attracted. I will not destroy your life on a fancy. I can't." He walked to the door.

It was time for her to leave.

At the door she paused, and then looked up at him. "Don't you get lonely, out there? Traveling those lines by yourself? Don't you wish you could share those adventures?"

He looked pained. "It is lonely out there, Tia. But few have the courage to truly abandon all they've ever known. It sounds exciting, but when it really comes down to it . . . they can't make that jump."

He'd been let down in the past.

Tia imagined him watching someone realize what they were doing and rush out of a train at the last second, leaving him alone inside, pulling away.

What would it be like to rip yourself out the guts of a city for good?

Her father sat in the chair by the entryway playing soligorithim at the family games table. It was odd to see him up this late. He worked an early morning shift at the calculating farms, running numbers on slide rules along with thousands of others.

He set his playing cards aside and held up a red letter. "This woke us up. It came through mail chute. Priority. For you."

Tia read it. A simple warning, generated somewhere deep inside the city's bowels, just for her.

It forbade her from seeing Riun for the duration of his stay. Any violation would result in his expulsion.

"Is there a problem?" her father asked.

Tia folded the letter up. "Did you read it?"

"I did." He looked back down at his cards. "Some of us have had friendships or . . . more, before our cardmates were revealed. People we knew and thought we liked. Over time, you realize you were mistaken. The city is wise."

"Did *you* want someone else?" Tia asked.

Her dad turned back to the cards. "Tomorrow is the banquet, Tia. You should focus on that."

Tia walked up the stairs to her room. In bed she lay down and reread the warning.

It wouldn't be fair to Riun to get him expelled because of her own confusion. He was a traveler, an explorer of new cities. She wouldn't rip this one from him, she decided.

Her cardmate sat across from her, partially hidden behind a staggering assortment of elaborate cakes, pots of loose teas, coffees, and fancy aerated drinks.

It seemed like half her street had boiled out of their multi-storied tenements bolted to the sides of the beginning the ravine's steep climb to celebrate.

And Tia found herself forcing her smile.

One of her aunts patted her shoulder sympathetically. "It gets better," she whispered. "Give it time. All of us are in shock at first. It's okay."

So apparently her smile was not very believable.

Later into the night Owyn found her, trying to hide behind a flower display.

"Are you feeling well?" he asked hesitantly.

"Everything is fine," Tia insisted.

Owyn stood awkwardly by her, then finally nodded and walked away. Tia sighed. He looked crushed and frustrated. And none of this was really his fault, was it?

Neither of them left the banquet happy. When Tia got home she just sat in the middle of her room, frustrated and getting angrier.

Her dad knocked and entered the room. "We have a problem," he said.

"I'm sorry," Tia said, looking down at the carpet on her floor. "The city provides. It calculates the best outcomes for us. We have jobs we are engaged with. Lives that are often fulfilling. And I know that Owyn is a good choice. I'm struggling, but I think I'll get through."

"Your aunt just sent a runner, he's at the door. She says a quarantine order has been issued for you." Her dad squatted down in front of her. "What have you been doing, Tia?"

His face was so full of concern it hurt to see. Tia flinched. "I haven't done anything since I came home."

"There must be probabilities or some new calculations the city has made," her father muttered. He sat down on another chair and rubbed his forehead. No doubt he was wondering where he had gone wrong in raising her. Or trying to figure out what he could do.

Which was nothing.

"Or," Tia said, "the city is right." It was strange to think of *the city* itself bringing its attention on her. It was more than strange: it was scary.

"What do you mean?" her father asked, looking up.

"I'm an ambassador. I'm exposed to things that come into the city. It's my job to stop them. It does mean there is a risk. And I know who I need to talk to."

"You can't leave, there are ambassadors on the way," her father protested, but Tia was already out of her chair.

She used a long black cloak with a hood to help her slip around the shadows of the streets and flit her way to the guest houses.

When Riun opened the door again, she pushed him back inside and closed the door behind her.

"What did you do to me?" she demanded.

"What are you talking about? What are you doing here?"

"There's a quarantine command on me. You've infected me with *something*; I want to know what."

"It's just me," Riun protested. "I'm not an agent. I'm not anything. I don't *have* anything."

"Then you must have gotten something from someone else," Tia insisted. "Do you have anti-city propaganda you've been exposed to or thoughts?"

"What? No!"

"What city sent you?" Tia poked his chest.

"It was my own idea. I wanted to see the world. That's all."

Tia threw herself down on the couch. "Then why am I suddenly a threat to peace and order? Why is the city going to quarantine me?"

"I don't know," Riun said. He looked just as upset as she did. "There's always a risk, being a traveler. That you picked something up somewhere. Some mannerism that a host city will get upset by. But I swear to you, Tia, I haven't set out to do anything to you. I would never forgive myself if I did."

She looked at him sharply. "You seemed quick enough to push me out of the guest house earlier."

"For both our sakes, Tia. You and I both know you have a cardmate. You have a place in this city. I won't jeopardize your life here."

But he already had. Just be revealing his existence, she realized.

She opened her mouth to try and explain this, and a loud rap came from the door.

"Open up!" shouted an authoritative voice. "Traveler Riun, in the name of the city open up!"

Tia stood. "I've ruined it all for both of us, haven't I?" The city had figured out she came here. Now Riun would be expelled.

"What will they do to you?" Riun asked, eyes narrowed. He didn't seem to be worried about expulsion. "Answer me quickly, for I've been to many cities, and the punishments for disorder vary wildly, Tia."

"Long term quarantine," Tia said. "Maybe a year. A recomputing of my personality profile based on an interview, pending release. Reeducation during the quarantine."

Riun grimaced. Tia stood up and walked over to him. "It's not your fault, Riun," she said. "It's mine for wanting something that isn't mine to have."

She touched his lips with her fingers. To her frustration, he didn't seem to be sharing the moment with her. His brow was creased with thought, as if he were struggling with something.

Then he gently held her shoulders. "And what is it you really want, Tia? Is it me or the traveling? Or to escape the city? Some want to leave it, but there always more cities, more places you'll have to navigate carefully. More places you'll be considered an outside threat by the city's Mind."

Tia looked into his eyes. He looked quite earnest at this moment. So she returned that with honesty. "I know I'm attracted to the outside. I think that's a part of it. And I think a part of it is you as well. I hope that's the greater part. But how am I to know? You are not my cardmate."

The hammering on the door stopped. They would be breaking it down shortly.

"If you truly are in love with both, and not just one of those things, then come with me," Riun said, and held out a hand.

Riun led her to his room and pulled on a coat, then swept his books and notes into his trunk.

"Lock my door," he said.

Tia did, hearing the ambassadors crashing against the outside door. It creaked, seconds away from breaking open.

"It's not uncommon for travelers to have to run for it when a city changes its mind," Riun said. "So we always have a way out that we note for each other."

He kicked at a panel, and a small section of the wall swung aside. They walked into the empty room next door and closed the false wall behind them. Outside, ambassadors trooped down the hallway and started banging on Riun's door.

Riun took them through two more rooms until they stopped at one with a window onto an alley.

They squeezed through, yanking his trunk along with them, and clattered out into the alleyway. Riun pulled his collar up, making to run for the street, but Tia stopped him.

"This way," she said, pointing at their feet. Wisps of steam leaked out from the edges of a manhole. "There'll be watchers on the streets. I know the steam tunnels."

Inside the dark tunnels they ran for the edge of the city, and emerged near the ravine elevators. Again, Tia directed them away from the street. "I know a faster way; my dad works around here," she huffed.

They broke through the doors and ran down the long halls of a calculating factory instead. Clean white, brightly lit, and filled with thousands of sober-faced men and women, leaning over abacus trays, flicking beads in response to equations being offered up to them by blinking lights near their control boards.

Their presence caused a rippling effect of commotion as they passed through, with calculators in clean white robes standing up to shout at them.

Tia threw open the rear doors, and they pushed past the handfuls of people waiting to board the city elevators. Curses and complaints followed them, but Riun shut the cage to the elevator shut and Tia hit the switches.

The elevator climbed up the side of the ravine, hissing and spitting as it passed street after street level, and the roofs of houses at the lower levels and clinging to the sides slowly slid past them.

There was a balcony on the High Road near one of the bridges that ran along under the glass roof that capped the city. Riun grabbed Tia's arm, and pulled her over to the railing. "Look," he said.

Tia did, and gasped. The city below was changing. People were spilling out onto the streets. Lights were turning on. It wasn't orderly, or staggered in shifts as normal. Instead, the focus of the disturbance was the calculating building they'd run through. People were wandering the streets randomly, not using the flowchart sidewalks and lights.

There was chaos in the Abyssal City and it was spreading.

Lights flickered randomly, and gouts of steam burst from below the streets.

"Did we cause that?" Tia asked, looking at the masses of pedestrians wandering aimlessly about, shouting and arguing. They could hear the grinding shudder of machines coming to a halt over the bubbling hum of discussions and arguments drifting upwards from the entire city. "Did *you*?"

She glanced at him, and realized from the look on his face that he was just as horrified as she was. "I'm just a traveler," he whispered. "Just a traveler."

They looked at the spreading chaos, rapt. "Do you think it'll bring the entire city to a stop?" she asked.

Riun shook his head. "No. No I've seen this before. It's a temporary fault. A system failure." Warning klaxons fired to life throughout the city. "Soon they'll order a return to homes, empty the streets. Stop all the machines then restart them. Order will return."

"I've never seen anything like it," Tia said. Not in all her life. It unnerved her. She'd always thought of society, the system around her, as stable and everlasting and solid.

Yet here she was, with Riun. And there chaos was.

In the distance, she heard the rumble of an intercity train.

They had to move through the sandbox and get to it.

"Listen," Riun told her, hearing the train and turning to face her. They were so close, their lips could almost touch. "If you leave with me, I can't promise you anything. I can't promise you a home or a city that you fit into. I can't promise you my love, I've only known you a week. All I can promise is a travel partner, and the fact that I do find you beautiful and interesting and I want to escape with you. Can that be enough?"

Tia pulled the silvered card off her neck and looked down at it. "Yes," she said. "I'm willing to take chance and uncertainty."

And then she threw the card out into the space over the ravine and watched it flutter away, down toward the steaming, chaotic streets of the city.

FOR THE LOVE OF BYRON

Mickey Zucker Reichert

Mickey Zucker Reichert is a pediatrician, parent, bird wrangler, goat roper, dog trainer, cat herder, horse rider, and fish feeder, who learned (the hard way) not to let macaws remove contact lenses. She is the author of two dozen novels and fifty-some short stories. Her other claims to fame are that she has performed brain surgery and her parents really are rocket scientists.

Night wind howled through the colonial village of May's Landing, sending a loose shutter slamming against a shop window. Elizabeth Holden wrapped her overcoat more tightly around herself, shivering beneath the red wool. The long, floaty fabric of her nightgown bunched beneath it, making her look bulky in odd places, but she appreciated the long sleeves and high-buttoned collar for the first time since arriving in the New World. She clenched her hands inside the rabbit fur muff and tried not to think about the growing numbness in her fingers and slippered toes.

The same village that seemed so bright and welcoming during the day now seemed like a strange forbidding place, rife with hulking shadows. The dark alleys drew her gaze more fully than the doorways now. Smoke streamed from every chimney, engulfing the village in a pungent fog. The machinery that usually spouted friendly billows of white steam now looked like huddled monsters prepared to spring at the unwary. Suddenly wishing she had never ventured out, Elizabeth glanced toward home. The mansion sat in darkness on the hill, looking as odd and uncomforting as the village itself.

Elizabeth forced an image of Byron to her mind's eye: an adorable armload of black, all huge brown eyes and clumsy paws. She had illegally dragged him across the sea, hidden in a basket of knitting. The law was strict about bringing animals to the pristine environment of the New World. It allowed for a limited number of domesticated cows, goats, pigs and chickens, all carefully cataloged and all ultimately intended for the dinner table. No exceptions were made for any other living creatures, although they encouraged the mechanical dogs and cats that had become the preference of the Old World as well.

Elizabeth had lost track of Byron nearly three months earlier. When he had grown too big to hide in her room, she had moved him to a clearing in the forest outside her window. There, she had spent many happy hours romping with the animal. Large, calm as windless sea, and mercifully quiet, Byron had grown from an awkward puppy unsteady on his saucer-sized paws to a gawky adolescent dog with a tongue that could wash her entire face in a single, happy lick. She had managed to pass him off as a mech-dog on the few occasions when someone had spotted her with him.

Then, one day, Byron had gone crashing off after a herd of bounding deer, their odd white tails flashing like parley flags. She had chased after him, but he swiftly outdistanced her. Elizabeth had not seen him since, though not for lack of trying. She had slipped away to call him at every opportunity. She listened breathlessly to all the passing gossip. If someone had discovered a living, breathing dog, news of its capture would have spread throughout May's Landing.

Elizabeth had nearly given up hope. When no news reached her, when no one spoke of an odd black carcass or the bones of some unidentified predator, she did not know whether to feel relieved or frightened. The thought of Byron lost and alone cut at her heart like a physical attack. Whenever she considered it, her chest hurt, breathing became a struggle, and tears flowed freely from her eyes.

Now, Elizabeth thought she saw a movement in the nearest alley. She stared, dark eyes attempting cleave the darkness, but she saw nothing more. With no other leads, she glided toward the alley, hesitantly removing her hands from the muff. Although she hated to lose its warmth, she worried more about falling on her face and having nothing with which to catch herself.

Not that it would make much difference, in Elizabeth's mind. She had never considered herself pretty, with her long narrow face, close-spaced eyes, and thin bird-like nose. Her stick-straight brown hair balked against the rags Peggy wound into her locks each night, refusing to curl. Elizabeth wore the latest styles because her parents insisted that their twenty-year-old daughter should appear suitable should a young man finally choose to woo her. Yet that seemed like a pipe dream. All the men of proper age and stature were already married or had their eyes fixed on Flora, Ruffina, Hope, and Hester. Men wanted girls with pert noses and sparkling blue eyes, lily complexions and rosy lips and cheeks, girls who could tighten their corsets to form delicious hourglasses: full, soft, voluptuous in contour. When Elizabeth cinched her corset, she looked more like a stick insect. Instead, she wore as many petticoats as she dared, trying to bulk up a curveless figure without sweating herself to death.

Elizabeth stepped into the alley, at first seeing nothing. Disappointed, she turned to leave, and movement touched the corner of her vision again. She whirled toward it, seeing a tiny, ragged figure staring at her from between a stack of crates. Recognizing it as a young boy, she crouched to his eye level. "Hallo."

The boy receded deeper into the darkness.

Worried he might run away, Elizabeth tossed him a penny. Moonlight struck an orange glint from the copper, and it pinged against a cobblestone, bounced, and settled on a corner of broken, wooden crating.

Elizabeth could no longer see the boy, but a small grubby hand eased toward the coin, snatched it suddenly, and disappeared.

"Please don't go," Elizabeth said urgently. She dug through her pocket to see what other coinage she carried. Her fingers sifted through florins and threepences to uncover a larger sovereign. She pulled it free. The gold would catch the boy's attention like no lesser metal could. "I'll give you this if you tell me what I want to know."

A filthy face poked out, surrounded by an unkempt mane of light brown hair. His gaze locked on the sovereign, probably more than he had held in a lifetime.

"I'm looking for a dog," Elizabeth said.

The boy continued to eye the coin. "There's dogs everywhere, missy. Every kid what can afford one's got a mech."

Elizabeth sighed. Even in the Old World, mechanical

pets had mostly replaced the flesh and blood animals of earlier times. Cleaner, more obedient, designed to love, they cost little to keep. If an owner forgot to feed it, it merely wound down, awaiting the single lump of wood or coal that would bring it back to life. The water needed replacement only once every few days, poured directly into a valve, not licked about and spilled. There was no excrement or urine to worry about, no training necessary. Random barking was never a problem, although an owner who wanted a protection animal could set it to warning mode. They could be calibrated to snuggle up at night or be tossed casually under the bed until the next play period without holding a grudge. They fetched, they wagged, they executed simple tricks, soulless automatons that performed their duties to the letter. They were also the only legal pets in the unsullied expanse of the New World.

"I'm not talking about a mech," Elizabeth spoke as softly as she could. As far as she knew, no one would overhear her if she shouted, but she did not want to risk the possibility. If the authorities found out about Byron, they would kill him and imprison her for smuggling. A terrified shiver traversed her. She hoped the boy mistook it for a reaction to the cold.

Even in the dim alleyway, Elizabeth saw a light flash through the boy's eyes. He licked his lips several times before speaking, still fanatically interested in the coin. Clearly, he knew something he did not wish to tell.

"I'm worried about him," Elizabeth said. "I love him, and I don't want anything bad to happen to him. Please. Help me."

The boy's gaze moved reluctantly from the coin to Elizabeth's face. He obviously tried to read the truth of her statement, the sincerity in the lines of her face. Apparently, he found what he was looking for, because he visibly relaxed. "Perry's got a dog."

Elizabeth needed more. "Black?"

The boy nodded. "As a raven. Huge beast. Bigger'n me."

Elizabeth hesitated. The last time she had seen Byron, his back had come up to the level of her knees. He was still a puppy, though. She supposed he might have grown to the size the boy specified. *It has to be Byron.*

"Can you take me to this . . . Perry?"

The boy receded back amid the crates.

Elizabeth's eyes had adjusted fully to the gloom, and she could easily make out his silhouette. He was still there. "I'll give you more." Desperate, she pulled nearly all the coins from her pocket. "Please, I'm not going to get anyone in trouble. I just want to see my dog."

In her rush, Elizabeth tore the edge of her pocket, and several copper and silver coins spilled to the cobbles. They rattled there, rolling on edge to settle awkwardly in the cracks between the rocks.

The boy darted out to gather them. In a flash, he had every coin in his hand. He looked hopefully at Elizabeth, then opened his fingers to display the stash.

"Keep them," Elizabeth said. "All of them."

The money disappeared into his ragged linen shirt.

"You can have the sovereign, too, when you've led me to Perry."

The boy gestured for Elizabeth to go deeper into the alley. Against her better judgment, she followed him, as her mind generated images of a gang of rough-faced boys ambushing her in the darkness. She did hear occasional scrapes and movement, but no one bothered them as she followed the unnamed boy through the alley, out the back, and down cobbled streets that would have looked familiar and relatively smooth in broad daylight. Now, they seemed more like random patches of road-like wilderness, with myriad hunks of debris on which to bark shins and trip even the wary.

Rats probably patrolled the alleys fearlessly, without enough cats to control their population. Elizabeth supposed that hunting the white-tailed deer, the foxes, squirrels, and muskrats might prove much simpler with real dogs to lead the way. She had even heard stories of strange, dog-like creatures that roamed the nearby forests. The huntsmen had described them as bigger than foxes but smaller than wolves, grayish brown in color, with long ears, small feet, and a yipping howl.

The boy led Elizabeth to the edge of the forest. There, he stopped. "Perry lives there." He pointed into the trees.

A blast of cold air stung Elizabeth's cheeks, reminding her of the upcoming winter. In just two days, the *Lucy Pearl* would weigh anchor, taking her family, and most of the upper class, to the warmer climes farther south. The governor and policing force would remain to keep the mansions safe from the rabble in their owners' absences. Elizabeth dared not leave Byron alone to the mercy of the harsh winter cold. "Perry lives in the forest?" Elizabeth gave the boy a searching look. Thus far, she had trusted him. Now, she suspected he had lied about seeing a live dog at all, saying whatever it took to get the money she had offered.

The boy nodded.

Elizabeth sighed. It appeared she had reached a dead-end, and now she had little more than the sovereign to start anew. "No one lives in a forest."

"Perry does," the boy insisted. "He has to, else someone'd find the dog." The hand snaked out to quietly demand the promised coin.

Elizabeth hesitated. The one-pound coin meant little to her, but she might need it to follow other leads. Testing, she called out, "Byron? Byron, come!"

Startled, the boy scampered several feet away before stopping. He stared at her, mouth hanging open.

Elizabeth refused to be distracted. "Come on, Byron. Here, boy. Byron!"

Something rattled in the brush. Then, suddenly, a massive black head thrust through the foliage. Ears limp as rags, tongue lolling, jowls trailing a rope of drool, an enormous version of Byron emerged, burrs tangled into his fur.

Joy soared through Elizabeth. Her heart tried to pound its way out of her chest. With thought of nothing else, she hurled herself at the animal. "Byron, by the Almighty! Byron." She enwrapped him in her arms, amazed by the sheer size of him. He had doubled his weight since she had last seen him.

Something tugged at Elizabeth's overcoat. The boy's voice went urgent. "My coin, missy. Where's my money?"

Though she hated to let go of Byron with even one hand, Elizabeth dutifully handed over the sovereign, and the boy immediately ran back toward the village. She unfastened the drool from Byron's mouth and let it drop to the leaves, then planted a kiss on his enormous muzzle. Big, sad eyes met hers, and the tongue came out to lash her face with doggy kisses. "Byron. Byron, I've missed you."

A breathless voice hissed from the foliage. "Rags, at heel."

Clinging to the dog so tightly the burrs jabbed every part, Elizabeth looked for the speaker.

A youngish man, perhaps a year or three older than Elizabeth, stood near the tree line. Presumably Perry, he wore a simple cotton outfit of gray shirt and pants with a black woolen overcoat, all of which had seen significant wear. Shaggy, sand-colored hair tousled over green eyes and a straight, fine nose. The long coat accentuated his thinness; he looked as much scarecrow as man.

Byron's enormous tongue swept the entirety of Elizabeth's face again. As she stared at the man, her hold loosened. Byron trotted off to greet him.

Worried she might lose him again, Elizabeth rose. "Byron," she demanded. "Come here, boy."

The dog froze in his tracks, twisting his fat head to study her over one shoulder.

"Rags," Perry said, his voice a confident tenor and his expression steely. "Come."

Byron's haunches dropped to the ground, and he whined softly.

Perry headed toward Byron, but Elizabeth got there first, twining her fingers into the thick, warm fur.

Perry stopped again, hands on hips, staring at woman and dog. "Who are you, and what do you think you're doing?"

Still clinging to Byron, Elizabeth straddled the dog like a boy on a pony. Byron's chest dropped to the ground, and he lay there with Elizabeth on top of him. "My name is Elizabeth Holden, and I'm taking my dog back home."

Perry rolled his eyes, shook his head. "I'm afraid you're mistaken. Rags is my dog."

Elizabeth knew there could be no mistaking Byron. She doubted anyone else had sneaked any dog to the New World, let alone one who resembled Byron so completely. "Did you bring him across the ocean?"

"No," Perry admitted. He slipped up gradually, until he could touch Byron as well. "I found him here, but he's been with me a long time."

Elizabeth stretched her legs, trying not to put too much weight on the dog, and hugged his neck. "Three months at the most. That's when I lost him."

Perry went silent, lips twisting into a frown. "I found him cold and alone, starving. I saved his life. That makes him my dog."

"So, if a doctor cures an infant, does that make the child his?"

"Of course not." Perry dipped forward suddenly to seize Byron by the ruff. "But that's different. A child is not a dog. And the child wasn't ill because her parents abandoned her."

Elizabeth's nostrils flared. She released her hold on the dog. "I didn't abandon him. I lost him. That's not the same thing."

"He ran away from you to be with me." Perry pulled suddenly. Byron lurched to his feet, unseating Elizabeth and dumping her to the moldy leaves and twigs.

Elizabeth rolled through the muck, outraged. She sprang to her feet as the stranger started to disappear back into the forest, dragging Byron. "Stop!" she commanded.

Perry ignored her.

"Byron! Come here this instant."

The dog lurched toward Elizabeth hard enough to unbalance the man. In the effort of catching himself, he let go of Byron, and the dog bounced toward Elizabeth. She dropped to a crouch and opened her arms to receive him. Before he arrived, however, Perry tackled him, driving the dog off his feet with a huff of expelled breath and sending them both skidding toward her. Elizabeth barely managed to scoot backward before man and dog jerked to a stop in front of her. His face now inches from Elizabeth's, Perry sprawled across Byron.

Elizabeth could not stop herself from slapping him, hard, across the cheeks. "How dare you! Throwing a lady in the mud and stealing her dog."

Perry rolled off of Byron, rubbing his stinging face. "I am sorry for knocking you down, ma'am."

"Elizabeth," Elizabeth reminded in a scornful tone. "And I'm a miss."

Perry executed a clumsy bow, clearly not accustomed to such gestures. "I didn't mean to make you fall, Elizabeth. I just wanted Ragamuffin . . ."

"Byron."

". . . and you seemed determined to keep him from me."

The full significance of the situation came to Elizabeth in that moment. She picked up her muff from the ground, never taking her eyes from Perry and Byron. "So what do we do now? It's not like we can hire counsel and set the matter before a jury."

That being self-evident, Perry bobbed his head cautiously.

"And I'm not going to agree to duel."

Perry snorted. "That didn't stop you from assaulting me."

"Nor you me." Elizabeth brushed dirt from her coat and nightgown with broad strokes.

Byron looked from one to the other, tail waving with enough force to sweep aside a semicircle of leaves at his back.

Perry scratched his chin and the fine wisps of beard growing there. "I suppose we let the dog decide." He glanced toward the village. "You go that way." He gestured toward the forest. "I'll go this. We'll call him and see who he chooses to follow."

Elizabeth liked the general idea, but not the execution. "Oh, no. Not in the woods. It's too easy for you to grab him and run." She turned her body toward the village and pointed her arms to make a V. "You go there. I go here. That way, we know it's us, not the location, that's drawing him. And I know exactly where you are at all times."

Perry laughed, the sound at once maddening and endearing. Elizabeth wondered how one noise could cause such contradictory feelings. "Agreed. Both of us remain still and call him. He has to come close enough for one of us to touch him before we determine the winner."

Still concerned about a trick, Elizabeth insisted on absolute fairness. "To hug him, not just touch. Your arms are longer." She added carefully. "And we have to call him from a sitting position. I'll make marks where each of us will sit, and your buttocks have to stay in one place the entire time."

Perry looked mock scandalized. "So you intend to stare at my buttocks?"

Elizabeth's cheeks went hot. "No, I . . ." she stammered. "I mean, I . . ." She glared at him. "You know, I could just forget the whole thing. Byron is my dog, and you have no claim—"

Perry groaned. "Not again." He gave Elizabeth a searching look. "I'm bigger than you. I could just beat you to a pulp and take my dog."

Elizabeth gasped in horror. In the excitement of finding Byron, she had not considered such a possibility.

"It's not like you could call the police and have me arrested, not without getting Rags killed as well."

Elizabeth glared. "So that's what it comes down to? Brute force?" She drew herself up to her full height and sucked in a deep breath. She had never fought in her life, and she had no idea how she would fare. She knew only that she would not give up Byron without a contest of some sort. She never would have selected violence; but, she might not have a choice.

Perry shook his head forcefully. "Elizabeth, I'm willing to stand by Ragamuffin's . . ."

Elizabeth's scowl deepened.

". . . Byron's decision. I'm just letting you know that I'm acting in the fairest way I can think of to settle a thorny problem. It's not like I could just get another dog to replace him."

"Nor could I," Elizabeth pointed out.

"You could afford a mech, I'd wager."

Elizabeth stiffened, seeing a possible way out of the predicament. "I can buy you a mech. And you can let me have Byron."

"Only if he chooses you. Otherwise, I'll have Ra–Byron, and I won't need a mech."

Elizabeth stared at Perry, her anger forgotten. Abruptly, she realized she had found a kindred soul, one who actually saw the value of a living creature over a steam-powered hunk of animal-shaped metal. When she tried to put the concept into words, however, they came out wrong, "You . . . love Byron. Don't you?"

Perry gave her a look of withering disdain, the kind she thought only the upper class had perfected. "No." His tone dripped sarcasm. "I just have a yearning for life in a prison cell." He sighed deeply. "How could anyone not love a real dog? The soft warmth, the unqualified love, the unmitigated faithful desire to do nothing but please."

Elizabeth closed her eyes, remembering the sweet bundle of puppy she had smuggled aboard the *Neptune*. Everything remained vivid to her mind's eye. "The tickle of fur against your lips, the sweet aroma of his puppy breath, the gnawing of milk teeth."

Perry laughed. "Most people would see those as the negative aspects: odor, shedding, biting."

Elizabeth grinned at the memory and huffed out a sentimental, "Yes."

Perry rolled his eyes and shook his head. "Very well. Shall we get started?"

Elizabeth saw no reason to wait. She marked out two open spots that looked equidistant from Byron's current resting place. The dog lay with his head on his paws, his big brown eyes tracing her every move, his brows rising and falling as he took in everything. Returning to Perry, Elizabeth pointed. "They look even to me; but, to keep things fair, you can choose your place first."

"All right." Perry accepted one of the positions and seated himself on the mark.

Elizabeth did the same. "Ready?"

"Ready."

Immediately, they both started calling. Byron lay in place staring from one to the other in apparent confusion. Always unusually sedate, especially for a puppy, he seemed in no hurry. Eventually, he rose to all fours again and yawned. Only then, Elizabeth realized how massive he had become. He had a regal head, with passive eyes and ears that hung like thick scraps of velvet. His long fur had a gentle wave that brought out streaks of bluish moonlight. His massive paws now fit his bulk, and his plumed tail split the air, waving back and forth gaily. He lumbered toward Perry.

Desperate, Elizabeth called louder, putting as much emotion as possible into her tone. "Byron, puppy. Byron, my sweet. I've got treats." She wished she had brought a scrap of venison from her dinner plate but had not thought of it. Byron loved her; she had not expected to have to bribe the dog to return home with her.

Byron stopped and looked toward Elizabeth. He took a step in her direction.

"Ragamuffin!" Perry glared at Elizabeth. "That's not fair!"

Abruptly light exploded through the clearing from several powered lanterns. Blinded, Elizabeth covered her eyes. An amplified man's voice issued from the village side, "What's going on here? Don't anybody move."

Perry shouted something Elizabeth did not recognize. She heard the sound of feet crashing through dried leaves. Then figures whizzed by her. She looked out just in time to see Perry lunging toward the forest and two policemen hurling themselves on top of him. The three men rolled together in a tangled heap of flailing limbs.

Elizabeth clutched her muff to her mouth, searching wildly for Byron. She saw only the black tip of a hairy tail disappearing between the trees. Two other policemen gave chase, smashing through the undergrowth, ungainly as moose.

"That was a contraband animal," the amplified voice informed them. Elizabeth tried to study the speaker, but the brightness of the lanterns hurt her eyes. "To whom does it belong?"

A moment before, they had been fighting over that very privilege. Now, Elizabeth fell silent, uncertain what to say. It was no use arguing that they had seen a well-crafted, furry mech-dog. She knew they would not believe her.

Pinned beneath the two policemen, Perry stopped struggling.

Elizabeth opened her mouth, not wholly sure what would emerge, but Perry spoke first.

"It's mine, sir. My dog. His barking awakened the young lady. She came out to investigate. I was afraid to get caught and led her here." The two men hefted him to his feet, clinging to each arm.

The amplified voice waited until Perry had finished. "Escort Elizabeth home," it instructed.

One more policeman emerged from the gloom. Careful not to look anywhere improper, he stepped to Elizabeth's side. "Come, young lady. Let's go."

Numbly, Elizabeth followed, uncertain what to think or feel. She wrapped her hands in the muff, her head low. She could not help wondering why Perry had confessed. They would never let him keep Byron. If they captured the dog, they would kill him; and they would imprison the man in either case. Perry had everything to lose and nothing to gain. Elizabeth glanced over her shoulder as she meekly followed the policeman. Arms held by two men, Perry remained wholly attentive to her, watching her trudge off into the darkness. No sound came from the woods, where Byron had crashed through and the two men had chased him.

He did it for me, Elizabeth realized, startled by the gesture. *He barely knows me. Why would he sacrifice his freedom for me?* Elizabeth knew sneaking out of her room at night was risky. She expected a scolding, a loss of privileges, perhaps a paddling. The idea that someone would catch her with Byron had never occurred to her. *Would they have thrown me in prison?* Elizabeth suspected they would have. And, now, Perry would go in her stead.

Despite the coldness of the night air seeping into her bones, despite the terrible danger to Byron, Elizabeth could not help feeling honored by Perry's decision. No man had ever done anything so gallant for her, and she wondered why he would do so now. Street people were not known for their manners or gentility, yet Perry had valiantly taken the full blame for something he could just as easily have shared or pinned fully on Elizabeth. If the guards had pressed, Elizabeth would have admitted to sneaking Byron across the ocean. *And to his death.* Elizabeth shivered, and not from the cold. She could not bear the thought of the sweet, gentle dog losing his life for no good reason other than her desire for his company.

I love you, Byron. Please stay hidden. Elizabeth hoped her thoughts could somehow waft to the animal, where he floundered through the brush or lay in quiet repose.

No merciful god could allow harm to come to one so faithful and innocent. Yet Elizabeth could not take solace from that thought. Every dog she had ever met demonstrated the same sweet-tempered loyalty, and bad things happened to far too many. *Farewell, Byron. May you live long and only joyful events befall you.* Tears stung Elizabeth's eyes.

Elizabeth's escort stopped directly in front of the mansion and kept his voice a bare hiss of sound. "No sense awakening the household. Can you sneak back in?"

Elizabeth managed a smile. "Thank you," she whispered gratefully. She had expected him to knock, to alert her parents to her misdeeds. Instead, he had given her the opportunity to avoid punishment altogether. It was a gesture of kindness she did not deserve any more than Perry's confession. "Thank you," she repeated.

The policeman gave her a silent bow. "I'll wait until you're safely inside, missy."

The idea of creeping around the house, then furtively returning to the forest occurred to Elizabeth, but it was clear folly. Grounded and watched, she could help neither Byron nor Perry. Instead, she climbed the same trellis that had allowed her escape and slipped back into her empty bedroom without alerting parents or servants. Shedding her coat, she fell into bed, tears pouring from her eyes. She refused to picture Byron's body lifeless, but her mind conjured images of Perry paraded to the prison, locked in a dank cell for a crime she had committed. *Why did he do that? Why, why why?* No answers came. Elizabeth knew she would have to ask them of Perry himself.

Elizabeth thought she would never sleep again, but the excitement of the day eventually won out over anxiety, and she fell into a dream-plagued sleep.

*   *   *

The May's Landing prison consisted of a stone building beside the butcher shop filled with half a dozen small cells. The three in front contained a short, nervous man who kept clenching and unclenching his hands together; Warren, the fat town drunk; and a burly stranger walking a treadwheel with a weary, fanatical step. Elizabeth's gaze traced the series of pipes and whoosh of water that benefited from his work. It would prove easy enough to power the system with steam, yet whoever designed it clearly intended it as a punishment for prisoners. No work, no water. They probably had to do just as much to earn their food as well.

Directed to the back, Elizabeth walked cautiously around the brick and iron cells. The odors of feces, urine, and vomit nearly overwhelmed her; and she found herself breathing only through her mouth. The other two cells on that side lay empty. Perry sat on the floor of the third, his head bowed. Apparently hearing Elizabeth's approach, he looked up. Then, recognizing her, he straggled to his feet.

In the gloom of the prison, Perry looked exactly as he had in village dusk: thin and fair with youthful features and pale eyes. In many ways, he fit the current vision of beauty, defined as much by light skin, hair, and eyes as voluptuous contours in women and straighter angles in men.

When Elizabeth turned the corner, it took her beyond the view of the other prisoners and the *gaoler*. They were, essentially, alone. "Why?" she asked, pitching her voice low so no one could overhear them.

Perry took a breath, as if to demand more information. Then he paused and smiled wanly. He knew from that one word what Elizabeth had meant. "Why should we both get in trouble? I figured I could handle the punishment better than you."

Elizabeth had no idea if he was right or not. She had heard that the *gaoler* did not discriminate between men and women, sane and insane, orphans or criminals. Anyone requiring housing who did not find a safe place on the streets eventually wound up here, sometimes crammed together in the same cage in leaner times. "Byron?"

Perry shrugged. "I gave him a 'run-and-hide' command. The men came back without him." Pain scrolled across his features. "Did they . . . get him?"

Elizabeth thought that, if they had caught the dog, news would have reached the entire village. "I don't believe so." She could not help grinning. "That means he's still safely out there."

"Yeah." Perry nodded thoughtfully. "Until he gets hungry or craves companionship." He turned Elizabeth a careful look. "Someone has to find him first and tend to him. Someone who . . ." He glanced around, as if afraid someone might overhear them.

. . . *loves dogs.* Elizabeth's mind filled in. She knew it had to be one of them. She was the only possibility, but she had managed to obtain something that could change that situation. Her hand slid into her pocket. She pinned the object against her palm and reached a hand into the cell.

Perry took her hand and held it, and Elizabeth transferred the key into his fingers. A startled look crossed his features, then they relaxed into normal. He hid the key inside his shirt. "Why?" he asked.

Elizabeth surmised the rest of the question as easily as he had hers. "Someone has to care for Byron. Someone who can keep him safe. Someone who knows the woods and how to live there."

Perry leaned toward her and dropped his voice to a faint whisper. "Come with me."

Startled, Elizabeth dropped to her haunches, speechless. Nothing in polite society allowed for an upper-class woman to slip away into the woods with a man, especially one of recent acquaintance. Traditionally, Elizabeth's family, and others of their standing, left the village as the weather turned cool. They traveled down the coastline southward, spending the winter months in warmer climates, to return in time for the thaw. The trip was planned for the following day, which was why her search for Byron had become urgent enough for her to leave her bedroom at night. She had planned to hide him amongst her gear.

Of course, at that time, she had not realized how much he must have grown. She now knew how difficult that task would prove, probably impossible. She regretted her ill-considered battle to take him home. It had only resulted in dooming both the dog and the one man who might have kept him safe in her absence. "I can't come with you," she said, almost laughing at the ridiculousness of the suggestion.

Perry did not share Elizabeth's mirth. "Why not?"

Elizabeth stared directly into Perry's eyes for the first time. He had an earnestness there she had not noticed previously, a kindness and depth of soul that well-suited a man who loved real dogs. Only then, she realized she found him strikingly handsome. "I'm . . . we're . . . from different worlds."

"Not so." Perry pressed his face to the bars. "I'm an Ashmore."

Elizabeth recognized the family name. They had Ashmores in their circle, even some bound for the ship. "You're an Ashmore?"

"My father was William, my mother Mary, and my sister Claire. Father made some bad investments; we lost the mansion. Before he could earn it back, the consumption took all three of them. I've been on my own about six years now, not so long I don't remember civility and manners."

Perry's face blurred, and Elizabeth blinked to try to clear her vision. Only then, she realized she was crying again. "I'm so sorry." Her voice emerged shaky. "How awful."

Perry pursed his lips. "I'm not looking for sympathy. I just want you to know we're not so very different. Your parents might not object to you marrying an Ashmore."

Elizabeth gasped. "Perry Ashmore, was that a proposal?" It seemed impossible on so many levels. "But we hardly know each other."

"People in arranged marriages don't know each other at all, yet they turn out fine." Perry reached through the bars for her hand. "I know you love dogs, especially Byron. That's enough for me."

Elizabeth found her hand in his before realizing she had moved. His grip was firm and tender, the perfect combination of strength and sensitivity. She knew exactly what he meant. Anyone who cared so much for a dog that he would risk imprisonment had a good heart. She would never forget how he had placed himself in this position to rescue her as well. The more significant obstacles came to her then. "This is insane. How could we marry with you in prison?"

Perry cocked an eyebrow, silently reminding her that she had just given him the means of escape.

Elizabeth had not forgotten. She had had little difficulty liberating it from its peg. But marrying a fugitive seemed even less plausible than marrying a captive. "And besides, why would you want a girl who . . . looks like me?"

Perry's other eyebrow rose to meet the first. "My mother was uncomfortable with her beauty, too." His fingers tightened around hers. "Elizabeth, you resemble her a bit. The same gorgeous dark eyes, a similarly shaped face, the same subtle curves. Not every man liked her looks, but my father did. And so did I." He drew her hand to his lips. "I see the same beauty in you." He dropped to one knee, taking her hand with him. "Elizabeth Holden, will you do me the enormous pleasure of becoming my wife?"

Elizabeth had waited so long to hear those words, ones she thought she never would. The sound of them thrilled through her until common sense took over, and she forced herself to shake her head. "I'm sorry, Perry. I can't."

He released her hand. His other knee fell to the floor, and his head slumped.

"It's not that I can't love you. It's just that I don't see how we could make a future together, at least not right away." Elizabeth hated to believe she could not survive without the finery to which she had grown accustomed. It seemed so shallow, so unimportant compared to love. However, she also doubted that she would have the stamina to spend eternity dodging the police, slinking through woodlands, tattered and cold. Perry knew the forest, knew how to survive in it, and loved Byron as much as she did. "Byron needs you. When I get back from the south, I'll visit you both as much as possible. I'll bring you warm clothes and food, whatever you wish. If we still feel the same way when Byron . . ." Elizabeth swallowed. She could not bring herself to say "dies," not even in euphemistic form. ". . . no longer needs us, then we can marry."

Head still bowed, Perry nodded. Finally, he rose from the floor, still clutching Elizabeth's hand. "You're right, of course. I have no right to ask you to live that kind of life." He gave her hand one more kiss, then released it. "Just promise me one thing."

Elizabeth would have granted him almost anything. She nodded.

"Tomorrow, before the ship embarks, come to the spot where we met. By then, I should have found . . . Byron. Let me show you he's safe before you go. It will ease your heart on the trip."

Elizabeth smiled. "Gladly. And thank you."

May's Landing seemed so much different in daylight that Elizabeth had a hard time finding the shadowy place near the forest where she had first laid eyes on Perry Ashmore. Although she had to dodge more people, Elizabeth had no trouble sneaking past the many shops and foundries through the clank of gears, the whoosh of machinery, and the hiss of vented steam.

Even far from the cacophony, Elizabeth barely heard Perry's quiet, "*Psst*." She stepped between the trees, only to find herself wrapped in his warm embrace. Elizabeth put her arms around him as well, enjoying the press of his body against her. Though inappropriate, it was also wildly exciting.

Something wet brushed the back of her hand. Elizabeth looked down to see Byron's enormous black form at her side, tail waving. "Byron!" She pulled loose from Perry to hug the massive dog and wondered how she could ever have thought she could sneak the animal aboard the *Lucy Pearl*. *Not in my knitting basket. Not this time.*

Perry waited until dog and woman had finished their greeting before taking both of Elizabeth's hands in a far more chaste and suitable manner. "We're both going to miss you."

"No, you're not." Elizabeth looked through the forest toward the place she had called home for the past six months. Smoke curled from the mansion's chimney.

"We're not?"

"Because I'm staying after all."

Perry shook his head. "Elizabeth, no. You were right. I escaped from prison. I'm an outlaw now." He patted the dog's head. "Byron, too. We have to stay on the run, hidden, and we can't ask you to do that with us. It's too cold for you, and I couldn't bear to watch another loved one die."

Elizabeth had thought the whole thing through the previous night. "I'm an adult, Perry. I told my parents I'm staying, and they can't really stop me. I can live at the mansion with the remaining servants. There're lots of empty rooms. If we're careful, you and Byron can even spend the colder nights indoors."

Perry only stared. The idea had clearly not occurred to him. Still several sentences behind, he finally stammered out, "You're not leaving?"

"Come on." Elizabeth grabbed his hand and pulled him through the forest in the direction of the mansion. She knew of a hilltop in the woods that would give them a reasonable view of the ship debarking. "I've already said my goodbyes. Now I want to watch them launch."

Perry stopped dead, nearly wrenching Elizabeth's arm. "You want to watch them launch? Come this way." He switched direction, racing through lowland forest on deer trails that forced them to duck limbs and dodge brambles, Byron lumbering at their heels. He ducked through a drainage tunnel to emerge at water's edge, just below the docks. Above their heads, Elizabeth could hear the shouting crowd, preparing the small iron steamship for its journey along the coast.

Elizabeth had never seen the steamship from the back. She got a spectacular view of the two large sidewheels as well as the row of metal screws on the stern, just beneath the level of the water. The wooden hull gleamed, cleaned and freshly painted. She could not see the name, but she knew it: the *Lucy Pearl*, much smaller than the ship that had taken them from the Old World to the New World. It had only a single boiler set near the back, and Elizabeth could see the full coal box sitting near it. The crew of ten planned to hug the shoreline. If they needed more fuel or supplies, they could easily obtain them.

Fifty-seven passengers boarded the *Lucy Pearl*, seven families and a selection of servants. Elizabeth watched them carrying their luggage, the children peering excitedly from every side, examining the wheels, the screws, the water with the same fascination. Until the previous night, Elizabeth, too, had looked eagerly forward to boarding, to leaving the icy winter behind.

Perry squeezed her hand. "You're sure?"

Elizabeth's thoughts had taken her in every direction but always came back to the same place. She had dragged Byron to the New World, a guiltless puppy who could not defend himself. She had no right to drop the problem she had created into a stranger's lap, even one as willing to accept it as Perry. Elizabeth could not help smiling. *Especially one as willing to accept it as Perry.* As little as she knew of him, it was enough to assure her that he had a good heart and a responsible head to go with it. "I'm absolutely certain. This is where I belong. With Byron, and with you."

Without looking, Perry scooped Elizabeth's hand into his own. His palm engulfed hers, warm, dry, and comforting. His other hand patted Byron's head, scratching behind the heavy, silken ears.

The *Lucy Pearl* took off with the familiar chugging noise that characterized all of the larger steam engines. Smoke billowed from the stack. The families headed southward stood on the deck, waving from the railing as a large group of people waved back from the docks and shouted their fare wells. In silence, Elizabeth watched the side wheels churn wavelets and the screws spin smoothly at the stern, leaving two wide wakes and several smaller ones to mark the ship's passage.

After a few moments, the crowd stopped waving and craned forward to watch the ship puff down the oceanway. Elizabeth could still see the silhouettes of people on the deck and vague movement that probably represented waving. She had just started to turn when an explosion shattered her hearing. She whirled back. Smoke and steam boiled into the sky. Fragments of boat and a few human figures flew in all directions. Screams of terror replaced the gentle noise of the steamboat's boiler.

The crowd gasped in unison, then started running and screeching in mindless chaos. Acrid smoke rose from the boat, ugly and out-of-place after the whiter puffs emitted by the smokestack. The *Lucy Pearl* lurched, and then burst into red-orange flames. The bodies hurled into the air fell back to the deck, driving holes through the planking, and the ship listed, sinking quickly into the ocean.

Terror clutched Elizabeth so abruptly, it was all she could do to keep from vomiting. *Mother! Father!*

A man leaped from the dock and started swimming toward the wreckage. Several others followed in a ragged, desperate lack of formation. Then an enormous, black shape hurtled past Elizabeth, into the sea, and paddled furiously after them. It took her a moment to realize what had happened. "Byron, no!" She lunged for the dog, seizing empty air. She tumbled into the shallows as the dog swam toward the burning ship with a speed the men could never hope to match.

Perry was stripping off his coat to follow Byron into

the ocean. Executing a shallow, graceful dive, he joined the mass of men headed to rescue the survivors.

Elizabeth wrung her hands, not knowing whether to worry more for her family, for the other victims of the boiler explosion, or for Perry and Byron. The latter two, at least, paid the risks no heed. Within moments, Byron seized a floating human form by the collar and dragged it vigorously toward the would-be rescuers.

A man accepted the unmoving figure from Byron, guiding the first victim toward shore. Byron executed a tight circle and headed back out to snatch a floundering child and carry it through the water toward another of the swimmers from the dock. The man took the child, who clung to his chest, freeing Byron to go after another.

Still searching for her parents, Elizabeth marveled at the strength and speed of the animal. Without ever being taught, Byron knew what to do and did it methodically and effectively, his strokes instinctive and his massive body allowing him to rescue even large adults. When it became clear what was happening, everyone joined in to help. The women lay down on the docks, reaching outward. The men collected the floating bodies on their own or from Byron, hauling them near enough for the women to grab hold, together hoisting them to the docks. Once there, the women rushed the victims to dry land, covering them with coats, rushing them to the infirmary, or waiting for them to join the rescue effort.

Tears flowing down her cheeks, Elizabeth waded into the shallows to help serve as a conduit between the swimming men and the hefting women, balancing survivors and bodies for the transfer. She saw her parents wading into shore, hand-in-hand, and an icy shudder of relief passed through her. No longer concerned for them, she set her mind to her own task, trying to banish the fear that, when the crisis ended, she would lose both Byron and Perry to their own courageous actions.

The *Lucy Pearl* slid beneath the waves, quenching the fires, until nothing remained to mark the spot but trails of smoke and steam. As the ocean claimed its prize, the men rushed back to the docks, worried to get sucked into the maelstrom of its plunge. But Byron remained, circling the wreckage. Suddenly, his shaggy head disappeared beneath the water.

"Byron!" Elizabeth wanted to shout, but only a whisper emerged. She saw Perry heading toward where the dog had gone, his strokes strong and sure.

Seconds passed like hours. Elizabeth could feel each heartbeat hammering her chest, every breath drawing in an agony of hovering smoke. Then, as abruptly as he had gone, Byron surfaced. In his mouth, he clutched a toddler, dragging her sodden head into the air.

As one, the crowd stilled, bodies half-drawn to the docks, strokes frozen in mid-movement. Perry reached Byron and took the child from the dog. For a few moments, Elizabeth could see nothing, as dog and man took turns blocking her view. She saw a few of the men start heading back out toward the sunken ship. Then, Perry raised the young child high out of the water. The child gasped, then coughed. Abruptly, she wailed in terror, grabbing for Perry.

She's alive!

The crowd cheered. Perry placed the toddler carefully onto Byron's back, and the dog swam back with a leisurely pace clearly designed not to dislodge his rider. As the child settled into place, she clutched the dog's furry neck in a death grip and stopped screaming.

Byron stepped out onto the shore with Perry at his side, keeping the child balanced. A woman, presumably the child's mother, seized the toddler and held her close.

The child snuggled against her. Once again, the crowd cheered.

Byron shook, sending a spray of water in all directions. No one seemed to notice or care. Most pressed in to embrace the survivors, to examine those who had not yet shown signs of life. A few approached the dog, touching his flag-like tail, his wet fur, his floppy ears now heavy with seawater. His tongue lolled, he panted heavily, and a string of drool dangled from his open mouth.

Perry flopped down beside Byron, and the dog collapsed to the ground, resting his head on Perry's leg.

From the corner of her eye, Elizabeth saw the police coming. "Go quickly." She waved at the pair. "Run!"

Clearly exhausted, Perry shook his head. Byron whined and rolled his gaze to Elizabeth, but he did not move.

Byron's face held the raw beauty and innocence of the universe, the eyes all-giving, the brows as expressive as anything human. He seemed to know what was coming, resigned, glad to sacrifice himself for the many human lives he had saved.

As the police drew nearer, Elizabeth threw herself across man and dog, burying as much of them as her smaller person allowed. She glared fiercely as the men drew up around her. "If you so much as touch a hair on either of them, I will attack. You will have to kill me first."

Those nearest the scene went silent, and the hush spread in ever-widening rings. Gradually, Elizabeth's parents stepped up in front of her, their faces pale, their clothing burnt and sodden. A scarlet line of blood trickled from her father's cheek where a piece of the ship must have slashed him. Others moved beside them, then still more until Elizabeth looked through a sea of dripping pants and legs and could see nothing of the approaching policemen.

A chant started up: "Save the hero dog! Save the hero dog!" As each additional voice joined the chorus, it became louder and louder until no other sound could penetrate.

Elizabeth hugged Perry and Byron in turn, tears once again coursing down her cheeks. Burying the dead and healing the wounded would take precedence over the next few weeks. After that, Elizabeth would finally have her wedding.

In the Cedar Falls Cemetery, amid the stone markers, stands a statue of a large, powerful-looking dog with long, wavy hair and a blocky head. Inscribed beneath it in Victorian letters is the following:

"Byron Ashmore
Hero of the *Lucy Pearl*
and the village of May's Landing.
Lived his first year in secrecy and his last ten
as every man's favorite son."

FOR QUEEN AND COUNTRY

Elizabeth A. Vaughan

Elizabeth A. Vaughan writes fantasy romance; her most recent novel is Destiny's Star, *part of the Star Series. At present, she is owned by three incredibly spoiled cats and lives in the Northwest Territory on the outskirts of the Black Swamp, along Mad Anthony's Trail on the banks of the Maumee River. You can learn more about her books at www.eavwrites.com.*

"**W**e are *not* amused."

"Your Majesty," the Prime Minister's voice held just enough sorrow to indicate sympathy, with a twinge of helpless regret. "I fear we have little choice."

I wisely kept my eyes down, focused on the rim of the wheeled chair beside me. I had performed my best curtsey when I'd been introduced, then sank to one knee, my black skirts puffing out around me. It had been suggested that I do so to avoid towering over the small, stout lady who ruled the Empire.

"Given the circumstances," the Prime Minister continued, "Miss Haversham's unique qualifications are the best and the only ones that will answer."

A pudgy hand with rings on every finger came into view and lifted my chin. I raised my head obediently, but continued to keep my gaze low.

The Prime Minister continued in the frigid silence. "Miss Haversham is also a recent widow, ma'am, in a sense. Her betrothed died on the eve of their wedding day."

There was an intake of air at that. I kept my face stoic and resolved, hoping that she'd not inquire about him. My fake betrothed had come into existence in the scant moments before this interview. For my life I could not recall his name. But he made a lovely excuse for unattractive mourning clothes and my hair pulled back into a severe bun.

The temperature in the room warmed. "The best, you say?" The hand was pulled back, and the chair creaked as she shifted within it.

"Highly recommended," came the firm response.

"Very well," Her Majesty said briskly. "It has been explained to you, Miss Haversham? What you are to do?"

"Yes, Your Majesty," I said.

"My godson is a genius," she continued, oblivious to my response. "You understand? Genius must be nurtured and protected. So far, he has resisted my efforts to see to his wellbeing. And his estates, such as they are ..." The queen shook her head. "He neglects himself," she continued. "And you will see to him."

"Your Majesty," I said with all due humbleness.

"We share a grief," she continued. "To have lost our dearest ones too soon. But mind your station, miss." The queen's voice was sharp as a blade. "Do not seek to rise above it."

Her hand gestured, and the chair wheeled off, out of

my vision. I waited until the door was closed before I rose to my feet. The Prime Minister let out a puff of breath. "That went better than I anticipated." He turned to me and raised a bushy eyebrow. "You are ready to depart?"

"Yes, m'lord."

"Then collect your weapons from the guard, and be off."

The carriage rode quite smoothly as it clattered over the rough country roads. I was taken aback by its comfort, since its appearance had given me no confidence. Dusty, unpolished, with seat cushions that were worn and frayed at the edges.

The horses were well-cared for, I'd grant them that, although the driver and footmen's attire left everything to be desired. Their uniforms were tattered at the cuffs, and the one had a patch at the elbow.

Clearly the task before me would not be an easy one.

We made excellent time from the station, and the carriage pulled up in front of the house before midday. The manor was large and lovely, but the grounds around the house had been sadly neglected. The shrubbery in particular looked like it had been savaged and partially burned recently. I frowned as I pulled on my gloves, adjusted my hat, and took up my parasol.

I alighted with the footman's aid, but there was no one to greet me at the door. I did not bother with the bell, but opened the door wide and marched straight in.

The foyer was dark, lit only by the light through the curtain gaps. I ran my gloved finger over the side table and *tsk*ed at the result.

"Ma'am." The voice was sharp, and I turned and faced the butler. "How may I assist—"

I held up my dusty forefinger. He bristled, but I cut off his response. "Lord Ashington," I demanded.

"His lordship is in his laboratory and is not to be disturbed." His voice was smooth enough, but his anger was clear. "Do you have an appointment, Miss . . . ?"

"Haversham. I am his lordship's new secretary." I raised an eyebrow. "Lead the way."

"His lordship said nothing of this to me."

I kept my eyebrow raised. "And you are?"

A dull red flush started to creep over the man's collar. "Jervis, ma'am."

I waited.

"This way, ma'am," Jervis said, his voice as rigid as his spine.

As we walked, I noted the signs of neglect. Clearly, the management of this household left a great deal to be desired. I didn't voice my observations, but Jervis's rigid back told me that vocalization was unnecessary.

He opened the door into the library. A large room with high windows filled with light and shelves of books almost made me smile as I stepped in. A delightful space, warm and bright, with the pleasing scent of old books and leather. A man's room, certainly, and one I thought well of until I saw the horror that lay before me.

The desk, a massive carved oak table, was covered in papers, strewn about in appalling disarray. In fact, the entire room was one large chaotic pile of correspondence, newspapers, maps, and heaven only knew what all. A secretary's worst nightmare.

"If you would wait here, Miss." Jervis said. "I will—"

I knew that ploy all too well. "No. The laboratory. Now." I didn't both with the "if you please."

Jervis resigned himself and obeyed.

We emerged from the house, walked down a lovely path through a formal garden to a large brick building with high casement windows.

At least, I assumed it had been a formal garden. The

large hedges had suffered the same damage as those in the front of the house, with great gouges in the earth and scorch marks here and there. I opened my mouth to question Jervis but decided against it at the last moment. Best to establish myself with his lordship first.

Jervis opened the door, and bowed me through with a malicious glint in his eye.

I stepped within and was met with a wave of heat, humidity, and noise. The skirts on my mourning dress wilted as quickly as the curl in my hair would have done, had I not secured it in its tight braid.

I took in air filled with the scent of grease and the acrid odor of hot metal. The entire building was ablaze with light, flicking in the lamps and reflected by the copper and brass of the machinery. Gears and pulleys turned and twisted above my head, and heaven alone knew what function they performed.

The wooden floor stretched out before me, with men and tables scattered all around two huge machines. More workers emerged from trapdoors in the floor with tools and plans, scurrying this way and that, clearly intent on their responsibilities.

Whatever the machinery was, there were also men high above us on scaffolding, climbing all over them, some waving tools, all of them shouting at once in an effort to be heard. Jervis stood by the door, but I advanced, determined to make my presence known.

I literally had to walk into the path of a workman to get him to acknowledge me, and I shouted my demand to see Lord Ashington. The cheeky fellow pointed up and darted off as I lifted my chin. Undaunted, I started up the ladder toward the figure at the top.

The man was stuffed half inside the top of the machine, bent over at the waist and cursing at the top of his lungs, banging at something I could not see. I arranged my hat and skirts and prepared to confront my erstwhile employer. "Lord Ashington," I started.

"Damn gear refuses to budge, Harkins," boomed a voice that echoed out of the oddly shaped canister. "Hand me—" The rest was lost in the roar of a steam valve, but a hand emerged and waved back at me as if requesting a tool.

I picked up a mallet from the nearby tool box and slapped it into his hand. There was another muffled explosion of words as it became clear that was not the tool he required. A head of brown curls emerged and glanced back at me.

I stood properly, my parasol firmly planted before me, with both hands on the handle. "A word, Lord Ashington, if you would," I shouted.

He stepped back and straightened. The queen is a small, stout woman, and I'd formed a mental image of her godson as roughly the same height and weight.

Lord Ashington was huge, towering over me, with a broad chest. He'd rolled up his sleeves, and the strength in his arms was obvious. His shirt was slightly opened, and his skin carried a sheen of sweat that was not unattractive. But his eyes . . .

His eyes blazed like brown suns, twinkling at some secret amusement that probably centered on my appearance in his domain. He ran his fingers back through those curls, and laughed. "Now, what's brought the likes of you—"

A klaxon sounded, loud and pulsing.

Lord Ashington's face changed in an instant. "Clark, are you on the damned boilers?"

There was noise below as men shouted and ran.

The scaffolding lurched beneath my feet. I staggered. Lord Ashington wrapped his arm around my waist to steady me and grabbed for one of the braces with his free hand. He clasped me tight in a most inappropriate manner.

"What?" was all I had time to say. The machine he had been working on moved, lurching to rise to its feet. It was an automaton, fully twenty feet tall, and it turned a copper face toward the klaxon.

There'd be no help from below, as men raced to what appeared to be a boiler on the verge of boiling dry. Once again the automaton lurched. Ashington released me, thrusting me behind him as he turned to confront his creation, wrench in hand. The platform shuddered beneath our feet. "We have to stop it," he yelled to me. "Or else it will—"

The automaton raised its hand, and whirling blades emerged inches from Ashington's face.

I gripped my parasol and leaped to the attack.

Silence fell over the ruins of the laboratory.

I stood amidst the destroyed automaton and slapped out the flames on the tatters of my skirt. Smoke rose around me carrying the smell of burnt cloth and my singed hair.

"Well, that's done it," Lord Ashington observed. His shirt hung in strips from his shoulders. He was bruised and bloodied but unbowed, hands on hips, looking about us. "Anyone hurt?"

The chorus of answers were negative as his workman scrambled around, putting out the rest of the fires. The scaffolding was a crumpled mess off to the side, having been destroyed by the flailing of the automaton during the battle.

With the reassurances of his men ringing about us, his smiling brown eyes focused on me. "Nice work with the parasol," Ashington said.

I glanced over to where my parasol was jammed into

the leg joint, mangled almost past recognition. "Thank you." I tried to straighten my bodice and arrange my skirts. "May I enquire as to why you equipped the creature with those whirling blades?"

"It was supposed to be a gardening machine," Ashington said. "To aid my groundskeepers."

"Ah," I replied. "And the beams of light shooting from its eyes?"

"I call them lasers. For trimming the shrubbery," Ashington said absentmindedly, as he examined the wreckage. "But the reasoning machine could never distinguish between 'gardening' and 'guarding.' Every time an alarm sounds, the thing attacks." Ashington ran his fingers through his curls. "No help for it, I'm afraid. We will have to start again."

"That may take some time," I observed. Strands of my hair fell into my face. I reached up to try to gather it back into its bun.

Lord Ashington watched my efforts. "Perhaps introductions would be in order? You already have the benefit of my name, Mrs. . . ."

"Haversham," I said. "Miss Haversham. I am your new secretary."

His eyebrows furrowed as he studied me. "I do not recall—"

"Her Majesty sent me," I explained, still struggling with my stubborn curls.

"Ah," his expression became guarded. "Did she now?"

"She did, m'lord." I gave up on my hair. "I am also here at the behest of Her Majesty's Select Ser—"

His face was a thundercloud. "I see." He stepped closer, glowering at me now with his full wrath. "I've told those idiots that my inventions are for peaceful purposes, not for the war efforts of the Empire."

He stood close enough that I could feel his breath on my cheek, but I refused to budge. I simply gave the chaos about us a pointed glance, lifted my chin, and met his eyes. "How could they draw such a conclusion, my lord?"

Startled, he threw back his head, and let out a ringing laugh. I waited patiently as he got himself under control. "I suppose I must endure you," he finally said.

"It would be for the best, m'lord," I replied.

"Perhaps we should discuss the matter further. Over dinner?" His brown eyes danced.

"That would be terribly inappropriate, m'lord," I replied. "But a cup of tea would be most welcome."

"Tea, then." He frowned as he watched some of the workmen lifting the torso of the automation. "Ask Jervis to see to it. I will be in shortly."

With that, he strode off, shouting orders to his workers.

Lord Ashington seemed even taller in the confines of his office.

Jervis wheeled in the tea cart, and Ashington bid me pour. The tea was weak and tepid. The scones had clearly been from a prior week's baking.

I took a few sips for politeness sake. Lord Ashington gulped his down and crunched through the scones, sending crumbs everywhere.

"So tell me," he said, those brown eyes intent on mine. "What is your real mission?"

I opened my mouth to deny, but changed my words when I saw his expression. Nothing but the truth would suffice. "To see to it that you are protected and given ample opportunity to develop your ideas and inventions without any harm coming to your person. To act as your secretary, and aid in the management of your household."

"The queen's not sent you here to try to get me to return to London?" he demanded.

"No," I said.

"Last time I attended her she tried to marry me off to one of her dumpy old ladies-in-waiting." Ashington shuddered in mock horror. "Heaven protect me."

I had to suppress a smile at that one.

Ashington caught it and leaned back in his chair with a satisfied look. "Very well," he nodded, accepting the situation. "But I want it clearly understood that this arrangement is on a trial basis, Miss Haversham. Shall we say three months?"

"With free rein, my lord?"

"Over the house and grounds, certainly. But the laboratory and the work we do here is under my direct control, is that understood?"

"Perfectly," I responded.

"Further," he said. "I will review any reports that you send to your superiors, before you send them. I will have your oath, Miss Haversham."

That caught me by surprise. I could hardly blame the man but . . . "My oath?" I stalled a bit.

"Yes," he leaned forward. "Your oath, or nothing."

I weighed the options before me and decided there'd be no harm. I'd not been instructed to keep anything secret, and his cooperation would make my task that much easier. "Very well, m'lord."

"Excellent," he leaned back in his chair and smiled. "I'm afraid you'll find I am not much of a paperwork person. I'll leave that in your capable hands."

I eyed the desk with a sigh and nodded. "As you wish, m'lord. More tea?"

That night I claimed a room in the servants' quarters, between the cook and the kitchen maids. It was a small, tidy room, with little else to say about it. But comfort was not my concern. An irreproachable reputation was.

The next day was a productive one.

An hour with the household accounts, and Jervis was sacked and in the hands of the local constabulary.

Another half hour in the kitchens, with a short presentation to the cook and household staff, produced a flurry of activity. There is something magical about the phrase "discharged without a recommendation" that captures everyone's attention very, very quickly.

It took two hours to pry the head groundskeeper out of his hiding place, sober him up with generous amounts of tea and sympathy, and offer reassurances that there'd be no further mechanical assistance with his duties. I assured him that I would hire some strong lads that would aid him in restoring the grounds. The fact that they had all previously served in Her Majesty's Service was a matter that I kept to myself.

That took care of the morning hours. After a delicious lunch with strong, hot tea, I turned my attention to the greatest of challenges.

His lordship's desk.

A few hours later, I sat back and sighed with satisfaction. In all honesty, it had not been as bad as it had looked at first glance. While his lordship was not the neatest of men, it appeared that his books were all in order, and the accounts of the various tenant farmers were accurate and up-to-date. Further, the bills for the laboratory supplies and sundry were current.

But his social correspondence was quite unacceptable. I shook my head over the small pile of invitations that I had organized on the corner of the desk. It appeared that he hadn't responded to a single one for months, and some of them were quite prestigious. Some of the letters were both purely social, but others were from other scientists and inventors from across the country and Europe. Really quite shameful.

I rang for tea, and then made myself comfortable on the settee to think for a moment.

It is a truth universally acknowledged that a single man in possession of a good fortune must be in want of a wife. And if that wasn't well established in the mind of Lord Ashington, it was in the mind of his godmother, the queen.

I had not lied to his Lordship, nor had I been entirely truthful. My orders were to see to his comfort and well-being, certainly. But that included—

The door to the office opened with a bang, and Lord Ashington walked in, his face smudged with soot and his curls in disarray. "I rather think I can save that knee joint." He threw himself into the settee opposite me. "But I will need to order some new gears for the reasoning machine. Seems there are a few bullet holes in the old one."

"Really, m'lord?" I raised an eyebrow.

"Odd, that, since I don't allow firearms in the lab," Ashington mocked me by raising his eyebrow. "Do you have any idea how—"

One of the kitchenmaids appeared in the doorway with a tea cart and a sparkling white apron, freshly pressed by the look of it. She pushed the cart close, curtsied with a giggle, and exited, leaving the door open as was proper.

"One lump or two?" I asked, reaching to pour.

Thankfully, Ashington was hungry. He accepted the napkin for his lap and his tea, and settled back into his seat. "You've been busy, I see."

I poured my own cup. "Yes, m'lord. There are a number of items that need your attention. Some invitations to—"

Ashington grimaced. "Burn them," he growled. "Card parties, for God's—"

I coughed.

"Yes, well, I am not going." Ashington declared. "No card parties, not soirees, no luncheons on the lawn, by all that is holy."

"As you wish," I said mildly. "I shall send notes declining the invitations, for those not yet past."

He gave me a careful look over his teacup.

I offered him the plate of scones, warm from the oven. "One of the notes was from a Dr. Hastings, who will be traveling through London on his way to Edinburgh."

"Hastings? Robert Hastings? He is a brilliant chemist." Ashington frowned. "I'm sorry I missed that one. I wonder if he's worked out his formula yet?"

"You might still be able to catch him," I said. "One of the lads could take a telegram to—"

"Yes, yes," Ashington waved his cup in the air, sloshing his tea. "Brilliant, Miss Haversham. Invite him for a few days, and I'll have him out to the lab."

"More tea?" I asked and poured as he explained his new theory. An excellent start to my first day and an answer to my difficulties as well.

The next few weeks gave me further satisfaction.

Dr. Hastings' visit went exceedingly well. I took notes of their discussion over tea, but declined any invitation to dine with them in the evenings. Besides, Mrs. Hastings and their two lovely daughters took delight in dining with Lord Ashington and cooing over him.

Ashington had given me a look of betrayal as they had disembarked from their carriage, but I ignored him. I'd already extended a dozen invitations to his fellow scientists and inventors, all with daughters of marriageable age. He'd agreed to them willingly enough before the Hastings' arrival. With any luck, one of those winsome lasses would have him in harness in no time.

I'd not wasted the rest of the time either. The new butler, Fredricks, was a gem, and had seen service in the Far Indies and Egypt. He'd fit into the household as if he'd always been there and hadn't blinked an eye at the various explosions coming from the lab.

After a token protest, Cook had relished the challenge of entertaining the new guests with her culinary arts. The kitchen maids were quite flush from all their efforts and the flirting they'd enjoyed with the new lads I'd hired.

Best of all, the head groundskeeper had come into his own. He had managed to hide almost all of the ravages to the gardens. I'd enjoyed a number of walks, discussing the plantings with the various new helpers. If we also discussed certain security issues, well, that was all to the good.

Ashington had a small desk added to his office for my use, and we'd developed the habit of using tea time to deal with the business of the day. It was very comfortable to have him pacing about, expounding on a theory, or some new outrage in the paper as I worked through his correspondence. Of course, the presence of guests meant he had the obligations of a host, but we still managed at least an hour or so each day. I rather enjoyed ...

I drew myself up short at that thought, and then drove it completely out of my head. Lord Ashington needed a wife of gentle birth, acceptable to his godmother, and willing and able to take her place next to him in polite society. I'd enjoy what I had and be grateful for it. The moment his betrothal was announced, I'd be on my way to a new assignment.

But until then ...

*   *   *

I fault myself for what happened next. I'd become complacent, at ease even over the last few weeks. It does not pay to let one's guard down for an instance.

In my defense, I should point out that Herr Doktor Girdenstein and his chubby wife seemed the last people on this earth to offer a threat. They'd arrived with two carriages filled with luggage and yapping lap dogs. I'd focused on seeing to their comfort, and not the number of muscular, grim drivers, footmen, and servants they'd brought with them.

On the second day of their visit, Fredricks had gone into town for errands with two of our lads. Ashington and Herr Doktor were in the lab, discussing the various methods of welding, when Frau Doktor Girdenstein came into the office with the terriers, asking for help with some correspondence. I'd been willing, of course, and was perusing her papers when she thrust the muzzle of her firearm up under my jaw.

She'd no compunction of searching under my skirts for my weapons, removing my pistol and two of my throwing knives. Then she frogmarched me into the lab, those damnable dogs yipping at our heels.

Lord Ashington looked up from his plans, and his jaw dropped. Herr Doktor used his astonishment to thrust a gun into his ribs.

"You will order your men to gather," Girdenstein's voice was low and calm. "We will see to it that they are secured, and no one will be harmed. We wish only the plans and your notes."

Ashington opened his mouth, but the Doktor pressed the muzzle of his firearm harder into his back. "It will not be you who suffers for any disobedience."

"There's no need." Ashington spread his hands, holding them open in a gesture of surrender. "You have us at your mercy. We will cooperate."

The devil we would. She hadn't found all of my knives. I shifted my weight slightly, eyeing Frau Doktor Girdenstein carefully.

"Haversham," Ashington snapped.

I glared at him for drawing attention to me.

"Get the plans, if you would. And my notes." He gestured to the trap door. "Quickly, if you please. I am sure the Herr Doktor and his wife wish to be on their way as soon as possible."

Frau Doktor pushed me hard, and I staggered forward. With a snarl, I turned, but she had that damnable pistol in my face.

"Please," Ashington said.

Startled, I looked over. His brown eyes held worry there and concern. Concern for my well-being. A tingle passed through me. I sighed, and started down the steps.

"Hans and the others are outside," Frau Doktor told her husband.

"Excellent," Herr Doktor rumbled. "They certainly can assist us in—"

Lord Ashington moved then, leaping forward to push me down into the cellar, jumping in behind me. He jerked at the wooden door and shouted. "Trim the shrubbery!"

The automatons both lifted their arms, and their eyes glowed as the door slammed down, and Ashington fell on top of me.

His weight pinned me to the floor and knocked the breath quite out of me. There was a crashing sound as debris fell around us. I couldn't see a thing, but I could hear the Doktor cursing, the squeals of the lap dogs, and the shrill screams of his wife.

"I was afraid of that," Ashington said in my ear. "Damn thing stepped on the door."

I gasped, trying to gulp in air.

"What's wrong?" Ashington asked. "Are you well enough? I'm too heavy for you."

"No," I couldn't seem to breathe. "My stays," I whispered, my vision going even blacker then it already was.

Ashington cursed. He shifted, and I felt his fingers at my collar. He tore my dress down the front, ripping it and my corset open clear down to my waist. I drew a deep breath, cool, dusty air filling my lungs.

"Better?" Ashington asked as the debris above us trembled.

"Yes, but," I squirmed a bit, trying to adjust. "But your toolbelt is digging into my—"

Ashington coughed. "That is not my tool belt, Miss Haversham."

"Oh," I froze, suddenly quite distracted from the distant screams.

"It would be a great help if we both just lie back and think of England." Ashington said. "Think of our duty to God and country and—"

"Your godmother is going to have me thrown in the Tower," I said.

"That's quite an effective method of quelling improper thoughts," Ashington said. "The image of my godmother bearing down on us. Thank you, Miss Haversham, that's rather taken care of the situation."

The floor above us quaked, and dust rained down as the rafters groaned. We were confined in the wreckage and darkness.

"Sounds like the Germans are having a rough time of it," Ashington observed. "Serves them right."

"It's my fault," I said softly. "They should never have managed to—"

"Who'd have expected Girdenstein of anything other than designs on my pot roast?" Ashington chuckled. "Besides, I am indebted to the man."

I blinked in the darkness. "Why on earth would—"

"Well, you are well and truly compromised, aren't you?" Ashington sounded very smug, and very satisfied. "There is no hope for it, and I shall do the honorable thing. We will marry immediately."

"We shall not." I said, trying to control the tremble in my voice. "Your position, the queen . . ."

"Even better," Ashington replied. "You will both stop throwing women at me."

"M'lord?"

"Ash," he demanded. "Call me Ash."

I drew in a breath of cool damp air. "I—"

"That last one, Dr. Conrad's daughter, she had a moustache," he grumbled into my ear.

I choked back a laugh. "She did," I admitted. "But she also is reputed to have a keen understanding of aerodynamics."

"Miss Haversham, science can only go so far."

I laughed weakly as dust drifted down on us from above. But I knew my duty too well. "Lord Ashing—"

He kissed me, his warm lips on mine.

A proper woman would have resisted. I moaned into his mouth, opening to him, wanting more, wanting . . . .

His hand eased up, cupping my breast under the torn bodice. "Yes indeed, well and truly compromised. The niceties will demand that we marry."

"Ash," I breathed. "I can't. Your godmother will not be amused."

"She will," Ash assured me. "Once I tell her that we are in love."

"We are?" I blinked in the dust and darkness, sure of my feelings. But did he—?

"Oh yes, my love." he kissed me again, as thoroughly as I could wish.

The trap door opened, and light poured in around us

as many hands pulled away the debris. Audible gasps could be heard from above. Ash raised his head and gazed into my eyes. "Aren't we?"

"Oh yes," I laughed breathlessly. "I rather think we are."

GRASPING AT SHADOWS

C.J. Henderson

CJ Henderson is the creator of both the Piers Knight supernatural investigator series and the Teddy London occult detective series. Author of some seventy novels and/or books, including such diverse titles as The Encyclopedia of Science Fiction Movies, Black Sabbath: the Ozzy Osbourne Years, *and* Baby's First Mythos, *as well as hundreds of short stories and comics and thousands of nonfiction pieces, this staggering talent is currently celebrating the fact he has now been published in some thirteen languages. For more facts on this truly unusual talent, the man to whom the Dalai Lama once said, "Don't stand in the doorway, fat boy, you're blocking the sun," feel free to head over to www.cjhenderson.com where you can comment on his story in this volume or even read more work if you're so inclined.*

Beware that you do not lose the substance by grasping at the shadow—*AESOP*

"Not much to look at this fine mornin', is 'e?"

Filimena Edgars had to agree with the captain. The man snoring on the floor before them was indeed a sorry sight. Of course, sleeping in a heap of straw on the wrong side of a sturdy set of prison bars has never been known to do much for anyone. This individual, however, managed to trump those minor discrediting affectations with an entire roster of others.

"I should say not," the young lady agreed, her previous list of reservations about their mission that morning suddenly seeming as inadequate as wine from the Americas or promises made by the French.

The object of Miss Edgar's disdain was indeed a sight—his hair long uncut, his body long unbathed. His unshaven face was covered in bruises, his feet were clad in neither shoes nor socks, and what clothing he did possess was stained with such a vast multitude of oils, fluids, and lubricants that their original colors were lost for all time.

"Wake him."

The captain's order was directed at a guard standing by prepared with a bucket of water. Its relatively quiet splash was followed by a shocking outburst of profanity, coupled with a violent thrashing of the no-longer-sleeping man's limbs, a display which sent wet straw, an assortment of insects, and a small family of mice flying in all directions.

"Roust yourself, lad," barked the sergeant of the guard, "these kind folk has taken enough interest in you to pay your debts, which means you'll be doing your decomposing somewheres else ... at least for a while."

As the suddenly slightly less filthy figure on the floor sputtered, working to pull himself together, the captain said: "AppleJack Stevens, you look like a cheese what got left in the sun too long. Shameful."

Blinking hard, shaking himself in much the manner of an ill-bred, and possibly drunken, hound, the sputtering fellow replied: "Captain? Captain Dollins?"

Ignoring Stevens, the older man turned to his companion. "There he is, Miss Edgars, the al'round best pilot and gunner the big wide world of lighter-than-air craft 'as ever known. One in a million, 'e is."

Turning her nose upward at the sight of Stevens as he burped, then used a finger to dig at some irritant caught between his teeth, the young woman responded: "Surely there is someone else we could use."

"No," answered Dollins in a somber voice. "There's not. And there's certainly no man I'd trust more . . . considering, that is, where we've got a mind to be goin'."

Burping twice more, rubbing at his eyes as strenuously as if they had been covered over with tar and left to dry, the pilot worked at focusing his attention on Dollins as he asked: "Unnn-hunnnn . . . and speaking of that, captain, sir . . . what god-forbidden pesthole did you have in mind for me guide the *Gibraltar* to this time?"

"The only one that matters, Jack, me boy . . ."

The pilot's head stopped moving, frozen in place by some inner property desperate to hear whatever Dollins was about to say clearly—correctly. Through eyes so bloodshot they appeared as an unbroken scarlet, he stared as the captain finished his sentence—

"Xibor."

And felt his eyes go clear as all the blood drained from his head.

Two days passing found Dollins and Stevens walking across an airfield to the northeast of London toward a massive hangar. The pilot had been shaved and shorn, bathed and outfitted to the point where he scarcely had any details in common with the figure that had been stretched out on the floor of the Bristol Debt House forty-eight hours previously.

"So, what landed you in the scut this time, Jackie—another set of eyes peekin' over a fan?"

"The last one, captain," growled Stevens. "Ever."

"Sounds a touch final, me boy."

"Final as a hat on your bed. Rose Beckett . . . she gave me a story I was puddin'brained enough to believe, took everything I had, pegged me for a tally she'd run the size of the empire . . . then laughed as they pelted me with their clubs and dragged me away."

"Feelin' a bit wary of the fairer sex these days, are we?"

"Just keep that over-educated trollop of yours on a leash," answered Stevens in a threatening tone, "or I'll show you six kinds of wary . . . Captain. Sir."

Dollins could not very well make much in the way of protest. The ancient taboo warning against the presence of women on ships was still strong, even in the enlightened days at the end of the nineteenth century, even regarding ships that plowed the ephemeral mists of cloud banks instead of the briny seas. Moreover, if he were truthful, the captain would be forced to admit he himself was a touch uncomfortable with taking a woman along on their upcoming voyage. His reasons, however, had less to do with superstition and more to do with the fact the trip upon which they were about to embark was no ordinary excursion.

But then, Filimena Edgars was no ordinary woman, either.

Miss Edgars was the head librarian at the Royal Academy, the youngest woman ever to have held the position. Coming from a family known for prizing education, she was a person of quite notable talents, even among her own relations.

Filimena was an accomplished linguist, musician, and mathematician. She spoke and could read some eighteen languages—ten of them flawlessly. She played five instruments quite well, nine more passably, and could hold her own with any accountant—Christian, Jew or Buddhist. And it was that exact combination of talents, along with several other lesser but notable aptitudes, which made her invaluable to the Gibraltar's upcoming voyage.

"Well then, Mr. Stevens," said the captain as the two closed on the massive hangar, "let's leave off such debate for a more proper setting, and instead get you to shakin' down this old girl of ours, shall we?"

"Whatever you say," answered Stevens sourly, the stench of Bristol still strong within his mind. "You do own me."

"Jackie," Dollins said, stopping the two at the hangar's entrance, "now let's you and me get all the lines straight between us. You're like a son to me, and I would 'ave paid to get you sprung no matter what. Only reason I found out you was in the can was when I start lookin' for a pilot for this voyage, everyone kept sayin' you was the only git crazy enough to go—"

"The praise of my peers . . ."

"And, when I said I would take you in a 'eartbeat if I only knew where you was, one of 'em told me. And then, as you know, you wasn't there no more."

Both men stood quietly for a moment, and then Dollins, his head lowered, his face slightly red, began again, saying: "So now, anyways, if you've reached an age where you've suddenly started worryin' about still breathin' on the morrow, then we'll just call it jake between us for all the times you pulled the *Gibraltar* through the fire and kept my own derrière from gettin' scorched along with it."

"It's not that, sir," answered the pilot honestly. "Hell and back, just to be standing here, adventure calling, a Robbins and Lawrence strapped to my side once more . . . you know I'm with you."

"Well, then, if you're in, you're in, for full crew wage, and half my share. And before you say anything else, go on inside . . . there's somebody there been waitin' to see you."

Stevens swallowed hard, looking for words he might be able to hand back to the captain. Dollins had been father, best friend, and confessor to the pilot for close to his entire life. The bond between them was as strong as steel and as welcome as Christmas. Which was, in the end, why Stevens did not want to see the captain risking his life in an attempt to reach Xibor. Not knowing how to say such, however, he instead walked into the hanger as directed, looking about for only a moment before crying out in excitement: "Spitz!"

His overwhelming joy was shared by the figure that came swinging and screaming down from the top of the *Gibraltar* on a length of chain. Hurling himself with a wild shriek, Spitz slammed into the pilot, knocking him roughly into the hangar wall behind. Hugging the forty-some pounds of uncontrollably excited chimpanzee to his bosom with a clear and honest joy, Stevens exclaimed: "Wherever did you find him?"

"Didn't. 'e found us. Don't know 'ow, but after that skirmish with the air pirates over Egypt, when 'e got lost after swingin' over and torchin' their balloon—again, nice work, Spitz, ol' boy—anyway, 'e found 'is way back to Mother England all on 'is own."

"He made it back here to Chelmsford on his own?" The pilot's eyes went wide with admiration.

Dollins explained: "No, but when I 'eard tales of a drunken monkey what could cheat at cards better than any thimblerigger in Torquay, well don't you know I was on the first rail car down the coast."

Stevens blushed for joy to have his dearest friend, as well as the best mechanic in all the British Isles, at his side once more. No one knew who had trained Spitz—a fact made especially puzzling considering his knowledge of steam engines seemed greater than that of Savery, Newcomen, and Watt put together—but he was an acknowledged master tinker, one who had gained the title Steamsmith to the Crown, at least once Stevens had taught him to wear pants on formal occasions.

"Look, Jackie," said Dollins, taking a quick glance at his pocket watch, "our time's runnin' like a poacher in the king's forest. What say we get on board? You give the ol' girl a quick white glove, and then the three of us will sit down with Miss Edgars and run our hash around our plates. I'll leave it up to you whether or not we set sail. Agreed?"

Stevens took a deep breath, set Spitz down on the hangar floor, and then stepped back to take a long look at the Gibraltar. Although the ship was registered as the sole property of one Albert J. Dollins, he considered the sleek and somewhat experimental, airship his—and Spitz's—as well. Aboard her the trio had delivered cargo to far off lands, battled pirates on both the sea and air, smuggled the last of the square eggs of the Andes out of the Southern latitudes for the British Museum, and come through more outlandish shenanigans unscathed than any band of adventurers had a right to expect.

She was, he knew, his ship, and if the *Gibraltar* was going to be sailing off into the greatest danger she had ever known, he could not let her go without him. Turning to his simian companion, he barked: "Mr. Spitz, are the nose cone battens rigid and secure?"

"Ook!"

"Has the air scoop been cleaned?"

"Ook!"

"And have you finally gotten that infernal squeak out of the lower vertical fin's rudder?"

"Ook, ook!"

As Spitz turned a gleeful somersault, Stevens turned to the captain and said: "If time's a'wasting, let's get her in the air. As soon as the course is set and we're level at five thousand, then we'll sit down with your librarian and have us a chat."

Dollins smiled, and then growled at the other crewmen there in the hangar to get the last provisions on board. Spitz gave the captain a salute, beat his chest for a moment, then grabbed hold of one of the many chains hanging from the ceiling and disappeared into the upper rafters. And Stevens, staring at the great ship and frowning, wondered if the madmen of the *Gibraltar* had finally bitten off more than they could chew.

"So, Mr. Stevens, why don't we make this meeting as brief as possible by having you make your objections so that I may put your mind at ease and we might set sail?"

The pilot raised his left eyebrow in response. Dollins and Spitz, both understanding his signal, sat back and allowed him to respond.

"Oh, *Miss* Edgars, you're so obviously my better in every way, why don't you simply explain away any objection I might have—in the interests of saving time, that is?"

Filimena knew when she was being baited, had suffered such nonsense at the hands of the men outside her own family all her life. Because she had been—to her mind, unfortunately—born fair of face and figure, even among those academics who were well aware of her vast accomplishments she had always been treated as just another female. Men like Mr. AppleJack Stevens, broad of shoulder and strong of chin, swaggering across the face of the land simply because they had been born with a few insignificant ounces of extra equipment, she was certain had judged and dismissed her to the point where she had simply had her complete and utter fill.

Still, she would not rise to his lure. She had learned long before how to keep such personalities, if not respectful, at least civil and at bay. Unrolling a large map across the table around which the four were seated, she asked for the edges to be secured.

When such had been accomplished, she took a pointer, and tapping a spot along the southeastern edge of England, she said: "We are here at present." Dragging her indicator lightly toward the east, she continued. "Once we've finally found the . . . time to embark upon our journey, we should make as straight a line as possible for this spot—"

Filimena moved the pointer gracefully, bringing it to a halt some two feet from her starting position, announcing: "Here."

"That's the middle of the Dasht-i-Kavir, the largest desert in Persia. There's nothing for hundreds of miles in any direction. Including the water and fuel we'll be needing for a return trip."

"In any other year of your life, Mr. Stevens," said the young woman, "you would be correct. Even most of the days within this current year of our Lord 1883. But, in a few days' time, and only for a few days, you will no longer be correct."

The pilot turned, looking toward Dollins imploringly. The captain gave him a slight nod, his head tilted, indicating he wished his friend would extend their speaker a few more minutes. When Spitz only offered him an indifferent shrug, Stevens merely asked: "Because. . . ?"

"Because it will be then that Xibor will reappear upon the spot from where it disappeared over a century ago, the spot where it has appeared on a precise and predictable schedule for thousands of years."

"Oh, Lord love a duck, Captain . . ."

"Miss Edgars," said Dollins to the young woman, ignoring his pilot, "if you would be so kind as to explain how you put together your timetable?"

Giving the captain a pleasant nod, Filimena turned the full power of her iciest condescension toward Stevens as she detailed how she and Dollins had come together in common cause. It had been the captain himself who had begun the entire affair, when he had stated casually at a mercantile association dinner that he had always been fascinated with the legend of the lost city of Xibor. Present at the modest banquet because of her family's involvement with certain banking interests as overseers and assurers of their accounting records, Filimena had struck up a conversation with the captain when the male members of her family had indicated their collective opinion was that he was nothing more than a nuisance in need of polite disposal.

Happy to assume Filimena was making herself useful by steering Dollins away from their far more important conversations, they quite forgot about her entirely as she spent the remainder of the evening in rapt conversation with the captain. What they did not realize was that she herself was even more fascinated with the idea of pinpointing the date, time, and location of Xibor's arrival back within the boundaries of the accepted temporal plane, and that she had been spending the better part of the preceding calendar year and all of the current one working toward that goal.

Discovering their common interest in the mythical city to be stunningly equal, the pair had formed a partnership. Dollins would supply the ship and crew needed to reach Xibor, and Filimena would provide the route and timetable.

Feeling some piece of the story had been left unmentioned, Stevens asked: "You'll pardon my insufferable ignorance, but what I don't understand is, to the best of my recollection, the greatest minds throughout history have been trying to crack the secret of how to reach Xibor. No offense to your skills as a human abacus, but what is it that gives you the reach over da Vinci and Copernicus?"

"A good question, actually, Mr. Stevens," admitted Filimena, upset with herself that she failed to keep her left eyebrow from rising in surprise.

"And the answer . . ."

"Music."

Composed once more, Filimena explained that the position to Xibor's coordinates lie not on a grid that could be determined by studying clues based solely on longitudes and latitudes, but by reducing the melody of the heavens to a mathematical constant. For years she had studied the lyric to be found in the movement of the clouds, the play of wind against the forest. She had charted the beat set by the incoming surf, worked out the syncopation in the minute variations of falling rain drops, identified the harmonies in the baying of hounds and the drum beat underlying the tread to be found in a simple line of marching ants.

"The melodic patterns of the solar system became clear to me of a sudden," the young woman said, the light in her eyes almost dreamlike, "and after I began to interweave the various threads of that concerto I began to understand the rhythm of the universe, or should I say, the universes."

"Meaning what, exactly?"

"What she's sayin', my boy," interrupted Dollins, "is that Xibor is where it is all the time, but it's not. Like a ghost what exists in another place, but on occasion slips into view when conditions are right."

Filimena made to explain further. Indeed, she seemed almost eager to do so, as if the pilot's opinion might almost be important to her. Cutting off any further explanations, however, Stevens turned to Dollins, asking: "And you believe all this, Captain?"

"I've worked with Miss Edgars here for over a year on this, Jackie. She's got me convinced enough to risk the Gibraltar. I've put everythin' I've got into this. She has, too."

The pilot considered for a moment, turned to stare at his chief mechanic, and then turned back to Dollins and Filimena, telling them as he rose from his seat: "Well, I'll tell you now, I think you're both stomping balmy. My opinion is, if you're wrong, we're dead, and if you're right, we're damned. But, my opinion apparently not being worth anymore than the monkey's, I believe my mechanic and I will retire to the inner skin for bananas and bourbon."

"Meaning what, precisely, Mr. Stevens?"

"Meaning Spitz and I have work to do, Miss Edgars, and neither one of us feels like doing it on an empty stomach or sober."

"Does that mean you're finally prepared to begin our voyage?"

Having started for the hatch, Stevens stopped and turned around one last time. Wearing a grin strained by frustration, the pilot answered:

"It means we've got to check our course. We've been in the air for hours, Miss Edgars. If I was half as incompetent as you seem to feel I am, you would have felt us lift off."

With that Stevens ducked under the hatch's low doorframe and stormed away in the direction of the bridge. Following his friend, Spitz loped toward the exit, turning just long enough to give the others a noncommittal shrug and grimace before disappearing into the hallway himself.

At the sound of a further hatch shutting behind the pair, a slightly embarrassed Filimena asked: "Have we really been in the air for hours?"

"Probably well over the Mediterranean by now. Yeah, Jackie really is that good."

Filimena merely nodded in response. Staring at the open, empty door, she sighed over her discomfort at having been wrong about Stevens' competence. As she sat quietly, a part of her mind wondered if that was the only one of her assumptions about the pilot that had been wrong.

Stevens and Spitz sat atop the *Gibraltar*, watching the night stars drift slowly by overhead. The pilot was there supposedly to verify their heading. In actuality he had a great deal on his mind, and needed both the crispness and silence of the late evening atmosphere to help himself focus. Spitz was present because he enjoyed being on the outside of the ship, and he sensed that his friend needed a companion at that moment. Sitting quietly in two of the large lounge chairs built into the *Gibraltar's* outer skin, a number of empty LaRaja's bitters bottles rolling around in concentric circles beneath their feet, the pair allowed the world to pass beneath them undisturbed. Neither said anything to the other. There was no need.

At least not for a while.

"Spitz, old lad, I hope we haven't gotten ourselves in over our shoulders on this thing."

"Ook, ook."

"You know Captain Al's been chasing the idea of finding Xibor most of his life. I've been over every scrap of information history has to offer about the place with him, and although it all makes claims that those what reach it all find their hearts desire, not a single bit of it ever says what happen to them what got there."

"Vootie?"

"You know it, mate. There might be those what reaches Xibor, but there ain't never been any what's come back."

"Couldn't we be the first?"

Both crewmen turned at the quite unexpected voice of Miss Edgars. Pulling herself through the Gibraltar's upper escape hatch, taking care to not snag her petticoats on its frame, she emerged onto the ship's crown, exclaiming: "Bit nippy up here, isn't it?"

"That it is," answered Stevens. "Most don't care for it. That's what Spitz and I like about it. The fact a body can be left alone in peace up here."

Settling into one of the lounge chairs, Filimena pulled the seat's built-in blanket from its side pocket and wrapped it about herself. The young woman found herself comfortable enough after a moment, except for the fact she had neglected to bring a pair of goggles along for protection against the wind. Shaking his head in amused pity, Spitz took off his own pair and handed them to Filimena as he ambled back toward the escape hatch. She accepted them graciously, stared at them for a moment as if she might be able to perceive any suspected fleas by starlight, then resolutely lifted them to her face and fastened their snaps behind her head neatly beneath her bonnet.

Pulling her blanket a bit more tightly about her shoulders, she asked, "Might I put a question before you, Mr. Stevens?"

"I don't rightly see how I could stop you."

"How gracious you are," answered Filimena before she could stop herself. Mentally cursing her temper, she reeled it in quickly then continued. "I've noticed you don't care for me very much. I'll not argue your right to do so, but for the sake of trying to maintain civility while we're all traveling together, might I inquire as to *why* this is so?"

Stevens tilted his head, lifting the flap of his leather flight cap so as to be able to stick a finger into his left ear and scratch at an itch that had been bothering him. Allowing the flap to then drop back into place, he took a draining pull on his last LaRaja, then sighed as he dropped it down to join its still rolling companions. "You're a quite lovely little girl, Miss Edgars, and your brain seems as wide as the ocean and as active as Vesuvius the day it arrested all attention in old Pompeii, but . . ."

"Yes, Mr. Stevens, 'but' . . ."

The pilot fought the dozen or so malicious utterances suggesting themselves as possible verbal cannonade, but rejected them all, holding his tongue for a moment until he could swim past the delicious influence of his many LaRajases, finally saying: "But . . . I owe the captain plenty—plenty and twenty pounds more. The only reason Spitz and I are here is to be there at the end for him."

"So," Filimena snapped, "you're just like all the rest. Pat me on the head, you will, for my accomplishments, 'so clever for a mere woman, isn't she,' but you don't believe I can actually guide us to Xibor, do you?"

"On the contrary, Miss Edgars," replied the pilot. Standing from his seat, stuffing his own blanket back into its pocket, he stretched his arms out at his sides, and then began to slowly stagger back to the hatchway. "I've no doubt you've got it all figured out. If you were just leading the captain on a wild goose chase, that would be different. A man's true mate will let him get into all manner of loony trouble so's he can rib him till he's tender then help him heal afters. But that's not what's happening here."

"Oh, and according to your narrow, male mind, what exactly *is* happening here?"

"In small words, the only kind I know, you're leading the man who's been a father to me most of my life to his doom. Albert Dollins is a good and proper sort what don't deserve to have ever met up with the likes of you. And Spitz and me, with all we owe him, well . . . tiny brains like we possess and all . . . we can't let him die alone."

And with that, Stevens caught hold of the hatchway's ladder and began to carefully maneuver his less-than-sober self back down into the *Gibraltar*, taking care not to strike his head against the jamb or his hair-triggered Robbins and Lawrence against anything at all. Seated in her chair, listening to the soft whir of the twin steam engines' turbines below propelling the great ship forward, Filimena Edgars stewed for a moment.

After all, she had only come forward as a proper, enlightened human being to try and propose the adoption of a touch of civility between herself and the pilot—and his monkey—so as to make their voyage more pleasant. And he had—

And then, while a number of comforting comments roared into the young woman's mind, several gentle whispers drifted in along with them, asking her to pause, and to reflect, on exactly what Stevens *had* actually done—if not from her viewpoint, than from his own?

The only answers she could come up with left Filimena feeling small and alone under the night stars, and filled with a shivering even the heaviest blanket could not dispel.

*   *   *

Despite the extraordinary intake of their beloved LaRajas on their night of departure, Stevens and Spitz managed to keep the *Gibraltar* straight and true, following each new course change as the captain and Filimena decided upon them. The pilot was perfectly willing to admit he could not begin to determine how playing a harp while singing mathematical formulas in a variety of languages could produce anything but a novelty act at which even Crabtree's Curious Carnival of Clowns—London's West End's oddest collection of performers—would roll their eyes. But, being an honest man, he also had to admit that, whether they would find Xibor or not, they were still headed on a true course for the middle of the Dasht-i-Kavir.

"I don't get it, Spitz," Stevens mused one morning, some eight days into their voyage. The pair inspected the port engine's piston assembly, "I mean, I know the captain's always had this seed stuck in his teeth over Xibor, but to buy into this dizzy business . . ."

Satisfied with the tightness of the galvanized lug nut he had been tightening, Spitz turned and gave the pilot a weary shrug, indicating he had no better explanation for their situation than his friend. Stevens was about to respond, when suddenly Filimena's voice sounded through the overhead speaker:

"Mr. Stevens, Mr. Spitz, your presence is required on the bridge, thank you."

The pair eyed one another, wondering what would require the both of them in the middle of a shift. Seeing no reason not to comply, however, man and beast wiped their oily hands dry for the purpose of safe climbing, hung their tools in their required positions, and then started up the ladder to the gangway leading to the bridge.

Once on deck, Spitz scampering up behind him, Stevens asked: "All right, we're here. What's so important you needed us to break our maintenance check?"

A most untypical impish grin on her face, Filimena turned to the captain. "Would you do the honors, sir?"

"Most 'appy to, my dear. Tell me, Jackie my boy, what would you expect to find at this longitude and latitude of the Dasht-i-Kavir?"

Checking his pocket watch, the pilot answered, "Assuming we haven't drifted any, we should be smack over the heart of the Kavir now. Which means there shouldn't be anything but sand in any direction for seventy, eighty miles."

"Then what," asked Dollins, stepping away from the bridge's front wind screen, "would you say that was?"

And, jaws hanging open, eyes wide, AppleJack Stevens and his pal Spitz walked forward as if in a dream, staring silently as the sprawling magnificence that could only be Xibor.

The approach to the city had been something out of a story told by an Irishman, a thing of glorious light and dazzling wonder. Spires that reached far into the sky from which gay pennants flapped in the breeze stood like the most graceful of reeds—delicate, towering. Xibor looked to have been constructed of every precious stone and metal known to man. Granite foundations gave way to bricks of jade, silver, and amethyst. Doorways were decorated with strings of gold and rubies, windows hung with drapes woven from dazzling silks and the most colorful feathers.

The *Gibraltar* made easy landing in a field practically set in the center of town as if it had been expected. Cheering citizens thronged the zeppelin, lifting Dollins,

Stevens, and Edgars onto padded divans. The crew was ordered to secure the ship and see to her provisioning. All but Spitz snapped to attention, saluted and turned to their duties, the mechanic stowing away on the open-air lounge transporting Stevens.

The parade through the streets of Xibor seemed to last for hours, and yet when the quartet was ushered into the main ballroom of the kingdom's great central palace, the four felt refreshed and invigorated. The sextet of men carrying each divan lowered them carefully before the throne of the king of Xibor, then bowed and removed themselves quietly. Standing from his throne, the mystic kingdom's ruler proved to be tall, large of shoulder and strikingly handsome. His features were the expected brown of the desert, his beard black and well-groomed, his eyes flashing with a fierce intelligence which made Filimena shiver.

"*Attention!*" The word brought all activity within the ballroom to an immediate halt. "We have returned once more to the world, and as always, we are greeted by the bravest of the brave—the cleverest of the clever. As always, our time here is brief, but until we depart once more, let the music play, let the wine flow, and may our visitors be rewarded with their heart's desire for daring all to reach us—to reach mighty Xibor!"

With a gesture from the king, the music started once more, dozens of Xiborians rushing forward to pull each of their guests into the dance. Within minutes the gaiety reached the level of near madness, a swirling, festive insanity which staggered the visitors beyond reason—birds with dazzling plumage, performers juggling flaming knives, acrobats seemingly capable of dancing up the very walls, tables heaped high with every delicacy from coconuts to hummingbird's tongues on toast—

"Guess I was wrong, Spitz," admitted Stevens. Reaching for a proffered goblet of wine, he added, "not that it would be the first time. Right, mate?"

"Ook, ook."

The pilot took a long pull from his crystal chalice, forced to admit that even the grapes of Xibor seemed better than any others he had ever known. As his eyes came in contact with his fellows, it certainly seemed as if the king's words were coming true. To one side he saw Dollins, surrounded by what appeared to be the leaders of Xibor's military. They all seemed quite complimentary, in awe of the captain and whatever tale he was spinning for them.

Shifting his gaze, he spotted Filimena, who looked to have attracted the attention of the magical city's intelligentsia. She appeared to be explaining how she had determined the location of Xibor, much to the appreciation and even admiration of those around her.

"Hell, even ol' Spitzie's been done proper," he thought, observing the chimp's antics as he danced atop a heaping mound of brilliantly yellow bananas and golden pineapples.

For a moment Stevens wondered if they might not have stumbled into something too good to be true, as if they were only being lulled into dropping their defenses. But, the pilot reasoned, not only would there be no need for such, considering the degree to which they were outnumbered, but also every face appeared to be filled with genuine joy at their arrival. It seemed little doubt that Xibor was willing to do anything possible to fulfill the king's dictate that the city's visitors be granted their heart's desire. And then, suddenly, he blinked, unable to believe his eyes.

Crossing the room before him, in a gown of shimmering white brocade, was his Rose.

"I don't believe it . . ."

More beautiful than he remembered her, her eyes
filled with a love he could scarcely believe, Rose Beckett
walked toward him, her white gloved arms extended,
her hair flowing behind her, woven with lilies, her mouth
forming the words of love he could barely imagine her
ever saying to him. Seeing her, his heart aching, he did
what he knew he had to: he drew his Robbins and Lawrence pepperbox, pointed it upward and pulled the
trigger.

The weapon discharged with an enormous sound in
the small area of the Gibraltar's bridge, immediately
snapping the others to their senses. As Dollins sputtered, Filimena shrieked and Spitz gibbered, Stevens
shouted into the relay tube: "All hands, ramming speed!"

Swinging the great wheel of the *Gibraltar* around, he
then aimed the massive airship at that which had truly
appeared upon the sands of the Dasht-i-Kavir, a staggering colossus of nightmare, a thing tall as a mountain
and wide as a river! A screeching black mound of teeth
and tentacles, it threw forth a thousand grasping feelers,
all of them covered in rough spikes of bone, looking to
tear the *Gibraltar* from the sky!

Dollins and Filimena searched the forward portal for
any sign of Xibor, but the city had vanished, somehow
replaced by the demonic monstrosity before them. Where
had the ballroom gone, they wondered. Their honors,
their glory? How could it have vanished? Even Spitz appeared dazed, unable to comprehend to where the peach
he had so recently been devouring had vanished.

"Ignite the gasbags," bellowed Stevens, "prepare the
explosive charges. It means our deaths, lads, but we'll
take that hellhound with us!"

And, as Dollins and Filimena looked on in horror,
barely able to comprehend what had happened to their

dreams, AppleJack Stevens steered the *Gibraltar* directly toward the mouth of damnation.

"I suppose you're feelin' pretty smug right about now?"

"Well, any reason I shouldn't, captain—sir?"

Not answering the pilot directly, Dollins turned to Filimena and said: "And that, my dear Miss Edgars, is why I said from the beginning there was no way I was 'eadin' off to look for Xibor without my boy Jackie at my side."

Downing a long pull from a LaRaja, Stevens added, "If I were modest, I'd disagree."

Seated across the table from the pilot, Filimena continued to stare downward, unable to raise her eyes to meet those of anyone else in the room. She had gambled all she had on proving her intelligence, and had been duped and used by some horror from beyond. As the bridge grew quiet, she felt the eyes of the others as if they were probing her—hungry. Waiting.

"I suppose," she finally said to Stevens in a whisper, "that our thanks should be given to you."

"Indeed," added Dollins, "but if I might, what exactly are we thankin' you for? What *did* you do?"

"Yes," asked Filimena. "How did you know? How did we escape . . . the ballroom, the crash . . ."

"I was just lucky," the pilot answered magnanimously. Taking another deep swig from his favorite brand of bitters, he explained, "That thing, whatever it was . . . it had a harder time with me that with either of you because I didn't believe there actually *was* a Xibor to reach. That whole thing about giving us our heart's desire . . . you two wanted to find it for reasons of your own. Me, well . . . my heart's desire was seeing us get home in one piece."

"But you were seeing the same vision we were, correct?" When the pilot admitted to Filimena's point, she asked, "If that's so, then what did it show you that you were somehow able to resist . . . unlike the rest of us?"

"Don't be too hard on yourself. The accolades it fed you and the captain, you deserve them. Why shouldn't you believe what you were seeing? But me, there was nothing it could offer me that I didn't already have, so it gambled, trying something I knew I couldn't have." Stevens took a draining swallow from his LaRaja. "Luckily for all of us I stopped believing I deserved more out of life than three squares and a monkey's friendship long ago."

"I won't argue with you at this moment, my boy, over what you do and don't deserve," said Dollins, "but I still don't understand what 'appened. I mean, one minute we're in that fancy throne room, then we're 'ere and you're lookin' to shove the *Gibraltar* down that thing's throat, and then of a sudden—bang—no Xibor, no monster, just us . . . floatin' over the desert like birdies with nothin' better to do."

"I took a gamble of my own, captain," answered the pilot. "When I realized this thing was playing with our minds, I wondered if we might not be able to fight fire with fire. So, after I broke its control by sending a round into the ceiling—sorry about the mess, by the way—"

"Just tell the story, Jackie."

"Sorry again. Anyway, having broken its dream for us, I . . . Gods, what would the word be . . . I willed myself to create one for it. When I threw out my blood and thunder images, I . . . our minds, well, they 'touched,' I guess . . . and I saw through to its heart, found that it does this on a thousand, a *million* different worlds. It shows creatures what they want, gets them in close, then eats them."

Filimena shuddered. Dollins laughed, slamming the

table with his fist as he shouted: "One in a million, you are my boy, and I'm grateful to you as Abraham when 'e 'eard 'e didn't have to slice up 'is son. Now, findin' myself famished, I'm 'eading to the galley for the biggest platter of anything I can find. Who's with me?"

When only Spitz volunteered to join him, the captain nodded with a twinkle in his eye and headed off with his chief mechanic to celebrate still being alive. Once they were gone, Filimena, her cheeks still red, her spirit still flagging, said quietly, "You've certainly have put me in my place, haven't you, Mr. Stevens?"

"Really, Miss Edgars," the pilot offered gallantly, "we, each of us, has to learn sooner or later we're not all we think we are. Me learning it and ending up in the Bristol Debt House is the only reason that thing couldn't get a handle on me like it did you and the captain ... and even Spitzie."

"Still," the young woman said, her voice warmer than he had ever heard it, "I feel I should offer you some kind of reward, for saving us all."

"Well," answered the pilot, his tone soft and understanding, "you know, when you were working with the captain on the course and all, I have to admit I did greatly enjoy listening to you play that harp of yours."

For the first time since their shared dream had ended, Filimena looked up, her eyes locking with Stevens'. The pair smiled at one another, and for their entire voyage home there was beautiful music between them.

GO FORWARD WITH COURAGE

Dean Leggett

Dean Alan Leggett is a systems analyst by day, writer and avid board gamer by night. He enjoys many topics of discussion; from ancient archaeology to quantum physics, any subject is open for debate. He currently resides in a small Wisconsin town with his wife Annette.

$\mathcal{S}$eeing the world below took my breath away. This is why I needed to be part of an airship crew, and this is why I came to the New World. Here it wasn't only the upper-class elite who could travel on an airship; here it was anyone willing to work, even the daughter of a German farmer. Sheila Ann Marie VonShelton. The name is fun to say, but to my friends "Sheila" is just fine.

My skills are not typical for an airshipman. You will not see me up to my elbows in grease. No, I bring the fine art of logistics. The best farms are finely tuned machines. My family ran one of the best in all of Germany. As the eldest, and the only daughter of nine children, I learned a great many things. Between the family farm, schooling, and helping raise eight siblings, I became a master of logistics, doing the most with the least and in the quickest amount of time. Father called me "gifted."

Looking down through the light clouds, I spied a V-shaped flock of geese heading south-southeast. I returned to reviewing the itinerary and the catalog of our current supplies. If you have a ship on the move you need to have everything in order. This is especially true on airships. Don't pack hundreds of things you don't need; it only weighs the ship down. Don't pack two months of food; you can stop and restock.

It was time to head toward the cargo hold to see what "miscellaneous important crates" really meant on the inventory. The *Akula* was not a large airship; it could hold a crew of a dozen if needed, with bunks for six that could be shared between shifts. Our cargo capacity was only two tons at best. For today's journey our crew count was four: the pilot, the mechanic, the captain, and myself. To be honest, they all gave me the creeps. No matter where I went they stared at me when they thought I wasn't looking. It wasn't that they'd never seen a girl before. During the interviews there were lots of young women looking to join airship crews. Come to think of it, most of the applicants for the *Akula* were women. Goosebumps shot up my arms. Great work, Sheila, you couldn't have thought about this *before* you were alone and over a thousand feet in the air with them. At least I could find some privacy in the cargo hold.

Entering the hold, I quickly shut the door, then moved one of the larger crates in front just to be sure they couldn't sneak in on me. Now who's being paranoid? The light from the cargo window provided just enough to read the clipboard. Wedging the crowbar into the nearest crate and pressing down, the nails gave a steady groan. Dark green wool blankets were tucked around the top. Pulling back the top blanket, I noticed a large camera. It was strange not to mark a crate with something so valuable inside. Then a thin sleeve of pink lace caught my eye. I gently pulled the camera, still attached to a small extending tripod, out of the crate. Underneath was a crazy assortment of clothing. Holding up the pink lace dress it was hard to tell the front from the back. The neckline plunged dangerously low. It looked like something you would see at a burlesque show. It was surprisingly small, oddly my size. Turning away, I threw the silken outrage aside and vomited in the corner of the hold.

My mind raced, certain they intended to put me in this dress and take my picture . . . or worse.

Three men I didn't know, a thousand feet in the air, and regrets for not taking my father's offer of a small pistol all flashed through my mind. Sucking in a deep breath and speaking a brief prayer, I focused. Maybe there was something else in here that would help me. If nothing else, at least I had the crowbar. Prying open the next crate I discovered random aviation gear. A heavy leather jacket way too big for me and a few sets of thick goggles wouldn't help.

I needed to confront the men. But if I could find a weapon, I would feel a bit more evenly matched if things went bad.

And speaking of bad, a metallic groan caught my attention. It was quickly followed by a vibration and a much louder moaning of metal as the cargo hold tipped to port. The crates tipped. Aviation gear spilled over the decking as my hands clung to the nearby cargo netting. I heard yelling above as the crates slid toward the front of the cargo hold. The nose of the ship must be pointing down at a severe angle. The crates gathered in front of the only door leading toward the inside of the ship. Following the netting, I made my way to the lone window. The ground was still a long ways off, but it was clear airships didn't descend this quickly unless they were going down for good. Something was wrong with the ship.

Chances were the captain was thinking about dropping the engine with the twin propellers. Suddenly the ship lurched up. I lost my balance and my backside met the wooden floor. I realized less than an inch of wood separated me from a long freefall. Pulling myself back to the window, I saw that the ground was still coming up fast. Crawling over the crates and miscellaneous contents, I grabbed the blankets and looked for that thick leather skull cap I'd found earlier. I put on the oversized leather jacket and strapped on the skull cap. It too was big, but I tucked my hair inside to compensate.

Wrapping the blankets around me, I made my way to the side-by-side cargo doors and locked my arms and legs around the thick ropes of the cargo netting. I managed to pull the pins out of the door and send it sprawling downward. My brilliant plan to jump out as soon as I spotted water was quickly forgotten as we broke through the clouds to find nothing but a few hills and trees zipping by.

I made my way back to the largest crate and wrapped some more blankets around me. Then I climbed inside the box. It was up to fate now. The blankets would provide little cushion. Pulling my legs in close, I prayed. Darkness followed . . .

Pain shot though me. I heard distant chanting and saw the flicker of firelight. We'd crashed . . . somewhere. I tried to sit, but the pain got worse. Everything went dark again.

No more chanting. There were voices, but no language I knew. I squinted, trying to make out my surroundings. There were round brass beams reaching toward the sky, meeting about twenty feet up. I saw the outline of the sun through the light cloth stretched around them.

"Welcome back, Shysie." Trying to sit brought a bout of vertigo. "Please remain still." The voice was male, strong but calm. "Here, have some water, but don't drink too much." There was a cool feeling on my lips and instinctively I started to drink. "You have returned to us once again. Please rest; you are safe here."

I knew that voice from somewhere, but couldn't place it. The voice wore dark skin and a bright smile. His hair was midnight black and pulled tight into a ponytail. His deep green eyes smiled back at me. He reached down, and I didn't shy away. He brushed some hair away from my face.

"You are a lucky woman," he said.

I smiled back. My mind said, "Where am I?" but my ears heard me say: "Water please, more water."

He gently leaned close, holding the skin of water to my mouth.

"That is the most wonderful thing you have said in days."

A cough sent water through my nose. "Days?"

He held me still while my coughing fit passed, then eased me back on the pillows. I placed my palm against his cheek and said "thank you" in my mind before falling back to darkness.

My next return to consciousness was greeted with peaceful silence. Dim light reflected off the brass poles. I noticed that the sun lit up the patterns woven in the shelter's cloth. The brass poles looked to be retractable in four-foot sections similar to a spyglass.

My mind was clearer. Taking a deep breath, I worked

through my injuries. My right leg was practically numb with pain, but I could feel my toes. My left leg was sore, but not as bad. My left arm ached and was in a sling, but with working fingers. I noticed my right arm was to my side and my fingers were interlaced with someone else's. This should have brought fear or at the very least a reflexive pulling away. It didn't. It felt right. The man was attached to my hand; he appeared to be a native of the New World.

He was awake, too. He tried to release my hand, but I held tight. This time I managed to speak clearly. "I assume it was you who found me."

His shirt was unbuttoned, and the definition of his muscles could be clearly seen even in the dim light. "You fell out of the sky days ago. The gondola shattered. The rear section snapped off, and there was debris everywhere. The main section of the gondola was pulled across the ground before the balloon exploded." His expression turned grim and he wouldn't meet my eyes as he continued. "If there were others on the airship with you, they . . . didn't make it."

Taking my hand out of his and placing it on his chin I turned him back toward me. "Whoever you are, I have a strong feeling I am alive only because of you." I saw that I was wearing a linen dress, and added, "I hope you had some help." He looked startled, so I added a faint smile.

"You may call me Kendo. Yes, I pulled you from the wreckage and brought you to the closest village." Motioning around the living area, "This is Mitena's home. She is a friend of mine and she helped watch over you. She is the one who tended your clothing and more delicate matters." Standing, he motioned toward the entrance. "I will bring you some food. You must be very hungry by now."

How right he was.

I felt strangely at home for the first time since leaving the farm. Here I was halfway around the world in a place filled with strangers, yet I felt at peace.

The end of the month brought the beginning of the village pow-wow. With my one good leg, I was helped outside and given a sturdy chair near the fire pit where many folks were gathered. They were shucking corn for tonight's dinner. I got to officially meet the rest of Mitena's family—her three daughters and numerous grandchildren. Everyone was very kind. They smiled and waved, never gawked at the blonde-haired, blue-eyed girl.

A child brought me flowers. She sat next to me. Kendo checked in on me from time to time and told me her name was Hanna. After Hanna's older brother called her away, Kendo returned.

"Is there anything you need, Shysie?" Earlier he'd left me his skin, filled with fresh spring water. I pointed at the leg of elk roasting over the crackling fire. He nodded and headed over to negotiate some meat for us.

After a few more days I felt much closer to like my old self. Only "Sheila" was gone; I decided I liked "Shysie" better. It was the name Kendo gave me when he carried me across north Texas and to this Indian village. He told me he'd set my leg and arm before wrapping me in dirty green blankets and dragging me for a day across the rolling hillside. At one point he mentioned even lugging me across a river. I placed Kendo at roughly my age, in his early twenties. One night he explained that his mother and father were city folks, but he returned to his roots and followed the clans north to Sequoyah, the Indian Nation. He said he preferred the freedom of the open air and rolling plains. In return, I told Kendo all about Germany and my father's farm, vividly describing the little towns nearby.

I liked waking up next to Kendo. My father would

not approve, believing in vows and marriage and probably not accepting the physical intermingling of races. Still, I thought I might drag Kendo to Germany to meet my family. But for that we would need some warmer clothing. A nice fur-lined coat would look good on him.

I ate my way through the Blue Lady Festival. The chili tasted amazing. Kendo brought me some cornbread pudding, and Mitena wrote the recipe in Kendo's journal so I could get it from him later.

I got around with the aid of a wooden crutch, essentially an elaborately carved cane one of the tribesmen made. Not only did it allow me to move around on my own, it doubled as a swatter so I could land an occasional whack on Kendo's backside for fun. Life was good in this village.

One day I awoke with the cheering of little children followed shortly after with a steady beat of drums. Looking around, Kendo was nowhere to be found. I reached for my cane just as Kendo rushed into the teepee with the large beaded backpack Mitena made for me. Reaching in, he pulled out a blindfold and my leather aviator cap. "Hey Shysie, your surprise day is here."

I ran my hand through my hair. "Kendo, I am not putting on that cap!"

"Shysie, we need to cover your ears and eyes for this surprise. This is where you trust me. Or maybe you don't really trust me yet?"

I sat quietly as Kendo placed that old large aviator cap on my head and adjusted the straps. My hair had been wrapped in a tight ponytail by Hanna yesterday, making the cap's flaps come down even farther. Even in the closest buckle hole the cap was still quite loose.

"We will need to get you a new cap. This one is too big for you." Giving up with the strap, he covered my eyes with a long silk blindfold, wrapping it around twice before tying it in back.

I waited for Kendo to hand me my walking stick. Instead, he slid his arms underneath me and lifted me up. He hummed an unknown tune, the sound competing with children clapping and cheering. After several minutes I could tell we were going up a hill. The children were shushed, and I heard faint creaking followed by a gentle bounce that had me imagining we were going up a wooden ramp. Kendo sat me in what felt like a large wooden chair. As he removed my blindfold, my eyes slowly adjusted; I was facing a large window that looked toward the center of the village.

My God! I was in an airship! My heart jumped. "What the hell were you thinking?" Without my cane I still managed to stand.

Kendo tried to calm me. "You cannot give up your dreams because of your crash." Kendo placed his hand on my shoulder, but I shook it off.

"I am not ready, not yet." Looking around, I could tell this airship was massive. This must be the lower observation area, as there were windows on all sides. This room alone could fit thirty chairs. A railing ran along the windowed area. My need to leave was slowly being replaced with a wish to explore this ship.

"If you must step out and get some air, we can do that. We have several hours before we lift off. Otherwise, we can meet Captain Tatianna Silveroak."

Mitena walked up the ramp at the side of a tall, dark-haired woman dressed in a finely tailored leather jacket and matching tight brown leather pants with a wide belt showcasing a bronze Q as a belt buckle. Her knee-high boots and moderate heels put her just above six feet. She closed the distance to us, holding her gloves. Mitena handed me the walking cane.

The captain spoke in clear English. "Welcome aboard the *Cherokee Princess*." She motioned around the observation deck. "She will not fall from the sky like your last airship. The Goddess Uelanuhi watches over us." Her eyes bore into me.

Kendo said, "Captain, we will need a little while to gather our belongings and say our goodbyes. But we will be ready before final meal." He gave a nod to Mitena, then he lead me back down the ramp.

The ship towered overhead, blocking out the sky. It was easily twenty times the size of the *Akula* and quite possibly the largest airship I had ever seen in both Europe and the New World. The *Cherokee Princess* was a long, tubular airship at best guess about four hundred feet. The overlapping swaths of fabric hung from both sides. Above the two-level gondola these huge banners of cloth bore symbols and writing in a language I had not seen before. They hung from the widest part of the airship and dropped down forty feet in places, almost to the ground. It created a skirt-like appearance. The sheet above the starboard side had massive lettering and underneath in bright red was written in English: "*Cherokee Princess*." Chills ran up my spine. I understand why Kendo took me inside first. I could make out large ballistae mounted in the rear. This wasn't a passenger ship; this was one of the legendary Sequoyah warships.

Even glancing back from Mitena's home, the massive ship it made me uneasy. "Kendo, the folks in the village are very friendly but—" I left the rest unsaid. Looking into Kendo's eyes, searching for some reassurance, I found little. He also appeared unsettled, but tried his best to hide it.

"Shysie, you need to understand my mixed blood and city-born background leaves me almost as much as an outsider as you in the eyes of Tatianna and her crew.

Still, she is a friend and distant family member of Mitena. Therefore, if we can trust Mitena, we can trust Tatianna. You want to visit the heart of Texas with me, don't you? I would not yet trust your leg or arm yet on an extended horse ride. The airship will make the voyage easy. Besides, Mitena thinks it will be good for you."

Packing up my few belongings, most of which were gifts from new friends, waves of sadness passed through me. "Kendo, what can I do to thank Mitena and the others in the village?"

Kendo turned his head as he gave it some thought. "You could send letters or postcards from our journeys. Some read English; they would enjoy the tales." Kendo's smile returned, making me feel safe once again.

In a show of strength for both myself and any who might be watching, I put a backpack over my shoulder and with my walking cane under my arm, hobbled off toward the ship. Kendo needed to finish negotiation for his horse Thistle, then would bring the rest of our belongings.

Captain Tatianna was talking with one of the local elders at the ramp, but nodded as I approached.

"Welcome aboard," she said.

I pointed up at the foreign words. "Captain Tatianna, could you share with me the meaning of those words; I do not understand the language."

Her smile lit up her face. It caught me a bit off guard, but I welcomed it. "Young one, the three largest words read, 'Return, Reclaim, Remain.'" She then spoke the words in her language as the elder nodded. "It is a long story. From what I hear, you are from across the great sea."

She offered to take my backpack. Accepting the offer, I followed her up the wooden ramp. Questions flooded my mind, none of which I had the courage to ask. She directed me up a spiral staircase that seemed to reach to the very top of the ship. We paused on one of the landings.

"You can store your belongings in your room here. Kendo will stay with the crew down this hall. Shysie, if there is anything you need, you can ask anyone. Every member of my crew speaks English." With a parting smile, she left me alone in my room, deep inside a strange warship.

It wasn't more than a heartbeat later that I heard a muffled explosion, followed closely by a tremor radiating through the walls and floor. Then another came quickly after the first, followed by a loud bell ringing from above. Tucking my walking cane under my arm, I made my way to the door. I heard people shouting in a strange language and feet pounding up the spiral stairs. Dare I open the door or wait here? The floor shifted strongly. We were taking to the air.

"Kendo!" I struggled to maintain my balance and fumbled with the door latch.

"Stay inside!" a man on the other side hollered. Then his feet thundered away up the stairs.

With the ship rocking so hard to port there was no doubt we were in the air. What was happening? Another explosion, much closer it sounded, ripped through the air. The concussive force sent me reeling back.

Time was a blur and was filled with shouts, explosions, and most of all fear. My chest was tight with it, my stomach rising up into my throat. A part of me was angry that no one had come to check on me, and yet I'd been told to stay put. Another part was happy they'd left me alone.

Finally—perhaps an hour or more later—I worked up the courage to head out of the room and down the stairs. A man pushed past me heading up. He spoke not a word. Limping down to the observation deck, I saw the rolling hills fly by. We were a few hundred feet in the air. To me it felt too close to the ground with a ship this size. Inching toward the window, I looked around for a village or any sign of civilization.

There was none. Just trees and hills passing by. It was entrancing, and I started to relax.

The familiar voice of the captain snapped me out of a brief trance. "A few of the crew said you were cursed and wanted me to toss you out. A blonde airship albatross or such, they said." She added a smile, but I was not amused.

I stood as straight and tall as my one good leg would allow and looked her in the eyes, "How long before we return to the village?"

Her expression gave me the answer I feared was coming next, "Sorry, little one, we will not be going back to the village." Turning away and staring out the large observation deck windows, she added, "We should outrun the three U.S. airships chasing us by nightfall. We will then rise and turn southeast and should be well above them after midnight. If there is no sign of them by late tomorrow we will plan to make dock near Gulfport. From there you can take a train anywhere you wish."

The taste of bile came fast. There was no point arguing with her.

As darkness descended, I headed to my room to sulk. This was a sign I had no place in the New World. Maybe returning home to the farm and my family would be best. I could book passage on a train to the coast where I could catch a steamer to Europe.

The bells sounded as we approached the Gulfport landing. Men below grabbed the ropes as we rotated to point into the wind. The landing was rough.

My legs were feeling stronger, but the cane still helped as I limped down the ramp and toward the low, flat-roofed station building. It was a sea of bright gaudy clothes and parasols. My beaded white shirt, leather vest, and matching layered leather skirt was not the typical Gulfport fashion, it would seem.

Kendo wouldn't know where I ended up.

I approached a busy train station. All the trains heading west were full, according to the notices. From overheard conversations I discovered that some folks had been waiting for a ride west for more than a week. The only open tickets were eastbound. It was just the New World's way of saying: "Sheila go home."

I didn't spot anyone I recognized among the crowd, not even the captain. I guess it just wasn't meant to be.

So with a heavy heart and the last of my coin, I purchased a New York ticket and a loaf of bread. I had my belongings in storage in New York.

The month-long boat ride from New York made multiple stops before reaching Rome. The long voyage should have dulled the pain of missing Kendo, but all it did was birth a thousand regrets. Why hadn't I searched for him? Had I run away from him instead?

The train station at the docks in Rome brought back memories. Two years before I'd come here looking for a steamer to the New World . . . a grand adventure awaited. Now I was going home. I was sad, but it would be good to see my family.

"Kendo, forgive me," I wrote on the steamy window next to my seat. Taking out my journal, I started a letter to him that I knew I would never mail.

Dear Kendo,
    Not a day passes that I do not think of you.
Your smile, your silly ways, brought more joy to
my heart than you can imagine. My choice to go

home wasn't an easy one. I now know it was a
foolish one. My leg has healed completely. I no
longer need the cane, but I keep it with me as a
remembrance of the village. My arm is as good as
new thanks to you.

You saved me.

There are no words to thank you. I pray that
one day we can be together again. I would like
that very much. You still need to show me Texas;
you promised.

Love Eternal,
Sheila, Your Shysie

I fell asleep, hoping to dream of being in Kendo's
arms once again. The whistle sounded sometime later
and I jumped up collecting my things. I'd sent word to
my family, hoping they would meet me at the train station. If not, it was going to be a long walk. Pulling at my
beaded shirt, making sure it was properly tucked into
my leather skirt, I headed for the door. Greeting my father in my Indian apparel might help me talk about
Kendo and my hope of one day returning to Texas. My
father would not take this well.

Stepping off the metal stairs, I spotted my father's im-
posing form in the distance. His massive build, his short
blonde hair and matching beard left him unmistakable.
As I made my way toward him the crowd thinned. There
was a shorter man with a wide-brimmed black hat standing next to my father, too short to be one of my
brothers.

It was my heart and not my eyes that made the connection.

I felt unsteady, but walked closer. My eyes darted
from my father's broad smile to the man with his face
hidden by the shadow of his hat. My father made the

first move and rushed toward me, lifting me high into the air. Still clinging to my bags I gave him a big hug on my way down.

Before I could speak, act, or even think straight, my father spoke. "Sheila, you wouldn't believe the story this man has told me."

Tears flooded out as Kendo looked up with his loving smile. "Shysie, you are a hard person to find! It is fortunate you talked so much about your father's farm, and equally fortunate I found a fast steamer and an airship."

I rushed into Kendo's arms, burying my face in his shoulder, "Kendo, how? Why?"

I could feel father's hand patting me lightly on the back. "Little Sheila, it is good to have you home. We missed you dearly, but I must say I feel we have missed you less than this young man has."

Smiling at Kendo, I mouthed, "I love you."

Kendo looked from me to my father. "Shysie, this may have worked out for the best. Texas can wait. There was something I needed to ask your father." Tears welling in the corners of his eyes, he dropped to one knee. "Sheila Ann Marie VonShelton, will you marry me?"

Glancing quickly at my smiling father and back to Kendo, I blurted out: "Yes. Yes!"

Pulling Kendo back to his feet I hugged him close and whispered into ear, "You don't know what you are in for."

He whispered back, "Together we will find out."

I playfully bit his ear, "Don't ever call me by my full name again!"

His reply: "I love you, too."

HER FAITH IS FIXT

Robert E. Vardeman

Robert E Vardeman has written more than eighty science fiction, fantasy, and mystery novels. He recently completed the novelization of the Sony PlayStation game God of War 2. *He has had short stories in the previous Jean Rabe & Martin Greenberg anthologies* Terribly Twisted Tales, Timeshares *and* Steampunk'd *(with another steampunk story, "The Transmogrification Ray"). Vardeman's collected short stories can be found in* Stories from Desert Bob's Reptile Ranch, *with original stories published in e-format. He currently lives in Albuquerque, NM with two cats, Isotope and X-ray. One out of three of them enjoy the high-tech hobby of geocaching. For more info, check out www.CenotaphRoad.com.*

For him she plays, to him she sings
Of early faith and plighted vows;
She knows but matters of the house,
And he, he knows a thousand things.

Her faith is fixt and cannot move,
She darkly feels him great and wise,
She dwells on him with faithful eyes,
"I cannot understand; I love."

In Memoriam A.H.H.—Alfred, Lord Tennyson

David Somerset elbowed aside two counts and a baron to stand at the edge of the dance floor. He could not take his eyes off her slender form, her trim waist and flaring hips, her surging bosoms billowing up from the bodice of the expensive ball gown so whitely, so enticingly. She floated like a feather on a summer breeze, whirling about in the arms of some British lord. Somerset hardly noted her partner was fourth in line to the British throne.

All that mattered was the woman, how she moved so delicately with a precise dance step. He agilely dodged the spinning couples in their expensive finery as they waltzed with gusto, turned slightly to the side and thrust his hip between the young duke and the vision of loveliness.

"My dance, I think. Sorry to have been delayed," he said, staring into her bright blue eyes. She was the perfect height. Her button nose twitched, at first with irritation at his boldness and then a knowing smile curled her lips.

"He is right, Duke Richard. Thank you for taking his place."

"I say, old chap," the duke said, puffing up so hard that the medals on his chest rattled. "You can't do this. She's Lady Kendall and I—"

"I'm bewitched." Somerset slid his arm around her waist and pulled her close. Too close to be seemly, and he did not care, but Lady Kendall did. She stiffened one arm and held him at bay. Her movement was subtle, as befitting a woman aware of her social standing.

"I know you," the duke cried. "You're that explorer fellow Somerset. The one who was in Africa."

"Yes, I was there, but left Allan to his hunt," Somerset said. His feet moved of their own accord. Lady Kendall matched his whirling step perfectly. Leaving the duke lost and sputtering in the mass of the dancers, Somerset turned his full attention to the woman in his arms. He felt the heat from her body, and her scent caused his nostrils to flare. Pearls glistened in her perfectly coiffed midnight black hair, in daring contrast to her sky blue dress that—almost—matched her eyes.

"You are a bold fellow," she said. "I suppose that is necessary for a soldier of fortune."

"Adventurer," Somerset corrected. "Lady Kendall, I have just returned from the Dark Continent and immense danger hunting for lost treasure, but nothing I faced there caused my heart to beat as furiously as your beauty." He contrived to move her hand to his chest. Her fingers pressed lightly into his tuxedo jacket, then returned to his shoulder.

"Mr. Somerset—"

"David, please, my lady, call me David."

"Then you must call me Mathilda," she said as they spun on the floor at dizzying speed.

For Somerset, the world receded and the orchestra might have been playing without strings on their instruments. Mathilda was all there was in his world, and her voice commanded his head and heart.

"Mathilda, the instant I saw you I was smitten by your beauty."

"Don't become too smitten, David," she said. They spun again. "Do you see the man in the wheelchair?"

Somerset took in the indicated man with a quick glance.

"He is a genius," she said in a level voice. "He designed the *Thunderchild* and oversaw its construction."

"It was destroyed by the fighting machines," Somerset said. "I heard about it while still in Africa. I tried to return to fight the invaders, but leaving the Dark Continent proved more difficult than I thought. My zeppelin was disabled for long weeks due to gearing problems."

"Charles could help you with that. He not only designed the *Thunderchild,* but was given permission to examine the destroyed fighting machines. He has learned a great deal from them."

"Did he build his wheelchair using the alien technology?" As he swung about Somerset caught sight of the man rolling away without obvious motive power in the wheelchair.

"Oh, no, that is his design."

Somerset looked hard at her. "How is it you mention him when all I wish to hear is your sweet voice telling me you think of me as I do you?"

"Charles is Lord Kendall."

"Your . . . brother?" Somerset felt a coldness build in his belly. Mathilda's face remained impassive, but there could be no other explanation than that coming from her bow-shaped lips.

"My husband. Charles and I were married some months before the invasion."

"You deserve more," Somerset blurted. It was an outrageous utterance, but he did not apologize for it. He believed it with all his heart.

"I know nothing more," Mathilda said simply.

"Was he in that contraption when you . . . when you married him?"

"All my life he has been so afflicted," she said.

The music stopped and so did Somerset's heart.

"Are you happy with him?" His words rang out across a now silent ballroom.

"He is my husband." She curtsied and walked away, regal and unaware of the eyes following her.

Somerset started to follow but a hand pressed into his chest, holding him back.

"You are impertinent, sir," said a mustachioed colonel. "Lady Kendall is not available for your trifling."

"This is none of your business."

"It is, sir. I am devoted to Lord Kendall. Without his scientific acumen, we would have fallen to the damned aliens."

"Germs did them in," Somerset said, distracted. He watched as Mathilda reached out to put her hand on Charles Kendall's shoulder. The man maneuvered his wheelchair and surged away, leaving her forlorn to simply stare after him. How he ignored her! How he mistreated her! And how could they possibly be married if the nuptials were not properly consummated?

"Lord Kendall turned their own devices against them and saved my entire regiment from destruction before they succumbed to God's will."

Somerset felt a sting of conscience. He should have returned to defend his country, in spite of the mechanical problems he had experienced. If only he had quit Allan's expedition sooner! Let him hunt for his chimera on his own. Somerset had doubts King Solomon's mines would ever be discovered, let alone by Allan.

"What can you tell me of Lady Kendall?"

"That you should not distress her—nor speak to her again. Do so at your own risk." The colonel puffed up his chest to show the Victoria Cross testifying to his bravery.

"I have no quarrel with you, Colonel," Somerset said.

"Think twice about attempting anything foolish. Lord Kendall has installed devices both new and diabolical derived from those bloody foreigners' technology on the grounds of this estate. No place in all of England is better defended against intruders."

"He has a precious jewel to guard," Somerset said, watching as Mathilda disappeared, dejectedly trailing after her husband.

The colonel harumphed, made a point of pushing past Somerset, and then went to a cluster of other military officers. All glared at Somerset, but he was oblivious. The more he learned of the lovely woman, the more he felt for her. What life could she possibly have being sequestered behind a defensive ring of weaponry with a husband who ignored her and could not possibly tend to her womanly appetites?

He wended his way through the dancers as they began a new step, one of which Somerset was unfamiliar. It would not have been good to attempt dancing with Mathilda to this tune since he would have stepped on her dainty slippers. He stopped at the narrow corridor leading away from the ballroom. Servants glided here and there with silent efficiency, bringing trays of food from the kitchen to replenish that devoured by the hungry horde of revelers. Somerset stopped one, who looked at him with dull eyes.

"Lady Kendall, where did she go?"

The servant silently pointed to a door set flush with the wall. Somerset might otherwise have missed it in his hurry to once more speak with the object of his amorous interest.

"Thank you," he said, but the servant had already turned and stalked away, his gait slightly askew. Somerset wondered if Lord Kendall hired veterans and this was a war injury. He pushed the notion aside as he pressed his fingers against the indicated door and slid it open. Quickly entering the dim corridor beyond, he found a ramp leading into the bowels of the mansion. Tiny rubber marks showed where Lord Kendall had taken turns in the ramp too fast as he descended.

He envisioned Mathilda dutifully following, a few steps behind as if she were some sort of Indian servant. Quick strides brought Somerset to the base of the ramp twenty feet underground. The sound of the orchestra above was drowned out by moans of pleasure from ahead that gave Somerset pause. He knew, as a gentleman and scholar of natural science, that he ought to retreat. The passion he overheard could be only the result of a husband with his wife.

But how? Charles Kendall was confined to a wheelchair that seemed propelled by some mysterious source, perhaps a small steam engine or more likely a new type of battery.

Hating himself, Somerset sidled forward to peer around a doorjamb into a spacious, well-lit laboratory. His eyes went wide at the sight of a comely maid, her skirts hiked high to reveal naked thighs. She perched on the edge of a black-topped laboratory table, propped up on her hands and her feet on the edge of the table. Her face was a mask of stark pleasure. Charles Kendall's head was thrust between her spread legs.

Somerset's hands balled into fists. Lord Kendall was a philanderer, having his way with the hired help while ignoring his own wife.

The thought of Mathilda struck him like a hammer blow. He stepped back, his heart threatening to explode in his chest. Pressing against the wall, he struggled with the moral dilemma of informing her. He had only seen her for the first time that evening and yet it had been love at first sight. Somerset had never experienced such a powerful feeling before, yet recognized it for what it was. He would lay down his life for Mathilda.

He started back into the laboratory where the maid was giving voice to even more intense passions, all generated by the man in the wheelchair.

Somerset stopped when movement seen out of the corner of his eye froze him. Coming down the corridor, a tiny smile curving her bow-lips, was the object of his infatuation.

Not infatuation, love!

He motioned her away, not sure what to do. She came on, her steps short and precise, unhurried, inexorable.

"Please, no!" He dared not call out loudly, but his words carried.

"I am glad to see you once more, David."

He stepped to block her view of her husband and the maid. Whether through tardiness or some unconscious desire, he failed. Mathilda looked past him to the amorous scene inside the laboratory. Somerset grabbed her shoulders and propelled her away.

"I cannot believe he treats you in such a scandalous fashion," he said, emotion causing his voice to crack. "Let me take you away from this, my darling Mathilda. I know it is sudden, but my feelings for you are true. Tell me you share my affection. Say you do!"

"I do," Mathilda said softly. Her eyes remained dry, but she did not look away from where Lord Kendall and the maid continued to wrestle about in their ardor.

"He is a cad. You must admit it. You see how he . . ." Somerset could not continue to torment the lovely woman. The evidence of her husband's faithlessness was manifest.

"I see. She is new. Not like the one before."

"Before?"

"He seeks to replace me. I do not want that."

Somerset impulsively grabbed her hand and pulled. Her flesh was cool and for a moment she was nonresponsive. Then she allowed him to tug her along the corridor, away from the laboratory where the maid cried out in one last convulsive spasm of pleasure. Immediately thereafter came curious sounds that drew Somerset back.

"No, don't," warned Mathilda. "He is chaining her down."

"What!" Somerset could not believe his ears. "The bastard!" He stared hard at Mathilda in disbelief. "Has he done this to you?"

"He has only chained me to his work table. Never has he done all else he has to Yvette."

"Yvette is the maid?"

Mathilda nodded slowly. This decided Somerset. He had felt pangs of guilt stealing away the wife of another man, subverting her affection for her husband, but no more.

"Come with me. My zeppelin is not far away, at the corner of the estate. We can leave, go away, fly to the other side of the world where no one can ever find us. We can go to Australia and find a lawyer to file for a divorce."

"Your zeppelin is on the grounds? Oh, no." Mathilda put one slender-fingered hand over her mouth in horror.

"The *Good Queen Vickie* is a staunch airship. He will not be able to stop us once we launch."

"The grounds are outfitted with diabolical weapons Charles invented. For the crown, of course, but he tests them here."

"I've flown through aerial barrage and even fought off air pirates along the Moroccan coast. My zeppelin is an aerial dreadnought. Do not fear on this score."

"His weapons are advanced. Charles is so very clever with his mechanisms and rays." Mathilda looked back over her shoulder when they reached the foot of the ramp leading up to the ballroom. "Yvette . . ."

"She must endure his perfidy, just as you have. It is vital to escape him. He is a madman! How dare he insult and humiliate a woman such as you?"

"I was here first," Mathilda said. "He has no right to replace me with . . . with her."

Somerset tugged harder and got the woman walking at her steady, imperturbable pace. She would not be rushed. They reached the top of the ramp, and then retraced their way to the ballroom. Many of the guests had already departed, but not the colonel who had accosted Somerset earlier. The officer spotted the pair and immediately made his way through the remaining dancers, a stormcloud of anger turning his face florid.

"How do we get to the south lawn?" he asked. "I would avoid that gentleman."

"Colonel Sanderson? He is Charles' friend and often tests the weapons invented below." Mathilda turned back in the direction of the doorway leading to the underground laboratory.

Somerset interposed himself between her and the hurrying Colonel Sanderson, then used his full weight to move Mathilda away. The shock of what she had seen slowed her. He had to admire her courage to this point, seeing her husband's infidelity and accepting a stranger's succor.

If only she would accept his love. From the way she looked at him, he thought it would not be long before her passion matched his own.

"There," she said. "We can go out onto the veranda, around the grounds and find where your airship is grounded."

"I say, stop there. Stop, you blighter! Unhand Lady Kendall!"

The colonel ran now, his highly polished knee-high boots reflecting light. The click-click of his heels drew near as Somerset herded Mathilda ahead of him through the French doors onto the quiet veranda. Barely had they stepped outside when the officer overtook them.

"Unhand her, you bloody git," he exclaimed.

Somerset turned, took in the situation instantly, and acted. The colonel reached for his ceremonial sword but drew it only a few inches, stopped by a sharp, hard right uppercut to the chin. His eyes rolled up in his head and he fell backward, at attention, his hand still gripping the hilt of his dress sword.

"This way," Mathilda said, slipping lithely over the low stone railing to the ground. She began walking in her unswerving fashion. "I hear it."

Somerset strained but could hear nothing but the music from inside. Some gay laughter echoed out, but less now than before. When the colonel was discovered or came to from his thrashing, all hell would be out for lunch.

He hurried to catch up with Mathilda. The wind blowing across the damp lawn was chilly, but when he put his arm around her shoulders to hold her close and keep her warm, he found her delightfully unaffected by the wet breeze. As they rounded the corner of the mansion, he heard the low hum of the idling engines aboard his airship. Along with the low hum he heard a louder clanking.

"Here, climb aboard," he urged, handing her up into the gondola to his pilot, Zellick. When she stepped onto the folding stairs, the zeppelin tilted slightly under her added weight. Somerset wasted no time following her.

He kicked away the steps, not wanting to take the time to pull them inside.

"We goin' for a midnight ride, Skipper?"

"Mr. Zellick, prepare to launch immediately." His pilot caught the tension in his voice.

"Might be a problem," came the warning from the back of the gondola.

"What is it, Cochran?" he asked querulously. Somerset wanted to get aloft quickly. He saw strange black mounds at the corners of the mansion he could not explain. On the lawn itself were other devices, with protuberances that might be barrels. It never paid to jump to conclusions, but both the colonel and Mathilda had said Lord Kendall used the grounds as a test range. Escaping from air pirates or even the small arms fire from the ground in Africa had turned him wary. The hydrogen in the bags was not easily set afire thanks to special baffles he had installed. A bullet would cause leakage but not necessarily an explosion.

But a tracer round? The *Good Queen Vickie* would explode like the sun coming up over the Sahara. One instant it would be dark, the next there would be dazzling brightness.

"His name's Corrigan," the pilot said. Then he frowned. "Or might be Cadigan. He never gives me the same name twice."

"He just came aboard a few days back," Somerset quickly explained to Mathilda, who stood looking at the engineer curiously.

"He is missing an eye," she said.

"But he is a wizard with the electromagnets," Max Zellick said.

"I know electricity," the engineer said, adjusting his eyepatch and studying Mathilda closely to the point that

Somerset considered tossing the man overboard, expert engineer or not. "And I know mechanical things. We got problems with the reduction gears. Stripped off a few cogs along the way."

"We can repair later," Somerset said. "Launch now."

"You aren't hearing me," Corrigan called out, over the revving engines. "We try to launch and the gears will end up curls of brass."

"It doesn't matter," Somerset said. "Now, launch now!" The colonel had been discovered and brought back to his senses. His bull-throated roar assembled lesser officers and brought them racing toward the zeppelin.

"David, look. We must avoid those," Mathilda said, pointing. The dark lumps mounted on the corners of the mansion were not gargoyle decorations—he had not dared hope that was all they would be. Cannons with curious twisting barrels were revealed. "Never seen the like," Zellick said, "but I don't think they mean anything but harm to us." He continued to apply power to the engines. The motors hummed, but the grinding of gears grew louder.

From the rear of the compartment came Corrigan's cry, "They're done for! We lost the main gear that controls the rudder!"

"We'll rise directly in front of that thing if we can't use the rudder," Zellick warned.

The cannons began to glow with a blue light. The crackling discharge at the tip of one of the barrels warned of a searing bolt that would ignite the *Good Queen Vickie* like a moth fluttering into a gas lamp's flame. The officers fell back at the sight of another cannon powering up.

"Release her and you will be allowed to leave," the colonel called.

But Somerset looked to the roof and the electric cannon. Outlined by the constant discharge was a man in a wheelchair. No matter what Colonel Sanderson promised, Lord Kendall would use his weapon to destroy the zeppelin.

"He would not dare fire if you are aboard," Somerset said to Mathilda.

Still calm, she contradicted him. "Charles is a man who treasures his possessions above all else. He will never permit me to leave. Rather, he would see me destroyed first."

Somerset realized the truth. Lord Kendall would demolish the zeppelin with Mathilda aboard so he could continue his illicit frolicking with the maid unhindered by a wife.

"We can fight." Somerset was thrown into the woman as the zeppelin lurched. The sound of tearing metal told him that the reduction gear had failed catastrophically. He didn't need Corrigan's verification.

"We can break out the rifles, Skipper," Zellick said dubiously. He looked from Somerset to Mathilda and back. "If you think it's worth it."

"It is. I will give my life for hers!"

"You willin' to give the crew's, too?" The pilot stared at him, waiting for an answer.

"Everyone off who wants," Somerset said. "The lesser weight will allow the *Good Queen Vickie* to lift faster, and we might avoid the weapon. If I have to pilot her, by God, I will!" To gainsay him, the cannon on the mansion roof fired, sending a coruscating blast above the zeppelin. If they had risen straight up, the craft and all aboard would have been killed. And without the proper gear he could not maneuver past the cannon.

"I love you," Mathilda said softly. "I did not realize it was possible."

Somerset swept her into his arms and kissed her. She responded, just a little.

Their eyes met. A tiny smile came to her lips.

"I *do* love you. I've never loved Charles, though he told me to. That is why he built Yvette, to remedy this flaw."

"Built?" Somerset stared at her. "What do you—"

New lighting ripped closer to the zeppelin. Somerset threw open a window and leaned out to assess their danger. If Lord Kendall succeeded in lowering the muzzle elevation any more, he would surely destroy them.

Somerset turned back to Mathilda, only to find her gone. He raced to the entry and looked out onto the dark grounds of the estate, thinking she had darted away to surrender and save him by sacrificing herself. But she was nowhere to be seen. Then he heard a loud exclamation followed by vitriolic cursing from the engine room.

He ran the length of the gondola and flung open the door to see what Corrigan did to the woman.

Mathilda looked at him, a loving smile on her lips. Her fancy ball gown had been ripped open. He surged forward to throttle the engineer, and then saw Corrigan half buried in the gear box at the stern. Mathilda reached down and completed the destruction of her fine dress and exposed bare white flesh. He cried out as her fingers curled into claws and she ripped open her belly.

Gleaming brass gears turned silently on jeweled bearings in her abdomen. Stainless steel wheels spun and copper wires wound about in tight bundles like sinews. Mathilda grasped one unit in her gut and yanked hard. It popped free.

"Here," she said in a voice lacking control, modulation, the dulcet tones he expected from her sweet lips. She handed the gear assembly to Corrigan, who took it, still swearing a blue streak.

"What do I do?" he asked. He spoke not to Mathilda but Somerset.

Before Somerset could tell him to replace it in the woman's belly, she screeched out, "Save the airship. Save David." Mathilda turned and tried to lift her hand but it flopped about, uncontrolled. "Charles is expert with gears and automata."

"You?" Somerset stared, too shocked to say more.

"Yvette replaces me. She responds more like a human." The screech of metal tearing against metal caused him to clap his hands to his ears. "Use my sacrifice. Save David," she ordered the engineer.

Corrigan tore apart the geared mechanism and yanked out a steel wheel before discarding the rest of the useless unit. He dived back into the guts of the zeppelin's reduction gear box. In seconds a whir sounded and the airship quivered like a thoroughbred in the starting gate, ready for the race.

"Got maneuvering back," came Zellick's cry from the prow.

Somerset slid across the floor and caught Mathilda up in his arms. Her eyes were glassy now and her face had gone flaccid. He lifted her into his arms. She was far heavier than he expected, but then she was not human. Yet he thought of her as more human than Lord Kendall ever could be. He carried her forward and gently laid her on his bunk.

"My love, I will see that your . . . your gear is replaced. You will be good as new. Better!" Her blue eyes fixed on him and she nodded.

The zeppelin suddenly veered to the side, sideslipping as the rudder spun them away from Lord Kendall's electric cannon blast. Somerset pressed her down into the bunk as she tried to rise and said, "Stay. You'll be safe here," then rushed forward to join his pilot.

The zeppelin surged, prow up and the rudder swinging about in perfect response to Zellick's expert han-
dling. The airship soared high above the Kendall estate
and away, but Somerset saw their real danger.

Zellick cursed as the cockpit of the zeppelin began
glowing a blue-white.

"The cannon. The ray has locked on us!" the pilot cried.

Somerset sprang forward but was pushed aside power-
fully. Mathilda had risen from the bunk and interposed
herself between him and the energy beam. He grabbed her
shoulders to save his beloved, but the metal under her flesh
seared his hands. He recoiled, then fell to his knees as Zellick applied still more power to the zeppelin's motors.

Somerset cried out as he saw the flesh burn from
Mathilda, leaving behind a metal skeleton that welded
itself to the deck. Then the ray extinguished her form
entirely in a smoldering ruin; incongruously, her head
remained intact. Somerset grabbed it and held it. Her
lips moved, although her eyes stayed closed. Then he
dropped the head as the superheated metal burned his
palms past human endurance. It bounced once and tumbled out the still-open cockpit door, tumbling a thousand feet to the ground.

He did not think he was deluding himself when he
heard clearly Mathilda's last words: "I love you, David."

"We're above the estate and out of range. Where to,
Skipper?" Zellick asked.

He took a deep breath and said, "Steer the *Darling
Matty* across the Channel. We have worn out our wel-
come in England." He looked at the estate far below.
Dozens of rays swept the sky seeking to destroy him.
Revenge would be his. One day. One day he would make
Charles Kendall pay for killing Mathilda. But not today.

"Glad to leave it behind," Zellick said. "That's a cold,
wet, inhospitable land."

David Somerset spread out a chart and began plotting a course to Italy. There were always treasure maps to be found in the Vatican catacombs, and he was anxious to leave Charles Kendall and his unholy contraptions far behind, even if he could never forget the man's greatest creation.

KINETIC DREAMS

C.A. Verstraete

Christine Verstraete is a Wisconsin author who's written children's books, short fiction, and nonfiction. A previous story on Alva Edison and her famous brother, Thomas, appeared in Steampunk'd, *also from DAW Books. Christine says she wouldn't mind going back in time to Tudor England, post-plague, of course. Visit her website at www.cverstaete.com.*

Alva Edison woke and gazed in confusion at her surroundings. Gone was the familiar *clink-clink tick-tick* of the cogs and wheels moving in the kinetic clock at her bedside. In its place, the small bedside clock hummed.

Gone was the comforting drape of the lace canopy above her. Her heart pounded as she stared at the maroon spread draped over the bed. She slid from beneath the cover and stopped, frozen, at the cool touch on her arm.

"Another dream?"

Her heart slowed as recognition poured in. She let

out a deep breath, relaxing as her husband, Doctor Pierre LaBonet, caressed her arm and pulled her close. "Yes, yes. For just a second, I thought . . . Never mind. It all seemed so real."

"Maybe we have to change your prescription, dear Alva."

For a moment her mind floundered. She tried to grasp what he'd said. *Per—? Oh, he meant a script.* She sighed again. Would this confusion never end?

"No, no. I'll be fine. It was just a dream."

"All right, but we'll keep an eye on it. Now how about we forget that for awhile?"

She welcomed his embrace and the forgetfulness his love offered, if only for a while.

Alva stood at the bedroom vanity later, marveling at her reflection as she did every time she combed her hair or applied a hint of color to her eyes and lips, an action that still felt a tad scandalous. Everyone knew that only certain women painted their faces. Well, at least that was what she thought in relation to her "other life," the one she only remembered now in bits and pieces.

She sighed. So many things had changed. A vibrant, healthy woman in her prime looked back from the mirror, a far cry from the ailing, prematurely old woman she had once been. She glanced at her hands, the knots and crippling gone, and flexed her fingers without pain. Amazing.

Even though her dear brother, Thomas, explained over and over what had happened six months before, she still had trouble believing him. She knew some things seemed, well, odd and different, and some things she simply could not remember after that nasty fall. Her arthritis had improved almost overnight from the new medications. And the rest? She didn't want to be mean, but she couldn't help but laugh when he'd brought up the subject again yesterday when they met for tea.

"Alva, I know you were pretty battered from the fall, but you still don't recall how we climbed aboard Mr. Wells's kinetic flying time machine and ended up here?" he'd asked. "You don't remember us making the adjustments so it worked properly?"

"Thomas, I think you've been hiding away far too long in that basement working on your projects! You need to get out more. A flying machine? Yes, I'm a whiz at math, but since when do I tinker with machines? How quaint!"

She shook her head at his crestfallen look. Her dear brother had to be tired from all the late hours he spent with his experiments. She worried about him, especially since he kept coming up with different takes on things that had already been invented. That steam-powered washer, for instance, and the oddly shaped light bulb. Why reinvent the wheel? She vowed to ask Pierre if he knew any charming young nurses they could invite over for dinner to meet her brother. They needed to find someone Thomas could spend time with instead of his being holed away constantly in that workshop.

The ring of the doorbell interrupted her musing. Finished with her primping, Alva rushed downstairs, wondering if Pierre had come home early. He'd been so thoughtful lately. She opened the door and gasped at sight of her brother, his hair mussed, his face and coat covered with soot and dirt.

"Thomas, what happened?"

He pushed his way in, his face worried. "Alva, we have a problem."

"We?"

"I need your help. Something's wrong with the machine. I've tried everything I can think of to fix the failed timing mechanism. I need you to help me make the adjustments."

"Machine? What machine?" She looked at him, perplexed. "Thomas, maybe you should talk to Pierre. Perhaps those chemicals you're breathing in that workshop of yours are making you ill."

He muttered a curse under his breath. "Look, I know how happy you and Pierre have been these past six months. That's why I've left you alone and let you enjoy your home as newlyweds. But I have no choice this time. I need your help."

"Dear brother, I'll help you anyway I can, even if I'm not quite sure what you're talking about. I know my memory hasn't been good, but you're really worrying me with this outlandish talk about flying machines and such. You have to watch what you say; someone might take it the wrong way."

"Just come with me. Please? I'll explain on the way."

She took in his disheveled appearance and hesitated but a moment. His eyes pleaded with her. Wetting a finger, she smoothed her brother's hair, rubbed the dirt from his face, and fixed his coat before grabbing her hat. "All right, I'll go with you."

The two-block walk to the towering brick building her brother called home would've been a treat if Thomas weren't so agitated. The last of the summer pansies smiled from pots in front of the other brick buildings. The streets sparkled after the morning clean-up. Even the sight of the two-seater, black steam-engine cars sitting at the curb that once seemed such a novelty made her smile.

She nodded in greeting and poked Thomas to tip his hat at the businessman striding by on a stately black Tennessee Walking horse. "Thomas, smile." He tipped his hat and fell back into his private funk.

Pausing on the sidewalk, Thomas looked first one

way, then another, before leading her to the door on the side of the building. He unlatched the padlock, pushed the door open, and pulled the chain hanging from the ceiling. The fluoresced bulb flicked on with a whoosh.

Locking them in, he grabbed a handheld torch and led her down the steps. The torch gave a bright, clear ray of light. *Flashlight*, she corrected herself, a word that still sounded funny on her tongue.

"This way."

She followed him down one long hall and then another. He unlocked and relocked a heavy set of wooden doors, then continued. "It's in the next room. Are you all right?"

She sneezed in response. "I'm fine, Thomas, except for the dust."

The next set of doors took Thomas longer to open as he hunted through his keys. The trio of locks opened with a click. Alva's questions about his extreme carefulness, maybe even paranoia, vanished as he gave her the light.

"Go on while I lock these behind us."

The light bounced off the device ahead, creating a golden glow that made Alva gasp and instinctively place her free hand over her womb in protection. Awed, yet curious, she stepped closer, trying to make sense of the majestic machine that loomed before her. It gleamed as if with an inner fire, the dash fitted with a breathtaking array of knobs and dials. Two bronzed arches flowed like liquid across the two seats to the back, where more knobs, levers, and buttons were arranged. The back deck held what looked like a giant fan fronted by a large storage box. Her mouth gaped open as she took it all in.

"Thomas. . . then, you mean, y–your stories are true?"

His gaze held hers. "Alva, never would I lie to you, ever. Yes, it's true." He directed her to sit while he went to the table in the corner. "I'll get us some tea and maybe we can figure this out, and hopefully jog your memory."

Alva sipped the tea he offered, then set her cup on the table as he reiterated past events. "All you remember when you woke up in the hospital, besides your charming doctor, was that you fell, right?"

She felt her face warm as she nodded. "I had nightmares for months about falling from the sky and landing in a cornfield. The dreams never made sense."

"How could they?" he asked. "When you see horse drawn and steam-driven vehicles on the roads, how could I explain that there really is another place in which airships fly powered by kinetics and steam? You already doubted my story of how you helped me adjust this flying machine. I know it's hard to believe that's how we came here, that we really do have another life."

Alva closed her eyes as the mathematical calculations ran through her mind. "I know the probabilities ... I just never connected my memory lapses and how things sometimes felt *wrong*."

He nodded and welcomed her to take a closer look, his mood lighter. "I knew at some point I'd get you to see. I knew it!"

"Yes, I understand, but I still don't remember it all. I guess that doesn't really matter."

"It'll come. Right now, I need your help. There's something I haven't told you."

"Oh?"

"I've been back and forth, several times."

Her eyes widened. "Now, brother, this is going too far." It was like when they were children, him always trying to take advantage of her gullibility. Her anger rose. "Thomas, I'm not a child any more. Don't do this to me."

"I'm not lying. Here."

Her eyes fell on the colorful newspaper he held out.

So unlike the black and white papers here with their flat, monochrome images. Headlines and colors screamed for attention.

"So different," she murmured. "So modern, but. . . "The feeling of familiarity faded when she spotted the headline:

Defore Jailed by Puritans; Charged with Witchery.

Thomas cleared his throat and explained, "There's the problem. Do you recall the huge change when the Inventors gained power over the Puritans? We were finally able to invent freely again?"

She shrugged. "No, but it sounds interesting."

"Defore tried to take over while I was here. He made the mistake of talking about my time travel and got caught up in a wave of witch-hunting hysteria. It's pushed all the inventors back underground. I was going back to help; then this happened."

Alva rose and eyed the machine, now noticing the pockmarks and punched-in sections of the metal for the first time. Black scorch marks wriggled around the dials like snakes.

"Smoke poured out when I started the machine up again. I've checked everything." His gaze held hers. "Alva, I know, you haven't been yourself, but your abilities are still there, just a little rusty. Will you take a look? Please?"

Despite her uneasiness, she couldn't resist inspecting the gleaming machine. Thomas opened the toolbox stuffed with bulbs, wires, and tools. She studied the dials and opened the compartment doors, her mind on autopilot as she tested wires and changed fuses. She realigned a cog here, tightened a wheel there, making adjustments without knowing why she did them, but instinctively knowing they were right. A few minutes later, she nodded and stepped aside.

"Okay, try it."

"Are you sure?"

She stared at him, hands on hips. "Now you doubt me?"

He smiled and pushed the button on the dash. The dials spun and lights sprang to life. The machine rattled and then steadied, the machination humming, the cogs falling into place with a *click*, a *clack*, and a high-pitched *ting*.

He let the machine run while he pulled over a leather bag, the sides bulging at the seams. "Alva, I'm afraid I have something else to tell you. The reason the machine went out of adjustment was that I accidently bumped the lever in mid-flight. It got stuck and sent me somewhere else, six months in the future."

A cold feeling settled over her. "Whose future, where?"

"Mine—and yours."

"Six months from now, you visited?"

"Yes."

"And you didn't tell me—"

"I tried to tell you before . . . before you got smitten with the doctor. Tried to tell you before you married him. But you were so happy and—"

The feeling of dread threatened to choke her as she decided whether to take the paper he held out. "B–but that doesn't mean something has to happen, or that it will happen, right? This paper from the future . . . it might not mean anything."

A shrug was the only answer he could offer. "I don't know that it will happen, any more than I know that this machine won't misfire and go hurtling into an unknown dimension. But it's still worth considering, isn't it?"

With a nod, she took the paper, unfolded it, and gasped at the black-and-white image before her. She read the headline, *Doctor and Family Found Dead After Break-In*. She didn't believe it—couldn't—yet it still struck fear in her heart. She folded the paper, not daring to read further, not wanting to learn things that she had no business knowing yet.

The sound of footsteps made her jump, and she thrust the paper at her brother. "Here, take this. Hide it."

"There's no need," the man said.

Alva gasped, stunned to see her husband come toward her. "Pierre? What are you doing here? How did you know?"

He wore a heavy black overcoat, his doctor's bag in one hand, their large trunk trailing behind. He set everything down and hugged her close.

"I hope you're not upset. Your brother told me everything. Of course, I didn't believe him, not until he showed me the machine."

She stepped back, her arms crossed in anger. "Y–you knew, yet you let me continue to wonder if I was losing my mind?"

"No." He reached out and took her hand. "I only learned of the machine two days ago, but I couldn't say anything yet. Not until everything was arranged. I went to the bank, withdrew some money for us and packed what we needed. I brought your jewels, the pictures of your parents, and your box of mementos. We have a couple changes of clothing and my medical supplies. It's enough for us to start over. I'm hoping that however this works, we'll be able to get the bonds and extra cash I left in our safe deposit box."

Alva staggered over to the chair, plopped down, and held out the paper. "You read this?"

He nodded.

"Then–then it must be true!" she cried. "It must be real or why else would you be here? We're doomed."

He came to her side and tenderly held her hand. "Alva darling, listen to me. That doesn't mean it will happen. As a man of science, I still have trouble totally believing all this—flying and time travel and what-not." He paused, waving a hand at the machine, "But I also can't doubt what my eyes are seeing. We have no choice. We have to take the chance that we can change the future. We must leave."

Her resistance died as he pulled the heavy cloak from the trunk and wrapped her in it, his hand pausing to caress the babe resting in her womb. "You'll need this. Thomas told me how cold it was his last trip."

Alva huddled next to him wanting, no, needing to ask the one thing she yearned to know most. "Pierre, the baby? Will it be okay? Please tell me."

"Yes, everything will be fine. You didn't read the story?"

She shook her head. "No. I–I couldn't. I want you to tell me."

Her face glowed as he whispered in her ear. Minutes later, Thomas took their trunk and bags, set them inside the storage box, and locked it. "Are we ready?"

Alva's hand tightened in her husband's strong grasp as they buckled themselves in, she sitting on Pierre's lap while her brother fastened two large belts around both of them.

That done, Thomas made one last adjustment to the meters and checked the notches on the time indicator before he fastened himself in."I don't know how everything with Defore will be resolved, but I've set the timer many months past the year we first left and beyond the time of the events in that newspaper, so we should be safe."

Alva leaned against her husband, her heart fluttering as flashes of that first ride returned. This time the stakes

were so much higher. "Pierre, maybe we shouldn't. . ."
Her words were swallowed in a plume of thick, black
smoke and an ear-shattering explosion as the machine
roared to life and disappeared.

A smile of contentment lit Alva's face as she helped her
eight-month-old son, Benjamin, finish his lunch. "Eat
your carrots, Benny, then we'll go see your daddy and
uncle. You want to do that?"

The little boy gave a big gap-toothed grin, his face
smeared with orange. "See Da, Unc!"

After wiping the boy's mouth, she picked up the in-
tercom phone and called the nanny upstairs. "Anna,
please bring down Benny's sailor suit. We'll be going to
the president's office."

She set down the receiver, still amazed at the recent
turn of events. Some things remained a blur, but the yells
of Thomas's rival Defore after he was sentenced to death
for plotting to assassinate President Thomas Edison and
Vice President Pierre LaBonet still rang in her ears.

The Inventor's Party was again in power and new de-
velopments like the arthritis medicine she took daily not
only improved her life, but offered relief to thousands of
other sufferers.

The incredible new steam-powered, kinetic land vehicles Thomas designed had caught the public's imagination and were being built from his plans. His kinetic
talking machine was also being reviewed for global use.

Alva caressed her ballooning stomach hidden beneath the flowing Victorian gown's folds and smiled. She
anxiously awaited the impending birth of her second
child, a daughter. Life was good.

FOR THE LOVE OF COPPER

Marc Tassin

Marc Tassin was enthralled by books from a very early age, and he often considered trying his hand at writing. Then, a few years back, Marc started attending the Gen Con Writer's Symposiums. Inspired by the advice and support offered by the panelists, Marc stopped thinking about writing and started actually writing. Since then, Marc has published numerous short stories, articles, and game materials and has loved every minute of it. Marc lives in a small town just outside of Ann Arbor, Michigan, with his wife Tanya and their two children.

The flickering lamp barely illuminated the little workshop, but it was enough for Christopher to admire his work. Ellie lay stretched out on the workbench's oil-soaked boards, little more than a skeleton of brass and wood, yet a thing of beauty to his eyes.

"Are you finished, Christopher?" Ellie asked in her tinny voice.

"For tonight, Ellie," Christopher replied.

He ran his hand over the feminine curves of Ellie's frame, feeling the gentle vibration of the spinning gears that lay hidden among the struts and crossbars. He wished that the queen hadn't called the Professor to the mainland to help with the war effort. How proud he'd be. More than once the Professor had commented on Christopher's talent. The fact that he'd left Christopher in charge of maintaining the household machines in his absence was evidence of his faith in him.

But of course, it wasn't the Professor that Christopher hoped to please with Ellie.

"Will I be able to walk now?" Ellie asked.

"I hope so," Christopher said, turning his thoughts back to the task at hand. "Assuming I've attached your legs properly, that is."

Placing one hand on the frame of her thigh, he gave one of the struts a pull with the other. It didn't give. Satisfied, he said, "Let's engage the drive, and we'll see if I got it right."

Christopher leaned close and slipped one arm under Ellie's shoulders. He pulled her to his chest, and reached around behind her with his other hand. He probed her lower back until at last he found the switch. With a click, Ellie's drive box rattled to life. The gyroscopes spun up to a steady drone, and the hundreds of interlocking gears clicked and clattered like metallic rain. He felt Ellie move in his arms, so he slowly released her. With awkward, jerking motions, Ellie sat straight.

"I feel strange, Christopher," Ellie said. She turned her lovingly sculpted copper face toward him. Her eyelids clicked open and shut, open and shut, over blue porcelain eyes.

"Well, that isn't too surprising," Christopher said, taking a seat on a paint-spattered stool. "It'll take some time for you to adapt to your new center of gravity, and your joints are probably a bit stiff. If it's too bad, we can loosen them up later."

Ellie turned on the bench and hung her legs over the side. She looked at them and experimentally raised and lowered one, then the other. Tipping her head, she studied her feet and pointed her metal frame toes.

"I like them," Ellie said. "Thank you, Christopher."

Christopher smiled. "You're welcome, Ellie."

Ellie continued to look at her toes, wiggling them one at a time. Christopher could hear the discs of the reason engine in her head whirring away.

"Do you think she'll like me, Christopher?" she asked.

The question was one Christopher had asked himself each time he worked on Ellie. If Eleanor liked Ellie, it might mean the start of . . . . Christopher pushed the thought away. He didn't dare hope. As Mrs. Arbogast, the estate's housekeeper, so often pointed out, he and Miss Eleanor weren't cut from the same cloth. "Every person has their place," she'd say. But he had to try.

"Of course she'll like you," he insisted.

"How do you know?" Ellie asked.

Christopher stepped back over to the workbench. He ran his fingers along the extension rods on Ellie's neck, checking for faults. "Well, in many ways, she's you. I patterned the template discs in your reason engine on Miss Eleanor's personality. You two will have lots in common."

"Oh, that's nice," Ellie said.

Christopher looked her over again. He frowned when he noticed Ellie swaying a bit.

"Maybe we should save the walking for another day," he said. "I'd like to recalibrate the gyroscopes first."

"Very well," Ellie answered.

Christopher smiled at Ellie. For a time he'd almost lost hope. It had taken much longer than he'd expected to construct her. Maintaining the hundreds of machines on the island took most of his day, leaving him with just a few hours each night to work on her.

The reason engine alone took almost four months. If not for the Professor's notes, Christopher might not have gotten it working at all. He had known that he wasn't allowed in the Professor's study, but Ellie was too important. He simply had to get her working, and the Professor knew more about machines than anyone Christopher had ever met.

Christopher sighed and looked out the window. He could just make out the feeble lights of the mainland. He wondered how much longer the queen would need the Professor's help and when he could finally come home.

"Do you miss him?" Ellie asked.

Christopher took a long, deep breath before he turned from the window. He started picking up tools and putting them away.

"Yes," he said. "I miss him very much."

Ellie placed her hands in her lap, hinged fingers intertwined, and looked at Christopher. She tipped her head gracefully to one side and said, "Perhaps you could visit him."

Christopher shook his head. "No, that isn't possible. The queen banned all sea traffic nonessential to the war effort. And the dirigibles don't land any longer. They just drop supplies as they pass."

Putting away the last of the tools, he brushed his hands on his pants and walked over to the table by the door where Eleanor's musiphone sat. The simple, polished wood box was a London Marvel Company creation that played hundreds of different songs, each as clear as if the orchestra were right in the room. It was one of Eleanor's favorite diversions, but it had broken down earlier in the week.

"I need to take this to Miss Eleanor," he said. "I promised. Wait for me here, Ellie, and don't try to walk. I'll be back soon."

"I'll wait for you, Christopher," Ellie said.

Christopher knocked quietly on the library's open door. The room was silent except for the soft hiss of the gas lamps. Their flickering flames sent shadows dancing across the thick oriental rugs and up the heavily laden bookshelves. More than once he'd heard Mrs. Arbogast thanking God that the Saxons hadn't cut the gas lines out to the islands. "Mark my words, Christopher," she'd said. "If those barbarians attack, that'll be the first sign."

Eleanor sat in one of the tall wing-backed chairs near the fireplace. With her back to the door, all Christopher could see was one fine arm. Even this slightest vision of the professor's daughter set his heart to pounding. For a time he waited, savoring even this simple view, fearing that if she became aware of him she might fade like a dream.

"Is there someone there?" she asked.

Christopher jumped. The musiphone slipped in his hands, but at the last moment he managed to catch it. Adjusting his grip on the machine, he took a deep breath, steadied himself, and padded into the room. He crossed the ornate rugs, the sound of his footsteps swallowed by the thick pile. He stopped just behind her chair. She hadn't turned to see who was there.

"I," he began, his voice sounding thin and weak to his own ears. He cleared his voice and tried again. "I finished the repairs on your musiphone, Miss Eleanor."

Eleanor leaned over and looked around the wing of

the chair. Christopher's breath caught in his chest. The light on her skin glowed like spring sun, and her gentle blue eyes glittered as if touched by the stars. Her raven hair was pulled back in a tight bun, highlighting the elegant curves of her face, and the ribbon of her pale pink lips reflected the perfection of the Creator.

"Thank you, Christopher," she said, smiling kindly. "You can set it over here on the table."

Christopher stepped around her chair and set the musiphone on the long, low table in front of her. As he positioned it and made sure it sat level, he dared another glance at Eleanor. She leaned her cheek against the wing of the chair and gazed out the tall window, a look of exquisite sadness on her face.

Christopher's heart ached to see her like this. When her father left, a deep, unabated loneliness had taken hold of Eleanor. With the sea lanes closed, she couldn't even go to the mainland to visit the other girls, making her a veritable prisoner on the island. He knew it wasn't his place to speak to her without permission, but Christopher couldn't help himself.

"Is everything all right, miss?" he asked softly.

"Oh, it's nothing, Christopher." She dabbed at the corners of her eyes with an embroidered handkerchief.

When she lifted her hand, Christopher noticed a letter on her lap. The Professor's dramatic spider-web script covered the paper. Christopher swallowed hard.

"Is all well with the Professor?" he asked, trying to keep the worry from his voice for Eleanor's sake.

Eleanor shook her head and traced the edge of the letter with her finger.

"He's fine," she said, her voice cracking. "The queen just wishes to retain his services a bit longer."

"That means . . . your birthday . . ."

"It's fine." She took a long, shaking breath. "We all need to do our part."

Before Christopher could say anything else, heavy footsteps rang out from the hall. A moment later, Mrs. Arbogast swept into the room. When she spotted Christopher, she narrowed her eyes and placed her fists on her ample hips. He bowed his head and put his hands behind his back.

"Christopher," she said sharply. "What are you doing in here?"

Eleanor stood and turned to face the door. "It's all right, Mrs. Arbogast. He was just returning my musiphone."

Mrs. Arbogast stiffened and performed a hurried curtsey.

"My apologies, Miss. I thought you'd gone to bed," Mrs. Arbogast said, recovering. "I was just coming to fetch the dishes."

"That's fine. No apologies are necessary." Eleanor turned to Christopher. "Thank you again, Christopher. You may go."

He nodded quickly. As he hurried away, Eleanor flashed him a conspiratorial grin. He flushed, his heart leaping. As he silently closed the door behind him, he heard Mrs. Arbogast say, "I'm sorry, Miss. Christopher should know his place. I'll speak to him."

Christopher leaned against the door, pressing his ear to the crack.

"You shouldn't be so hard on him, Mrs. Arbogast," Eleanor said. "Anyway, he's really quite sweet."

Christopher grinned hard enough to make his ears hurt. Almost skipping, he hurried off to the workshop. He'd have Ellie ready by Eleanor's birthday if he had to work all night, every night, for the next week.

*   *   *

Kneeling before Ellie, Christopher reached around and placed one hand on the small of her back. With his other hand, he pressed gently on her abdomen. A soft click told him that the last of the plates that made up her skin was secured. Standing, he stepped back and looked her over.

"How do I look, Christopher?" Ellie asked.

"You look beautiful," he said, smiling. He stepped over and gently rubbed a smudge from her copper cheek with his thumb. "Eleanor is going to love you."

For a moment, he let his hand linger there. He could feel the soft vibration of the reason engine's discs whirring away inside.

"You like her very much, don't you, Christopher?" Ellie said.

"Who? Miss Eleanor?" Christopher stepped back to lean against the workbench, his cheeks flushing.

"Yes," Ellie said. "She is very special to you, isn't she?"

"Yes. Yes she is."

"Am I special to you?" Ellie asked.

Christopher laughed. "Of course you are, Ellie. In fact, I'm going to miss our conversations. I quite enjoy talking to you."

He hadn't expected it, but as Eleanor's birthday drew closer the thought of seeing Ellie go weighed on him. He placed a hand on Ellie's shoulder, letting his fingers drift over the smooth curves of her metal skin.

"Yes, I'll miss you very much, Ellie," he said.

"That's very kind, Christopher," Ellie said. "I'll miss you."

For a moment they stood in silence, Christopher and his creation, alone in the half-darkness of the workshop.

"Oh!" Christopher exclaimed. "I almost forgot. I have something for you."

He dashed to the closet, pulled it open, and lifted out a hat-box sized package.

"What is it, Christopher?" Ellie asked.

Christopher, beaming, brought the box over to Ellie.

"Go on, take it," he said. "It's for you."

Ellie tilted her head to one side, then reached out with her long, graceful hands and took the box. Every motion spoke of precision in both action and purpose, and Christopher felt pleased with how quickly her reason engine had adapted to motion. Ellie, balancing the box expertly in one hand, removed the lid. She tilted her head the other way as she examined the contents.

"Do you like it?" Christopher asked.

Reaching into the box, Ellie took out the dress. It unfurled before her, the hem swishing across her toes.

"I like it very much."

"I made it myself," Christopher said. He reached out and took hold of the edges of the dress. "Here, let me help you put it on."

The process was a bit awkward, as neither of them had any experience with putting on dresses, but after a few failed attempts, and more than a little laughing, they managed it. Ellie turned her back to him, and Christopher slowly fastened the long row of buttons from the copper cleft of her buttocks up to her neck.

When he'd finished the last one, Ellie turned back to face him. The dress bunched a bit around her waist, so Christopher reached out and smoothed the fabric.

"How do I look?" Ellie asked.

"You look stunning," Christopher said. "Miss Eleanor is going to love you."

Ellie did not reply.

"Come in," Eleanor called when Christopher knocked.

He opened the door just enough to enter, then closed it behind him.

"Excuse me, Miss Eleanor," he said. "Do you have a moment?"

Eleanor stood near the window, looking out across the sea.

"Of course, Christopher," she said, without turning. "Do come in."

He walked over to her side. As he approached, he noticed a single, half-eaten piece of cake sitting on a china plate. An empty tea cup sat on a saucer beside it, and under the saucer he saw a birthday card. It was open, and the writing on it was Mrs. Arbogast's, not the Professor's.

"The fighting is getting worse," she said.

"Excuse me?" Christopher asked.

"The fighting," she said, as she turned to him. "It's getting worse. They say the Saxon navy is planning a major attack."

She walked over to the little table, gathered up the hoops of her skirt, and sat on one of the small cushioned chairs. Absent-mindedly, she played with the little silver spoon in the tea cup, tinkling it against the delicate china.

"There are even rumors that they're planning an invasion," she added, looking out the window again.

Christopher struggled to find something to say.

"Mrs. Arbogast says they wouldn't do that," he offered weakly. "She says we've got many more soldiers, and more money, and much better equipment thanks to men like . . ."

He stopped himself too late. Eleanor looked up at him, sadness painted on her face.

". . . like my father," she finished for him. "Yes, I know. It's unlikely he'll be home before Christmas now, what with things as they are."

For a time, she said nothing more, and Christopher

remained silent. At last, Eleanor looked up and smiled a sad smile. "I'm sorry, Christopher. I shouldn't go on about such things. You had something to tell me?"

Christopher swallowed hard and wrung his hands. He fought back a shiver before speaking. "I made you something for your birthday, Miss Eleanor."

"You did?" Eleanor's smile took on an air of real happiness. The sight warmed Christopher's heart and eased his nerves. "Why, Christopher, you didn't need to do that."

"Oh, it was my pleasure, Miss Eleanor."

Eleanor rose and stepped over to him. As she drew close he imagined that he could feel the soft tickle of her breath on his skin.

"Well, what is it? You have me quite excited." She looked to see if he was hiding something in his hands.

Christopher hurried over to the door. Grasping the handle, he pulled it open, and Ellie stepped into the room.

"Christopher!" Eleanor gasped. "That's incredible."

Eleanor rushed over and danced a circle around Ellie, looking Christopher's creation up and down. Christopher grinned foolishly.

"It's for me?" she said, unable to take her eyes off Ellie.

"Yes, Miss."

"How on earth did you manage this?" she asked.

"The Professor taught me quite a bit before he left. I built her mostly using spare parts from the workshop, although I saved up my wages to buy a few pieces from the Marvel Company. They arrived just before the queen closed the shipping lanes."

"It's wonderful," Eleanor said. "What does it do?"

"Oh, anything really," Christopher said, coming over to stand beside Eleanor. Christopher struggled to stay focused. Standing so close to Eleanor was almost more than he could bear.

"I know you've been terribly lonely here," he continued, "so I thought you might want someone to keep you company. Another lady, that is."

"Keep me company?" Eleanor said, looking at Christopher in wonder.

"Yes. She talks, you see. Say 'Hello' to Miss Eleanor."

"Hello, Miss Eleanor," Ellie said.

Eleanor squealed with excitement. "What do you call it, Christopher?"

"Um, her name is Ellie," Christopher said. "She knows lots of things. She can talk about stories or politics or music or just about anything really. And she can play games and read and knit and do a lot of other things too. And if she doesn't know how to do something, you can always teach her."

"I'm looking forward to being your friend, Miss Eleanor," Ellie said, and she performed a perfect curtsey.

Eleanor lifted her hands to her mouth. When she turned to Christopher, she had tears in her eyes.

"Oh, Christopher," she gasped. Leaping forward she wrapped her arms around him, laid her head on his chest, and hugged him tight. The feeling of her pressed against him, her delicate hands on his back, her cheek to his heart—it was the most wonderful thing he'd ever experienced. Without thinking, he put his arms around her as well. He wished, desperately, that the moment would never end.

"Miss Eleanor," Ellie interrupted. "Would you like to play a game?"

Christopher felt a sense of helpless panic as Eleanor pulled away.

"Oh, yes, Ellie," Eleanor said. "That would be wonderful."

Eleanor turned to Christopher one last time, and going up on tip-toes she kissed him on the cheek.

"Thank you so much, Christopher," she said. "This is the most wonderful birthday present anyone has ever given me."

With that, she spun around, ran to Ellie, and took her by the hand.

"Come on, Ellie!" she cried, and the two scurried out of the room.

For a long time after they left, Christopher just stood there, unable to move. He didn't know how he felt, but the emotions that caught in his throat were a bit like joy but strangely like sadness at the same time. He couldn't have dreamed of a better response from Eleanor, yet he felt as if he'd lost something very important.

At last, with nothing else to do, Christopher returned to his workshop.

The boom that awakened Christopher rattled the windows so violently that one of them cracked. Christopher leaped from his little cot in the corner of the shop and stumbled over to the window. The water between the island and the mainland was afire with specks of wavering orange light. At first, his half-sleeping mind thought that it was odd for there to be so many fireflies this time of year, but then he understood.

Ships. An armada of ships.

Christopher raced across the room and grabbed a lighting stick from the embers of the stove. He lit his little lantern and tossed the stick back into the fire. He ran to the door, shoved his feet into his boots, and threw on his coat. Another boom shook the workshop and sent dust raining down from the rafters.

Christopher bolted out the door. The distant thunder of a hundred churning steam engines thrummed in the air. Streaks of fire tore across the sky. From some-where far away, he heard a woman scream. He sped to the house, nearly falling twice in his haste before he reached the back door. He didn't knock or ring the bell but charged into the darkened kitchen. Reaching for one of the gas lamps, he tried to light it, but no gas came out.

"Mrs. Arbogast!" he shouted.

His voice echoed in the darkness. No reply came.

"Eleanor!" he cried.

Christopher charged down the hall and into foyer, but he found only darkness and silence. Another explo-sion thundered, and the foyer chandelier tinkled and swayed. Up the stairs he ran, cringing at the sound of more explosions, each one nearer than the one before.

When he reached Eleanor's room, he found the door open. Forgetting his place he rushed in. "Eleanor! Elea-nor! Where are you?"

"She isn't here," a soft, tinny voice said from the darkness.

Christopher spun around and found Ellie sitting on a chair in the corner. She was wearing one of Eleanor's day dresses and had her hands folded neatly in her lap.

"Ellie!" Christopher cried. He rushed over and pulled her to her feet. "The island is under attack! Where is Eleanor?"

"They left not long ago," Ellie said. "A man in a navy uniform came. He said they had a dirigible and were evacuating everyone."

"What?" Christopher said, aghast. "But they didn't wake me. Where are they going, Ellie?"

"I heard him say the airship was moored by the old boathouse," Ellie said.

Christopher shot from the room. He could hear El-lie's footsteps behind him. He had to get to the boathouse before the dirigible left. What if he were already too late? What would the Saxons do to him?

Down the stairs, across the foyer, and out the front door he ran. He sprinted down the lane, his feet crunching on the gravel, punctuated by thunderous explosions from the water's edge. A fiery flash went up somewhere on the mainland, filling the sky with orange light. Christopher ignored it and hastened along the winding trail.

The flash of another explosion lit the sky, and he spotted the dirigible, just beyond the trees. It was still quite low, and he felt hope rise in his chest.

"Wait!" he shouted, still running. He knew it was foolish, that they couldn't hear him from there, but he was unable to remain silent. "Please! Wait for me!"

Down the hill, through the little stand of trees. Within moments he stood on the wide concrete patio above the boathouse where, in happier times, revelers danced and music played during the Professor's summer parties. Above him floated the dirigible, but already it was ascending into the sky. Its massive engines rumbled with a low throb he could feel in his chest.

"Wait! Wait!" Christopher shouted, his panic rising. He saw that a sailor was pulling up the dirigible's rope ladder.

"No! I'm here! Please! I'm here!" he cried. He dashed over under the ladder, jumped, tried to reach it, but fell short.

The ladder stopped. Christopher looked and saw the sailor begin lowering it, but a moment later another man came and put his hand on the sailor's arm. The second man shook his head, motioning for the sailor to raise the ladder again. The sailor looked surprised but followed the order.

"NO! Oh, no! Please! I'm here!"

The ladder rose and rose until it was pulled in the

door. The sailor stepped back, and the door swung shut. Slowly, the dirigible turned and began to float away. Christopher chased it, waving his arms.

"Eleanor! Eleanor!" he cried.

He saw her, just for a moment, her hand pressed against the window, her face lit by a dim light from within the gondola. He thought she looked sad, and she mouthed something to him, but he couldn't tell what. A hand reached out and pulled her away, then pulled the shade over the window.

"Eleanor!" Christopher cried.

A crushing wave of noise and light shattered Christopher's senses, and a force struck him in the chest like a hammer. It lifted him off his feet and tossed him through the air before gravity sent him crashing back to the ground. Like a marionette with its strings cut, he slid and rolled across the jagged slabs of concrete that were once the patio.

When he came to a stop, a high-pitched screeching filled his ears. Heat swept over him, and fire burned all around. Christopher tried to move, but his limbs refused to respond. Another boom, a little further off, shook the ground.

"Eleanor," he murmured.

It was too late. Christopher slumped. The world began to fade, shadows creeping in along the edges of his vision. Sound faded. The explosions fell silent. His eyes closed.

A hand grasped his and pulled, and the world came flooding back with it. Up from the ground it raised him, out of the ruin and the flames, and then an arm wrapped around his waist. It pulled him close and held him with a firm, comforting grip.

"We have to go," Ellie said. "They'll be here soon."

Christopher looked at the dirigible. Like a dark cloud

against the night sky, it slowly floated away, growing smaller with each passing moment.

"They left me, Ellie," he said.

"I know. I'm sorry, Christopher. Please. We need to go."

"Why would they leave me?" he said, turning to her. "Why would they . . ."

He caught sight of himself in the reflection of Ellie's polished copper face. Parts of his skin were torn away, revealing smooth, polished copper underneath.

Christopher pulled away from Ellie, stumbled, and fell hard to the ground. Shaking, he looked at his body. He ripped away the shreds of his shirt and found a torn layer of something like skin over an elaborate copper shell. Here and there, the copper had peeled back to reveal spinning, whirling gears.

Christopher opened and closed his mouth. Unable to breathe, unable to think, a wave of despair washed over him. With a force as powerful as the blast that had destroyed the patio, the truth crashed down on him. He gasped, and air and burning acrid smoke poured into him. Shaking, shuddering, coughing, he lifted his hands and looked at the torn, bleeding flesh. Human flesh. He turned them over. Copper shone beneath the shredded skin of his palms.

More explosions rocked the ground.

"Christopher?" Ellie asked, her voice calm. "Christopher?"

Christopher put his head in his hands and squeezed as if he could crush the truth, force things back to the way they were. But, of course, nothing changed. Slowly, so slowly, the sobs faded. The hole in his heart, however, remained a dark, empty thing.

"That's why," Christopher murmured.

Ellie, standing behind him, said, "That's why what, Christopher?"

Christopher lifted his head, and stared vacantly at the wreckage of the patio where he'd once watched dancers spin while the orchestra played.

"That's why she never loved me, Ellie."

Another boom, this one farther off, echoed across the grounds.

"I'm sorry, Christopher," Ellie said.

The sobs threatened to overwhelm him again. He fought back the worst of it, but the tears still came. "That's why *no one* will ever love me."

Ellie touched his shoulder, lightly, tenderly.

"*I* love you, Christopher."

Christopher turned to her. The firelight glowed on her perfectly sculpted, copper face, glittering along its graceful curves. Her blue, porcelain eyes shone, and the ribbon of her lips reflected the love of her creator.

He reached out and took her hand. Hinged, metallic fingers intertwined.

Climbing to his feet, Christopher took Ellie in his arms. He looked into her eyes and raised a hand to her lovely cheek. The gentle whir of the reason engine's discs purred beneath his palm, and Ellie inclined her head, ever so slightly.

"You'll stay with me?" Christopher asked.

"Of course, Christopher," Ellie answered.

Together, hand in hand, they disappeared into the darkness.

CASSANDRA'S KISS

Mary Louise Eklund

Mary Louise Eklund grew up near Asheville, North Carolina, and frequently went to Biltmore House and Gardens on school field trips. Since then she has made pilgrimages back to see more rooms as they have opened. A special thanks is extended to them for their inspiration of daydreams growing up and for Mr. Johnny's home in "Cassandra's Kiss". Mary Louise now lives in Wisconsin where she's working on her own multitomaton to shovel snow once her teenage son leaves for college. If that should fail she's attempting to convince her husband on the virtues of a snow blower.

Johnny flopped onto the blue leather chaise, gingerly holding a flannel ice pack to the left side of his face. The cool flannel formed to the cuts expertly stitched by Tom, his multitomaton butler.

"I should have just thrown him out." Johnny spoke to the bust of Molière peering down from his perch on ornate bookcase. Rolling his good eye away from the smirking marble face, Johnny glared at the white mock ribs of the blue ship keel ceiling. "Sure old man, you'd find humor in this situation, but Syd is going to kill me." He closed his eyes. "Like I said, I should have just thrown Cheeky out instead of punching him for wagging his pow."

There was a soft scrape of the heavy mahogany door on the plush Karabagh rug, followed by the gentle hiss of well oiled joints moving. "The dirigibles carrying our guests are now visible. The ground crew is in heliographic communication with them. Lady Espear is in the lead and shall be landing in a quarter of an hour. Will you go out and greet her?" Tom's expressive brass eyebrows moved fluidly; he'd never been able to keep them as noncommittal as the rest of his copper countenance.

Johnny dropped the ice pack onto the silver butler's tray next to him. Looking out the door to his library table covered in material only twenty-four hours ago he'd been anxious to share with Sydney, he screwed up his face in disgust.

"Dammit, Tom! Why am I such a shortsighted sod?" Johnny stood and stomped over to the window that looked over his estate. He slammed a button on the wall with his palm. The linen shades dropped, diffusing the light. No one could see in without pressing their face to the glass.

"Sir, what you did was a chivalrous act—defending the honor of Lady Sydney from the disparagements of Sir Cheekbalm. I understand from your other guests you gave him a chance to retract such unpleasant innuendoes, but the man didn't take your gracious offer." Tom picked up the ice pack and emptied it into a champagne cooler. He lifted the lid to the ice bucket, picked up large chunks of ice, and crushed them to snow allowing it to fall into the pack.

"Thanks for your unwavering support, Tom. I should have only thrown him out and not let it get to fisticuffs." Johnny angrily shoved his desk chair out of the way as he watched the landing field from the window. "No, I won't meet her out there. I think it best she get the shock in private before we explain it to the guests. Show her here." He took the refreshed pack and collapsed on the chaise. "I am NOT letting her know what vile gossip a drunkard spewed about her. I'll just have to skirt the truth as best I can and deal with my appearance rather than the cause of it."

"Very well, sir, I shall convey her directly from the landing green." Tom exited with a quiet whirl of cogs punctuated by the click of the door.

The dirigibles circled the estate in large lazy ovals awaiting their turn to land on the south terrace. Lady Sydney Espear was the first to disembark.

"Good morning, Tom!" Sydney approached the butler in wide confident strides. "Where's Mr. Johnny?"

Tom's brass eyebrows lifted with a soft swish. "Mr. Johnny would like to speak to you in his office while I tend to our guests." He proffered his arm to escort her up the broad stairs and deftly guided her across the terrace and into the library. One brass eye clicked in a conspiratorial wink before he departed into the wisteria shade of the terrace once again.

"So that's it." Lady Sydney sighed heavily, pulled off her ostrich leather gloves, and slapped them across her palm before grasping the door to Johnny's private office. Her eyes landed on the knife-carrying friar panel in the door. "You men and your drinking . . . even when in the service of God!"

As she entered, ready to bluster at Johnny for getting into his cups, her words were cut short upon seeing his face. It was framed by the familiar parenthesis of black hair, but the left side was swollen. It bore multihued bruises and stitched cuts. He raised a flannel bag in apologetic greeting.

"Syd, I'm so sorry. I've been trying to ice it to keep it to a minimum." He shrugged. "I'm not sure it's working."

Tossing her gloves onto the sofa, Sydney rushed to sit on the ottoman next to him. "Johnny, what happened?" She proffered her hand to his cheek, but he waved her away, taking her slender hand in his.

"Let's just say I fell while playing cards last night and leave it at that." He squeezed her hand before letting it go. "I'm sorry this happened just as you bring society to my door. I was on the verge of being acceptable again due to your efforts."

"It seems I'm doing the job of Sisyphus." She leaned back, removing her wide brimmed hat. After sticking the gray pearl tipped hat pin into it, she tossed it onto the sofa next to her gloves. "So was anyone else injured in this fall?"

"Lord Cheekbalm sends his sincere regrets that he will be unable to attend." Johnny did his distinctive head tilt and grinned, flashing his gold teeth.

"Oh Johnny, if you weren't such an excellent investigative partner I'd not try to reform you." She heaved herself up from the ottoman. "I'm glad you didn't attempt to greet the guests looking like this." She removed her ostrich leather coat and tossed it onto her hat without noticing it crushed the black egret feathers. Her traveling suit was the usual dark heather gray to match her eyes.

"I'm so grateful for your attempts at reformation and pledge to be a better pernor of your efforts."

He put the compress back to his face. "You look

lovely today. Perhaps your radiance shall make my deficiencies less noticeable."

"At least you're contrite. But flattery won't get you out this mess; we need to offer something more plausible than a fall." Sydney walked over to the long window facing the landing green. "The guests are busy being shown to their suites, and that will distract them for now. So tell me, was Cheeky's fall worse than yours?"

"I certainly hope so, considering he's got thirty years on me. Syd, as I said I deeply regret this and will do anything you say to make amends and improve the situation."

Her heels clicked on the Italian tile as she paced off the edge of the carpet. "What started all this?"

"I'd really rather not say. It's offensive to even think about. Let's just move forward from this unfortunate lapse, shall we?"

Taking his seat behind the large desk she pulled out a sheet of paper, then drew the pen from its inkwell. "Very well, either you had a misadventure exploring or a riding mishap; which shall it be?" The nib began making soft scratching sounds on the paper as she wrote.

"I like the misadventure. I'll inform Tom and we'll go from there." He went to the brass call plate behind his desk and pushed the butler call. "What are you writing?"

"Your apology note to Cheeky." Sydney said without looking up. "You will copy it into your own hand and have it delivered to him. He's to understand that you regret the events that led to his unfortunate riding accident and extend him an open invitation to enjoy the hospitality of the Plebeman estate once he is well."

"I won't do that. He's no longer welcome here or anywhere that I have a say." Johnny tossed the ice pack onto the desk with a clatter. "He deserved what was dealt to him and a great deal more in my opinion."

Sydney rolled back in the large desk chair. "You just promised full cooperation and then refuse the second thing I request."

"Look, Syd, I did a wrong thing for a right reason." The door to the office opened and Tom entered. "I won't say what went on because I—I just won't." He looked away from her piercing gaze. "I'll tell my guests I was injured performing a preliminary investigation of the Bell Witch. I'll be charming, sober, and restrained—the perfect host reentering society. I'll write Cheeky offering best wishes on his healing from his riding accident, but I'll warn him not to forget that horses will buck under ungracious masters." Johnny turned and looked at his beautiful best friend. "I will not extend an invitation to that rude, barbaric churl of a man. I'm yours to mold except in apologizing to Cheeky. That's the only limitation, really."

Tom's head turned in several jerky movements while his brass eyebrows raised then settled into his normal expression. "I too am here to serve and make this fete as enjoyable as possible for all."

Sydney sighed and shoved the pen back into the well. "Then injury from misadventure it is. You shall pen a letter to Cheeky letting him know discreetly and extending my regret that he's unable to attend because of his unfortunate encounter with an ass." She looked curtly at Johnny.

"Very well put. I couldn't have said it better myself." Johnny smiled roguishly.

"You will not drink beyond what is socially expected during this week. You will turn into your room at an early but polite hour. You will not call Mr. Pickney Pinky. He detests that! You will reenter society repentant and gracious. I require it because doing so will facilitate connections to improve our investigations. Once those who hold esoteric objects trust you to not pawn them or lose them in a bet then they will share them with us to study." She strode to the door with purpose. "I will show myself to my room. Tom, see that Johnny is presentable and on the loggia at three for tea."

"Yes m'am!" both replied as she made her exit.

That evening Johnny tugged at his waistcoat and longed for a good Irish whiskey as Mrs. Pompenroy prattled on about how wonderful it was he'd finally grown up. The side of his mouth was becoming raw from biting it to keep from offering what was truly on his mind at the asinine comments he'd endured since tea on the loggia.

The only respite from the tedium had been when it was time to change clothes. The selections had been left to Tom. He now stood in a cutaway jacket made of the same black gabardine as his trousers. The shawl lapels and the detail down the trouser leg were black matte satin. The V faced waist coat and all too snug small bow tie were an ivory blend of silk and linen. He flexed his toes against the point of new black oxfords and pondered what pointy-toed fool designed the damn things. To top off his total discomfort, his hair was pomaded heavily to keep it from falling forward as it was prone to do. He pulled at his diamond cufflinks to keep them from poking his wrists. When he'd voice a complaint about any of this Tom would play the recording of Sydney's voice saying, "Tom, see that Johnny is presentable."

He watched Sydney descend the main stairs on Dr. Chickering's arm. The crowd followed her as she glided with the dashing doctor onto the temporary dance floor that had been installed in the winter garden. He selected a cup of punch from the tray of a passing footman. The music started as the lights dimmed, allowing the full moon's light to stream in the octagonal dome over the dance floor. Johnny pursed his lips noting that Chickering's hand was too low on Sydney's waist. Her midnight blue gown glimmered in the light—tones of blue with twinkles of sliver thread. She expertly managed her train to make it appear she was effortlessly floating in the man's arms.

"They do make a handsome couple." Anson Wetmore had sauntered over to Johnny's left. "Everyone on the dance floor will imagine themselves looking so fine."

"Eh, she can make any bloke look good." Johnny sipped his punch and made a face at the sticky sweetness of it.

"That's true," Anson said. The Jamaican shipping magnet looked dapper in his white tie with the dark red embroidered waist coat. "Speaking of looking good, you look like a miscreant lapdog groomed within an inch of his life."

"That's how I feel." Johnny motioned over a footman and returned the punch cup. "My head is pounding and my stomach is unsettled from all the polite crap I've been choking down."

"Surely she understands you were defending her honor. The man was disgusting. Anyone who knows Sydney knows she's a fine lady." Anson turned to face his friend, "She treats everyone with the best of manners, except those zombies she got with that Phoenix feather flame thrower you made." He smiled, his white teeth sparkling, "Whew, I'll never forget her covered in mud wearing my brother's old riding suit while torching those poor buffers."

"Even in men's clothes and covered in swamp muck she can cut a striking figure. You should have seen her using the stake gun in Transylvania catching vampires on the wing. That woman is one hell of a shot."

Tom approached with the distinctive mechanical purring sounds. "Harry has insisted I inform you immediately that the Cassandra plant will be blooming at three AM."

"Tell him Lady Sydney and I will come to view the blooming."

As Tom departed, Anson turned toward Johnny. "I thought the Harry multi was the cook."

"That was the intention, but multis have personalities. Harry was much better at gardening. Richard has a knack for French pastries. Blew the whole mass production theory. For best results each multi has to be matched to the right task, then trained." Johnny bit his lip, "Now to get a moment with Sydney to tell her about the blooming."

"Think you'll see the future?" Anson's eyes were wide with interest.

"Dunno, ol' chap. Even if we do, who'd believe us? That was part of Cassie's curse, wasn't it?" Johnny patted his friend's arm and moved forward in the crowd in a more chipper mood.

Try as he might that night, Johnny could not get a moment with Sydney. She was always out of reach, laughing at some fop's joke while tossing her head back so that the sapphires and diamonds in her hair sparkled gaily.

That evening, Johnny paced in his bedroom. The heavy baroque furniture only added to his dark mood. Staring at the roaring fire in the black marble fireplace, he reviewed the frustrating night of Sydney deftly avoiding him. He'd been unable to tell her the about the Cassandra plant they had both almost died at the hands of a Yeti to bring back. His brooding was interrupted by a metallic knock on the door. "Come in."

Harry approached looking cleaner than usual. "Sir, I did all the rechecking you requested." He was nervous—if a multi could be nervous. "It's definitely going to bloom at three. We're you naught able to inform m'lady?"

Johnny sighed. "Blast it Harry. No, I wasn't able to inform her. It appears I'm reduced to sending notes in my own house to my business partner." He strode over to the table and kicked one of the large twisted legs before sitting down to toss off a note. "Leave the damn flower alone. If I can't get Lady Sydney down there I want no one, not even you, there to see it bloom. We will be the first to experience its effects. I won't be robbed of that!"

"Yes sir." As Harry backed toward the door his joints squealed in protest. "I'll inform the garden and conservatory crew to be elsewhere tonight."

"Thank you Harry." Johnny attempted several notes, wadding up each before throwing them under the desk. "This is ridiculous! I'm going up to her room and tell her. If she doesn't want to come with me, fine—but I'm not going to miss this."

He kicked off his plush carpet slippers, pulled on his brogans, and marched up the back staircase. Arriving at the door to the south tower room, Johnny knocked. Tilly opened the door. "Good evening, Mr. Johnny."

"Show him in, Tilly," Sydney called. "Then finish brushing out my hair. These rats are driving me insane." She pulled one of the padded hair forms from her hair and cast it upon her dressing table. "I dare say you feel the same way about starched collars, don't you, Johnny?"

"Very much so."

He looked about the room. The soft cream furnishings only served to make the deep blue of Sydney's gown more vibrant. All was tidy in the soft floral oval, except around the dressing table. There, Sydney's jewels rested on a velvet pad where she'd dropped them, and her delicate dancing slippers were kicked off to the side. Sydney's eyes were closed in enjoyment of the brushing.

"Harry has informed me that the Cassandra plant will bloom at three."

Sydney's eyes snapped open as she spun on the damask covered bench.

"Yes, I am going down to the conservatory to watch the process and came to inquire if you'd like to accompany me."

"I'm exhausted, and it would be tonight." She held out her bare feet and wiggled them. "Yes, yes of course I want to see it. After all we went through to get the damn thing I'm not waiting for its next blooming."

Johnny couldn't help but smile at the dainty feet wiggling. "Very well, I'll have the cart at the library's entrance in an hour. We'll ride down to save your feet."

"Perfect. See you then."

An hour later the ponies trotted perkily as they pulled the cart across the pea gravel paths. The pair sat quietly as they entered the walled formal garden. The large conservatory's glass roof shone in the full moon light.

"You know, Johnny, I'm always amazed by this place." Sydney was now dressed more practically in a blouse and traveling skirt with her hair in a loose ponytail. "It's amazingly beautiful; the ramble, formal gardens, then there hidden from the view of the house this huge conservatory where plants from all over the world thrive."

"Mom loved being surrounded by fresh plants. Dad had this built so that she'd never run out of blooms no matter the season."

"He must have loved her dearly." Sydney looked up the façade of the building as if seeing it for the first time.

"She was the dreamer, the colorful one. He was the one that made those dreams fly. That's what they used to say. She designed the custom gondolas and Dad made the dirigibles."

"What a perfect match. You were lucky to have such wonderful parents."

The grinding of wheels on the gravel gave way to the clip-clop of the ponies' hooves as they pulled onto the brick patio. They stopped at the main door opposite the kitchen garden. Johnny didn't regret his impulsive order for all garden staff to keep away. After an evening of being shunned by Sydney he now had her all to himself.

"I've sent the staff away since we don't know the range or effects of the bloom."

As they entered into the balmy palm court, the heady scent of tropical blooms engulfed them. The centerpiece was a group of grand palms rising stories high in the center point of the pitched glass ceiling. Around these giants were wrought iron tables filled with tropical plants of all sizes and descriptions packed as tightly as their health would allow and ornately arranged.

Sydney walked along the plants, caressing leaves and leaning in to sniff the exotic blooms.

As he watched her, the sprinklers and misters turned on. In seconds they were soaked to the skin as they dashed through the nearest door. They stopped in the small glass vestibule between the palm court and the desert house. Here were implements of care for various plants and a small bench.

"I should have thought that would require a lot of moisture to keep the plants so lush." Sydney pulled her hair to one side and began squeezing water from it.

Shaking his head to shed water like a dog, Johnny

agreed. He looked more like himself as his locks fell forward to frame his face. "We can cut through the desert wing to the tundra wing where the plant is."

"Lead the way." Sydney untucked her white shirt. It was now transparent, showing that she still wore her evening corset with the detailed decoration. Johnny tried hard not to look, but failed and consoled himself that at least he didn't stare. He opened the door to the next room and a welcome blast of dry heat wafted over them as they entered.

Just as she let go of the door, Johnny turned with a warning, "Don't let that door slam." It did anyway, shaking the whole white-washed wrought iron frame of the desert wing. "It's most unpleasant and hard on the glass seals."

He sat on one of the rock walls that held the sand for the various forms of cacti. "I've never really gotten why Mum wanted this prickly collection. They are interesting, but weren't ever used in the house. Great place to get needles to stick your brother with during dinner time."

Sydney let her hair loose and attempted to flap her shirt dry. "I can see collecting the plants. They are interesting. I'm sure your mother sketched their unique shapes."

"I wouldn't know. I've not gone through her portfolios. I haven't the heart." Johnny shrugged against the itch of cloth drying on his skin.

Sydney busied herself tending her hair. "Shall we be off?"

Johnny led the way to the opposite end and grasped the door handle to exit the desert wing, but the door didn't open. "It's locked. The staff must have locked all the back doors when I ordered them away for the night." Turning, he looked through the panes to the palm court.

"The water has stopped in there now so we'll just go that way."

Sydney led this time, but was stopped by that door. "It appears when I let the door slam one of the implements fell blocking it. I can't open it."

"Bloody hell. Can anything else go wrong viewing a damn flower?"

"Not just any flower, but one whose pollen cause you to see the future." Sydney pushed with her weight against the door.

"I'll just punch out a glass pane and reach through." Johnny took her arm to move her aside.

"Oh, just what we need! Then we'll explain how we were caught alone in the conservatory late at night with me in a see-through blouse." Sydney pushed him back. "That wouldn't cause a bit of gossip."

"Fine." He looked around the room for something to break the glass. "Nothing." Taking a deep breath, Johnny sat on the rock wall and held his aching face in his hands. "Guess we just have to wait."

Sydney sat next to him. "Head hurt?"

"Yes."

She gently massaged his neck. "I know why you got into the fight, Anson told me. It was really very sweet of you to defend my honor."

"I should have just thrown him out," Johnny mumbled through is hands.

"Ahh, well if you'd told me why, I'd not been so gracious to Cheeky." Her hand traced his arm before moving away. "Now he probably thinks I'm after his paunch and his wallet."

Johnny snorted. "He's a catch if you like the bellicose sort."

They sat in silence. Johnny had run out of things to say, something that had never occurred with Sydney before. Suddenly, his head whirled from the realization he loved Sydney in a way he'd not admitted. He'd always enjoyed the free and easy exchange with her. They had always gotten on so well; neither held back. Looking up at her profile he spoke in almost a whisper.

"Syd, will there ever be an *us?*"

She cocked her head. "I thought there was an *us* . . . as in here we are now. We're a team."

He smiled wanly, "I know that but I meant as a proper couple, an *us?*"

Sydney looked directly in his face. "I don't want to be one in a string of women."

Johnny turned to face her. "I do love you. There have been no others since we started working together. Surely after all these years you know I've reformed from my charlatan days in that manner."

"In all manners. A gentleman plays cards and defends his lady's honor. It's a far cry from what you tell me you used to do."

"*His* lady?"

"Yes, if you'd want to settle for just me instead of keeping your options open for someone better."

"I honestly can't think of what better would be." Johnny leaned in toward her.

She leaned forward ever so slightly to accept the kiss. During the embrace that followed as the clock stuck three a bright opal light burst forth in the neighboring wing.

"We're missing the blooming." Sydney now wrapped in Johnny's arms whispered watching the radiance over his shoulder.

He glanced at the light, then gently with his index finger directed her face to his. "I don't need a flower to show me our future is bright. I've got all I need right here.

DASHED HOPES

Donald J. Bingle

*Donald J. Bingle is the author of the novel Green-
sword, a darkly comedic eco-thriller about global
warming. He has written short stories about killer bun-
nies, Civil War soldiers, detectives, Renaissance Faire
orcs, giant battling robots, demons, cats, time travelers, ghosts, time-traveling ghosts, a husband accused
of murdering his wife, dogs, horses, gamers, soldiers,
Neanderthals, commuters, little kids, kender, and se-
rial killers. He is the author of the near future military
sci-fi novel, Forced Conversion. He is a corporate and
securities attorney. He has a fascinating website at
www.donaldjbingle.com. He rarely gets steamed, but
his work colleagues find him rather punky.*

"Coals to Newcastle," harrumphed Ogden Suttington,
as he flung an invoice down on the huge rolltop
desk dominating his office space at Suttington Coal
Works and Mining. "Coals to *bloody* Newcastle!"

Genevieve Suttington gave him a hard stare. "Really,

Father. Mind your ulcer. Mother, God rest her soul, would never approve of you getting so upset about business—and you know what she used to say about such language."

Ogden pushed his spectacles down his nose and looked over them at his daughter. "If your mother were alive, I wouldn't be the one dealing with these blasted invoices. I could be spending my time seeing to the revision of the mine plans and the expansion of the business into newly discovered seams."

"You know I'm doing my best to help, Father," replied Genevieve. "I've almost gotten caught up with the correspondence that fell in arrears after Mother's passing. I should have time to help with the payroll and accounts soon."

She wanted to help, truly she did. Father and Mother had been so good to her—never leaving her wanting for anything as she grew up, providing for a university education for her, even though, in these allegedly modern times, such extravagance was normally reserved for the male heirs of the well-to-do. Still, it was hard to muster too much enthusiasm over paystubs and equipment orders after studying Aristotle and Archimedes and Newton.

Nor was she likely to meet any suitors in the business office to Father's mines. While she held no prejudice against the miners or the salesmen and such who visited the office, she did crave the affection of a man of education and sensibility, not the slick, pushy, middle-aged hawkers of wares or the coarse, rough men of the mine. What a pity she would have no more time for the Literary and Philosophical Society now that she was taking an active part in the family business.

Father's face turned red as he held up yet another invoice, his hand quivering with rage as he scanned its contents. "Fire and damnation! Again! Coals to *bloody* Newcastle."

Genevieve did her best to put a tone of disapproving shock into her response. "Father! Such language ... Why, I never ..."

Father turned toward her in a quick motion. "Don't say you've never heard such language before. I won't have you telling a bald-faced lie just to admonish me." He gave her a mischievous wink. "Go ahead, admit it. You've heard such phraseology before. I dare say that if you work at the mines, you'll hear the same and much, much worse often enough."

Of course she had heard such language before. She was a college graduate—from a university filled to the rafters with young males, whose tongues could be as quick and vulgar as their hands—but there was no reason to rile her father further. "Of course I've heard the phrase 'coals to Newcastle' before, Father. It is an exclamatory recitation indicative of redundancy. To wit, no one would bring coals to Newcastle, since it is the center of the entire English coal industry."

She did her best to force a blush. "As for the other phrases, Father ..."

Father cut her off with an abrupt motion of his hand, still holding an invoice. "Well, it's an exclamatory reci ... dundancy or whatever you said, no more." He brandished the invoice at her, as if she could read it across the room in the dim light afforded by the gas lanterns ensconced on the wall. "Here's the proof, more to shame. A second invoice relating to the steam-boiler for the Shaft 37 crusher-sorter, *importing* coal to Newcastle from Rhineland. We mine coal, for heaven's sake, yet we are importing coal to fuel the device that crushes and sorts our own coal. What's the world coming to? Demand for coal is enormous, what with fancy newfangled machinery, inventions, discoveries, steam-powered transportation, steam-powered factories, steam-powered plumbing . . . Where will it end?"

"I'm sure the invoice is just reflective of a temporary dislocation in the timing of shipments from our own mines, Father. Customers come first for all our production, after all. Nothing to worry about, I'm sure. Business is strong."

Father released his iron grip on the invoice. "Too strong, I fear. In between sorting out the accounts payable, I took a look at the mine plans versus usage and anticipated mine life. The invoice isn't a temporary reflector . . . or whatever you said . . . it's a harbinger of the future. With all the steam-power, England's running through her coal reserves in record time."

"You mean the country could run out? The company could run out of coal to mine?" Her prospects of meeting an educated, sensitive suitor as a penniless victim of mining bankruptcy would be practically null.

Father screwed up his face and picked up his pipe, chewing on the stem for a few moments before answering.

"There's one thing. I've resisted it because of the dangers involved, but the engineering men, they say it can be done."

Genevieve did not like the look on Father's face. "Go deeper?" she asked in a whisper.

He shook his head. "The coal's not deeper; it's farther afield."

She didn't understand. All of the subsurface mining rights in the area had been granted long ago. "What do you mean?"

Father took the pipe out of his mouth to squirt a pittance into the spittoon on the floor near the corner of his desk.

"The coal seams keep going from here, beneath the North Sea, with no sign of stopping. We'll have to mine under the waves if we want to keep producing steam."

Coal mines had extended beneath water before, of course, but rivers and lakes are not as deep nor so broad and heavy and fraught with waves and tides and motion as the sea itself. The new project took years of planning and organizing to put into effect, with consideration for the economics of the mine plan and the safety of the miners who would be toiling beneath the sea. Not only were enormous steam-powered pumps needed to clear out any seepage into the workings, but the sea above complicated everything else. No ventilation shafts, no escape shafts, no rescue shafts would be possible beneath the ocean. Air would need to be pumped in. The long horizontal shafts extending from the on-shore entrance shaft and mine workings would mean getting to and from the coal-face could take considerable time and communications would be difficult—almost as difficult as finding love in an office shared with Father.

That changed the very first day she met Trevor Moynihan.

At first, she thought Trevor to be just another of the many tradesmen and sales people who came to the office to pitch their wares to Father, albeit a younger, cleaner, better-looking specimen than most. But Father had been called to one of the nearby pits to handle a minor difficulty and so Trevor was left to cool his heels awaiting the mine owner's return. As she explained the delay, he smiled briefly and then averted his gaze—stammering a few phrases about how it would be no trouble to wait in order to see such a busy and important man. He fidgeted and looked about the room, as if seeking something safe and neutral and inanimate to look at instead of at her. She decided to have some fun.

"You're not like the other salesmen," she stated simply.

He stared at her as if shocked that she was addressing him, then quickly looked away. "Er, how so?"

She shrugged. "The other salesmen are generally older, for one thing."

"I'm sure they were young once."

She laughed. "Yes, but the company is an important client, so only the most senior salesmen usually come calling. There's nothing young about them. I'm sure Father was young once, too, though he shows little evidence of it anymore."

"Every journey has a beginning and an end. Change is the mark of a journey's progress."

"So you are saying that with enough time, all salesmen become pushy, serious types, with no sense of humor? You've not pictured a bright future for yourself, Mr. Moynihan."

"Oh, I'm not a salesman, at least not except in the most incidental way. I'm an inventor."

His posture straightened almost infinitesimally as he said the word "inventor."

"And how does one become an inventor, Mr. Moynihan? Do you come from a long line of inventors?"

"Er, no . . . I mean I don't know. My parents died when I was very young."

She flushed at the thought she may have discomfited him. "I'm sorry. I didn't know. That must have been very terrible."

"I suppose. I was very young."

"Still, I'm sure you had a hard life."

"A bit lonely in some ways, but not so bad. I was

taken in by the Anglican Charities of Newcastle upon Tyne. They even sent me to college, by special dispensation of the vicar—one of his 'bright boy' fellowships."

"And is that where you learned to invent?"

"It's where I learned a lot of things—math, science, engineering formulas, and mechanical drawing. But you can't be taught to invent. You either invent things or you don't. I've met a few other inventors, though, mostly at meetings of the Literary and Philosophical Society."

"And so you've invented something you think could be useful to our company?"

He flashed a smile. "Er, yes. The Pressure-Sensitive Steam Fixed-Communicator."

"I haven't ordered anything like that lately. What does it do?"

"It allows one to communicate over great distances using a code transmitted by extremely high-pressure steam."

"By code?"

"Yes. By fluctuating the pressure contained in the extended steam line by rapid stops and starts of a release valve, someone on the other end of the line with a pressure gauge can read the fluctuations and decode the message remotely."

"Doesn't pressure in a steam boiler fluctuate on its own, due to variations in the heating elements and such?"

"A keen observation," replied Trevor, nodding with a nervous smile on his handsome face. "You speak truly, but by keeping the pressure at an extremely high level, those natural operational variations are not noticeable compared to the more significant variations from starting and stopping the release valve."

She frowned. She had hopes for the lad, but his invention sounded outlandish, even dangerous.

"I've seen the victims of boiler explosions here at the mine. Maintaining such high pressure over a pipeline of such great length as to be useful in our undersea mine shafts would be quite dangerous. Releasing massive amounts of steam to send even the shortest, simplest message would be dangerous and disruptive. Besides, it would require immense amounts of energy to maintain pressure over miles of pipe. Why, we might as well take our production straight from the mine face to the boiler for the communicator with none to spare for customers."

"No, no. I fear I am a better inventor than salesman. You see, the pipe is extremely small in diameter—more like a pipette. A small, commercially available steam-engine produces sufficient steam to maintain high pressure over an extended length because the total area of pressure is actually quite moderate. I could show you the math . . ."

"I can calculate area given diameter and length myself, sir."

"Oh, yes. My apologies. I'm sure you could." He glanced at the door, as if hopeful his prospective client would arrive. "The key to the invention is the pressure release regulator and gauge system, which allows rapid release and re-establishment of pressure, creating short or long spikes or dips in the reading, which can be read as a simple code. Alfred Vail invented such a code for use in connection with Samuel Morse's telegraph system . . ."

Father burst through the door, sweaty and with his jacket off and his shirtsleeves rolled up. "Bloody thirty-seven winch, never dependable in cool weather no matter how much the foreman tinkers with it. Remind me never to purchase anything from Fairfax & Wilmington again." He looked at the young man standing in front of his desk. "Who are you?"

Trevor jumped lightly and stammered as he responded. "T–t–trevor M–m–moynihan, Mr. Suttington. I've come to t–talk to you about my P–pressure-Sensitive S–s–steam F–fixed-Communicator . . ."

Father fluttered a hand toward Trevor as he moved behind his desk and started unrolling his sleeves. "Yes, yes. Read your prospectus, or 'p–p–prospectus' as you would say. Works like a telegraph, I understand, but without electricity. That correct?"

"Y–yes s–sir."

"Can't stand electricity. Passing fancy. Dangerous stuff. Packs a shock. You could probably kill an elephant with it."

"No electricity, s–sir."

"Great. Steam, that's the power of the future. Great idea this Pressure-Sensitory Fixer Gizmo of yours. Genevieve will arrange everything for you. Mind you, you'll have to work the mine-side communicator yourself until we have someone trained."

"Er, I thought I might operate the topside end, myself, sir."

"Nonsense. No room in here for a third desk, so Genevieve will have to do that. Nothing wrong about going into the mine for a bit, son. Men do it all the time."

Genevieve communicated a lot with Trevor as the installation of the Pressure-Sensitive Steam Fixed-Communicator was fabricated and installed, running from a steam-engine outside Father's office, through a release valve regulator and gauge at her very desk, then out to the mines, down the vertical shaft and then lateral almost two miles under the North Sea to within a few hundred feet of the working face of the mine. There it hooked into a second release regulator and gauge in a mobile underground office used by Trevor.

In person, under Father's baleful glare or her own smiling countenance, Trevor was a bundle of nerves, but on the steam pressure line ... online ... Trevor was confident and well-spoken and witty and full of hope and ideas for the future and interested in her life and her studies and her future plans and dreams. They chatted constantly, at first ostensibly because of the need to test and regulate the system, then to practice, practice, practice her coding, until she could manipulate the release valve in a staccato of dots and dashes prescribed by Vail's code for Morse's silly electrical invention.

Eventually, they chatted just to chat, to learn about each other and talk about inconsequential things. Their chats were undoubtedly a needed respite for Trevor, who was teased and worse endlessly by the miners for his bookish ways and his relative intolerance for the conditions in the mine. Given the pressures of the rock and waters above, the ambient temperature of the natural coal seam was nigh unto 90 degrees Fahrenheit. Worse yet, the frequent use of steam-powered equipment and seepage from above drove the humidity high.

Hot and steamy.

As for Genevieve, she longed for companionship and intellectual stimulation and more from Trevor, but was under the constant eye of Father and the constant stress of her office duties. Only when she and Trevor were pulsing one another online did she have a life of her own and hope for a future of her dreams.

She and Trevor never touched, but felt each other's every move, every mood, every thought through a three-mile column of pressurized steam in heavy-duty half-inch diameter copper pipes that also contained their growing love, released in brief dots and dashes over weeks and months.

Hot and steamy.

*   *   *

And yet, all was still and pleasant on the day Genevieve's life changed forever. No explosion reverberated through the mine office when the collapse of the North Sea adit first occurred. No voices were raised above conversational tones as the critical moment came and went. No shaking of the earth or subsidence of the ground beneath grimy Newcastle hinted at what was occurring miles away in the gloomy depths of the North Sea mine.

No doubt all of that occurred beneath the ocean when the bedrock encasing the coal-seam burst, however. No doubt a deafening crack rang out as the roof collapsed. No doubt the bellow of the earth subsiding joined with the thunderous roar of the ocean depths flowing into the shaft to blot out the full-throated screams of alarm and agony of the miners in the midst of the watery chaos engulfing them. No doubt the frigid water of the North Sea hit the hot rock and the hotter steam-powered machines with an angry, shattering hiss. No doubt the men ran and fell and drowned or dove into pockets still sufficiently air-tight to hold back the water, although instantly pressurized to a nearly lethal level, to wait for death.

Up above, however, all Genevieve saw at first was a broad dip in the pressure of the Pressure-Sensitive Steam Fixed-Communicator as the cold water far below surrounded and cooled a considerable length of sturdy pipe. A moment later, the steam engine outside whined as it ramped up to maintain the prescribed pressure. She knew instantly something was amiss.

Once the pressure level of the device re-attained its specified mark, Genevieve frantically pulsed the release regulator to inquire.

No response.

She tried again, then again.

Nothing.

She tried yet again—barely forcing herself to wait be-tween pulses, to give Trevor a chance to respond.

Finally, a pulse came. "Ocean breach. Trapped."

She ran to the wall near Father's desk and pulled the alarm cord. A mournful wail of steam-powered anguish drowned out all other sound across the offices and the workings and the mines and the town. She let go of the cord and rushed back to her desk to reply, looking up for only a moment to shout "North Sea" when Father and a few others came in to find out why she had sounded the alarm. They immediately rushed back out to organize help and she was left alone.

"Help coming," she pulsed.

"Not possible," came the reply. "Under pressure."

She was an educated woman, one of the few in this working-class town. She understood the physics, the math. If Trevor was under pressure, there could be no hope of rescue. The North Sea had flooded the shaft, forc-ing its way both directions along the shaft from the point of breach. Moving shoreward, the water pushed air ahead until the pressure dissipated as it found the ventilation shafts and vast, interconnected underground workings of the older portions of the mine, above the level of the sea. Seaward, the water had flowed through the shaft, obliter-ating everything in its path (except a study copper pipe too small to create much resistance and too strong to be overcome by the external pressure), until the column of air before it had compressed to an equalizing pressure.

Even if someone could somehow drill down from above to the pocket of life beneath the floor of the ocean, releasing the air pressure would allow the sea to move in. And even if completely unblocked, there was no way to move through miles of submerged tunnel to escape. There was no hope.

Only life.

Tears flowed unabated down her cheeks, wetting the high, starched collar of her maroon and white gown. "I understand."

She received no immediate response, so continued after a few moments. "What can I do?"

"Send for their families. I will send the names of those men still alive here."

She ran to the door and called for one of the messenger boys to gather his counterparts and report back as soon as he could. Ten minutes later, there were ten boys waiting outside the office, and twice that in family members who had already headed for the mines when the alarm had sounded.

When Trevor finally transmitted again, she could almost feel the tremble in his hand from the way the gauge quivered as it dipped and dropped as he pulsed the names. Six. Only six, including Trevor, were still alive. As the names came in, she wrote each one on a separate piece of paper and waved for one of the boys at the door to come forward and take it. By the time the last had been given out, the wife of the first miner named had arrived, physically supported on the arms of Father, who was pale and disheveled and who seemed to have aged twenty years in the past twenty minutes.

Genevieve explained in simple, stark terms to the frightened woman that her husband, Daniel, was alive, but not for long. They should say their goodbyes. She would transmit the words to the mine and Trevor would transmit back the words of her husband from the other end.

The woman started to wail and cry. Father moved to comfort her, but Genevieve cut him off. "There's no time for that, you understand. There's no time. Mourn him when he's dead. Cherish him while he still lives. Tell him you love him while you still can be heard."

The woman nodded dully and composed herself enough for a brief farewell. Each of the other four women did the same in turn. The conversations were heart-wrenching, though unsurprisingly simple and similar to one another.

When the goodbyes of the women were finished, the vicar came in and Genevieve dutifully transmitted the words the Church required to see to the care of the doomed men's souls, along with a few private words from the vicar to Trevor about how the investment in his education had been paid back a thousand-fold.

And then it was Genevieve's turn to speak with Trevor. She asked the vicar to wait outside and sent Father to deal further with the grieving widows-to-be and shut the door.

"Alone," she pulsed.

"How I wish that word could be 'together,'" he replied.

"We have been. We will be. We are."

"From afar," came Trevor's shaky reply. "Same country, same town, same office, yet always and only from afar. I have spent hours coding I wish I had spent cuddling."

She wished the same, but now was not the time for recriminations. She had to remain strong. "No regrets. Sight, sound, touch. Merely signals our brains interpret to convey reality. We have made our own signals, our own reality. We have known love, even if we have never spoken it aloud."

His pulsed reply came quickly, as if afraid there was no time for even a few brief dots and dashes. "I do love you. I have loved you since we first met. Know that. Remember that."

"I always will."

She received no reply for more than a minute and she

feared time had run out, but finally an increasingly shaky signal returned. "Daniel has gone unconscious. Pressure, CO_2. Not long now."

"I will always be here," she answered.

"I've nowhere to go," he pulsed.

She looked up at Father's desk and the mine plans and the business ledgers and all the mundane trappings of life, suddenly hating what progress and business and commerce had done to Trevor, to her, to them. "I'm sorry Father sent you into the mines," she signaled.

"I'm not," he replied. "I never could have told you I loved you except online."

"I know."

"One last thing."

Her throat caught. "Anything."

"Marry me."

She was so adept at coding that her hands reacted at the speed of thought. "Marry you?"

"I know you are educated, rational, scientific. So am I. But I was also raised in an Anglican orphanage and I believe there is nothing irrational about forever. And if there is any chance at a forever with you, I will do anything in my limited time and power to assure it."

"So will I." She smiled at him through her tears, though she knew he could not see. She let her hands try to convey her mood, her love through a quick dance of dots and dashes. "Yes."

Genevieve rushed to the door and called for the vicar, asking him to marry them as quickly as possible. She could see the hesitation in his eyes, hear the theological wheels turning in his mind as he considered the implications.

There was no time for this. She would transmit her own words of marriage regardless of what the vicar said if he did not respond. "Now," she pressed. "Don't desert him in his last moments."

The ancient Anglican nodded and came inside. For a few moments the regulators pulsed and the gauges twitched and dipped.

"I do," she said.

"I do," he replied.

"Husband and wife," said the vicar, who then retreated discreetly out of the office.

"Alone," he coded. "Everyone else has fallen."

"Together," she replied. "Forever."

"Now what?" he signaled back, the letters coming more slowly as dots and dashes became longer and more irregular.

"We consummate the marriage," she pulsed, "as best we can, in our own signals."

"My invention was never meant for that," he answered, the last words almost indecipherable.

"I can see the possibilities, though," she pulsed. "Just lie back and watch the dial on the gauge and I'll do the best to bring you heaven until the real thing arrives."

He did.

She did.

And they were together. Hot and steamy.

... --- . -. -.. ... - .... - .- .-.. . --- ..-. .... --- .-- -.. .. -- .- -.
-.. ..-. --- .-. -.-. --- .- .-.. .-.. .-. -.. - --- - .... .. -.. ... .-. - .. --- -.
--- ..-. .... . -.. - .. -. -. . .-.-.-

ABOUT THE EDITORS

Jean Rabe is the author of more than two dozen fantasy and adventures novels and more short stories than she cares to count. She relishes editing anthologies . . . this is her seventeenth . . . almost as much as she likes tugging on old socks with her dogs (and she likes that a lot). She resides in Wisconsin, where the winters are too long, the summers are too short, and the football and steampunk are just right.

Martin H. Greenberg is the CEP of Tekno Books and its predecessor companies, now the largest book developer of commercial fiction and non-fiction in the world, with over 2,250 published books that have been translated into thirty-three languages. He is the recipient of an unprecedented four Lifetime Achievement Awards in the Science Fiction, Mystery, and Supernatural Horror genres—the Milford Award in Science Fiction, the Solstice Award in science fiction, the Bram Stoker Award in Horror, and the Ellery Queen Award in Mystery—the only person in publishing history to have received all four awards.

Gini Koch
The Alien *Novels*

"This delightful romp has many interesting twists and
turns as it glances at racism, politics, and religion en route.
Darned amusing." —*Booklist* (starred review)

"Kitty's evolution from marketing manager to member of
a secret government unit is amusing and interesting
...a hilarious romp in the vein of 'Men in Black'
or 'Ghostbusters'." —*Voya*

TOUCHED BY AN ALIEN
978-0-7564-0600-4

ALIEN TANGO
978-0-7564-0632-5

ALIEN IN THE FAMILY
978-0-7564-0668-4

To Order Call: 1-800-788-6262
www.dawbooks.com

DAW 160

Seanan McGuire

The *October Daye* Novels

"...will surely appeal to readers who enjoy my books, or those of Patrica Briggs." —*Charlaine Harris*

"Well researched, sharply told, highly atmospheric and as brutal as any pulp detective tale, this promising start to a new urban fantasy series is sure to appeal to fans of Jim Butcher or Kim Harrison."—*Publishers Weekly*

ROSEMARY AND RUE
978-0-7564-0571-7
A LOCAL HABITATION
978-0-7564-0596-0
AN ARTIFICIAL NIGHT
978-0-7564-0626-4
LATE ECLIPSES
978-0-7564-0666-0

To Order Call: 1-800-788-6262
www.dawbooks.com

Once upon a time...

Cinderella, whose real name is Danielle
Whiteshore, did marry Prince Armand.
And their wedding was a dream come true.

But not long after the "happily ever after,"
Danielle is attacked by her stepsister Charlotte,
who suddenly has all sorts of magic to call upon.
And though Talia the martial arts master—
otherwise known as Sleeping Beauty—
comes to the rescue, Charlotte gets away.

That's when Danielle discovers a number of disturbing facts: Armand has been kidnapped; Danielle is
pregnant; and the Queen has her own Secret Service
that consists of Talia and Snow (White, of course).
Snow is an expert at mirror magic and heavy-duty
flirting. Can the princesses track down Armand and
rescue him from the clutches of some of
Fantasyland's most nefarious villains?

The Stepsister Scheme
by Jim C. Hines
978-0-7564-0532-8

"Do we look like we need to be rescued?"

DAW 130

Laura Resnick

The Esther Diamond Novels

"Resnick introduces a colorful cast of gangsters and their associates as she spins a witty, fast-paced mystery around her convincingly self-absorbed chorus-girl heroine. Sexy interludes raise the tension as she juggles magical assailants, her perennially distracted agent, her meddling mother, and wiseguys both friendly and threatening in a well-crafted, rollicking mystery."
— *Publishers Weekly*

"Esther Diamond is the Stephanie Plum of urban fantasy! Unplug the phone and settle down for a fast and funny read!" —Mary Jo Putney

DOPPLEGANGSTER
978-0-7564-0595-3

UNSYMPATHETIC MAGIC
978-0-7564-0635-6

To Order Call: 1-800-788-6262
www.dawbooks.com

Celia Jerome

The Willow Tate *Novels*

"Readers will love the first Willow Tate book. Willow is funny, brave and open to possibilities most people would not have even considered as she meets her perfect foil in Thaddeus Grant, a British agent assigned to look over the strange occurrences following Willow like a shadow. Together they make a wonderful pair and readers will love their unconventional courtship."

—*RT Book Review*

TROLLS IN THE HAMPTONS
978-0-7564-0630-1

NIGHT MARES IN THE HAMPTONS
978-0-7564-0663-9

To Order Call: 1-800-788-6262
www.dawbooks.com

DAW 170